'Brilliantly written. Truly addictive. Michael Tobias is tuned in and here proves that you don't have to be the victim to feel the pain. The detail, the feeling, the emotion, the passion, the burning desire for retribution. Oh the retribution ...

'The journey of our heroes is the stuff of dreams and of nightmares depending on which species you align yourself with – the nonhuman, the subhuman, the humane. I'm with the former and the latter for the record.

'For the uninitiated the motivation of the warriors herein will be a revelation.

'*Nineteen Eighty-Four* for animal abusers.'

Keith Mann – Animal Liberation Front activist, currently imprisoned for 10 years for "terrorist" activities

'Who hasn't raged at injustice? Or fantasized about snuffing out those who knowingly kill all that is good? Should it matter whether the victims are black or white, innocent children, helpless animals, streams, or forests?

'Michael Tobias gives life to such desperate thoughts, melding morality with high adventure, and action with anguish. A terrific story, told from the heart, its soul rich with knowledge. Some people and corporations should lose sleep wondering if *Rage And Reason* will ever become a real life thriller for them.'

Ingrid E. Newkirk – President, PETA: People For The Ethical Treatment Of Animals

'Rage and Reason is a compelling book that reminds us of our tendencies as a race to act without reason or recognition of consequence. Traversing the bridge between the sacred and profane, we are made deeply concious of the true nature of life, and of the importance and necessity of compassion.

'Michael Tobias has consistently hit very close to home by bringing us face to face with ourselves.'

Steven Seagal – actor/producer/director

'This very personal narrative is at once a riveting and troubling journey that deals with humans' continued abuse of nonhuman animals. It is one of the most controversial works of its type and is a must read as we head into the 21st century. To be sure it will force clarity for those on all sides of these difficult issues.'

Marc Bekoff – Professor of Organismic Biology, University of Colorado, Boulder; editor of *An Encyclopedia of Animal Rights and Animal Welfare* (Greenwood, 1998)

'*Rage And Reason* has hit a bit too close to home ... So compelling are the human dynamics of a tale where terrorist carnage takes on a life of its own.'

Dr. Tom Marks – Academy of the Pacific, Honolulu

'Murder, mayhem and mystery – all in the context of animal rights. Think it can't be done? Read this book.'

William Shatner

Rage and Reason

Rage and Reason

MICHAEL TOBIAS

Edinburgh • London • San Francisco

AK Press, P.O. Box 40682, San Francisco, CA 94140, USA
AK Press, P.O. Box 12766, Edinburgh, Scotland EH8 9YE
AK Press, London

Library of Congress Cataloging-in-Publication Data
A catalog record for this title is available from the Library of Congress

British Library Cataloguing-in-Publication Data
A catalogue record for this title is available from the British Library

ISBN 1-873176-56-2

For JGM

AUTHOR'S NOTE

The following is a work of beleaguered fiction, an utterly minority voice, the product of a painful convalescence in a distant land. Its characters were created in the mind of a fictitious protagonist for purposes of self-help, general therapy and unavoidable reflection. No deliberate or subconscious malice, ill-will, defamation, smear, opprobrium, belittlement, shame, dishonour, deprecation, humiliation, disparaging innuendo or harm – public, private or financially-related – to any product, or by-product, brand name, trademark, patent or food type, biological process or industrial image or intellectual copyright is intended, either by implication or deduction, deliberately, inadvertently or otherwise. Nor is any possible or plausible likeness to – any of the above, or to any one human being, or group of such beings, either living or dead; to any small business or multinational, government agency, President, employee, contractor, subcontractor, high school, college, university or staff, research lab, or laboratory staff; to any farming or ranching community, State, city, or city council or local government, agribusiness, or corporation – premeditated, wilful, pre-contrived, intended, planned, considered or designed. Nor has any deliberate, accidental or coincidental likeness been favoured or fashioned, planned or intended, in any way, for any purpose.

While fictional characters in the book cause harm in adherence to a perspective they – as mere characters in a novel – apparently believe in, let it be *unambiguously asserted by the Author, and herewith understood by the Reader,* that *the Author in no way condones such violence,* or seeks its realization in real life; nor presents it in this fashion as any kind of model or tactic to be adopted by anyone, anywhere, at any time. The violence in this book has been purely invented and conveyed as a warning of things gone wrong, terribly wrong, in our society, and for purposes of throwing some dark light on the tragic, psychological forces at work that compel people to kill; as well as for purposes of medical and psychological expiation, of venting the inevitable frustrations inherent to being a sensitive person -which we all are; members of a species that has collectively waged relentless war against defenceless creatures that were here long before us, and, with a little luck, will be here even after we have moved on.

The Author would forcefully submit and remind readers that there are *nonviolent* options for working with that frustration. The human destruction of other humans, and of the myriad other life forms with whom we cohabit the Earth, can be halted, and the world healed, through dedicated effort targeted at changing human systems – of law, of consumption, and of perception. By other names, through consciousness raising. Active compassion, tolerance, peaceful campaigns, patience, education, extraordinary forbearance, and art, are all corollaries of the nonviolent psyche, of a conscience organized around effective and transforming techniques for mending a human world gone awry.

Violence need not beget violence. Love can conquer even the most widespread and very real of evils, even of the kind imagined and portrayed throughout this novel.

MT

A BROTHER'S PRELUDE

The Germans have said, at least since the days of Schiller, that great souls suffer in silence. Over here, we explain that you have the right to remain silent. But you have *no right* to remain silent when the suffering of others is at stake. It may be noble, even spiritually uplifting, to forgive one's own personal enemies. The Dalai Lama appears to have done so. And Christ certainly exemplified that ideal. But it is sheer complicity to forgive the enemies of *other* innocent victims. If Thy name be truly hallowed. In sum, that has been the message of my strange and terrible, my sublimely fulfilled brother, who for better or worse, I have kept.

He loved Puccini, scored better than average on his college entrance exams, had a girlfriend, worked part-time for a vet, loved our parents with an atypical conviviality.

He was no subversive; not in Pueblo, Colorado where we grew up. But being my only, my older brother and protector against the mob out there, he was my rightful obsession, in a metaphorical sense. My own inner double who would talk to me in my sleep, give me wings to fly, a private guided missile. His increasing chaos, private hells and glorious estrangements in real life shadowed my own unconscious evolution as a young boy. We walked railroad tracks together, rhapsodizing insects, girls' tits, card games, and Puccini, what I mistook for years to be a kind of squash. But even then it seemed to me that I was doing most of the talking, that Dirkson (he actually preferred, oddly enough, to be called by our family name, Felham, a request I honour) was always engendering my own internal dialogue. I knew he was preparing for something grand and expeditionary. I fantasized a number of *Lost Worlds*. I was a movie buff. But what was it, really? In the beginning, I hadn't a clue.

When he first heard a rendition of Puccini's eccentric duet for cats, with hisses and scratching on an old gramophone recording which he purchased precociously at the age of eight at a second-hand store, I guess he figured he'd discovered his first Everest; arranged his own Lento molto rendition of the 'Donde Lieta' aria from *La Boheme* which seemed to break his heart ... *Donde lieta u-sci al tuo gri-do d'a-mo-re tor-na so-la Mi-mi al so-li-tar-rio ni-do* ... I succeeded in finding the translation ... *Once again I'll return to my own scentless flowers, lonely as once before to live with all my memories* ... How bizarre of him. He sang it for Mom's birthday, giving her a large bouquet of black roses. Why black, I wondered.

Years later, when he came home the first Christmas after leaving for the Air Force Academy, everything about him had changed. The metamorphosis occurred during that time away, I assumed. It was at one of those Midwestern Christmas parties – so American, so white and plastered, in his case so courteous and obligatory – that I detected a deeper syndrome, one that had begun long, long ago, out on those railroad tracks, amid the deep-running agonies of a Mimi, a Caravadossi, and all the other tragic figures of his Puccini.

As everyone joined in, belting Christmas classics– *Hark the herald angels sing, glory to the newborn king; peace on earth and mercy mild, God and sinners reconciled* – his face went ashen, whey, a disastrous colour ... – *sorrowing, sighing, bleeding, dying* ... one Noel after another ... *word of Father now in flesh appearing* ... *the ox and lamb kept time* ... *Angels tell the story of this day of glory* ... *four calling birds, three French hens* and so on – I stood watching his increasing – what? – Disgust? Pain? – averting eyes, squirming ungracefully away from social kisses, struggling not to mingle, as if adjusting to a life that was already pathological, a desperado mentality. And I knew then and there that he had done something wrong. Something dreadful, perhaps. He was dying out, fading away. Who are you? I implored.

And as the harmonies mounted that Christmas, the carolling more and more rancid, he sank further away – I observed – until I too was locked out, the distance between us becoming unrecoverable.

There was but a single option available to him – no one else would ever know, could ever understand – which was a slow suicide. He meant to accomplish great deeds in the process. A glory unto God. And thus the logic of what is normally termed terrorism began. Launched according to a serious and deeply-considered motive, his own inner demolition, a worldly and empathetic condition, timed to self-destruct; love of animals that was, considering the human odds – I shudder – the mores, against it, insane. Why you?

And where does a life split apart? Or become so philosophical and questioning, so brutally frank as to be properly called a state of crisis, painful, and life-threatening? When does the seeing of the way things really are, suddenly mean that we can no longer be what we were, or would like to be? In other words, when does seeing condemn, and realizing destroy, forever more? Like the motions of help, or belief, a *witness* is forever subverted. His insides gutted. Don't doubt this theatrical flair for one moment. Even with the space of years to make light of it, and then to try and ignore it, to rout it from one's insides, I was ultimately caught out unawares, feeble and full victim. *Destiny* is another one of those words.

Was it Felham's first year biology class in high school that triggered the mental quake? That was a very modern institution, after all, its motto chosen in the name of Descartes, with a very special field day in store for those who stomached the preliminaries. Forget frogs. That was endearing kid's stuff. Forget guinea pigs and hamsters that hadn't yet been flushed down toilets the first time they nicked the child or shat on the master bed; forget the has-been cats, the ones picked up off the street and left famished and desperate and caterwauling at the backdoor of Biology 101, expecting sympathy and warm milk, not vivisection. And the fish and salamanders and toads. Hundreds of external gills, pulmonary arteries, aortic arches, venous systems, tiny little crania, toad digits severed like there were no tomorrow. That was all early in the day, the larval stage of secondary education, to separate the squeamish with no future in science, from the real novitiates.

Later on in the course, Biology 101 was on to the dog. Not the family dog, the sleek, well-groomed, well-fed variety, but the half-wild with anxiety subspecies, hair matted, eyes frazzled and, well, desperate jaws arthritic from hunger. A German shepherd whose hips were disintegrating, a mongrel that had clearly lost its way months before, the scrap from biological supply companies, the ones stolen under false pretences, or shipped in from the pound expressly for the purpose of dissection. But they had all been family dogs, once. And it showed in their manner of want, of hope. Sentiments flared in the lab, because students found it hard, at first, to separate feelings from *science,* as it was all deemed. But in the end they mostly managed it, cutting into the amateurishly anaesthetized being, fighting to keep it down, the squirming dog, their own vomit and tears, and ultimately making the grade. Oh but it got worse, at the end.

Macaca mulatta, otherwise known as the Rhesus monkey. This was a time, recall, when Blacks were still forced to sit at the back of buses in America; when in Australia the law still favoured dogs over Aborigines; well before countries like India banned most exportation of the little Rhesus (though even then the U.S. Government could intervene on behalf of national research labs). But in those days, twenty-thousand a year were apparently being shipped over to this country for any and every purpose. They were not expensive. Our local junior college got two of them, as well as an Indian mongoose. Half of our biology class took an excursion to the college to take part in the killings, a kind of reward at the end of the term. I don't know what laws were circumvented, or overlooked, if any; how it could have happened that fourteen-year-olds should have been condemned for the rest of their lives for having participated in the cold-hearted murder of those two gentle, pitiful primates. It's beyond my comprehension. When I think back to it, I imagine every black and white Frankenstein movie I ever saw, primitive villagers, my peers, chasing the frightened and confused monster into the misty graveyard carrying pitchforks and torches and shotguns. No reason. Only hatred that surfaced from ... from where? From everything they were, had been indoctrinated to be, their parents, their grandparents, their religion, to have made monsters out of two helpless little monkeys ...

Why not keep them as school pets, mascots? the vice president of the high school student body had inquired, prepared to make it an issue. Because they could carry diseases, came the absurd, but unexamined reply from the Dean of Arts & Sciences at the college.

Those hamburger-raised brats, pre-med., pimply and pubescent teens, skinned the two sensate beings damn near alive. There was clearly vengeance in the act; something so complex and atavistic that I can't begin to flush out a meaning. Human behaviour in high school and college should well be the model for every worst-case scenario. The monkeys cried just like little babies; their wrinkled fingers grappled in the air for rescue by another primate, God, Mother; they looked with big dark eyes up at the obscene and fumbling juveniles whose sharp instruments were already raised, pleading and convulsing, strapped down indifferently, no sense whatsoever that high school students equated with living beings. Rather, the monkeys were staring into the eyes of Hell, of demons at work seeking revenge on all goodness, beauty, perfection. A few girls might run out of the lab, to cry and puke in the johns. But the vivisections were only accelerated. It was like trying out for the football team. There was hardly a discussion of human sex education in that school, yet there were these kids castrating the male monkey with their junior college peers (the school had gotten a breeding pair, all the more remarkable considering their sad fate) dangling its balls in front of the young ladies – a real turn on, you might suppose. You'd even begin to ask yourself whether the Rhesus wasn't more sensitive, could feel more pain, had greater needs and more lasting desires, unquestionable insights, than those sudden sadists who thought nothing of taking knives to them. Who would never understand what they had done unless the cards should one day be reversed; until such time as knives were taken to *them*. And thus the link to Felham, to my present sunspot, a brash explosion in the hearing mechanism, something so tangled in the human skein, so complicated by trembling soul and contemplation, half-thoughts, inhibitions, rotten luck ... And no remedies.

That was my understanding of American manifest destiny, played out in a small Colorado cow town. The administration of ether, or whatever the hell they used, was never an exact science. And it was erroneously claimed by the instructor that monkeys bred like flies and had few feelings. The cost, about eighty dollars a piece in those days. One dollar per student, or the price of a movie ticket. The stupidity on everybody's part was monumental.

But even so, even taking into account that slurred holistic decay of sense and reason; even acknowledging the decline of a young man's West – and by implication, every facet of the system, from parents to teachers, schools, jobs, civil workers, neighbours, peers, all involved in perpetuating what has become, with shit on one's ears, unadulterated madness – how could I have missed the moment he became so infected with it, so strange and dangerous?

Something induced him to press that trigger a first time. A revolution inside him. That was the apple falling from a tree, the midnight ride of Paul Revere, the first rat that ever made it through a maze. Every trigger after that moment was a piece of cake. He was free. Who would have surmised such ontologies?

How could Jessie have predicted what *her* day would bring, turning on the ignition, heading down the hill? Or you, a few pages into something leisurely picked up? Who is Jessie? She's the woman that was his undoing. She's also the woman who guaranteed, in a certain allegorical sense, his survival. And who are you? What have you done? Someone, at some time, is going to inquire, will find out. Perhaps at Judgment Day. Or maybe that's what one should call *Felham's Law*.

There is complicity, as defined under the law, any law, and I have to go through each day fearing that something terrible will happen to me, as it happened to him. They're going to come and take me away, or ambush me in the night, as I return home late from work. A world must be conspiring all around me, enclaves of hateful people you can't imagine, people who really exist, not just in the movies. I hate him for showing me that, for bringing it so calamitously close. My life is not my own. Which was always the one thing I had prized above all else – to be free of any hassles.

I just wish he'd die already. Or let me know that he is really in permanent exile. Or volunteer for witness relocation. I can't stand not knowing. Always expecting a bombshell. I can see why so many infants born during the Dresden bombings grew up gay. I mean I don't truly understand, but I can imagine. The constant overhead. The never knowing. The clutching to tits, the shaking shelter. Always wondering when it will be all right to venture outside, and what the street will look like.

Sometimes, I think I'd like to turn him in. If I knew exactly where he was. To end this purgatory. This incessant state of goddamned apprehension. I don't need this. It's simply untenable. And he should know it. He should be more sensitive to me. I mean, I'm also an animal, if you want to talk on that level. And I've worked hard. And I've got an MBA. And I deserve some peace of mind. And I'm like some unpredictable jerk atop a building in the wind. Afraid of heights. And I don't know whether I'm going to jump, like that would cure the vertigo. I don't know whether Felham is getting to me. Or if there's shit on *my* ears and the sickness, the howling, is beginning to unhinge my nerves, as well. The neurons are dynamite, and every day I move cautiously through a no man's land of mine fields and live wires.

I'd asked him if he wouldn't mind baby-sitting my son Bart for the morning. Iyura, Bart's mother, my wife, had to have two wisdom teeth removed and I needed to be out of town. He was not crazy about the idea but acquiesced, taking the kid to one of those Gymborees where babies are brought by their mother to be socially enriched.

So there was Felham sitting akimbo on the floor, surrounded by all these buoyant mothers and felicitous infants, and his ankle started to bleed.

"Is that blood? I'm sure that's blood ... Someone's bleeding!" a fair-haired woman exclaimed, her lips heavily smeared, eyes thickly painted, suggesting the violent, chariot-coursing brush strokes of a Rubens.

A shadow figure in the room. No sense that destiny was being shaped, here; my brother's tale, streaked like the rain against a getaway car.

Felham had inadvertently knocked one ankle against the other in his awkward shenanigans with my boy. And this was the beginning of his doom. Flight. Lucky stars.

"Dammit," he muttered, getting up, moving over towards the wall, a string of droplets following him, where he took off his other sock and wrapped it around the oozing ankle. This implacable fact of himself, separating him out from among the others. One of the few lousy times he actually tried to commingle, like a normal person.

All eyes in that room stared at the ankle. Irate with aversion; aghast with premonition ...

Like a grenade going off in the whorls of his head, the shattering fiasco of inner blood. Blood thoughts ...

It did not hemorrhage, but could not be easily checked, either ... drops of blood that came from nowhere. Who speaks of blood, outside of medical brotherhoods? Blood feuds, thirsty, cold, out for, blood, blood money, blood pressure. Blood meal. The great unending plains of blood. All of it. In me. That moment.

A world that dreams, acts, sees, hopes, believes and remembers because of blood, but dismisses it as unfavourable, undiscussable. The perfect spherical drops, a sentence across the seven feet – he moved towards the wall –

... a passage of tortured remains, minute, as holy as any Grail smearing the floor. A telltale sign that danger has trodden here ...

Again, in his head, it starts to scream. *The crackling horror-scented howls, a rapturous litany, that flow of blood which suffers no intelligence, no decorum.*

Because you see he'd come to identify his own blood which spilled onto the floor of newborns and their mothers, with the abuse of animals. With their blood. The equation is obtuse, admittedly. But he was surely living according to certain sacraments of his own devising. Responding in kind. 'An eye for an eye' – that did not come even close to catching the magnitude of Felham's eucharistic connections to the animal world.

My heart thinks of his ankle in that way; to the destiny closing in all around him; the vast geography of turmoil whose only legal defence, or right of counsel, or Bill of Rights, however one describes it, was my older brother's heart. He was in a sense, the last possible appeal, a governor's signature staying execution. Not at all what Jessie, who sat ten feet away on the floor, watching the unfolding, would have expected.

The kills from Lapland to Amazonia. Every day. Every day. A civilization based upon kills. AC current, ice, butcher paper, plastic wrap, foam trays, industry and chemistry, oligarchies engendered for the purpose of preserving kills.

They all point to the same ankle of calamity. They move away, grabbing their babies. Only Jessie remains steadfast.

How often have I gone through the steps that must have brought him to this abyss of pain in a San Francisco Gymboree? The smug, jeering, bureaucratic posse eternally after him, never a moment of breathing space, forever writhing in his gut. I think individual pain is the individual's, period. And each one of us can look forward to entering the same ring and getting knocked out by the final round. There is to be a final round, make no mistake. Some box young, forced into it, hit over the head when they least expect it. Others are dragged in, or seduced. And still others find that a fist is suddenly lodged in their gut, like a cancer, and they've got to fight right where they are. How the hell did that fist get in his gut, and now in mine? Why me?

The point Felham drove home was that the fist is inherent to life. One might as well accept it earlier than later. His Irish.

Did one freckle detect another? Did the odd autumnal strands of red hair in Jessie identify a kindred autumn in my brother? Irish to Irish?

Just four days before this incident, this blood amidst swaddlings, Felham had pushed his way through customs in Thailand, his ankle layered with gauze, the inside of his tennis shoe awash in blood. Moments later, shuffling through line, a guard had sniffed the air and looked him right in the eye. The eye of oblivion, about to snap, blast furnace of queries, malignant with wonder, man to man. A thickset, inscrutable-eyed stranger with his pistol, able to kill unpredictably, governmental and sworn to duty, while Felham had everything to lose, standing in line in the sweat of unaccustomed defencelessness. *Will I kill myself? Will I take out others? How far am I willing to* go? he churned inside.

Felham didn't waver. He had to get out of that sordid country, had to banish from his nostrils the amalgamated scent of torment, masked as food. Masquerading victuals, twelve-year old Burmese AIDS-carrying slaves, scents, spices, all precious and odoriferous – kill. Remains. Gushers of blood jettisoned at the jugular, the point of decapitation. Goats, bulls, pigs, chickens, ducks, dogs, birds, who knows, the occasional Hmong rebel tribesman cut down in the purgatory alongside the Cambodian border. Every living thing subject to the knife. Thai food, in other words. Tom kai kai. Pad Thai. Mee krob. All the congested dishes of flesh. Of legs peeled, skins broiled, eyes gouged, bones ground into the exotic-sounding. The squeals near the floating flower marts of incarcerated little ones, white fluff, or blue-black feathers; yellow eyes, groaning foreknowledge, intelligence quivering for days, weeks in anticipation of the sorry moment. And all the while delegated to the short end of a tether, kicked, teased, fly-harangued, fed nothing, scraps out-of-reach, water tepid and foul. Every back alley dampened with the blood of long-term victims. A trade from the outer jungles to the inner city. Tens-of-thousands taped, tied, bundled, burlapped and shipped off in oxygenless crates to Germany or the Canaries or Cuba or Mexico. To easy ports and borders where officialdom could be bought; that looked the other way and smiled, blandly discounting it. That toothless lawless smile of countries goaded by the taste for blood. Fast money. And not a single tear across the human landscape.

Those picturesque views of Thailand, high white hotels with edgeless swimming pools and scantly done-down goddesses on burlesque afternoons patrolling the air, sustained by the lust ever expectant. All a hot and languishing window-dressing for those incapable of seeing beneath the veil. Refusing to look. A Thailand deep in darkness and death. How few native species actually remained, including the Karen tribesmen, the last vegetarians, dying out in the jungles.

Which may prompt the reader to ask how I could accurately describe Felham's desperate exit from Thailand.

There had, in fact, been previous exits, some of which he had detailed to me in moments of sad laxity, multiple personae (?) or boyhood panic.

On one such occasion, the description led us into what I now recognize to be a maze of logic.

"Why, I mean how ... WHY?" I pleaded with him at the time. "And why are you telling me?" I was angry, appalled, incredulous, and it was the first night of a long irrefutable heaviness. He had just come out of the French-tiled bathroom with wide cloth bandages all over his hand. And he smelled peculiar, somewhere between a fish market and a dead game animal.

"Because I need you to know, that's all. Because you're my only brother."

The words rebounded, a Bryce Canyon between us, and for the first time my own situation reared up, family connection, hateful link to the unwanted, and I felt disgraced, impure, dirty. I would never forget the feelings of having been implicated. Thailand was merely the most recent of a string of implications.

"There is evil in this world," he had quietly reminded me. Now the prophecy resurfaced.

"And you're adding to it," I impugned.

"No. I'm trying faithfully to stop it."

"By killing people?"

"I'm doing my part to minimize the overall violence. We dropped atomic bombs on Japan for the same reason, not because we thought it was a good thing to kill a few hundred thousand Japanese, but because we figured – and we were probably right – we'd be saving more lives than we destroyed, in the end."

He said this fearlessly, in spite of the fact of his Japanese sister-in-law, whose uncle was in the war, working for the other side. But there was nothing personal in his thinking. I knew that much.

"That's different. We were a nation that had been attacked, and had made a national decision to revenge. I don't mean revenge, I mean – "

"You mean punish."

"To get even," I said, "It was just." I might have taken back that word. Because justice and war, any war, have never quite been reconciled in my mind. And yet what else is there to justify killing?

"Punishment is the force at work," he went on. The verb that makes us do things – the *desire* to punish. The purity of punishing, the intense satisfaction which comes from punishing. You can't deny it. We wanted to cripple those bastards. To make them suffer. It's fine to speak of reconciliation half-a-century later. But Pearl Harbor happened."

"And who are you punishing?" I demanded. "The human race?"

"I don't know where to begin," he said, exhaling with a sigh burdened by impatience. "You and I have such utterly different views." He spoke with some defeat in his voice reacting to the fact that I had turned my back on his activities in the past; decreed my total non-involvement, my censure of what little I knew about him. What little was more than enough. Enough to make a wreck of me.

"I'm listening," I said curtly.

"We're all equal here on earth. Every living animal that surely feels as much pain and joy as anybody I know. Their neurological systems are essentially as complicated as our own, down even to as simple a creature as a sea slug."

"You've talked to sea slugs, lately?"

"I don't know their language, but I don't know Tibetan either, or Japanese, for that matter, and that has not prevented me from admiring Tibetans and Japanese."

"I would have expected a more intelligent analogy from you."

"Listen little brother, animals are the *core* of all intelligence, all analogy. Every metaphor in art, in literature, in human thought. Do you doubt it? You want intelligent analogy, look to the animal kingdom. They're smart, kid; smarter than any of us can possibly imagine, that's been proven on countless levels, in tens-of-thousands of situations."

Kid ... It was a former life. Except I wasn't so gullible any more. And my childhood was no longer relevant, under the current conditions. "Give me one example?" I said.

"You're baiting me."

"No. I mean it. One example." I was not ignorant of the literature, though certainly vague in terms of particulars. But I was aghast at how slippery he seemed, diverting attention from what were, to be clear, his crimes against humanity.

"Washoe."

"The chimp?"

"Yeah."

"I read about it."

"Him."

"Okay, him. I read about him years ago in some science periodical or someplace. You could argue the data in any direction, if I recall. They didn't convince me, anyway, that the words weren't memorized, without any real understanding."

"You're diddling. And you weren't there."

"Were you?"

"No, but I have been in labs, lots of them. I've spoken with chimps and I can tell you that Washoe knew what he was talking about, and that's a working vocabulary of hundreds of English words and concepts. The average American has a working vocabulary of under fifty words a day. How many words of chimp do you know? And the same with Koko the gorilla. An utterly expressive, articulate animal. Big brain. Big thoughts. Big heart. Loves cats."

"I think you're reading into the research whatever you want to read."

"No, you're just being stubborn and blind because you don't want to accept – fundamentally – a premise that would force you to think differently."

"*Thinking differently* does not quite capture the context of premeditated murder, now does it?"

He closed his eyes, then opened them with the reticence of dignity. Felham's ire, the haste of generals was tempered by his genuine protectiveness of me. As far as he was concerned, I was still living at home. "When I was in the Amazon I heard about a species of rare parrots that dwelled in the trees above a tribe of indigenous Indians up along a tributary in the northeast. Eventually word reached the outside as to the existence of these people. The first anthropologist ventured into the Indians' camp hoping to get to know them. But he was too late. The Indians had already gone extinct. Most of the parrots had died out as well, but one old bird was left, and upon seeing this anthropologist, it got all nostalgic for people, flew down from the high canopy and began speaking the Indians' language to this scientist, who was then able to learn about the tribe, down to important details. Think of it: a bird being the last living spokesperson for an entire people."

"It sounds like hearsay."

"No. In Paris, police relied upon a bird's description of two thieves to make a prosecution stand in court. The bird had been home, sitting on its perch, as the burglars sacked an apartment, speaking to one another."

"That stuff's really true?" I doubted it.

"The Brazilian parrot had observed for years, decades, genetically, perhaps, for millennia. It missed the company of people. They have souls, little brother; they are individuals with strong eccentric personalities, they dream, they love – they make love passionately. They mate, often, for life. You've seen them preen one another, with their eyes half-lidded in ecstasy.

I'm not keen to go on standing here teaching you all the basics of wildlife biology because ... well, frankly, I can see that your own opinions are like cement, at the moment."

"You're entitled to any opinion under the sun, as long as it doesn't hurt anybody," I concluded. I had to cut him off, to sever even the possibility of concurrence, otherwise I could see myself losing distinctions, slipping into the morass.

"Well it's my opinion. I believe it, I know it to be so, in my gut, I feel it as much as anything." He was mad, I thought. "As much love as I had for Mom and Dad. The shared destiny of all life forms is basic. And being human in my book connotes responsibility, empathy, love."

"Big words. Easy words."

"They're not easy."

"Tell them to a jury and see where they get you."

"Are you with me or against me? I need to know," he pressed.

"Of course I'm WITH you, you dumb ... You're one to talk of love ... " I was over the top of some fierce, inexpressible exasperation, wanting but having no right to admonish him, mistrustful of so noble a speech. How could cold blooded murder come across as eloquence and reason? "They say Ted Bundy had a high IQ as well."

"It's love that I'm talking about."

"I don't kill people. Jesus, Felham. What do you want from me?"

"To know that I believe in what I'm doing. These are people who have escaped justice." He was using my turn of the phrase. I realized that. It made our differences more difficult.

"If they're guilty, they'll eventually get caught. You're not the law."

"I am a law."

"Oh fuck ... you're crazy! You're fucking crazy!"

"I am a law, little brother. The law of my heart. You've got to live for something. You've got to be able to say you tried to make a difference in the end."

"Well this isn't the end, or not for me. Though it doesn't sound like you've left yourself much time."

By no means was he unaware of his situation. His whole being was electric, a calculating solemnity that bristled with awareness, a hubris totally outside culture. A solitaire, a dogmatist, a man without a dust mote of humility. Working on sheer guts, on fear. Just being near him over dinner relayed much of that adrenaline. By his proximity, I felt the bounty on my head.

"Look, you've got to try to understand this," he went on, adopting a relaxed air. I could see his drinking hand tremble.

"There are other ways," I interrupted. "Thousands of people concerned about animal welfare are making a difference, and they're doing it peacefully."

"They're doing very little."

I knew that there was an *Endangered Species Act*. An *Animal Welfare Act*, because average, feeling people protested conditions and persuaded Congress to do something. I told him so. Though to be perfectly forthcoming I didn't *really* know anything about such laws, or what they did, or didn't do.

"Those same activists, with the best intentions, have been reduced to pleading with other environmentalists to write twenty cent postcards to Congressmen, and letters to Governors threatening to boycott their States, and all products coming from those States, until such time as they have ended every manner of abuse, from killing grizzly bears, to turning their back on illegal laboratory experiments. Section nine of the *Endangered Species Act* forbids the killing of any threatened or endangered species."

"There. That's a law."

"And every State government breaks it by condoning the killing under murky, hard to trace guises, every hour, every day. Some don't bother with circumvention: they condone the killing outright. There are more laws pertaining to the manufacture of bubble gum, or lipstick, than there are relating to all the animals on this entire planet. I could tell you things. But I'm not sure you'd even care."

"That's just bullshit. Of course I care. Why the hell do you think I'm a vegetarian? Because of you. I had a million dollars to spend. I could have done anything with it– " Mom and Dad were killed in an automobile explosion and Felham and I joined others in a class action suit " –but the vegetarian restaurant seemed like the best, the most moral– "

"Fuck. You did it for the money."

"That's not true, dammit! I was the one who suggested naming it after Dad. Not you!"

Ralph. Ralph David Felham. A mere fifty-five when he perished. A great Dad. Macho, this is true; military hero, decorated, all that. But turned liberal. Gentle. A perfect paradox that you could live with and comprehend and almost envy. A small-town, Colorado version of Leonardo Da Vinci, I liked to think – art and submarines; machine guns and nudes. And I felt tears and wanted to punch my brother in the chest for insinuating ... but I didn't. Not a murderer. No way. No telling what he might do. That's how crazy I thought he was. I was in total jeopardy.

"Okay," he murmured.

I'd become impervious to his argument, just as he knew I would and I basically told him to get out. I didn't want him coming near me, my wife, my child – I wanted him away forever. I was more tactful only because I was scared, scared of the older brother whom I had emulated half my life. "Given your dilemma," I said – I used the word conscientiously – "you can't expect us to remain in business together as if nothing has happened?"

"What would you propose?" he asked.

"I don't know." I was stalling for the words. Afraid to exile a person who was, after all – and more so on account of the folks being dead – half of myself. My only living kin.

"It's my other life. I need the cover," he admitted with a hint of humility after some moments' thought, referring to the restaurant and our relationship.

"Cover?"

What was right? What do I say, what am I supposed to do? Can you understand that there was nobody to help me in this? My life was over.

"You will not!" I finally broached, reprimanding out loud, firmly planting my will where I thought it belonged.

"Only good will come of it."

"Only good will come of WHAT?" I appealed.

"You're facilitating– " I heard no other part of it. *Facilitate.* That's what the jury would remember. Dirkson's brother and business partner facilitated the whole operation. Guilty.

"I cannot allow you to drag us with you," I resolved.

He sat on the couch, his head utterly downcast. I had to say no, but by doing so I felt as if I'd given him time to drum up some threat, something I'd already done without knowing it that he could hang over me. Some warning reaching back to our childhood, perhaps, an emotional hook from which I could not extricate myself. The death of our parents. Would he use that? As he contemplated the moment, I began to panic: what if he's going to tell me I'm already in it up to my nostrils. That by being in business even these last four years together, he being the minder, a sort of glorified bookkeeper, that I'd *already* facilitated. Had he used the restaurant's profits to finance his, his ...

"Okay," he repeated, somberly.

I just looked at him, waiting for certainty. Then nodded. "You'll walk away?"

He said all right. He'd go. Forget he ever mentioned any of it. I could take him off the company record. Tell the lawyer he'd changed professions. Moved, I didn't know where, obviously. And then, completely ignoring the tension, he asked if he could fix us dinner. We were at home. Iyura and Bart were at Iyura's cousin's house.

Later, after concluding the hellish drama of our little talk, I nearly could hope that Felham had been exaggerating his morality play, elocuting some dark wish fulfilment that had come to naught. I knew he was hurting, worse than I'd ever seen a living person hurt. Or maybe *that's* an exaggeration, in as much as he was patient, rather stolid-looking. And what did I know about hurting? But his story bore little resemblance to any reality, or character trait, or family history. It came from nowhere and led nowhere. It couldn't be my brother, but had to be some sinister verbal diversion away from what was really at the bottom of his avowed anxieties.

"You want to tell me about what's *really* going on?" I volunteered the next day. "Is it about the deaths of Mom and Dad".

To my eternal regrets, he did. He started all over again, or he tried to, stumbling through much of it, step by step. In that Thailand of his hatred, Felham was stricken with a toxic and overpowering clarity.

There was no particularly strong family tie providing him an easy out, other than myself. I was a like a magnet for him. He knew he could get to me, because he knew me so well. Furthermore, he stood firmly by the realization that he had already outlived most Neanderthals, Romans, indeed, most pre-nineteenth century peoples. That might not mean a thing to the living, but in Felham's mind, the remaining days or months, or years were gravy. What a way to view it. Good way, really. Historical and neat and fair. I don't know where he came by that enlarged sphere of thinking. Certainly not Pueblo. Swimming at Jake & Al's Sports, consuming fast food and root beer floats and working out elaborate plans to cop feels along the river in Silver Creek on Saturday nights with girls picked up at the bowling alley. Fast drives down Big Thompson Boulevard. I could tell you things – the apotheosis of the mundane. Comfort. Love. Security. Little things. Cicada at night in the cottonwoods. Great nature. Little struggles. His first encounter with Sartre, and our highly literate Grandmother, Dora, despairing of his exhaustive analysis of Sartre's novel, *Nausea.* She feared it might wreck the thirteen-year old in him. The one who used to play games of gin rummy and cheat like a fiend so as to let her win. He was sweet that way.

Now there stood before me this colossal change from all that. Call it personal growth. More than a mere metaphysical problem, in Felham's case. I needed to know whether my brother at any point questioned himself, stopped long enough to register fear and trembling, or whether the decision was taken on the front lines of his ruminations to go forward, not in the vain hopes of some Purple Heart, or stopping the war against animals, but for the survival of *himself.* Did he think about a soul? Was it his *soul* that concerned him, or the souls of others? And if so, what is the soul? I ask this here not to belabour the inadmissible, but to admit to my own utter confusion on all matters religious, or pertaining to motive. I have become a mental victim of the laws closing in around me. Not that I think he was acting in any religious manner, although he might have been. But because I would be greatly surprised if Felham actually did what he did on account of the soul. But then how else am I going to explain it? What the hell am I going to say?

On the other hand, he was already a dead man in the eyes of the law. That's right. He had nothing, absolutely nothing, to lose. Absolutely free.

All I could see, in sum, was that my brother was on the run from the FBI. And he would be so forever, until they caught him, and tore him ligament from sinew. And suddenly my insides were on the lam with him.

I won't argue that there isn't a little quadrant in me which thrills to Felham's charter. A psychological Corpus Juris Canonici which imagines his next move, or wonders when I'll read about him, finally, in the newspapers. It's the same foreboding I go to bed with, dream about, wake up fearing. A foreshadowing that is my brother's highest ideal. And maybe mine, too. But it's a small part, not one I'd talk about, or live by. I'd rather it didn't exist. Like I said, sometimes I just wish they'd get him, before he gets to me.

My wife, who has just come home with Bart, does not know anything about all this. That I have to live concealing so much from the woman I love is oppressive. Iyura works at a classy gallery downtown, specializing in eighteenth and nineteenth century American and European masters. She did her MFA on a painter named Federico Zandomeneghi whose blues and shadows she was mad for, and had spent years refining her impressions and parleying her passion into a viable lifestyle. Imagine: a profession built up of shadows! Black-eyed, svelte-loined Iyura, from Kyoto. I have no intention of destroying her confidence in the family unit. To plunge her from the safe aesthetic realm, from lovely openings and showings into the hell that Felham has ordained, is not necessary, if in fact I can somehow avoid it. That it should be my own martyrdom is enough for one family.

So I told him he could keep the cover of our restaurant. It was the least I could do. A whim fulfilled in the smothered silence of an old routine.

And fortunately he was often away somewhere. I never asked. We maintained a strict decorum of ease and of discretion.

He came back the other day and I inquired how he was doing.

"Fine," he relayed. "Never felt better."

"Perhaps you wouldn't mind– " and that's when I asked him to spend a couple of hours with Bart at the Gymboree on account of Iyura being tied up with her teeth business. There was a need in me to bring him in closer.

However outrageous his misadventures, he seemed – somehow remarkably – to be pulling them off. And I was beginning to have this strange fantasy that he'd never get caught. Or that perhaps I really had imagined everything. This irreality induced me, finally, to press my inquiry. "By the way, where were you?" I just had to find out.

"You really want to know?"

"Sure. Why not?" My easy capitulation already belied the worst descent, a treasonable move on my part, though I hadn't even figured that out, yet.

"Thailand," he said in a surprise whisper, behind the closed doors of my linen-upholstered office.

I see him entering a complex with wire cutters and a machine gun. He would have carried enough rounds slung over his camouflaged shoulder to take out a battalion. There were slimy, lotus- and snake-congested moats along which whole families of grebes made their way, past the honeysuckle and raspberry. They would be caught and eaten later on by locals. Palm trees swayed and were infested with red ants. I hear a distant sound of the highway, of fast-moving lorries filling the sky with diesel.

He had a bowie knife beneath his nylon sling belt, and suddenly makes his first hit on a stout, moustachioed, rifle-toting guard. I see him nearly severing the head, and easing the crumbling body without a ruffle into the water, where he washed off the enormous blade, then continued forward. A second similar execution, this time a woman. Long black hair. A Thai beauty. Slits her throat with great expertise before she feels anything, on account of his speed and there being no nick in the steel, just as Biblical literature commends. No nicks. He goes forward to the main compound where it would not be so simple. Lots of people, and something like an acre-sized greenhouse, filled with corroded cages and a gamey fetor that was already detectable. The birds themselves are not audible. He knows what to expect. A grim, hunched silence, the condition of birds wearily between life and death, that have been tormented beyond what any human being could ever survive. Oven-like jails.

Felham takes in the difficulties at once. There is much ground to cover. He'll have to run. His car is parked in the jungle, just off a main thoroughfare heading north towards Pathum Thani. From the compound back to the car, it is half-a-mile. Three minutes. By that time, how many others will have been alerted? And how many are there? He waits, watching for the pace of things from the protection of teeming tropical cover.

He counts eleven men and two women, not that he distinguishes between them.

He screws on a muffler to his piece, having logically decided to start by taking out stragglers from a safe, silent distance, one at a time. With the first scream, he'll move in, his heater blasting away. Felham knows his weapon.

Three bodies go down. Through the face, or the heart. He never misses. But the third hit is accompanied by screaming and a general alarm. Now they're swarming.

He plunges forward, taking out four men engaged in cards, one slipping away behind the door. He shoots out the windows, punctures tyres on nearby vans. Fire is returned. Felham dives to the dirt, rolling towards the side of the house and facing up in a barrage of marksman's compliments. Returning deadly spray. Eight down, he reckons, racing towards the greenhouse. Fire pursues him. Again ducking down, spinning over, taking out those right behind him with a roar of blast fragments. But more howls are coming, in mutant, nasal Thai; a volley of enraged hornets. Other foul-figured men are running into the compound, all heavily armed. Men in jeans, men in suits, young women looking like the Viet Cong.

He attains the greenhouse. The stench is terrific. Felham kicks open the door and realizes his worst apprehensions. Easily a few thousand rare birds. Cooped up in encrusted cages decades old. Never cleaned. Disease-born acreage. It will take at least ten minutes to free them. That could be a problem. He hadn't counted on so many birds.

Felham lunges beneath a window as it shatters with incoming bullets. Wrestling himself to the entrance, covering his own movement with an avalanche of machine gun spray, he peppers the outsides, catches sight of two advancing females and wastes them. Men are zeroing in to the sides. He blows away one of them, then tosses one of several grenades on his chest harness at the two jeeps parked in tow in a turnout, and a second at the house. He must be sure that the house burns down, and all of the records of transactions with it. The explosions leave few combatants. But Felham knows that the fire will attract authorities sooner or later.

He goes after an escapee who wears a suit and is probably one of the four notorious brothers Felham had learned about poking around at the many bird markets in the city, pursuing him through the jungle adjacent to the front side of the house. At long range, Felham downs him, then returns to his task.

One of the women he'd hit lies before him in the dirt. She is alive, groping for air. Her throat is hemorrhaging. Felham doesn't pause. He puts a bullet through her head to ease the animal's misery in her, then enters the bird house. Normally, he would have left the human misery alone; left it to suffer. But he doesn't have that luxury of revenge this day. Too much happening. Too much exposure.

Rapidly he sets about opening every cage and flushing the live ones out towards the east, away from the city. He recognizes some of the species, birds that have been captured from all over Asia, from the Mergui Archipelago, Hainan Island, Burma, Assam, Bangladesh, Tibet. Derbyan, Emerald-collared, and Plum-Headed parakeets, a Grey-headed Fishing Eagle too weak to strike out at him, a pale Celebes Hanging Parrot – worth a fortune in Los Angeles; the strikingly beautiful Flamed Minivet, probably from Borneo, all of nine inches, brilliant red, screeching for all it's worth. He's got a chance back in the wild. But not a Black Drongo, crow-like, sullen and Javanese, not moving, probably a female, won't make it. Several maroon and black-naped Orioles. Animated, no doubt recently brought in. Endless prey. Many can not fly. A familiar scene, though on a larger scale. Huge numbers of the birds have already died, their bodies festering. Beaks, crania, little claws lie scattered like distant feathers. Some manage to fly away, with wizened cries and withered wing. Some might even survive.

The house is on fire, dark smoke swirling into the sky. Soon there will be helicopters coming to investigate.

He finishes his job, tosses his weapons and grenades into the back of the burning jeep, save for his rod, and runs towards his own vehicle.

As he crosses the outermost fence, where he'd clipped his way through, a single bullet tears into his ankle. Felham half-twists down, whips around, his machine gun discharging a bevy of death. But he sees no one and then flings his weapon into the water, where it sinks. Throwing himself into the passenger side of his rented Mercedes, Felham swings a wide U-turn and races south towards Bangkok. Within minutes, as the first chopper appears overhead, Felham recognizes a vehicle in pursuit.

It is down to the minute now as he sees three cheaply attired toughs trailing him in their polyester knock-offs of some Italian tailoring. Felham can detect their gun hands at the ready. He has no doubt that given a clear aim, crowd or no crowd, they will shoot. Can he take on the whole blasted airport, lacking the weapon which he'd tossed on the run? It is not his intention to die this day.

There's no end to it, he knows that. The spreading disease, a metastasis of entrails dovetailing across every border, a world showered in the lack of caring. He must have known that it is impossible. Even a Mother Theresa has to contend with nothing more numerical than a local hospice here or there.

But he has no time to consider the problem, giving off instead that air of nearly missing his connection. A safe veneer, not out of step with other tourists, beachcombing debauchees on their way to Puket. Breathless, passing through customs, a great price on his head. *The line is going to*

*take ten minutes ... no choice but to force your way on the pretext of missing
a plane. The guard will ask for my ticket and note that I'm on time. What's
all the hurry? Something's wrong, he'll think, smelling the blood.*

"Ticket?" asks the official, a rifle-presenting guard by his side, the
weapon at alert, pointing upwards from the military-banded waistline.
"Passport?" The security is greatly increased as a result of a recent airline
crash, cloaked in the lingering controversy. Reverse thrust or deliberate
tampering?

Felham, nerve-hardened, extends falsified passport, with the obscure
European name and likeness, as well as his boarding pass. The passport is
scrutinized, checked on computer, and somehow – thanks to Muppet –
enjoys easy clearance. Yet there is a moment, the stumbling heart-stopping
reflex: there's no more room, it's in need of extra pages.

The customs official frowns, half shakes his head, then studies Felham.
Felham mumbles *Is something the matter?* He never uses the word
'problem'. Problem increases the problem.

But the customs official says nothing, passing the time by examining
the far-flung record of an itinerary before him. He sees much of this, Felham
assumes. Though the passport in his possession is particularly fraught with
a nomad's restless wanderings, all trumped.

Felham senses his assailants in the rear and cringes impatiently at the
sluggishness of the official before him, who seems to be wanting to divine
Felham's life story.

"No more room," the official says with irritation unable to find a place
for the exit stamp.

Felham smiles calmly. The official stamps his ink on top of a Burmese
one. A week before, Felham had done his business just south of Rangoon,
where the delta throws up enormous mudflats and estuaries serve as mating
grounds for innumerable migratory birds of the Himalaya, a popular hunting
ground for the Thai operation. Poachers easy to knock off from their own
camouflaged bunkers with a long-range laser-guided rifle. At the right time
of day or night, the bodies would sink into the mud without trace, as the
incoming tides with their twilight-frenzy of sharks promptly covered them.
Good sport. Almost a vacation. These Thai bastards were going down. He'd
cut out the heart of what was one of the largest operations of its kind in the
world.

"Blood!" a second young mother cried out, averting her eyes, pulling her
baby away from what, in the city's parlance, smacked of an AIDS thing.
Disease derangement that topples the calms of a baby gym; fury directed
at the culprit; fury of a mother's protective urge, like no other rage.

The hulking bleeder, annoyed, apologetically caught out in the awkward stance of evasion, denial, trying to cover up.

First one, then other infants started pissing, scared, in their diapers.

"Can I help?" the only unsqueamish of the ladies offered – Jessie – holding up her talcum powdered, symmetrically wrapped and squirming bundle, while lending a shoulder for him to lean against. Standing ill at ease, the massive man in Haight district trews, a tribal tartan of bland and intertwining nondescript tweed from the sixties, his out-of-sync Banana Republic khakhi safari jacket against the wall, fiddled with the bandages and put back on his black canvas basketball shoes, not a gimmick or trim of leather to be found. Professional. Rugged. A collector, she thought.

"I'm all right," he gesticulated, slipping back away from the centrifugal force he'd unleashed.

"What happened there?"

"Rubbed the wrong way." Felham groped for an explanation.

Then she noticed a scar on his neck. "You don't look like the clumsy type." The young woman was at once arrested by something in his pride.

She was all-American, pretty like some part-time model for one of those photographs on the back of low-cal popsicle packages. *Have I ever seen her, was I once attracted to her?* Though she had something else, as well, Felham thought; something rugged and unpredictable in the precise colour of her hair and way she held herself.

Irish-Scottish-Idaho descended Jesilia (Jessie) Moran was baby-sitting her best friend Astrid's fourteen-month old infant, Squirter, not inappropriately nicknamed. This was one Gymboree she'd never been to, though several others in this part of town were familiar to her. She had obviously noticed him at once, he being the only man among mothers. A black, delicately trimmed moustache, and that distinctive scar. The scar, along with the clothes, suggested that he'd perhaps been gored by a rhino, or endured surgery for throat cancer. Maybe he had a run-in with a gang.

The gang theory held little water. He was too big. Of course, she'd also seen how gentle he'd been with his baby, who'd taken outrageous liberties with his largesse, hitting him, making a veritable mockery of all that was muscle-bound and masculine about him. The man had reacted like a drunken linebacker, laughing, out-of-sorts, obviously loving every minute of it. Possibly new to mothering. A recent divorcee?

He's sensitive. The squints in his eyes were the give away. He'd obviously been through that divorce, she reckoned. There was the smooth-skinned machismo of a happy, unsullied marriage suddenly shattered, bringing out the vulnerable child in him. He was fending for himself now, probably for the first time in years, doing his own laundry, having to reacquaint himself with his own kid. Probably got the diapers on wrong.

Or maybe he was a widower? Maybe his wife was the one who died of the throat cancer. His eyes were a dark and Antwerp blue, though far from clear. They were bloodshot, even at ten paces; dark shadows beneath, bushy, Kalahari eyebrows that spoke success. You could discount the normal professions right off. This was no banker. The frayed tweeds were anything but Montgomery Street apparel. Lecturer in history? Perhaps. Realtor? Never. This guy was tanned, well-travelled, probably even monied, given his humility and almost chic disregard for cohesive clothing. Interest rates were disastrously low but still not low enough to save California real estate. Lawyer? She knew no lawyer who looked that sloppy. Doctor? She would have heard about him. Accountant, manager, car dealer? Get serious. But she kept wondering.

While he smiled weakly.

He's out-of-sorts, she determined. A good start, even if the precise coordinates or adjectives lacked precision. But her instincts were well-founded enough to make no mistake. Definitely. Ill-at-ease. Brute softened by hurt. Probably Pacific, Stanford-league, two-hundred-ten pounds, like one of those well-equipped Peloponnesian statues, given his height and certain equipoise; explorer, cattleman, perhaps aviator, she squared up in a glance gently.

Removing all impediments. "My name's Jessie. And this is Squirter." She took a yellow plastic spoon out of the baby's mouth, diverting the temptation of these newborns to swallow half the world.

"Good name, I guess," he said, half-avoiding her penetrating look. He didn't want to have to confront signals, male-female stuff. He wanted no contact, but didn't have the act of aversion on the ready. She surprised him. He was out of his element, this being the first time he'd ever baby-sat.

The woman in charge of the toddler session walked over to him. "You better take care of it." Her insinuation was clear. He had best leave NOW! Felham was glad to oblige.

The woman's assistant had gotten lots of paper towelling from the bathroom and had politely instructed Felham to clean up the mat. She turned over the towels to him with an exaggerated reach, as if she were near to a bomb that could detonate at any moment.

Felham put down his little boy, and on his knees made short business of the blood on the floor. Then he deposited the paper towels in a waste basket.

"Come on, Bart," he said to the kid, lifting the noncommittal brat. The other women had gathered up their babes-in-arms and skirted all sides of the Gymboree mat.

He thanked the solicitous Jessie and departed. She watched him go past the door, and wondered about his dignity in the face of such weird embarrassment. He had shown a meekness that did not exactly correspond with his physical size. His eyes had remained discomposed. She sensed trouble about his person, blushing, locked, electrifying, and had allowed her mind to carry the sequence and physical syllogism of this secret inner man beyond the justifiable confines of those few minutes. Jessie lived more and more in the idea of things, a means of separating desire from hope, from proverbial disappointment, in other words. Too often she'd been left with the bitter boredom of a fancy, an idea of a man, that was going, and would go nowhere, and which left her lonelier than before. She was tired of defeat.

An hour later, Jessie's grocery cart crossed paths with the same man at a neighbourhood store in West Portal.

"Hello again!" she hastened. Jessie's chest was pounding. Upward coincidences seldom happened in her life.

"That was embarrassing," he said right off. "Your name was ..?"

"Jessie."

They chatted, awkwardly. He said his name was Clyde Maybe.

Finally "Where's Mom?" she ventured.

He volunteered (to his own amazement) that he'd also been baby-sitting for someone else, for his sister. Of course, there was no sister.

They pushed their carts side-by-side. "If these things aren't a coincidence, what are they?" she registered out loud for his benefit, more by way of general postulation.

After a moment's coy consideration, Felham said, "I don't know."

Jessie never dithered. "Look, are you married or what?" She saw no ring.

Felham reared back. "Yes, of course."

"Ahh. Well, that's nice." She felt no further inclination to pursue this moment, but was unclear how to excuse herself.

When, to his horror, he suddenly retracted. "Actually, I'm not."

"Married? But you said."

What are you doing! his mind roared. *I don't know.* He was human, after all. "Just a defence, I guess," he said.

"Against what? Me? Or just in general?"

"In general."

I'm glad I hadn't been present for the exchange. Inanities cascading in a downpour of shyness, two adults behaving like twelve-year olds at their first social.

She went on about her insecurity, which had been triggered in the presence of all those mothers. Ten years of discretion had gotten her nowhere particularly cosy, she implied. Jessie was hankering to go out and this man seemed good-hearted, not to mention, sexy. Anyone who would take time off from his day, his job, his whatever, to baby-sit for his sister had to be okay. Even if his name *was* Clyde.

"Then a man like you shows up, big arms, nice smile ... How'd you get that scar, anyway?"

He stood perplexed. Felham was not only attracted to her physically, but he found this flower of free inquiry too inviting for words. For a few brief minutes it made him feel like his old self, prior to being a half-dead man. It made him remember what it was like. To be free. And attracted to a woman without any fear that life was no longer possible for him. It made him forget what was necessary, and what he had been doing with cold systematics and fanatic diligence for nearly a decade. Like a Priest.

"You're a kick!"

"That's what my mother always says. I guess I was a real hell-raiser during her third trimester." She stood back to assure him she was no captive of the senses, then turned, saying, "See you around." It was an abrupt coda.

"Come on, Squirt," she added. Squirt hung on to her shoulder as she walked towards the cash registers.

He realized, this killer brother of mine, that he had inadvertently inflicted hurt. She was a dignified creature, alert to the abstract, the slightest innuendo.

"Wait a minute," Felham called back, tracking behind her, Bart standing on the shopping cart riding First Class in the upper berth, like Washington crossing the Delaware.

"I'm late," Jessie stated, getting out her cheque book in line.

"I mean maybe we could ... "

She feigned impatience, a moment's testiness. Then she relented. "You have a preference?"

"For what?" he said.

"Food," she reminded him.

They parted. He smiled with slightly pained relish.

Shit! Felham cursed to himself afterwards, rubbing his eyes in the dirt of this disastrous regression.

So Felham, flattered by a pretty woman's forwardness, having tried to avoid the connection, without hurting what in his mind was an obviously sensitive nature, had failed.

I find the failure intriguing, if only because he had not failed for over fifteen previous years, apparently. That is to say, my brother (this 'Clyde Maybe') had not looked at a woman with any personal attention, during all that time. Or, that's the impression he's left with me. And yet suddenly he found himself inviting her to dine with him at a restaurant in Marin County. Not any restaurant. But our own. The dumb shit! Though he didn't confide any of that to her, or not yet. As if it would be possible to keep such a secret.

You could just call and cancel, he thought. *Tell her something came up, something unexpected. People understand such conflicts. Nothing to feel bad about.* It wasn't like he had a contagious disease. It was that Dirkson Felham was more than he appeared to be, as can be divined by now. And what he was, what he had become, required the complicity of silence, of an anonymity he had ruthlessly and systematically engineered over a period of years. Only one other person knew anything about the real Felham, other than myself, and that was a mastodon of a man, a Falstaff in Levi's who went by the not unappealing monicker of Muppet.

Muppet. The two of them had been in the Air Force Academy together, for all of a year. I can not tell you how this paragon of reason, music of the spheres, numeric whiz-kid, aeronautical prodigy, Puccini look-alike, came to be ensnarled in such high-level scandal, cheating, in as much as I had lost contact with my brother when he went away to school and as yet knew nothing about his best friend, Muppet. But that's exactly what happened.

It turns out they had managed to slip answers to a friend of theirs who was in the Academy on scholarship, Mickey, the son of an emblazoned career officer who never let up on his boy. Mickey was one of the best pilots in the armed services but had no head for mathematics. Both Muppet and Felham had already talked themselves out of military careers, according to Felham's much later rendition of the affair: they were soldiers of fortune, and they hated authority, desiring more stimulating and financially lucrative adventures than bombing raids in Nam and fifty dollars a week. And neither had anything against Communists. By that time, my brother had already come to some major conclusions.

Muppet, who at first glance had nothing in common with Felham, other than brains, had a bad-seed distant cousin in Peru who was cashing in on the cocaine market, long before the war against drugs was in vogue. The last thing Muppet cared about was drugs, but he was anxious to travel, particularly to a jungle. It is incredible to me that both of these boys, prestigious military or corporate careers open to them, shared so complete, so furtive and unexpected an aversion to the system. It was not common then, other than among North Beach beatniks writing poetry. So, with Lima on their minds, Muppet and Felham opportunistically took the rap for their friend. I suppose it was a clever way of getting the hell out of the Air Force overnight. And their expulsions could not have come at a better time. It was early 1968. The Secretary of Defence, MacNamara, was having what some described as a nervous breakdown over the quickly-escalating war. He was resigning for a job in banking. And his likely replacement, Clark Clifford, was equally nervous about the war. According to the press at the time, he was deeply depressed over LBJ's erroneous dream of a domino theory. LBJ viewed the war like a hitchhiker through a Texas hailstorm, all machismo, and he was preparing to call up 206,000 additional service men for active duty in Asia. Felham and Muppet did not view the war as attractive hunting ground for a soldier of fortune, even though most of their friends, I imagine, did. I don't know how these two were able to distinguish one kind of hunting ground from another.

"But how could you take the rap for a jerk?" my flabbergasted parents had demanded. Felham and Muppet stuck together on their response, changing the allegation from that of their own trivial misdoing, to an all-out assault on America's involvement in southeast Asia. Their prescience in this matter was little appreciated in Missouri, where Muppet came from. Within days of the revelations of his *malefaction* at school, Muppet's parents essentially disowned him. They felt no keener disgrace. Our parents were more lenient since they too had opposed the war, supporting instead one Eugene McCarthy, who was primed for New Hampshire. Dad had already sized up Vietnam. It had none of the rationale of World War II, he said. And he held to those views. He had lodged quiet apprehensions about his son having gone to the Academy in the first place. As for Mom, she would have preferred him to study music, I think, given his obvious talent.

Felham didn't care about the cheating. He and his friend were just under nineteen years old. Muppet had accomplished resounding results on his SAT exams, higher than my brother, perfect 800 scores on both Math and English, a fact little absorbed by others on account of Muppet's sheer physical presence which tended to confirm the cultural stereotype of a big eater, slow-wit, congenial moron. He had already achieved his bouncer's girth. His warm embrace could be dangerous. His weight, then, was well over three hundred pounds. He played football on account of his proportions. His fat was mostly muscle, though. In addition, he suffered from a rare medical condition whose one noticeable effect was his near virtual immunity to pain inflicted on his appendages – hot stove, needle, bullet, it didn't matter. All had the same benumbing impact, a dull itch which warned him of the danger but was never sufficient to cause much discomfort. He inherited the nervous affliction from his father, a southern Ozarks farmer. It had something to do with mixed signals between the anterior commissure and the lateral spinothalamic tract to his brain. That otherwise harmless physical disability, which he would turn to his advantage, coupled with his size, strength and adroit crack shot capabilities on the artillery field, gave him all of the characteristics of a killing machine. Save for one: Muppet shed tears more readily than he cared to admit, whether at family reunions or reruns of old movies like the *Miracle on 34th Street* and *Lady for a Day*.

As his girlfriend in Colorado Springs put it, Muppet was a *big hunk a' lovin'*.

The two of them rode motorcycles throughout the Rockies that first Spring, prior to Muppet and Felham taking off.

The tattoo of a mermaid on Muppet's right bicep, the result of a wild night in Mexico City, added to his new image. By the time the two ex-cadets pulled up in their VW bug before a high-security fence at Muppet's cousin's house in Lima, they had talked themselves through the first year Berlitz guide to Spanish, were fluent in Hispanic women, and were wanted by the Guatemalan constabulary for failing to pay at a gas pump (they were not thinking coherently, having consumed inordinate quantities of tequila, even granting the 550 pounds of metabolic energy between them). An iguana they'd picked up en route they presented to Danny as a sort of belated housewarming gift. A money order for twelve dollars was mailed to the gas station in Mazatenango.

Danny – also from Missouri – had come into millions of dollars according to the family buzz, but he was not his own man any more, as would be discovered. His bribes, debts, and pay-offs more than negated the blood money which he'd made. Despite his big barricaded house in the dry hills, his half-dozen housekeepers, Danny was in trouble. He needed protection, trustworthy protection. Both Muppet and Felham fit the bill. They didn't know what they were getting into, it must be said. It was all part of their fantasy search for adventure.

In the eastern jungles Danny's 'colleagues' turned on him while he was touring a crop. Felham was taking a leak behind the Cadillac when the gunfire broke out. The only thing that saved Muppet were all those years of greasy french fries and Rocky Road ice cream. Felham took out four men. His first kills. The artillery training at the Academy had paid off. Danny took a hit to the shoulder and went down hemorrhaging. Muppet got the other two, then passed out. Several bullets had rocketed somewhere through his pelvic region, sprayed from a small machine gun. The Cadillac was riddled with fire, useless. The three men escaped through the jungle by foot. At night they were swallowed up in gnats and blood midges. They saw by sundown the docile aquatic rodents known as the capybara, feeding in a delicate single file beside a river. They saw dangling snakes and mating cockatoos inhabiting the upper canopy, and packs of romping coati foraging in the shadows. It took them five days to reach a village where the big thing was radio soap opera. There an apprentice herb doctor patched up Danny and sprinkled Muppet with red ants. Within minutes the itch in Muppet's gut had ceased, and with the itch, the blood. Later, the swelling disappeared, or at least was no longer visible. Danny, meanwhile, had sufficiently recovered to be plotting his revenge. As for Felham, he was deeply involved with the four men he'd shot down.

"I thought about them the whole time in the jungle," he eventually told me. "They had families, brothers, sisters, moms and dads. They were as scared as I was. Somehow, at the moment of their death, their fear came over to me, was transferred. I carry all the fear now."

I didn't really understand. I don't know if he did. How can a teenager actually *understand* the murder of four men? It's much easier to kill than to understand, a platitude wasted on the young.

"It was self-defence," he stated carefully, beginning to form some theory that would account not only for instances of self-defence but, I imagine, for that pantheism to which he was increasingly headed. He and Muppet were falling in love with the jungle. Everything about it.

Revenge came, and with it more troubles. Danny got arrested. A senator from Missouri, a friend of Danny's uncle, managed to have him extradited to Los Angeles. A cocaine shipment had been intercepted in the Owens Valley. Danny's lawyer plea-bargained. Justice was swift. He received a sentence of fifteen years with no possibility of parole.

Felham and Muppet had missed all the excitement. When thirty heavily-armed federales carrying bullet-proof shields surrounded Danny's fortress in the pre-dawn hours, tossed smoke bombs and then plowed through the adobe walls with two army tanks, his two sentinels were sipping piña coladas on a dirt airstrip way to the east, near the Brazilian city of Manaus. Danny had done business with a sandy-haired, soft-spoken European there who supplied the drugs to one of the wealthiest industrialists in the Amazon; drugs which were, in turn, dispensed as gifts, partial payments and bribes for a variety of nefarious activities in the rainforest.

But Felham and Muppet were not blind to destiny. They went to work for Bijou, the industrialist.

So why had a valedictorian contrived to get himself thrown out of college only to work for druglords and reactionary money-grubbing whores in the Amazon? Because Bijou worshipped Puccini. And because my poor brother was a hopeless idealist. Did he realize that his boss was an environmental rapist? Apparently not. Because he saw more pristine environment than he thought even existed on the rest of the planet.

Brazilians were not yet swarming the northern jungles. There were still over a million native indigenes, primeval peoples; there were still fish in the rivers, birds in the trees, and little smoke covering the horizon. It still rained in the Amazon. The four generals who would conceive of a plan to 'save Brazil' by tapping the wealth of the rainforest, had not yet sold their bill of goods to the country's President. The roads had not yet been hacked into the forest. But the problems were beginning.

For three years, Felham and Muppet were immersed in the ordeal of the jungle, becoming acquainted with every weapon known to deliberate carnage, both primitive and high-tech. They learned to read the jungle. They fought any and all of Bijou's growing competition for what were in fact legal Brazilian markets. They took snipes at rubber tappers, intrepid gold miners, other zealous druglords, anyone who got in the way of the Company. And what was the Company? According to Felham, it was one of the largest employers of poor people in the Matto Grosso. It did no business with cattle ranchers, replanted forest, gave large grants to local Xingu and Ge-speaking Indian tribes in order to help them preserve the delicate balance, well in advance of the Green Movement in South America. Felham was taken in by the Company's image. The drugs bothered him, and to the best of my knowledge he never even tried them. But he viewed such matters as the trivial vices of others, compared with his own *experience* of the upper Amazon. It's rather clouded for me because he emphasized only those incidents which begged of the later pattern of vigilantism.

The mists hovering over the rivers in the early morning. The sounds that ricocheted and spoke to one another in an orbit of secret slangs and plangent know-hows. He'd heard of the various El Dorados, rumoured waterfalls, mouldering ruins, and he himself witnessed rarities among insects and colours; stripes, fangs, bird wings, the enormity of trees, the sensuality of tribal women, all of which must have confirmed his reason for being there, in his mind.

Felham – who stood six feet three inches and could run a hundred yards of Amazon in just under thirteen seconds – in the meantime curtailed three assassination attempts on Bijou. Felham and Muppet both earned thirty thousand dollars a year, a considerable sum in the early seventies. They had lavish quarters, Indian mistresses, and while there was no health plan, or pension and profit sharing, they did have the use of Bijou's pool, tennis courts and private jet. Incongruities surrounded by jungle. These benefits were hype, as far as Felham was concerned. Anyway, he didn't play tennis.

Eventually, Felham grew up, began to sour on his strange and powerless employment. He'd seen and done things that had made him quite ill. He finally saw through Bijou and the whole enterprise; outgrew boyhood adventure, in other words.

All this queasiness reached a point of no-return when Coocoo, an injured baby jaguar that he'd rescued from the wild, nursed back to health, and raised as a pet, was stolen. Felham tracked the thieves many miles through the jungle, to one of the employee camps. They were employees of the Company, low down on the ladder; miserable mestizos living in a tent city on the fringes of Bijou's gold-mining operation. It was his description of the Jaguar which first alerted me on many fronts: here was the young man that I remembered, sensitive to the point of inverted frenzy. It meant trouble. Trouble dogging me at both ends of the thinking, feeling stream.

It was raining. Three in the morning. Felham's attention was instantly turned towards the dogs, who were already straining after him, tied, flimsily perhaps, to opposing stakes. The mottled *fila brasileiro,* champion scent-hound, used by the conquistadores to recapture escaped slaves. Several of them. And the white, hundred pound *dogo argentino,* equally noted for being a killer, the only *Pero* alive that could stalk a jaguar.

The workers were ill-tempered. There'd be no fessing up in this place. Felham carried a large hunting knife, and a pistol, but these counted for little here. He was surrounded by some fifty armed workers ready to turn what was still sleepy hostility into an execution. Felham had never been to this particular camp. A few of the mestizos knew who he was, and there was submerged chortling, in Indian. They were not impressed with one bodyguard. Felham recognized the local boss and spoke to him in broken Portuguese, while looking around, sizing up his situation.

There were dozens of animals strung up by their hooves and paws and talons. Some were alive, more or less, curling in the misty late night darkness, breathing erratically. Others hung still and lifeless beneath tarpaulins, over slow burning fires. Nearby, a crematoria's remains were piled up – butchered carcasses, dispersed bones, the ashes of long-mingled life forms. Soon any trace of them would be erased. Felham didn't understand it yet, but Bijou's spoils were not simply the result of standard industrial dispossession of the local Indians. There were other such crematoria all over the Amazon – hundreds of them.

"Where's my pet jaguar?" Felham demanded.

"No jaguars here," came the sinister reply.

Behind the spokesman issued an annoyed fart.

Felham stepped up to the farter and repeated his demand.

The man yawned, then spat and turned his back. Felham knew this was the prick. He kicked open the flap of the man's tent from whence smoke was rising. There was the flayed pelt, alright, with its butterfly pattern – where an arrow had once pierced its kittenish fur, a pattern that only got larger as Coocoo had grown up in Felham's care. The pelt was wet. The body had been barbecued and mostly consumed.

This time, however, Felham checked the impulse, swallowing his revulsion. Muppet was back at the compound sleeping. Felham didn't like the odds.

As he left the camp, laughter, and the ravenous barking of dogs, followed him.

He waited several days, then he did what no one could have expected, not even Bijou – to whom word quickly circulated. Felham returned to the camp, this time with Muppet. It was the middle of the day and most of the camp-hands were gone. Felham had not slept for two nights, thinking things over.

Those two nights were certainly a prime catalyst. And when I imagine them over to myself, it's like picturing Pascal, or Margaret Cavendish, or Jean-Jacques Rousseau in the Amazon. Felham had already tasted a deathwish. He'd seen and done things that few people would ever deem feasible. How he reconciled murder and self-defence for druglords; how this early talent had come to vanish in the mire of the jungle; and how the confrontation with poachers stood out against this backdrop of treachery, does not, in my mind, necessarily lead to philosophy. It beggars total disgust. But Felham contemplated, all right. And the results of his thinking were to have dramatic consequences.

He and Muppet were resolved to right the barbarism to the extent possible. They took out what little resistance they encountered, killing several men, then proceeded to cut loose the animals. Most of them were already dead. A few were able to get back into the doomed jungle on their own. One of the creatures – a black panther – lashed out at Felham, ripping his upper torso and throat with a single terrified swipe. From that time on, Felham knew to wear protective clothing. But he would always cherish the wound. For Muppet, the freeing of pain, seeing those animals run into the wild, was the high point of his own life. Muppet, too, had been preparing for this moment for he had also crossed his own River Styx in high school.

It was the end of their days with the company, and the beginning of their secret journey.

Some might simply chalk it up to one more search for self. I don't think that's what it was at all. Felham was beyond simple anodynes. He had trained in decisiveness. He was no longer the Felham I grew up with.

The restaurant was crowded. Jessie was twenty minutes late. Felham had spent the previous hour going over the books in the back, upstairs, then had a spread of antipasto laid out in anticipation.

"Hi Clyde," she said quietly enough. Their table was situated off in the corner, directly above the water. Felham had taken the precaution of leaving the name of a party – *Clyde Maybe* – with the hostess, Liz, up in the front. "There will be three of us," he'd informed her.

He stood up and helped Jessie to her seat. She noticed a scar she hadn't seen before on his left hand. The tissue was jagged, as if he'd been cut by glass and the wound had never really healed. She was surprised that she hadn't detected it in their first meeting. It was ugly. The question mark lingered in her mind long after the pleasantries passed. She looked around a number of times, admired the setting, then returned to his gaze which was right there to meet hers.

"Nice spot."

Felham toasted coincidence.

She noticed yet a third scar on his knuckles.

Still no point asking, she thought, trying to gauge his career. *Lumberjack? Football player?*

Finally, she could no longer hold back. "You played football, right?"

"No." She acknowledged his hands. "Well, you certainly don't dress like someone who works on cars."

"You're wondering about the scars."

"Hard not to."

Felham exerted a most conscientious manner. "I used to fix helicopters."

"Really?"

He lied. "In Vietnam," figuring his evasions need last only a few more hours. By then he'd have tasted his fill of the feminine, recalling, perhaps, the Indian mistress with her oiled breasts and burning eyes, and awakened to the clean slate to which he was committed. No major harm done. This was not an issue of faith or celibacy, after all.

As for Jessie, that was enough of an answer. She didn't need to pursue his lack of eagerness which must be the normal twenty year aftershock Vietnam syndrome. Common horrors, she intuited. Her first cousin, Seamus, had died over there.

Ten minutes later, he found himself opening slightly, buoyed by her quiet enthusiasms and beautiful wiles. He ventured his own query, though he already knew the answer. "No man in your life?"

"I'm just lucky, I guess."

He couldn't help warming to this injured creature.

There was mutual seduction. She didn't know what she was doing any more than he did. He made her fear her deliberations. The slightest desire was choked by way of habit. She'd played it safe for years. Her facial muscles revealed their inherent ambiguity, pulling for the distance of a bystander, while giving him every encouragement that sudden affection can muster – all in the face of previous disappointment and resulting scepticism. He seemed to take the bait. She knew she was staking out new territory. Of course, one can imagine anything.

"So where's your brother?" she asked.

"Up in Toronto for a day or two."

"Why's that?"

"Something to do with his business."

"What's he do?"

Felham blurted the first thing that came to his mind. "He's a lawyer. A District Attorney."

What if, by chance, she's been to the Gymboree before? What if she knows Iyura, you dumb shit! his insides reeked. "Actually, he owns this ... this place." His tone fell away weakly.

"Well, what do you know!" she said.

Felham's mind was racing backwards. *Why did I volunteer such information! If she had been to the Gymboree she would have at once known Bart and asked about Iyura. She hadn't.*

"So who's looking after Bart?" she motioned.

"My brother's married. Nancy, his wife, wasn't able to get away this morning. I love kids." The words sounded so strange to him. Almost mesmerizing, beyond the mere audible; a harbinger of remote, implausible realities.

"None of your own?"

"Maybe someday."

"Maybe." She grinned. "Clyde Maybe. What's Maybe?"

"Huh?"

"I mean the etymology?"

"Etymology ... Flemish," he again blurted.

"Interesting."

"What do you feel like eating?"

She pondered the menu, looking up to ask him, "So how long have you been a vegetarian?"

"Most of my adult life," he replied.

"I have to tell you – and it's probably the end of our budding romance – I do eat animal flesh every so often. Not meat, but fish."

"I can tell."

"How can you tell?" she squirmed.

"Your body odour, and your complexion." He knew what he was doing and why.

Not just the words, but the way he uttered them, rather astonished her. It was mean, and intended to be so. More than that, she thought, there was something terribly schizoid about the comment. She smiled, putting down her menu. "Anybody ever tell you you're a real charmer?" She said it with little jest and thought to put a graceful end to their date, not appreciating his tactlessness, then changed her mind, determined not to walk away from unfinished business. *Give him one more chance,* she decided. She didn't want to have to close the book on yet another mysterious stranger who turned out to be just one more weirdo.

"You really have a way."

"Look," he started coolly, "I didn't say *bad.* I just implied distinctive. Flesh sits in your intestines for nine days. That amount of strained digestion accounts for its own blend of body trace."

She simmered in an incredulity, half chuckle part wriggle, turned past him, looking out at the lights over the water.

"I'm glad you came tonight," he went on, aware of a faint pleasure, already, in pissing her off. *Jesus, Felham* his head vibrated. *What are you doing?*

"Brutal honesty," she said. "I suppose I could do worse." The waitress came, they ordered a double noodles al dente. Felham drank his wine without making eye contact.

He then asked her about her work, when a beeper interrupted the conversation. Felham had a portable phone brought to the table. She called in to her clinic, then informed Felham she had to leave.

"You want to meet Squirter's sister?" asked Jessie

"Squirter's ..?"

"She's about to be born, at my birthing clinic."

It had been Jessie's dream to establish the first natural home birthing clinic in northern California. By now, some four hundred babies had come into this world in the Victorian mansion, scented with jasmine, dimmed by Vermeer lighting and the presence of no doctor, no oxygen canisters or injections or anything smacking of technology. Jessie was dedicated to fostering life's happy footsteps in this world, plain and simple.

Felham did what he should not have done, according to his own rules. He continued into the night, following her in his own car. They crossed the Golden Gate Bridge, turned up Nineteenth Avenue, took it through the Park and headed out towards the beaches, where the clinic was. Jessie drove fast.

It was nearly ten when they walked in on the delivery. Jessie's best friend, Sarah, a single mom, had practised kundalini yoga everyday for an hour throughout her pregnancy. Now, seated in a large warm tub of water, she jettisoned her little girl effortlessly, crying out in what resembled the throes of an orgasm.

Sarah took the newly-named Olivia out from under and clutched her to her breast. Two midwives oversaw the procedure. When the umbilical cord was finally cut, a piece of it was offered to Felham.

"It's edible," one of the women alleged.

"I'm vegetarian," he said grimly, stepping away towards the bathroom adjoining the clinic's main entrance. "I'll be back in a minute."

Felham looked into the mirror, caught in the grip of an attraction against which he'd worked diligently for years to immunize himself. He opened a stall and sat on the toilet for lack of a better place to contemplate his new found feelings.

This is fucking insane! he repeated silently.

When suddenly, someone entered the lavishly-done rest room. The door to the lavatory closed. There was the sound of a metal pail striking the painted tiled surface. Felham couldn't see who it was through the narrow crack in the stall. But he could make out the shoes. They were no janitor's shoes. Crocodile. A janitor? In a birthing clinic? Felham heard the water turned on. Hot blowers were activated. Sound was being drowned out.

An alarm bell went off in his brain. Thai crocodile? He silently shot upwards on the metal handrail that had been fitted for the handicapped and waited in hanging position over the toilet, motionless, breathless, out of the line of possible fire.

Felham was carrying no weapon on his person. He'd left it in the car.

There was no movement from the crocodile shoes.

The lock on his door started to jiggle. Felham contracted his whole body, ready to spring.

There was a pause.

A mop swathed the floor beneath him.

The lavatory door opened again, and this time remained open.

"Hey Jess!" the man's voice spoke.

"Hi Tom. Clyde?"

Felham breathed deeply and righted himself, opened the door and stepped out. The janitor was a student, tight pants, long hair, crocodile shoes.

"I'd better get going," Felham said, mustering a nervous smile.

"Why don't you come with me to my office for a minute," she said.

Felham followed her. He noticed a picture of Jessie standing with her arms around a man, beside an impressive array of medical books. There were dozens of photographs of infants all over the comfortably attended room.

"My Dad," Jessie clarified, noticing his look. She stood in front of her desk, at a friendly distance from Clyde, just shy of close.

"Ahh."

"So what do you think?" she began.

"Think?" He was not playing dumb. He was still addled.

"Should we try a second dinner sometime, vegetarian, same place?"

"I've got to go out of town."

"When will you be back?"

Felham didn't expect to have to confront decisions like this.

"Um ... in a few days."

"Great." She kept up her zeal. Jessie had already decided not to be swayed, or dissuaded, as the case may be. She thought she more or less understood this species of reticence on Clyde's part. He had suffered something in his past. Something with long-term tentacles. She was not wise to men, particularly. No distinct reason to hate them, or to love them. Neither a healer-obsessive, nor one of those Bay Area Earth-Mothers – she despised the very notion, with its distinct tarnish of overweight, group therapy, soapy chants and the New Age. That was not Jessie. Vermeer lighting had nothing to do with the New Age. My brother, on the other hand, was profoundly interesting to her, the reasons not altogether clear in her mind. She really knew nothing about him. Unlike other men, he had boasted of nothing, cracked no jokes, made no stupid asides, seemed utterly disinterested in work or money or pedigree. Most of all, he was direct.

"Call me when you get back?" she asked.

"Really?"

"Yeah. I'd like that."

"So where do you live?"

"Marin County," he said.

"Well, here's my card. You know the name of the clinic if you lose it. I want to see you again." The resolve irked him.

He kissed her on the cheek. She smelled good, he thought. Not at all like dead animal flesh. Her hands touched his sides lightly, afraid, charmed. "You smell good," he said out loud.

She grinned. "Make up your mind."

"Good night," he voiced, reassuringly.

Felham checked under his hood, as he did routinely and then drove his cobalt Vantage Vilante Aston-Martin back over the bridge, past Tam junction and past the Amidha Center, a Zen Buddhist farm where he lived some of the time in a small, three-tatami-mat room with a king-sized futon and a view looking out over the sand garden. Aside from a tea table with a vase, and a low, teakwood cabinet for his gardening clothes, he had no other possessions at the centre, his only known place of residence. Felham's papers were also efficiently limited to the annual books, which Jason's accountants maintained at the Sausalito branch of Ralph's Restaurant. Other than his Aston-Martin, which he picked up used for $175,000, he seemed to be a man who had given up most material things. Muppet always laughed about how the car made up for everything else.

There were nearly one hundred residents of the centre, most of them western students on the road to monkhood. The community was self-sufficient, indeed, possessed invaluable properties that had been donated to it by a prospering Marin County Zen Buddhist population. Felham had donated his share.

He spent most nights at the centre when he wasn't travelling. Unbeknownst to anyone but Muppet – I didn't ever know – he also owned a rambling, rundown farmhouse twenty miles beyond the Amidha Center, just off the road a bit toward Point Reyes, between Bolinas and Dog Town. And that's where Muppet lived. Felham never drove there except before a trip, and only late at night. These were rules that they lived by. There was nothing arbitrary about them, nothing at all.

It was after midnight. Felham had taken the high road over Mount Tam, on his way to the farm. A fog on the water's edge, two thousand feet below, had risen up the forested slopes. The circuitous two-lane highway, wet from the weather, was densely cloaked by scudding mists. In the headlights he could make out deceptive ghosts clustering around the redwoods. He loved this road, with its daytime ocean views, wild peacocks, occasional jutting rocks.

Felham began the windy descent towards Stinson Beach several miles below. A set of headlights appeared behind him at a distance, the first Felham had encountered since leaving Tam junction. Immediately he sped up. It was the same reaction which, as a kid, impelled him to dash behind trees or dive down into the grass, the cold dark lumbering grass, and remain pressed hard against the ground so as to disappear until the car passed. These instincts are forever. They're important.

Within minutes, the vehicle had closed in. Felham saw a man driving a Porsche. As it pulled in closer, the man's face came into recognizable view. He was Oriental. Felham raced forward around a turn, a blind manoeuvre at which his vehicle was adept, even on wet pavement. The Porsche stayed with him. The driver was a professional.

Felham's mind shot upwards. He floored his vehicle while removing a hidden semiautomatic from under his seat. The last thing he wanted was a dent on his new paint job, let alone a bullet hole.

The Porsche tried to corner him on a turn. Felham saw the gun rising in his rear-view mirror. Both vehicles were taking the turns at sixty miles an hour, freely using both lanes. The speed limit was ordinarily fifteen on such curves.

Felham went faster. He had the advantage of knowing the road. He preferred not to have to use the gun. If he could only reach the straight-away.

Felham zig-zagged within the turning manoeuvres. He gained distance from the Porsche. The man was taking aim. Felham disappeared. The Porsche disappeared after him.

Now the road was clear. Felham clocked ninety miles an hour, holding it through the dense night until his gut told him it was time. He did a seventy degree turn, braking maniacally. It was short. He hit the dirt embankment on the other side, spun out, but kept from flipping. He saw no vehicle behind him, and managed to downshift without breaking as he descended around the second radical turn. His brake marks were in the dirt.

Suddenly, the Porsche flew over him. The man had trailed at the same speed, but unaware of the coming hairpin turn. He'd gone off the hill, the vehicle twisting in the air.

There was an explosion in the lower meadow.

Who did you think you were dealing with, fuckhead! Felham intoned.

"Jason? Jason, honey, what's wrong?"

"Huh??"

Iyura had sat up in bed, gently putting her fingers into the rainstorm of sweat.

"You're having a bad dream, sweetheart."

I stared out in the darkness. Felham did not stop. There were homes nearby, the Stinson Beach fringe community. He slowed to twenty five, lest a cop be out on duty. He pulled to a near halt at the stop sign before the general store, then continued. Stinson Beach was asleep. Felham drove along the lagoon. The mist had cleared at this zero altitude and the moon shone on the surface of the ocean. He made a mental note to scrap the tyres and get an entirely different brand of radials. Tyre marks had a way of being traced.

"It's okay," Iyura repeated.

I had no doubts who the assailant was. My brother had no doubts. The man's associates back in Bangkok, the ones that had trailed Felham to the airport would know of their cohort's early retirement by morning. That left Felham very little time.

FEATHER

He was churning inside. What idiocy, what weakness. To permit a flirtation. In others, the most normal dalliance. In Felham, the kiss of death. To what end? TO WHAT END? That teasing nausea, a prelude to real and disastrous acquaintance. The later pursuit and explosion had brought him to his senses. There is no easy accounting for this one blip on Felham's chart. An anomaly as rare as erbium or works by Carel Fabritius. And yet, there was a reason he should have slackened his grip in such a manner.

Felham parked his Aston-Martin in the broken down garage in the rear of their farmhouse, an uninviting redwood structure hidden behind lumber, drowning in strawberry vines and lilac, and told Muppet about the incident coming home. His nerves were raw. Was he followed from the restaurant? Muppet asked, more than a little annoyed. They seldom fought, but this was too much.

"Goddammit, that was stupid!"

"I know. It just happened. I'm sorry."

Had he been spotted at Jessie's clinic? How did they contrive to track him? Were there others?

"The tyres'll have to be replaced. Keep the car in the shed for at least a week," Felham said. They were both thinking of the police as well as the Thai. In all these years, no one had come after them in their own territory.

"Or longer," replied Muppet. "That's too close. What went wrong?"

Felham described the three men who pursued him to the Bangkok airport. So now they'd use the old red Range Rover.

Felham retraced the tracks along the dirt roads leading to the house in the Rover, repeatedly driving one set of tracks into the other, at angles, backing up, racing forward, until the Martin's tracks no longer existed. He walked the track with a rake to be sure. Not a single radial showed through.

Muppet, meanwhile, had done his homework at the Mill Valley Library, speaking with a trusted contact in Anaheim. He never checked out books, however; never even applied for a library card. He kept no notes for more than an hour or two, and always written on checkout cards in pencil, in his own cryptic shorthand, an illegible scrawl, then burned them discreetly, usually in library bathrooms, flushing the ashes down at least two toilets.

There was no record, no book, no magazine, no computer, no trace of an identity, at the farm, as they called it. The farm was an old Czech homestead which Felham acquired anonymously through three separate foreign brokerage firms, one of them a cul de sac dummy corporation. There was no phone. All calls were placed from phone booths. There was no address. The region was unincorporated. No mail ever got delivered. No children came on Halloween. The nearest neighbour was two miles away. The house sat quaintly, entangled in undergrowth, far off a dirt trail through the woods, not really a road, off another dirt road which led to a ridge, then dead-ended, off the main two-lane road to Point Reyes. They simply didn't exist. The ridge offered no tourist possibilities. There was no view from above – no helicopter surveillance or landing possibilities. The beaches were over the mountain ridge, obtainable via an entirely different route. And so it was that this non-existing cabin maintained its pristine nothingness. And it was almost a pleasure not existing. Going through the world not as modern men in a city, but like wisps of transpolar cloud, ascetics, transcending boundaries, without any connection. Free and wild and desperate.

"You get a truck, okay?" Felham asked, slipping out of his clothes in the bathroom, then stepping into the shower.

Muppet, calmed down now, nodded. "Big sucker. Licensed to carry zoo animals. Should be more than adequate."

"What's the story?"

"It'll be sitting in long-term parking, H-ll, at LAX. It actually reads "Mordechai's Kosher Cucumbers" on the outside. It's had many uses. You'll leave it any time before sunrise in the back of Taneki's Market on the main drag in Aguanga, on the northern road to Mount Palomar. There'll be a map with your tools, as well as a key for the motorcycle which you'll find inside."

"What about the weapon?"

"Mac-10 with silencer. She'll be in the same place. She's loaded."

The Mac-10 was Felham's favourite machine gun. Muppet always hid the weapon, or weapons, along with any tools needed for the job, in a metal container behind the driver's seat.

Every aspect of a rental, a purchase, a temporary connection was handled through moles, who in turn were paid in cash anonymously and kept their own fake ID's. Third parties were dangerous, of course; but so far Muppet had a nearly perfect score. Not that it was a game.

"How many am I looking at? Where the hell's my favourite ginger soap?"

"Here." Muppet reached in a cabinet for a bar, then turned, sniffling the air. "You're wearing cologne. Jesus!"

Felham turned on the water.

"Tell me there's nothing to it," Muppet repeated.

"I told you." Was he lying?

"Her name?"

"Jessie."

"And yours?"

"Clyde Maybe."

"Anything else?"

"No."

"It's just never been part of the plan."

"I said I was sorry. Now forget it."

"It was a mistake."

"JUST LAY OFF!"

Muppet had had no difficulty renouncing women years before, when he and Felham agreed to their mission. That's what it was, a mission written in stone and concrete, historic and evangelical as any labour-intensive edifice in the annals of Christendom. Who, or what, were they converting? The World's suffering, Muppet might charge. He had forsaken not only women, but perhaps deliberately lost his parents in the upshot. War-abiding patriots who believed in every ounce of American fire power, soldiers of Christ who felt sorely cheated by their son for not having a family representative at the Tet Offensive. Muppet had sent word to his Mom, via his ex-girlfriend, some years later, that he was okay, living in Newfoundland, sheep farming, penitent about the old days, but resolved to his new livelihood, an exquisite little eclogue of fabrications. But they never spoke again. And, in fact, at that time he was in Rio conspiring with Felham and plotting the downfall of Brazil's growing trade in endangered species.

These strong-willed Gullivers had kept to their celibacy, not from lack of desire, but from the fear of complications. That and their unconditional hatred of meat eaters.

Muppet could look a man or a woman in the eye and know if animals had been consumed by that person. There was shiftiness, he'd say. You could see it in their lips, their teeth, in the movement of their joints. Certainly in their odour, their aura, the thickness of their adam's apple, he avowed. There were many ways. The manner in which such people grabbed hold of things, or probed the distance, or reacted to a threat. Carnivores the world over shared a common language that was brute and graceless and unmistakable.

He could venture down any fast-food street in America, Route 140 through Fresno, for example, and begin to pale and wilt just as sure as if he'd been a fireman working Chernobyl. His pallor mounted, no recovery, mildness into madness, hot blood, fume, and spit. He'd rant inside, hang up, or lather and stew and sizzle and fester, a storm cruising the normal byways of American culture with a rapier in his breath. All three hundred high dudgeon herbivorous pounds of him.

Surprisingly, given the anthropological, the physiological paradigms of most thinking – weight connoting meat – Muppet was a gourmet vegetarian cook. He was big on tofu, grilled, sauteed, braised in peanut sauce. He loved avocado, papaya, black mustard seeds, Gujarati khanui, quesadillas, varieties of hummus and bulgar and barley and bran; big on mezze, prepared robustly with scallions and chives, coriander and Bulgarian yoghurt, dill and mint et cetera. And Caesar Salads. Or baby lettuce with roasted pinons, walnuts and tomatoes. Tomatoes and mustard. Any kind of wine-spiced, French, English or German mustard. Sambal Kechap, crushed chillies, chutney, vegetable rolls and moo shi spreads – sprouts, fried peanuts, in plum sauce. Beans with coconut. Fried lentil cake curries. Roasted cauliflowers, spinach, green pepper, red onion and pineapple pizzas, escarole, fontina and marinated garlic dishes, green chard, leeks baked in parchment, buckwheat noodles, savoy cabbage, pumpkin soup, black bean and zuni stews, vermicelli with curried courgettes of eggplant, summer gazpacho osterized with cashews, mozzarella salads, and late night french fries. Couldn't help himself on that one. They ate only those rare dairy by-products that were absolutely home grown, small-time afterthought enterprises, the sort usually given away free, due to excess, in places like Santa Cruz or Eureka or Grass Valley. Organically-fed, humanely cared for dairy. Animals that were loved. They were no saints. Both Muppet and Felham were addicted to chocolate and Ferrarro's hot sauce; chocolate raisins at movies, kisses, truffles, fudge bars. Huguenot Torte. There's no question that Muppet was the real eater of the two. My brother might have passed on food altogether if it were possible. He fasted frequently.

"Fill me in," asked Felham.

Muppet regained his regularity, breathing more melodically, through his gut. He continued with details, like a heavy mechanic slowly turning a wrench on a rusted pipe. He did things completely, sharply, unerringly. And because he felt little or no pain, Muppet was by far the more dangerous of the two, in any dark alley. He could run one hundred yards of Amazon nearly as fast as my brother. That speed, coupled with his weight, gave him the equivalent mass of Boris Pasternack's locomotive tunnelling through the night with its headlights turned inward.

"In the daytime, there are two keepers, and one security guard."

"You're sure?"

"That's the word on the street. Security dude'll be Thai, carrying a holstered Magnum. There's also two additional cleanup people and the occasional U.S. Department of Agriculture rep who allegedly makes spot checks but don't you believe it. They're all in cahoots."

"Naturally."

"That's the daytime scenario."

"Night-time, Mup." Felham was impatient.

"Night-time should prove simpler, depending how fast word travels on that Oriental creep of yours. Were there any witnesses?"

"Hope not."

"You better be prepared. The weapon should do."

"That doesn't worry me." He was crack behind his sights.

"But if you're lucky, you should only have to contend with the security guard, and the keeper – who usually hangs out in his own room in back, apparently. Keeper's the problem, though."

"Why?" Felham was speaking up above the spray of the shower.

"I found out only today. This night shift guy's new on the job. Probably innocent. Might want to consider leaving him alone if possible."

"Fast-action tranquillizer." They respected the innocent. That was basic to what they did, however complicated arrangements might get.

"No."

"Why not?"

"It's too late to provision it."

"We got a plastic shell outback, right?"

"Yeah but–"

"So I'll carry it on board."

"Not on Air West, you won't. X-ray'll pick up its shape."

"What about packing it, and sending it same day delivery?"

"Brilliant. Deliver where?"

"That was stupid." Felham rubbed his eyes.

"Give me a towel. I got soap– "

"So what do you want to do about the keeper?" Muppet said.

Felham slipped into a white cotton bathrobe and checked the time. It was 1:20 a.m. He wanted to be in Los Angeles by 6 p.m. the next evening.

"I'll manage him."

He'd managed such problems before, though he didn't like taking that level of risk.

"Here's the layout."

Muppet drew the interior of the bird quarantine station from memory. "Take out the security at the side door, here. You'll need wire cutters. They're in the truck."

"Video surveillance?"

"None."

"What about the alarm system?"

"Simple clip wire."

"Trusting bastards, aren't they?"

"Yeah. Now there's approximately a thousand birds in there. They process that many every week."

"I thought every month?" Felham declared.

"It's supposed to be every month, of course; the germination time for Exotic Newcastle's Disease. But they've got the system down. Apparently, they're not treating for psittacosis either. Ninety percent of them die in this hell hole. Those that do make it to pet stores in Los Angeles and San Diego are pretty far gone."

"When was the last shipment?"

"Yesterday. You'll be getting them free of steel leg cuffs, which is the point. Think you can handle eight hundred parrots?" Muppet asked.

"You want to come?"

"Not if you want me to have the Maryland thing in order."

"Right. Is there something else? Are we clean on this, Muppet? Gas, registration, licence plates?"

"Hope so."

"What about Mr. Prick?" Felham went on, referring to the kingpin.

A real family-run operation. Dr. Alick Prawkaow. First cousin of the hit in Bangkok."

Felham started to repeat the name.

"You'll find his address circled on the map. You can make your hit after picking up the birds, on your way into the hills. It's apparently a normal neighbourhood. Not even an electric gate."

"How come they're so confident?"

"Because they've been running the operation without any resistance from the Feds for three years. Definitely one of the largest suppliers of illegal wild-caught parrots in the U.S. by alfie's estimates."

"Who from alfie?"

"Edward."

"Edward?" Felham had never heard the name.

"Someone new."

"What do we know about his level of information?"

"Alfie's been all right in the past."

"Someone on the inside?"

"Possibly. There's a newcomer there. Could be the one."

Alfie was their general in-house name for the animal liberation movements, an investigative entente of contacts in many countries from whom on occasion they obtained crucial data, or details. No member of alfie had ever gotten close to either Muppet or Felham. Names, locations, actual intentions – none of it was ever gleaned.

"We'll have made a considerable contribution, Dirk."

Felham headed for bed. He was restless on account of that woman, Jessie. Felham knew that he had committed a grievous sin, the worst folly, the one, the most difficult taboo, in his current life. He had no business leading her on, or tempting himself.

"You want a beer?" asked Muppet, ready to be conciliatory.

"Yeah." Felham said, lightening up from sheer exhaustion. He dug out his reserve stash of M&M's and plopped down on the heavy Burmese monk's bed – teak wood and silver – in his room.

The next afternoon Muppet drove Felham to the airport in the Range Rover. Felham flew to Los Angeles, carrying a small rucksack on board, in which he kept a skintight black mask and gloves, a beeper (they used the number of a phone booth at the John Muir Cafe six miles from Dog Town, avoiding portable phones for tracing reasons), and an effective pocket-sized heat-seeking laser device of plastic that resembled a lighter, detected 98.6 degrees plus or minus at a hundred metres in the dark, even around corners and through thick walls. A virtual reality gadget much like the NASA helmets. It could be quickly readjusted to seek out and read computer screens at half-a-mile, also through most walls. In addition, Felham carried a handy electronic lever which fit on his key chain and was the size of a key. It instantly opened nearly any lock on the market. He'd gotten the know-how from a book entitled *Insecurity And Stealth*, the Bible of the field, by one W. R. Cram, safecracking genius, and legendary wit.

Felham had not been to Los Angeles in over a year. He tended to avoid the city about which countless prose poets have waxed or despaired. But what Felham hated about it was more instinctively enumerated than facile thought can conjure in word. All that could lend form to formlessness was his hatred. Hatred of size, of inorganic expanse (more steel and concrete and chemicals, dirt, disease, garbage, and man-made things, than live things), of environmental depletion. This total lack of inner knowing which only cities encompassed. Matter. Anti-Christ. These qualities combined to make most of Los Angeles inhospitable for most life forms. One might argue that birds and people, poodles and coyotes fared rather well north of

Sunset. And it may be true, at least as far north as Mulholland Drive, in island clusters and vegetated retreats of the rich. But the city was bigger than the north of Sunset. The city was far bigger. Tens of thousands of animals, lost and dire, were killed every day. Tens of thousands of humans died every year as a direct, or indirect result of environmental pollution in Los Angeles, a fact little appreciated. Nearly as many as the number of those American GI's who died in the Vietnam War. All of this computed in him.

Felham had seen dogs trapped in the median of a freeway, straggling mile after mile, thirsty, confused, terrified, and slowly sinking from hunger, exhaustion and car exhaust. No hope of ever – EVER – getting across the freeway. In one instance, along the Harbor 110 downtown, a passing policeman noticed a German shepherd caught in such circumstances and he shot him rather than stopping his patrol car to rescue the desperate canine. A little editorial was published in the *L.A. Times*, voicing a complaint at the officer's atrocious lack of humanity. The next day, the voice was gone. The dog was dead, and life went on.

Typically, after nine days in a pound, a dog or cat is put to sleep. In that action, a life rudely snuffed out, pain and anticipation discounted, a miracle of sensate connections betrayed, the city excels. Mass kills, mass cremations, enough ash to fertilize a desert. But there is no fertilizing in LA of that sort. Children are not invited to witness the death of these myriad former pets; the nightmare never gets out. The dog is dragged, huddling for last ounces of protection, pleading, really, with people – who are all it knows in this final concrete shelter, the name a travesty; and failing in its final pleas. What has it done, this utterly healthy, life-defending champion? Good looks, fine hair, deeply sensitive eyes, warm breath, warm blood, once a baby, once a youth, once in love, still in love; what has it done but be free, maybe for a day, or a squalid garbage sniffing week, in Los Angeles? Free and then captured, flung into a net, dragged away, given little water, little food, molested, and prepared to be killed. With an injection. A cowardly injection. This gulag of dogs and cats. Down the street, slaughterhouses, glue factories, pet stores. In every gutter, the decapitated birds. Around every corner, the fallen opossum, spleen ruptured, guts exploded from the anus or mouth or eyes. All part of the scene.

Los Angeles hated animals. Cities hate animals. Felham hated cities.

He arrived at long-term parking, discreetly examined the tool kit, studied the map, and proceeded. The truck was enormous, clumsy to drive. He slowly maneuvered it to the exit, paid for two days and two parallel spaces, and made his way out to 405 South. The on-ramp was interminable, the truck difficult to handle. He had a headache. He was scared. An early-warning system in his nerves was blinding him like so many headlights and blaring horns.

At nine o'clock Felham finished his dinner at a Good Earth restaurant and headed for the so-called quarantine station. He parked a block away at a busy truck stop, as luck would have it. There he put his things in his pack and walked the remaining thousand feet or so to the building.

The structure was exactly as Muppet had indicated. It stood adjacent to a baseball field whose immense lights were fortunately dark, across the street from a gas station and a Methodist church. Adjoining the field was a residential street, in whose tree-lined shadows Felham put on his mask, gloves, shouldered the rucksack, and proceeded to the building with machine gun in one hand and wire cutters in the other. He wore soft ballet slippers. He was not unaware of the fact his gloves and slippers contained leather.

A dog came up to him and sniffed, prepared to bark. Felham stroked its mane. "Easy boy."

There were lights all through the building, and four parked cars around the side. With no obvious entrance and nothing written on the dwelling, this warehouse specializing in death disappeared in a nondescript way. A residential street. No precise zoning. Only the birds knew. Birds, whose voices were muffled by apparent insulation gave themselves away to one who was listening up close. Traffic was light. Felham stalked the structure. He was good at that, keeping the weapon along his leg, out of profile. The dog followed him.

There was a man across the street. Felham acted cool, keeping to the dark, maintaining stride. The man, pushing a grocery cart filled with tin cans, moved on, missing Felham's figure. There were birds in the sycamore trees, attracted perhaps to faint throes from within the structure beyond. They clearly sensed that far-flung relatives were trapped inside. Around the corner was a ramp. That's where the truck would have to pick up its load. Next to it was a security door. There was a wire mesh over that entrance as Muppet had indicated. The door was evidently never used. Security, and all personnel, apparently kept to the front.

Felham scanned the exterior and saw no video. Then he used his laser.

"Dammit!" he muttered, picking up four thermal shapes. *Who were the other two?* He felt for his gun. The dog, sticking to him, sniffed at it.

"Go on, get!" Felham whispered intently. The dog moved on, sensing trouble.

Now older brother worked fast, working with a bartender's fluency; cutting the fence, stepping up to the door, slicing right through two deadbolts, and silently administering his special key to a third lock.

He withdrew a contained plastic squirter of oil from the rucksack – it had been in the truck's kit – and applied a squeeze to the door, to prevent it from squeaking.

Squirter, he thought.

He pushed it slightly open, his Mac-10 raised. Felham peered inside. In a glance he saw the whole joint. Suddenly, his gaze was riveted: not fifty feet away, talking to a large, gorgeous Hyacinth Macaw, was an equal eyeful, a college student in jeans, her long brunette hair tied back. Felham trembled with anger, anger directed at that fucking alfie connection. Why hadn't he known about her?

Suddenly another woman came into Felham's purview. Probably the keeper. She was sweeping, but it was a futile task. The place was disgusting. Years' worth of excrement, dust, debris, feathers floating in the air, permeated the facility. Forty to a cage, Felham estimated. That meant these bastards processed four thousand per month, fifty thousand a year, of which probably forty-five thousand of them died.

Cages piled in three tiers stretching easily one hundred feet. It was a large building. He figured on half-an-hour to get them all into the truck. Already, from the side door, he could see many lifeless animals among what was supposed to be a new crop.

Felham loved birds, needless to say. I don't know where he came by the sentiment, because we never had them as pets growing up. I presume it was the Amazon, some other jaguar-like experience. The stories he'd heard. Miraculous tales. He'd read some literature, knew the science of parrots quite well, and was thoroughly convinced that such birds exceeded, in intelligence and wisdom, all other animals, including most people. Their emotional capacity was legendary he averred – and he meant any birds, whether emu or sparrow. That such affectionate members of the biological community could be brutalized beyond description, shot, chopped up, the remaining live ones hauled away in nets from the primeval forest, drugged with tequila, suffocated in fenders, or taped fast to bodies so as to be concealed at borders, was too horrifying. That their lives – which, in the wild, could last a century – were reduced to suffering, every moment, in the hands of gangsters and bureaucrats, greedy insensitive bastards, and – at the end of the criminal chain – of all the moronic owners of these so-called pets, left him outraged and unstoppable. A bird in a cage was even worse than a man in a cage, for the bird did not know what was happening. A bird cannot be alone. A bird needs the company of compassion. Whereas most human beings can think their way out of compassion and still survive, are wont to survive. Genetically, morally, humans have known slavery, domination. But their generations have been fuelled by that slippery, alluring word, hope. A powerful antidote that is probably absent in all other species.

For Felham, the plight of birds symbolized the general plight of all animals. But there was no question that he had this special place in his heart for winged critters. Because they were meant to fly, to be free, their incarceration was all the more humiliating and disgraceful. If we cannot even free a bird, he would maintain, we will never free ourselves. The slavery will continue. Blacks. Jews. Whites. Yellows. Every organism on Earth is subject to the same laws of physical and emotional and moral reciprocity. He speculated that way.

Now he heard additional footsteps and crouched low to the ground. A security guard, and a second man with him – both Thai – were coming up towards the women.

Felham had been confronted with moments like this before, I know. His heart was pounding. Mine would be bursting. He did not kill innocents if he could avoid it, that much I can vouch for. He backed away to grab time. Something gave way, a large pebble. He caught himself against a centre post. There was a grating sound upon the gravel. A thud where his wrist connected with steel.

One of the guards swung around and stared at that side door, noticed a change, the crack, shouted out loud – "Whey!" – drew his gun, as did the other, and ran towards the spot.

Felham stuffed his laser device in a pocket, checked his weapon, and stood his ground just outside the door.

The first guard inched along the inside wall. Felham heard the creaking and kept low to his stance.

Suddenly, the man burst out. Felham plugged him in the head. The second man followed and received a similar discharge – bullets to the back of the skull and neck, before they could even pull their triggers. They didn't suffer. Though Felham never searched for meaning or compensations for the dead.

His body was burning with indecisiveness. Goddamned women! Muppet's revenge, he figured. Felham made up his mind. He'd wait.

"John?" one of the women called out. "Deensau?"

"What is it?" the older woman said in a loud whisper. Felham could make it out, even above the din of the birds.

"Should I call for help?"

"No," the college student replied. "John? What's going on? Hello?"

Felham heard one set of footsteps walking to the door.

"Maybe you better be careful," the other woman said. "This place ever been burglarized?"

But she kept coming. Felham read this to mean exactly what he'd feared. Two innocents.

He was in a real pickle. He never took confederates, and had vowed never to trust. Trust had never worked.

She stood on the inside by the door, three feet away, motionless, waiting. She couldn't see the bodies. They'd fallen outside, out of line-of-sight.

"John, what is going on?"

Now she came closer. Felham stood back, his head frazzled. He clenched his automatic.

She walked out. Felham threw his arm around her, tightly sealing her mouth with his non-gun hand. She couldn't see him.

"Joanne?" the second woman called.

Joanne managed to squeeze free an inch. Enough for Felham to glimpse her face a second time. A lovely, scared girl, probably twenty-five. Their eyes met.

Felham heard running. Now he had no choice. He stepped inside, pulling his hostage with him, took aim, and shouted – "STOP! NOW."

The other woman froze and crumbled onto the floor, her hands outstretched.

"What do you want?" the girl named Joanne cried out. She was motionless against him.

Felham was burning up, frantic. This sequence of events was far from what he had planned. He never got into such scrapes; never had to speak; was never seen. Bullets to the head, rapid, efficient release of the animals, out of there. Maybe he was getting too old for this.

"Please ..." she begged.

Felham continued to hold the brunette with his gun aimed at the blond woman on the floor.

"You killed them," the brunette muttered.

He did not intend to speak, but the urging was there; an impulse between attraction and pride. "I'm here to rescue the birds. Plain and simple," Felham declared in a calmed voice.

Then she said, "I'll help you!"

Felham jerked in surprise. "Shit." His head spun, thinking.

"I don't need your help. Why did you two have to be here, anyway?" he carped roughly.

"She just started yesterday. She doesn't even know the troubles here."

"And you?"

"And I've been trying to help."

"Bullshit."

"Hey, I know what goes on. It eats me up inside. Please, Mister. I'm on your side."

"Doesn't look like it to me."

"I'm on the inside to investigate what goes on in places like this. You've got to believe me. I used to be in veterinary medicine at college before dropping out to work for animal rights groups."

"Why'd you drop out?"

"Because I couldn't stand what they were doing."

"What were they doing? Fast." Felham knew exactly what they did.

"Uhh ... Well ... They'd gather animals from the pound and cut them open, almost for sport. Vets! Strictly brutal stuff. It's all for money. Worse than medical school. Never any anaesthesia. None. The professor said there was no funding for anaesthetics, and it was better for the students to see animals squirm. Thousands of animals tortured to death in the name of veterinary training. I was asked to go to the pound, select a cute little perfectly healthy dog, newly arrived– " Felham held her tightly by her hair, his machine gun pointing up at her throat, as she rifled through memory, speaking frantically on her feet " –and cut off all four of its legs. Amputate is the word they use. No anaesthesia. The worst torture on earth in the name of science. You gotta believe me. I've seen vets break the necks of birds that people have brought in, behind their backs, rather than waste time and money putting them to sleep with an injection." She was whining now, terrified. "I'd walk down hallways and hear animals howling in all directions. Please. You're hurting."

"Alright, that's enough," he said. Careful. Move quickly. He'd wasted too much time. No more unnecessary talk. No getting any chummier. He was way, way over his head, his limits of fraternization.

"Is there any rope or wire in the back?"

"Yes. With the packing materials."

Felham ushered Joanne by the arm and plucked up the second woman from the floor who'd been listening silently. Now he moved both of them into the back room.

"Please, hurry up!" he asked, amazed by his own courtesy.

Passing the cages, Felham could gauge the sickening brutality with which these hundreds of creatures had been captured from their nests, stuffed without air or water into every imaginable container and illegally smuggled across borders, to arrive here, in deplorable holding tanks, separated from blood relatives and mates, deprived of everything that gave them life and had given them life for millions of years of evolution, since the time of their ancestors, the dinosaurs. The birds cried out. They looked to him, eyes puffy, and dazed. Feathers and pieces of feathers cannibalized by other scared birds, drifted through the warehouse. Such conditions routinely aroused aggression but many of the birds were not wont to fight on account of their weakened states, and they would sink away into themselves, like catatonics, their energy evaporating, and with it their will to live. Birds died every night, their eyes slowly closing.

The few private inspectors charged with overseeing such quarantine stations around the country were in fact eager to see all the birds die out, week after week, because that constituted proof that there was an alleged disease that would not get out into the open market place. The worse the conditions, the more birds that died, the better the inspectors felt. And this syndrome thus perpetrated an increasingly brutal assault on the wild nests, as the numbers decreased and the market for the birds correspondingly increased. The financial rewards were considerable. End users – the pet owners – were typically oblivious to these behind-the-scene horrors.

Even the transport of such birds in cars and trucks was swathed in bizarre motor vehicle rulings that permitted birds to be plucked during transport, for whatever insane reason. Feathers from live birds could be tossed out of a moving vehicle without coming under any illegal category of littering. Water and feathers were not considered littering.

Felham knew that less than six hundred birds had been seized by the Feds the year before, out of probably a few million that were illegally smuggled into the country. Regulations, and the minuscule size of the regulatory force, constituted a charade. The rare smuggler who was caught got fined, and one time in a thousand served a few meaningless years behind bars. Meanwhile nearly all of the exotic birds were going extinct to service this bribe-ridden industry. They either died because their whole territory was crumbling, or at the moment of capture, in transport, or in these execrable holding stations. Legal holding stations. Once the smuggled bird reached quarantine, it was considered legal. No endangered species bill on earth could stop it. Only the spread of disease and cruelty.

Frequently, the owners or inspectors simply killed the birds inside the station, except for the bigger ones, worth as much as $100,000 to some collectors, sick or not. If there were an outbreak of any disease, all the birds were sold off quickly or, if the Feds had their way, drowned, or gassed, or thrown into a bonfire. Bribes could easily postpone genocide by a week or two, enough time to sell the more costly species.

For the Prawkaows, the business had been worth an easy ten million dollars a year.

Felham quickly shut the door behind him, forcing the two women to sit on the floor beside one another, back to back. He noticed a walkie-talkie on the table. He put it on the floor and crumpled it with his foot. He found hemp, as well as tape, and then ordered the younger girl, Joanne, to tie up her companion. She did so. Felham secured the knots. Joanne stared at him.

"Don't look at me," he said.

"You're the one," she stated, curiosity mingling with fear.

"Don't talk."

Felham started to tie her up, then decided it was best to keep her tied in a separate room, in the event the two of them somehow managed to help each other.

He pulled her away and forced her to walk out into the main holding facility.

"I can help you," Joanne whispered. "I know who you are."

With that Felham spun her around. They separated. "What are you talking about?"

"You're the one who saved the Delaware chimps. You murdered that anaesthesiologist."

"I only did to him what he did to the animals. I used the same chair. Same clamps. The same smashing device. A primate's a primate under the law. Some are innocent. He wasn't. Now get over there."

"Please let me help you," she went on, not wanting the other woman to hear, unaware that she already had heard. Felham was attentive to the discrepancies.

"You're crazy," he said.

"Why do you think I'm here? I'm undercover with alfie. I can't believe they didn't tell you. Who was your contact?"

Felham said nothing. The last thing he wanted was a groupie. He looked at his watch then stated, "It's late. Sit down. Don't move and I won't tie you up. All right?"

She was urgent now. "Let me help you. You don't think I haven't studied the techniques of government anti-poaching in East Africa? Of Earth First! types? You need my help."

Felham blinked, perplexed. He was already so far beyond the rules of his own game that he figured he was immune to further surprise, further transgression. He let her speak. But there'd be no more reliance on alfie, that was for sure. And no more doing things alone. Muppet would have to get the hell out of libraries and come back into the fray where he belonged. This R & D business was just so much crap.

"Alfie fucked up," he said, flummoxed.

She registered both hurt and astonishment. "I don't understand it."

He was mumbling angrily to himself now. "All right. Help me get the bodies inside."

She worked with him. They dragged the two corpses to a position along the inside wall, leaving a thick blood smear. Felham used one hand, keeping his other on his weapon, the trigger un-cocked.

"Get wet rags. Clean up the blood. Come on!" There were extraordinary amounts of blood in pools on the floor, and outside the door. Bathing the concrete. Inching in all directions.

Felham now made a detail past all the cages to inventory the next phase. He noticed several un-Asian birds, including a huge Imperial Amazon of Dominica, from the Caribbean, in a small cage by itself. It looked sick, hopeless. Probably worth $75,000 on the market, if it could be fenced before it died. It might have a chance in the hills of southern California. And there was a second lone bird, even worse off, no longer having the strength to stand on its perch, but crammed up, a shivering ball of mauled feathers in a corner of its cage on the shat-upon newspaper. Felham believed it to be a St. Vincent Amazon, unimaginably rare. There was supposedly only four hundred in the wild. Now, three hundred ninety-nine.

More than half the birds were not moving. Some clung to the wire meshing. Others lay stiff, while still others tried feebly to gain comfort from the corpses around them. Such comfort had developed to the elemental; a touch, a look, even a second's glimpse might hold back a bird's tear for the night. Birds cried. Not with tear ducts but with voices as sullied and orphan-like as any abandoned child, inconsolable like Bach's Mass in B Minor. They reared in the dark cavities of their little bodies, unimaginable proof of feelings. And to have that sentient feast of love confined to such cages was the worst evil. The cages were steel, awkward, but moveable.

"Alright, Joanne is it? You want to help, you can help. I'm taking these birds about an hour and a half from here, into the mountains, where there are plenty of wild fruit trees and very few people. And I'm going to let them all go. I know it's not biologically the ideal situation for them, but it's a hell of lot safer than in here. I killed those two because they were guilty. And because the message will get out."

"Yep. It will." She did not evidence much surprise about that.

"Now I have a truck down the street. You can help me load the cages inside. And then it's up to you. I'm not going to hurt you."

"Thanks."

"Walk with me to the truck."

"Okay."

Felham put away his things in his rucksack, and held his Mac-10 under his sweater. He never stopped pointing the weapon at her. They walked out the side way through which he'd entered.

Now there was considerable traffic on the street. Mostly teenagers, probably coming home from a game, cruising. Felham felt self-conscious beside the girl, and she beside him.

"Walk normally."

"Obviously," she said, with a conspiratorial hint.

Felham got into the truck, while she stood on the passenger side, waiting for him to unlock it. If she was going to run, this was the time. The pit stop had a 24-hour restaurant. She'd have all of seventy-five feet to make for it, across the gravel. There were other trucks under which she could disappear. These thoughts must have passed through her mind. Felham took the chance. He figured she was with him on this. If she'd been with the cops, or if the Thai had found out about their dead compatriot on Mount Tam, the place would have been swarming.

She fiddled with her bra, then climbed up into the passenger seat of the truck. Felham drove out of the parking lot, up the street, and then backed down the building's access ramp. Joanne hopped out and guided him with her hands so that the vehicle was flush with the loading dock.

Felham told her to open the main doors while he stood with his gun. He pulled out the motorcycle, then they set to work, dispensing with dollies – too time consuming – but rather dragging the cages into the truck. The phone on a front table was ringing.

"Answer it," Felham ordered. She did so in a normal tone, while he listened, his gun in his hands.

"Get Deensau. Hurry up," the voice speaking to Joanne said.

Felham motioned to her. She caught the logic.

"He's out getting coffee with John."

"I'll call back in five minutes. If they get in have them call me, you understand?" It was a woman's voice with a thick Thai accent.

"Who was that?" asked Felham.

"The boss's wife," Joanne said.

Felham sighed, wrapped in a blizzard of incredulity. Another omission. Another woman to deal with.

Working together, Felham and Joanne got the birds into the truck quickly. The girl saved him time. Felham put the motorcycle against the last of the cages inside the vehicle. He closed the door, turned around, and found himself staring at a gun.

"Don't move," Joanne said coldly. She'd had the weapon hidden in her blouse. Now, she clutched at it with both hands. It was aimed at his face. She stood directly in front of him. The phone rang again. She was forcing control into her hands. Carefully, she picked up the receiver. Felham dove down, rolling away.

She got several bullets off, which dug into the floor, blasting large chips out of the oily concrete. Then she too hit the floor, her body peppered with spray from Felham's Mac-10. The throat fell apart, blood burst in gushers, and her face, pretty seconds before, now more or less lay in distorted fragments. Parts of it were ten feet away. Splattered titbits dripped off the wall even further from where Felham stood, having risen to his feet. The weapon was powerful.

She was a professional, all right. As smooth as he'd ever witnessed.

He ran into the back room, kneeled before the blond who was shaking, placed his gun up against the back of her head, intending to finish her off. She shivered out of control.

He hesitated, then turned her towards him. She could only see his mask, but the four eyes met. Suddenly, he still sensed her innocence. She looked like a working mother. Someone who didn't have a clue as to what was really going on in this place. Was ignorance punishable? Neutrality, yes, if it meant turning one's back on the needy. But ignorance? He'd never thought so. Certainly not in the case of one woman. Her stupidity appalled him, but he imagined that she must have her reasons for not knowing, or not wanting to know. Whatever he thought, he was evidently not prepared to kill her.

He took a chance, and whispered something unto her ear, the tone of his voice as different as before. He had masked the tone, enunciating like a foreigner. She nodded compliance. Her breathing was unsteady.

Felham ran out to the truck, and pulled away with sixteen squealing tyres. There was no question about the other hit, now.

He drove at a normal speed all the way to Taneki's, a hole-in the-wall country store on the fringes of a deserted town in an empty quarter of southern California.

Felham kept going, past the store and out of town ten miles into the mountains. It was after midnight when he pulled off the highway, turning up a dirt road into the forest. He drove a few hundred feet further, until there was no chance of his being seen.

The night air of California, up in the southern hills, in summer, is mild and perfect. The stars poke around the white granite boulders, just as they do on Mars. The crickets play jazz. The raccoons bicker and toss their spoils. Deer nuzzle the bark and duff, while an occasional cougar saunters uninhibited across the road. The madness of San Diego and Orange County is far away; far enough to ensure a few more years up in these hills.

This night, Felham's task was easy. Release them. Pray for them. Nudge them on their way, into a new wilderness that one could only hope they'd make their own. The fruit and nuts were scarce, compared with South American varieties. The land was relatively hard and ungiving. There were competing organisms, other birds, raptors they would not know about. Yet it was freedom. Open sky. The chance to react to the universe again.

He opened all the dozens of cages. Many of the birds did not want to go, or were so sick they simply couldn't move, trembling and scared and pathetic in the dark. It broke Felham up to have to force these sick ones out of the cages. Where they plopped onto bushes, or cried, or rolled onto the cold earth and just waited, waited for a snake to devour them. Many had died during the drive. Within half-an-hour, the live birds had walked or flown away. The dead ones – which numbered at least a hundred – Felham piled under some trees, kicked humus, pushed dirt, rocks, and branches, until the funeral mound was concealed.

One bird, an animated, cherry-headed conure, its bright emerald green wing feathers upright in a tingling pompadour of frenzy, weighing no more than ten ounces, its beak bigger than the rest of its face, long, agile, ancient-looking talons, alighted on Felham's jacketed shoulder, grabbing hold determinedly. It promptly commenced preening my brother's neck, clicking like a lighter, trying to find food on his tongue, right there under the Milky Way. Cooing busily, twisting its little head adoringly in erotic ardour to signal a perfect match. Just like that. Felham called him Feather. Feather called my older brother 'Wa-wa'.

They then got into the truck and drove hack to Taneki's. Felham – still in skin mask and gloves – locked up the vehicle, leaving the keys where instructed. He then got on the motorcycle and with the little bird holding on just inside his collar – Feather-bent-for-leather – sped back towards LAX.

THE MAINE WOODS

Wes Madrid, an excitable, cocky, strapping, thirty-nine year old former cowboy, presently a G-7 Fed, drove his older associate, Special Agent Robert Jerrasi, to Dulles International. Madrid – never beaten at arm wrestling (well, once, by Jerrasi) and never thrown from a steer (he used to ride rodeo in Wyoming) – had obtained a degree in law enforcement from Denver University before landing a job at the FBI in Washington. It was 11 p.m. He'd affixed a portable red strobe to the outer roof of his Dodge Impala which flashed rhythmically now as they accelerated through a summer drizzle at eighty-five miles per hour.

"You ever hear from your ex?" Madrid wondered out loud, just to break a pensive twenty-three minute drive.

They both were expectant, focused on the telephone call which had alerted them to the killings. Time was tearing at Jerrasi's insides. Ripping to shreds, second by second, a hope which had not arisen in over six months. The trail had gone dry. Now he was intent: he had a feeling about it this time.

"No?" Madrid remarked, pursuing Cloris idly.

"Cloris? She's alright. No reason to see her. This is not a bull. Slow down."

"You don't have a lot a time, Bob."

"Now listen Wes, I want you to run a complete financial on these Thai."

"We don't have authority."

"So get the authority. Get Kinesey outta bed. He ought to do something for sixty thousand a year. By tomorrow morning, first thing. Who they're doing business with. Inside and outside the U.S. I don't expect and I don't want the LAPD getting involved. So get me local bureau surveillance on the place, round the clock."

"Give me your LA mobile number."

"I wrote it down for you."

They looked at one another. "Write it again, here, on the back." Madrid handed an annoyed Jerrasi a pack of matches.

"I'm staying at the airport Hilton. That's it." Eventually they skidded into curbside at the airport.

"Call me," Madrid said.

The two men were not what you'd typically describe as rivals. Madrid had passion, Jerrasi punctiliousness. The younger man had dreams, unburdened as yet by failure. The older one was pushing his luck and knew it, had few friends, was a sexual misanthrope, and had been nearly ruined by the professional object of his desires, after more than 2,700 days of futile searching.

Jerrasi, five feet eleven inches of swarthy muscle, moving through crowds with a blunt, ungiving stride, narrowly made the overnight red eye, flashed his ID for his upgrade, downed 15 milligrams of Dalmane in a shot of gin and tonic, and put himself to sleep reading *Crime And Punishment*. He'd begun recently to atone for all those years of magazine browsing, radio and TV grazing, and the perpetual dozen or so florid and embossed bestsellers from which to select at airport bookstores. He was tired of bestsellers. Which all seemed dictated by the same computer; pages lifted straight out of law and aeronautics libraries. There was innocence and there was guilt. No compromise, in Jerrasi's universe. No fudging, no surrogates, no plea bargains, no parole, no mercy. Embrace your friends for as long as they are friendly, destroy your enemies. A simple, no-nonsense approach to enforcing a Democratic way of life. A mean-spirited approach to life? Not necessarily.

Dostoevsky seemed to Jerrasi to be a notch or two above the airport and grocery store paperbacks. The man was deep, psychological, different, at times incomprehensible, he thought. Jerrasi had never before delved into what he believed to be 'classics', save for Capote's *In Cold Blood*, the Norman Mailer book about Gary Gilmore, and an early futile attempt at *Titus Andronicus*, recommended once by a now deceased partner. Life had modelled art in the case of that friend, who succumbed to a gang-style murder in Baltimore Harbor. He was dismembered in so disorderly a fashion that fish and gulls got to his floating bits long before the police. Jerrasi from then on chose to distance himself from so-called great literature, figuring that Shakespeare was somehow to blame for the killing, that the greater the writing, the more dangerous it was, if one were prone to suggestion.

It was a superstitious interpretation of art. Jerrasi was rather proud of it and now, for reasons in reverse, approached the moribund nineteenth century Russian for help in picking up the trail once again. He needed all the help he could get. He'd managed a few pages every night and was well into the case, acting the moves as he would have played them, literature or no literature, already into the recollection of bloodstains, delirium, and that psychology which cuts both ways.

By 7:15 a.m., Jerrasi was headed straight for the Los Angeles Police Department pathology lab downtown. He had a nostalgic feeling about Los Angeles. He'd put two PCP freaks out of their misery in this city a few years back, part of a secretive nationwide manhunt, and presently he drove with a renewed and vigorous intention, bearing down in the centre lane, deviating not left nor right but working his way through morning commuter traffic by sustained and systematic animosity. His thin lips gave away their purpose. His eyes, shielded by '*Terminator*'-style shades, were grey. He drove with one hand on the wheel, his other hand in a plastic bag of pistachios. He hated plastic bags. They did not tear easily, nor predictably. One day he'd crack a tooth trying to get through these bags.

Jerrasi was his job, his job was Jerrasi, and this tour of duty, as he likened it, was nothing short of a perk. Not what others might look for in a 'perk', but then Jerrasi had few equals. Criminals were on a high in this city, and so were lawmen. Like fishing in Guaymas. For the killing. Together, they struck a nervous, highjazzed, cosmic arrangement, in Jerrasi's mind, that ensured continuous, armed combat. War zones. The promise of spoils. It was nothing less than addiction, like entrapping hookers ('escorts') a minute or two after they'd gone down; or gorging oneself on sushi. To hell with the worms.

Raised on *Dragnet*, Jerrasi felt very special goose bumps riddle his irregularly shaped shoulder blades (his spine was diagnosed as curved since second grade) and hairier than normal forearms, at the sight of the Parker Center at 150 North Los Angeles street, 'The Glass House' as local cops named the central police headquarters downtown. It had the television air that lent to his profession ... what? Unique dignity? Self-worth? Purity? The rite of eugenics was consecrated inside a police station. He could detect the ritual trappings blocks away whilst wading through the disenfranchised slime that slithered in and out of the constabular complex, mostly from city buses. Anyone badly dressed within three blocks of the LAPD was, in Jerrasi's estimation, no longer a pedestrian, or a citizen with rights, but a possible suspect. Foul. Black. Degenerate. Doper. A cunt of troubles. An ungrateful parolee. Defalcator. Movie producer. Con. Sodomist. Bomb-thrower and child molester. The culprits flocked in from downtown flop houses, or raunchy hotel dens, or pads squirrelled away from ex-in-laws or others on the prowl. Jerrasi was familiar with every possible dive and shithole. Or they drove down in old stolen, or scraped-together heaps, '57 Chevy's or low-rider get-ups. Jerrasi saw the cars queuing up along the curbs, with waiting wives or girlfriends doing their nails inside, at the ready, so as to save their ex-cons from paying dimes and quarters in the meters. The women, some teen-types, all looked like they were having their periods, frayed hair, besmudged make-up. Seedy broads. Usually in deep. Thousands of repeat offenders, on the street, off the street, through an impossibly overworked system of revolving doors that incorporated a disinterested nod from the Watch Commander on duty, past a labyrinth of patrolmen, traffic officers, narcs, RTOs and the medical evaluation unit, district and city attorneys, shrinks, and drivers charged with taking nutcases over to Unit 3, the psycho ward at the USC Medical Center, or locking them up at some other facility that could handle the overflow.

The FBI man parked in a special VIP section and strode evenly beyond the madding crowd, flipping his ID at two paunchy Afro-American security guards, one male, one female, thus avoiding a long line at the magnetometer. He turned open his vest to reveal a chest harness and his 9mm Beretta semiautomatic, his standard sidearm. You could kill sixteen assailants with this weapon, the 92-F, without reloading. Unlike the older 38 calibre Smith & Wesson Model 15, the previous revolver issued to numerous police departments around the country, as well as the U.S. military, the Beretta had a sexier feel. The trigger, the ease, the balance of weight, balance of power, in Jerrasi's mind, and probably in the minds of many others who carried the little bitch, was sensual, a female orgasm, inherent to the touch. It could have been a body part, all right; quivering with readiness to detonate a charge that guaranteed complete satisfaction. This weapon exposed, he was still frisked, however, by the woman, which he accepted with professional evenness, saying only, "What are you looking for?"

"Bombs," she replied.

"Bombs?"

"We've had our share of pissed off cops."

"Better lose some weight," he added.

"I'm workin' on it," she said with an unfazed smile.

He'd left the pistachios in the car (under the seat) and now toyed with a cinnamon-coated toothpick to get at the between-teeth slivers, while heading towards Chief Sutton's suite of offices on the eighth floor. He'd never met Sutton. They'd spoken once on the phone, during which Sutton had highlighted the incident. There had been little discussion of details because of the jurisdictional thing. Jerrasi did not want, or need, his help. And he'd made that largely clear. Normally, he'd have gone straight to the scene. But the bodies were here.

The elevator swelled and rocked, it stank of sweat and steel. During the irritatingly intermittent ride upwards, he noticed four out of seven people that he definitely did not care for: a bursting Irish policeman who looked like an extra, and did a disservice to the stereotype. "Don't you guys have a nautilus anywhere on this building?" he asked him pointedly, receiving yet another smile in return – and two obvious parolees in torn blue jeans, smelly unshaved slobs, useless to society, should never have been let out. He took the Irishman's smile and turned it into a glowering flourish of energy and respectability that managed almost at once to intimidate the others. They sidestepped a foot away from Jerrasi in the crowded elevator, taking some comfort beside the Irish cop. Coming up just to Jerrasi's chest was an old badger of a woman, improbable spite written all over her, ugly and short. Jerrasi hated ugly and short. There was an Asian stuffed-shirt in cheap polyester leggings and a jacket too tight for him, probably a dumbshit lawyer who got off keeping hardened criminals, like the parolees, free of justice. And finally there was a young red-haired secretary, from another planet, whose tightly wound dress revealed shaven legs, legs which suggested to Jerrasi a wet and wanton diversion.

"How are ya?" he said.

"I'm fine, thank you," the secretary replied in the voice of a diligent telephone operator, hardly looking at him.

Never mind, he thought, walking briskly from the elevator, crossing in front of the old badger, working his way down the corridor to the Chief's door. There were bars on the clerk's window at the entrance. Security stripes on every corner.

"What is it?" a less friendly blond cop standing behind the bars inquired.

"What is it? What is it?" Jerrasi harangued, turning his head in some derision. "Now what kind of greeting is that?"

She paused, buckling up her chin. "You gotta problem, buddy?"

"Yeah, you. Why don't you be a sweet little lady and go tell your boss his visitor's here."

"And who might that be?" she carried forth, prickling.

"The visitor, or your boss?" Jerrasi said in his inimitable way. He delighted in the bait. If there were baiting-bees, baiting clubs, baiting societies, he'd be famous. "Your boss, beautiful. Sutton's his name, in case you forgot."

"You have an appointment?"

"Sure do."

"Have a seat. He's busy."

"I'll stand if you don't mind. Get him. Now."

She twisted her head slightly. Jerrasi relished the gesture. "Your name?"

"Jerrasi. FBI."

"Let's see some ID."

He flashed his card. She studied it for a priggishly long duration – he figured maybe she was just plain stupid – examining the face on the picture with an abnormally indulgent suspicion.

"Something wrong?"

"Just making sure," she went on.

He in turn glared across at her breasts, which were bursting beneath a tightly-clad blue uniform punctuated poetically by her brass badge. "That's Armstrong," she said, turning.

"Well, Judy," he declared. "Either you need glasses or a high school education. Probably the education would make more of an impact."

Armstrong picked up the phone and called to the rear in a most audible voice. "We've got an asshole here from the FBI wants to see Sutton. He around?"

Jerrasi smiled like a little choir boy. He had to hand it to the women here. They confirmed their reputation; a punchy force. He was just putting on his best airs, playing along, no harm intended.

The Chief appeared and motioned to have Jerrasi let in. An electric buzzer sounded and the clerk's entrance gave way to the visitor.

"See ya later, sweetheart," Jerrasi said acerbically, passing by Armstrong.

"Eat shit!" she muttered, countering an attitude with an attitude.

"Good morning. I'm Sutton. Long night, I suppose? See it in your eyes. Or below the eyes." It was his oblique manner of suggesting Jerrasi remove his sunglasses, which Jerrasi did not. He kept his style intact, along with the bolo, certainly uncharacteristic for Washington. It was hammered out of Zuni silver, a purloined souvenir from an Indian thrown into the slammer for forty-four years, the result of a reservation mix up, a killing in other words. The creep's wife, on the government dole, wasn't exactly asking about the item.

"Robert Jerrasi, FBI," he said in measured solemnity, extending his hand in a disinterested greeting. "Very attentive staff."

As they walked back towards his office, Sutton explained how Armstrong's thirteen-year old daughter had recently been raped in the bathroom of her school. "She's understandably angry."

Jerrasi let a tiny lump of guilt dissolve quickly in his throat.

"Want some coffee?" Sutton asked.

"No thanks."

Sutton was new here and Jerrasi could see he was up to his eyeballs, having assumed responsibilities in the wake of a predecessor who had plunged from grace. Brown loafers on large feet, wrinkled off-white cotton slacks, matching 100% Egyptian pressed cotton shirt, and a tie the colour of anthracite, gave him a distinctively smart comportment.

"Sorry about the airport business, but we just don't have the manpower or funding to run a limousine service back and forth from LAX. It's not like the Mayor's office, here."

"No problem."

"Come on in. File's on my desk."

"If you don't mind, I'd rather see the bodies, first."

Jerrasi caught Sutton on a bad day. They stood jaw bone to jaw bone, perhaps eight inches apart, turned to each, slightly; not entirely opposing, but ill-at-ease forces from the start.

"All right," Sutton acquiesced. He could see that Jerrasi was going to live up to his reputation. But he had his own reasons for being easy, and other, more important things on his mind.

The three bodies had already been confined to the refrig for nearly half-a-day. The lab technicians in white smocks rolled them out and lined them up.

"You guys got anything cold to drink in there?" Jerrasi asked.

Nobody knew whether he was joking or not. Finally, to break the silence, one of the two, a long-haired Korean ducked back into cold storage and withdrew a Diet Verner's which they kept in a little white cupboard between corpses.

"This'll be fine."

Jerrasi unpopped the can as the party continued into the laboratory where all three bodies were relieved of their white coverlets.

Jerrasi took off his sunglasses and placed them in the breast pocket of his grey linen Armani jacket look-alike. Now he could register with his own eyes that the dead Joanne had been riddled with nine millimetre cartridges from a Mac-10 machine pistol, a familiar weapon that left a devastating signature, or path. Jerrasi had been following the pistol as much as the man.

"Yep," he mused out loud with ironic restraint.

Chief Sutton already knew that this was a case well outside of his own bailiwick. Not only the fact of it having occurred in a Federally-sanctioned avian quarantine station, but by the manner of death, which was sufficiently dissimilar from two other existing serial killer cases in Los Angeles to exclude it, even, from local follow-up. No body parts had been severed, no urine or feces laid to rest in the woman's mouth. The FBI would be taking over and he felt unburdened by it, though already there were some in-house hotshots voicing frustration, questioning the Thai operation, vying to get their hands into it. But Sutton had tried to stifle such enthusiasm, having carefully gone through the summary files. He knew that this was

Jerrasi's own Golgotha. It was all in the make and calibre of bullet, which seemed to fall right into an existing pattern. Not to mention the animal connection. No other serial killer was consistently hitting up on the animal connection anywhere, in any State or country, that he knew of.

Jerrasi remained fixed upon the young woman, who lay naked like a cannibalized mannequin on the steel table before him. But like all mannequins, her body, despite its upper obliteration, was moulded of desire. Jerrasi felt attracted to it. A vagina the colour of sunburn. Dark pubic hair rimmed with frost. The hint of her questioning lips. Saying something at the very moment of her demise. But there was more, indomitably more to her allure.

He thought he recognized the sign – the eighteen bullets which had blown away her chest, neck, face and right hand. A chime of recognition as momentous to Jerrasi as, well, say the discovery of Agamemnon's death mask of gold, the mud-caked bodies of Pompeii, or those perfectly preserved Inuit mummies found beside a glacier in Greenland. Little decomposition. The face of a six-month old infant wrapped in furs, staring out across frozen time. The same question on its lips: Why?

Among the remains of her face, some that had been lifted from the wall of the quarantine station with tweezers and placed in a jar, an eye remained. He looked at her eye. Baby blue. Still bright. Scared, or surprised. The eye seemed to took back at Robert Jerrasi.

The two Thai security guards had suffered simplistic deaths by comparison. A bullet through the head, and through the head and back of the neck. They were more or less in place, these faces, blood having gushed out the usual orifices of mouth and nose. He tossed the consumed Verner's into a waste basket.

"What's her name?" Jerrasi asked.

"Joanne Jerome," Sutton replied.

"Turn her over," Jerrasi said.

The assistant did so, knowing her liquids had been well drained. Jerrasi admired her firm yet shapely buttocks. He felt around the base of her hairline, nudging the sides of a cavity where at least two of the bullets had shattered her skull. He could feel the weight and shape of the cartridges and sense the speed at which they had shepherded her to oblivion. He closed his eyes, fingers in place like a healer, divining the fingers which had pulled the trigger. Sutton queried Jerrasi what he was doing.

"I'm getting close to him," the FBI man uttered dryly. His eyes remained closed. And in the no-man's land of bullet holes, of hair blood-soaked and limp, of flesh torn by velocities in the thousands of miles per second, he remembered his boy.

Eight years before, during the first week of the hunting season in Maine, Jerrasi had been toasting with friends at the dirt parking lot, before a roadhead not far from Baxter State Park. It was 4:30 in the morning. The sky was tossed in gold and cobalt speculai, very Hemingwayesque. Enough to embolden any man. A cold wind whipped against their wolverine fur-lined jackets. Jerrasi and his eleven-year old son, Tom, each carried a Winchester 86 chambered for a .375 H&H Magnum calibre. All-American weapons. Jerrasi would have preferred a 105 Howitzer.

"Isn't that gun way too big for Tommy?" Jerrasi's wife Cloris had agitated.

"It's time he started behaving like a man," Jerrasi discoursed, eluding the self-evident cliché, by cloaking what was a tired refrain in a tone of retribution. He was having problems with his wife. She was sexually frigid, according to him, but he was afraid as yet to impugn her outwardly.

As for Cloris, who couldn't even water the lawn straight, let alone shoot, she couldn't have been more bored by her husband's fixation with guns and hunting and justice and putting away bad guys. Jerrasi, whose work dictated he wear a 9mm Beretta 92 strapped to his chest, was a collector of dark steel. He spoke the language of gauges and bores and calibre. Their unfinished basement was a veritable arsenal of pieces – varmint guns, Brownings, Rugers, DA and Colt SAA revolvers, auto pistols, shotguns, and machine guns. He relished the to-do of black powder in an old Walker percussion revolver. But his real prize was the 1935 .357 Smith & Wesson Magnum his father had given him. '35 was the year it came out and the year his father – then a Pinkerton – was wounded in the leg during a memorable shootout with members of a mob in Joliet.

Jerrasi saw little of his father. And some of their time together was not memorable. On occasion, Dad would drag him down the thinly-carpeted stairwell, out along the concrete path, through the dirt, and into the garage, all by the collar, or the back of his shirt, and beat him unmercifully with a hard leather belt. *You no good piece of shit!* he'd scream, often toppling over lights, throwing a table, smashing a vase. Such behaviour had nothing to do with alcohol or even insanity. Usually the provocations were more ambiguous. Jerrasi, even as a kid, picked on girls, pulled down their pants, or set their braids on fire. Sometimes he'd gouge his knife into school property and declare his deepest frustrations which, of course, concerned his father. The shirt by which he'd been dragged would be torn to shreds and he'd have welts all over – his neck, his waist, his chest, legs, even his face. It was never abuse, always punishment. Sometimes he was forced to sleep in the basement – a cold, damp place with rats. Dad was a lawman and that made whatever he did proper, according to Mom, even according to the young Jerrasi himself.

Family traits endured. Jerrasi had gotten into the habit of slapping his own Tom more vindictively as he got older. Mother had softened him. Tom reeked of unnatural aversions – aversion to the cold, aversion to sports, even to girls.

"You've become a goddamned sissy, Tom! Just like some homosexual. You know what that is?" Jerrasi laid into him one evening, straightening the lad's shoulders, and smacking him playfully on the cheek. He'd swipe him once, left to right. Tom would duck. Jerrasi would hold him rigid, taking his head between his hands, then smack him again, right to left. Tom hated those smacks, which sometimes came in waves. But he had come to believe, as Jerrasi himself had believed, that he deserved them. That the law was infallible.

"Send you to military school, how about it, Tom?" He'd changed his son's name. Tommy was history.

Tom was not altogether disenchanted with his father, in spite of his tough man act, because among his own grade school peers, the FBI was considered 'far out'. And when Tom's Dad came one day to school to speak about law enforcement and to warn them against drugs, and the danger of their weenies (a word he did not actually use but every boy and girl in the auditorium knew what he was referring to), he pulled out his chest gun just like in a duel, just like a metal weenie, a duel with the whole auditorium, and it caused an unforgettable commotion.

"There's one thing we at the FBI most cherish, ladies and gentlemen." Tom knew that his friends would all be impressed by that! "And that's order. You know what the opposite of order is? Huh? Anybody?"

Needless to say, no one chose to raise his or her hand.

"Disorder. That's what. Sounds like the word disease, doesn't it? That's because it is a disease. Just like when your body gets sick, that's because it's out of order. You step out of line, you stray, you do something bad, you take drugs, you read sex magazines, you skip out on school, or Church, you get bad grades, you steal from the neighbourhood grocery, or from your mother's purse, whatever it is you do that's wrong, you'll have your body to answer to. Just like the FBI. That's right. Your head will tell you at night. You won't be able sleep you'll be so upset. You'll get headaches. Bad dreams. You'll puke. Your skin might break out in acne. Or worse, venereal disease. Look it up. And before you know it everybody around you, everybody at school, in your family, they'll know you've been up to no good. They'll see it in your eyes. They'll smell it on you. That's right: bad deeds smell bad! Your face tells the truth. Pimples. Cavities. Bloody noses. Remember that. The first policeman who sees you is going to know:

that child did something wrong. Let's get him! Because you can't hide from the law. Any more than you can hide from God. Or your parents or your teachers. That's why the FBI is what it is. That's why I carry this gun ... and this other guy ... "

He withdrew them both with John Wayne's panache – *Wow!* – he spun the empty barrels, even pointed them dead-on at the front rows accusingly.

"You! And you! What about you!"

Children were raising their hands all over the auditorium. Within seconds, Jerrasi had the whole auditorium hostage, except for Tom who sat in morbid dread, his hands down, unsure what to do. Teachers were very uncomfortable with the situation, needless to say.

Jerrasi smiled and put down his guns, and the mood of gaiety and fascination, which had preceded his sermon, returned.

It was a big day. The school's president was very grateful. There was no secret: they had a drug problem (as well as a few pregnancies and cases of clap). Random searches of the lockers had yielded scandalous provisions. Hashish. Hustler Magazines. Uppers and downers. LSD and several knives. Lots of impenitent, spoiled little pricks. Jerrasi had arranged for Tom to be bussed in, though the school was actually out of their family's district. But he thought the harder edge was just what Tom needed. Get to know more of those Afro-Americans. Hispanics. Street kids.

And Tom had now assuredly gained in his friends' eyes. He clearly had inroads, secrets, invincibility. Best of all, he had protection. After Dad's visit, Tom was suddenly endowed with an aura, as if he too were a little bit of the FBI. Tom started acting like he had a hidden chest harness and carried 'a piece', as he now called it.

In the pre-dawn hours, after a night in an all male lodge, with its pussy and jerking-off jokes, they toasted with three of Jerrasi's college-friends, before starting up the trail. Jerrasi had been looking forward to this vacation for months, having twice cancelled it on account of sudden calls in the night.

"You cold, boy?" Jerrasi asked Tom, with a quick slap to the face. That hurt.

He didn't say anything. He had a bad earache on account of the wind, but he forced silence upon himself.

"That's good," Jerrasi boasted, proud to be there with his son. "It'll do wonders for your constitution. You'll always thank me for this."

The idea was to reach a well-known knoll by dawn, scope out the valley on the far side, and stalk a moose.

Jerrasi remembered the sweetest of sensations – spotting the bull, resting the cross hairs of his gunsight on top of the enormous hump of that gorgeous beast, hanging from prone toes, inching onto the trigger. The explosion ricocheted for miles. The moose bolted. Jerrasi and his boy ran down the hill, high on the chase.

"Come on come on! Move it!" he ordered in anguished fast whispers, frost detonating from his lips, rifles raised in an anticipation tantamount to lust.

Tom tumbled, unaccustomed to the size of his boots or the rubber soles that, once caked in mud, were no good on more mud. The gun must have hit him in the head when he fell.

"You're lying in the mud, son!" Jerrasi said, standing over him impatiently. "Get up!"

Tom was scared. He didn't want to get up, not ever. There was blood on his scalp, he felt it with his fingers where he hit himself.

"Let's bolt!" and Jerrasi yanked him up to his feet, goading him methodically into the battle.

"Don't worry about it. I used to trip all the time. You all right?"

"I guess so," Tom implied.

"You know, don't you, that I think you're the best kid around?" Jerrasi said out of the blue. "Some day you're gonna make a fine law enforcer, just like your grandpa."

"Just like my old man," Tom rallied, aping his father's style. His ears hurt badly.

Jerrasi poked him in the gut with his rifle, meant to be a loving gesture. "You bet."

They stood silently, so Dad could fix their bearings.

"Just smell that Davy Crockett sap in the air. That's *National Geographic* light you're witnessing, son!"

And indeed, as Jerrasi remembered it, a sunrise that combed its way down through chequered clouds into his earth-hunkering heart, up his curved spine, honing his mind. He savoured the hunt in early morning, though it was all too infrequent those days that he got to hunt four legged animals in the woods. Most of his hunting was done on concrete, or tarmac, where one left skid marks, powering through neighbourhoods in fifth gear, empowered by a bullet-proof vest and wailing backup.

The itch of steel, of cold mahogany handles and the expectation of a blast that thundered across miles of open season, was nothing short of religious. And so much more pure than killing on a street, or inside a tenement, where a hidden and surprise witness was likely to confound an otherwise smooth, unambiguous conviction.

The animal kill made him tranquil, pantheistic, full of intense emotion. He believed that hunters came as close to nature as you could get, and he intended to inculcate that supreme passion in his one offspring. In his wildest imagination, he saw himself winning the Weatherby Trophy, impossible, of course, given his salary. But the idea of bagging big-game on six continents was certainly appealing. As was the Weatherby .460 calibre rifle, the only weapon of its kind capable of bringing down a charging rhino. Short of the Weatherby, Jerrasi had his heart set on the Grand Slam of North American Game. You had to kill twenty-nine large mammals. He knew he had a long way to go.

He'd earned the right to kill, he thought. He'd fought hard in Vietnam, and came home only to be subjected like so many to scorn, imposed guilt and the hyperbole of those faggot bastards and whores who'd protested the war.

They could never be vindicated, even if America were willing to engage in recrimination twenty years later, and Hollywood was intent upon betraying movie-goers, by awarding those same faggot bastards its cowardly accolades. That was Hollywood's business. But there was no excuse, in Jerrasi's mind, for arguing ethics and philosophy when defence of one's homeland was involved. He was not quite to the point of love it or leave it, in as much as he acknowledged mediocrity all around him. But he had assiduously followed the President, out of a sense of genuine enthusiasm for discipline, even if the President later turned out to be merely mortal.

He found the FBI the perfect solution for one pissed off veteran. His older brother had also gone to Nam but he remained in the military. His father, meanwhile, had retired to Tarpon Springs, Florida, with his mother, before passing away. Mom still lived there. He harboured less than one hundred percent affection for that woman, on account of something she once said that he never forgave her for.

"You have a *weak chin*," she declared, the subtlety hidden in her intonation, which was more of a question.

Maybe she expected him to stand up to her husband, since she never could. But that was not the best way to urge him to do so, he was sure.

One day after the war she had the ill manners to refer to the chin in front of his FBI friends following a morning of mock-heroism that had even brought out a few members of the press. Jerrasi was interviewed. He was being lauded for his courage and commitment; an up and coming star within the department. Mom was asked to comment. *You must be proud, Mrs. Jerrasi. He's just like your late husband* the reporter commented. Her response was more or less a loving quip, conveyed with her own special brand of sentiment, or irony. Or maybe she was stating for the record once and for all what she really thought of the wife-beating man whose thirty seconds of seed had once, long ago, made another younger man in his belligerent image. *Yes* she replied. *And even with that weak chin of his! You see it?*

Jerrasi exploded, and told her never, NEVER, to mention the chin again. She never did. But he never got over it. Photographs of him all seemed to emphasize, in his mind, that useless chin. And when a cop once made a wisecrack about it, Jerrasi decked him. And since he couldn't grow a normal beard – genetic insult added to injury – he was stuck with his soft chin and his deep suspicions that his mother didn't really want him. His best defence, he figured, was to return the compliment. He hardly ever saw her now.

Meanwhile, Jerrasi rose quickly through the ranks. He put dozens of creeps behind bars. He had a legendary sense of smell, better than 20/20 eyesight, and one of the steadiest trigger fingers in the business. His wife stayed at home and sold Avon products by phone. She loved her job, loved her son, put up with her husband, and the neighbourhood in Columbia, Maryland, a community to which they'd recently moved from Alexandria. The ten-block, rectilinear enclave boasted its own security guards, and more fountains than any townhouse development on the East Coast. The Jerrasi's, like their neighbours, had a beautiful front lawn, and two storeys of solid baked brick, and were only four minutes away from Pac'n'Save, Tom's school, three beauty parlours, a Cinoplex, four gas stations, and a huge shopping mall that included a Saks Fifth Avenue. Yet they were out of earshot of the freeway, and dogs were not allowed anywhere around the nine-hundred townhouse complex. So there were no feces to be seen anywhere.

It was an orderly way to live.

Jerrasi and Cloris were not high school sweethearts. She'd had a first marriage that her parents had annulled when Cloris was twenty. She'd run off with a biker to South Dakota for one of those annual Hell's Angels affairs. Her month-long binge out on the road in no way corresponded to the picture of Cloris that Jerrasi had long cultivated, nor was the *'horrible, horrible'* affair (his description of it) ever referred to, except when Cloris sometimes at night, if they'd been sullen with one another, seemed to drift off into a vengeful dreaminess. Jerrasi knew that she'd be feigning that Jack shit. Jack was the fuckhead's name who 'banged her up' just barely one time, hardly counted, according to Cloris, and married her in a group perversion near Dead Wood. Fortunately, his bang was hardly even a spark. Cloris got no disease of any kind, and certainly didn't get pregnant. Or if she had, Jerrasi never knew about it. He'd never have married her if that had been the case. Of course, as it was, Jerrasi only found out about Jack after he'd solemnly sworn, "I do" up on the tulip-studded altar.

Jerrasi commuted to work by Amtrak, which was also close by. When he wasn't on a case, he volunteered his time speaking on behalf of the understaffed, under-budgeted Institute for Legislative Action, the NRA's lobby in Washington, whose task it was to kill any and all anti-gun legislation in Congress. Jerrasi was quite vocal on the issue of good versus evil.

"You all know the difference," he flapped.

His biggest claim was the Chinese suppression of the student rebellion, which would never have come about, he insisted, if the Chinese had had their own Second Amendment, granting them the right to own and bear arms. Sometimes, privately, he questioned that right; whenever a gun was aimed at him and the owner happened to be some beast out of his mind on drugs, or panic, or hate, or revenge.

He had stared them down, blown a number of them away in heroin dens, in freeway shootouts, even on college campuses – the sickness was spreading – and those which he'd spared, he'd seen back out on the streets, sometimes within hours. He knew that the system was letting down law enforcement. If he and his partners didn't take care of a situation whenever they got the chance, the system might, or it might not, invoke justice. It depended on the shit ass lawyers involved. That meant never, never, granting the benefit of doubt. A shoot first, ask later frame of mind. Jerrasi had a motive. His friends lived by it, he lived by it, fed his family by it, and read it into the Constitution.

It was all in the gun.

Tom had had little practice with a weapon before that day, in Maine. He was a born flincher, in his father's eyes. But a few kills would ween any kid, in spite of his having kept pet rabbits, and been reared on petting zoos. He was a momma's boy, sickeningly chivalrous, even at that age. It was not dignified, his father explained. Jerrasi had been embarrassed when his son was the only boy who did not know the first thing about hitting a target during an annual FBI family picnic. That's when Jerrasi volunteered to speak at Tom's school. Maybe it would motivate his son.

When she later divorced her husband, Cloris, icebound and remote, portrayed Jerrasi before an arbitration hearing, as *'insanely stubborn and too self-righteous for words'*.

Did the condemnation change him? He was not immune to the feelings associated with his divorce. He hated cooking for himself. Cloris imbued food with taste. Jerrasi microwaved everything to death. The realization that he'd now have to hunt down his sexual pleasures depressed him after a few failures at the local nightclubs. His two weekends a month with Tom were precious, now. And that was perhaps the one benefit of the break-up. As for the rest, Jerrasi knew he'd been right. The battles had been her making. The complaints dated to her genes, not his. No question in his mind: his mother-in-law and Cloris got the same pimples in the same corner of their necks at the same times. Symbolic understatement. It explained everything.

If there was any lingering doubt about the veracity of Jerrasi's side of things, one merely needed to look at his professional life. His record was deliberate, engineered. Flawless. Internal Affairs had checked him out – reports of brutality – but concluded that there were no unusual grounds for further investigation. He was a model FBI man, they alleged, and for the record proclaimed that Robert Jerrasi had made a significant contribution to the department.

They sighted a lumbering buck and held back since it was moose they'd come to bag. Jerrasi loved the taste of moose. One large bull was worth a year of steaks for his family and friends. Though that was just hype, of course. It never really worked out that way. Jerrasi's brother's family didn't want the meat for reasons having to do with his sister-in-law's diet. Doctor's orders. She was forgiven. And more often than not, they'd go out for dinner because Cloris always found it too taxing to fry up frozen moose. It meant dethawing, days in advance, and if you dethawed too long, the drainage stank. Often, Jerrasi would change his mind, return the thawed steak to the freezer so that the next time Cloris dethawed it, she found freezer burn and had to toss it. There were any number of similar complications to wild meat.

They pursued their lost victim for an hour, then settled on the notion of going after new prey. The first one had gotten away and they found themselves deep in dogwood. Tom had trouble moving through such a thicket. It had rained for several days before, and the mud made maneuvering more and more difficult for him. He took other falls. Though with eight hundred hunters out that morning, nothing would get away for very long.

"You're sure her genitals were not tampered with?" he asked.

Sutton looked to the pathologist in charge.

"We checked carefully for penetration. Nothing."

It was the nakedness that made him remember. Standing over the naked corpse of Joanne Jerome, Jerrasi remembered how that morning long ago in Maine had made men naked under God.

He heard the screams of a hunter suddenly rifling across the aggregated forests, like a crack in a frozen lake that proliferated with the dull, whipped ingredient of sound. At first, Jerrasi and to a much lesser extent, Tom, thrilled to the image of a triumphant hunter standing over his felled moose. They were envious, as they'd seen no other live prospect for hours. But then the blood-curdling wails exploded with a sense of deja vu in Jerrasi's brain.

"Come on, Tom!" he ordered. He and his son ran in the direction of the screaming, and as they ran, other screams, confused shouting, ululating curses, pierced the still air of the wilds.

The screamer's partner had just been shot through the head by a stray bullet. The dead man sat quietly against a tree, like a sleeping shepherd from a Renaissance pastoral poem. Except that his companion was groaning – "Oh God" – beside him, in a muddle of paranoia.

"Don't shoot!" Jerrasi shouted, pushing Tom down so that they were both concealed behind umbrage. "It wasn't us!"

The hunter didn't know who to trust.

"Someone fuckin' blew away my buddy! We had the moose in our sights, goddammit!" And he aimed his weapon in all directions.

"I'M A COP! DON'T MOVE!" Jerrasi hollered, holding his place, not sure how to handle the situation, when abruptly another voice started bellowing at a distance.

"Oh Jesus ... Jesus Christ somebody please help us ... "

There were echoes of gunshot all over the woods now, no way to decipher any pattern, deliberation, or motive.

"Dad??" the boy cried out.

"Shut up and do exactly as I tell you!"

The dead man's companion, Jerrasi and his son moved through the forest, crouched and feeling cornered. The volume of dire calls for help was quickly escalating. Suddenly a piece of wood the size of a brick rebounded off a white pine, not three inches from Jerrasi's head. They all dove to the ground. Jerrasi shot out into empty air. He saw nothing.

"THERE'S PEOPLE HERE!! DID YOU HEAR ME!" He paused. "I SAID THERE'S PEOPLE HERE!"

They slowly got up, started to move. Another eruption banged off at close proximity. They ran, they pressed the ground in a sloppy frenzy, they ran again. Another whiplash of steel into bark. They gained cover behind a rock. The three of them were breathing in more harsh air than they could handle. Tom was blue in the face from fear and confusion. Jerrasi, lacking for his normal backup, hearing his wife's later censure, started hollering at whatever irrational offenders were out there.

"DID YOU SONSOFBITCHES HEAR ME?! THERE'S LIVE HUMAN BEINGS HERE – NOT MOOSE, FUCKHEADS! THROW DOWN YOUR WEAPONS! YOU'RE ALL UNDER ARREST!!!"

Silence greeted his demands, then more hits out in the distance. Expanse surrounded them, yet they were cornered in a claustrophobic nature. Trees concealed them, but also made them more vulnerable. The large granite erratics, castoffs of Maine's long-ago Ice Age, sheltered them on one side only. In the orgy of gunshots that surrounded them, no shelter was very meaningful. They were far away from the parking lot. Far away from friends. Jerrasi even sensed that they were lost, and he did not have the presence of mind to use a compass, to think straight, to react professionally to the situation because, as of yet, he could not make out the situation. No black and white parameters. No good guys and bad guys. Someone had made a bad mistake and it had triggered other reactions.

"We've got to keep moving!" he informed the dazed man who had now become part of their trio. His ulterior motive was to drive this stranger into the lead. Let him be the hero; let him be the first one out.

"DO IT NOW!" Jerrasi implored, pushing the stranger out ahead, beyond the rock.

"It's clear," the man yelled, his voice many decibels louder than it needed to be, at ten feet.

"Go Tom!" Jerrasi said.

It was instant. Tom took the hit to his throat. The muzzle energy of the incoming bullet threw him like a stuffed doll. His head smashed at a horizontal speed back against the rock, and the body lumped over and dropped.

"NO YOU FUCKING!!!!" Jerrasi, checking the impulse to lunge for his son. Then dragging himself with lizard speed through the mud after him. It was thus in Vietnam.

And the two men – Jerrasi and the dead man's partner – started shooting wild into the four winds. And the winds picked up the battle sound of exploding powder, screeching horror, and touched off an additional spree of gun terror, turning hunting season into a desperate Lebanon.

Fearing the other guy, hunters by the droves continued shooting. No questions. Within minutes, screams had multiplied across hundreds of acres of hardwood. From every direction. Up above at the knoll, in hiding places all over the valley.

They were all being stalked, and stalking. In the midst of the mayhem, Jerrasi dragged his hemorrhaging boy through the woods in the direction of the trail head, he thought.

Tom was silent, losing blood faster than Jerrasi could drag. They came to a creek which they'd never seen before.

"D'you see this creek before?"

"What?"

"DID YOU SEE THIS CREEK BEFORE??" Jerrasi ranted, grabbing the stranger by the bullet pouches on his outer vest with his free hand and shaking.

"NnnNo!" the stranger stammered.

"We're lost. SHIT! WE'RE LOST! YOU FUCKING COCK FUCKING SUCKING SHIT! CUNTS! SAVAGES! GODDAMMIT!" and his brains and words and demons spewed out of him. Dreams disintegrated. Perennial philosophies, safe platitudes, the level ground of forty years, all thundered away beneath him. Chasms opened up. The profound disappointment of finally being a condemned man.

"Help me," he mumbled to the stranger, trying to hold his limp boy.

Jerrasi and the stranger dragged Tom for miles. Dawn became twilight. Jerrasi and the stranger tried unsuccessfully to build a fire. They had one pack of matches between them and it was not enough. Jerrasi had not come prepared for an assault. He carried no flares. Darkness brought with it twenty degree nightfall. The wolverine fur kept them alive, but not Tom. His small figure evanesced briefly, the skin tone turning to the substance of light itself, Belleek-softened, reflecting the tranquillity of unscathed spirit, or unconsciousness.

Jerrasi still had some ammo and was prepared to fight his way back to the parking lot at dawn. But that proved unnecessary.

"Drop your weapons!" the voice in the megaphone cautioned, above the din of approaching helicopters. It was the State police.

Jerrasi and the stranger raised their hands to the sky.

The chopper hovered, then set down, as troopers leaped out, covering one another Vietnam style, in attack formation.

"FBI!" Jerrasi screamed, his ID card extended in his palm.

Fifty-eight hunters in all were found dead. Nothing like it had ever happened. As for deer and moose, not one had been taken.

"We deeply regret the tragedy, while not failing to note the windfall for our wildlife," a local radical radio station reported.

The State police discovered that at least ten of the victims, eight males among them, in addition to two females (mothers), had been killed by the same, common make of big game bullet, a 300 Weatherby magnum. But there were dozens of other makes as well. The bullet that plowed through Tom Jerrasi's neck at nearly 2900 feet per second was a Nosler 120-grain ballistic tip. Autopsies revealed dozens of .30-30's, as well as the .405 WCF, whose impact on a forehead can be nicely demonstrated by dropping a watermelon from atop the World Trade Center in New York and onto the pavement below.

So despite ample suspicions of a deadly psychopath on the loose, there was never any proof that that first stray, and the horrible carnage it unleashed, had been anything other than tragic mishap, a risk inherent to the opening day of any hunting season. The press got hold of this incident and turned it into one of the grandest critiques of human folly in recent years.

But Jerrasi and his colleagues at the FBI drew their own conclusions, which were augmented later that week when the owner of a restaurant chain specializing in Maine lobsters was found boiled to death in a large cauldron in the kitchen of her establishment. Her skin had turned to the consistency of the rare tats bota, or Brazilian armadillo. Sixty-five live lobsters had been stolen, their whereabouts and state of health unknown. No message had been left. No reason for the murder stated.

"What do you suppose the guy had against lobsters?" Wes Madrid had wondered aloud. Madrid had been brought up from Washington, just three months on the job, to work with Jerrasi.

And that was the beginning of the trail. Lost in Maine. The blood of his hemorrhaging son, coating the dogwood and alder and evergreen, for thousands of feet. Dragging the memory even now, through the same thick underbrush. Just like his father used to drag him out into the shed for a good beating.

He couldn't shake the phantasms, analogies, echoes. He hadn't been able to carry Tom because he was afraid to stand up. That's what it was. Bullets were flying throughout the day. A night with a manic stranger. *If you're a cop then do somethin' damn you!* he kept saying. An eleven-year old's blood by starlight. The evil wilderness. The way Tom had been thrown backwards against that rock, with a speed that was uncanny, as if the rock were coming at him. It could have been Jerrasi just as easily. He was plagued by the knowledge that he had urged the stranger first, then his son. He truly believed at the time that second position would be safer. Or had he only been testing Tom, forcing him into the line of probable fire so as to become the martyr that Jerrasi always believed himself to be, beneath the terrible lashings of his father? He had endured all those years by clinging to the foreknowledge that one day, when he was larger, he'd take his revenge.

But then his father died and revenge became meaningless. Unless he considered his mother. But not like this.

His personal life, his tormented thoughts, were all assbackwards. What he still had was his job, and a mushrooming vengeance that now took on a realizable focus.

A month after the burial, a CEO's severed head was found beneath the domed lid of a silver platter at a banquet table in New York that had been prepared for board members of a large company which specialized in hoghead hydroclippers. The man's head had been sliced off in a maximally efficient instant. The manufacturer's blade had been approved by the U.S.

Department of Agriculture. It consisted of seven inches of tempered chrome-molybdenum; its lightness and ease of handling nearly eliminating the risk of operator tendonitis. That was the company's big edge in a marketplace that disposed of nearly 100 million pigs every year in this fashion. And they were merciful clippers. Upton Sinclair might have called them even *wonderful* in their manner of facilitating instantaneous death to the animal (if one ignored the hanging up by a leg, the trolleys, the long march to the killing ground ...)

Whoever had gotten into the building had done his homework, staked out the offices, knew privileged information, and had access to the elevators past the security guards.

The FBI was obviously intent upon finding whoever did it, believing the culprit to be the same person or party from Maine. Jerrasi was put in charge of the investigation.

Now he had new purpose that was clear and exhilarating; a chance to vindicate personal history, Tom, the Vietnam war, his broken marriage, and the U.S. Constitution, all in one thrust. He felt no guilt over his son's death – that sensation had passed through him, then dissipated, not quickly but with slow reasoning powers; but his hatred towards the man, or men responsible, was now irrepressible. Whatever twinges of regret he might have felt were abandoned, as he reinforced a lifetime of militancy, vanguarding the battle to defeat evil, in a world which seemed bent on personalizing the war.

The enemy was clearly hung up on animals. But he ruled out Seventh Day Adventists, Quakers and Unitarians right off. Furthermore, the vendettas were incomparably more studied and lethal than those of the various animal liberation movements, whose tactics precluded harming people.

But if it was the culprit's intention to stir up the American consumer, or the environmental movement, then he had failed thus far. The outcry against such terrorism was overwhelming. Even many vegetarians openly condemned the killings and vowed to 'get him'.

Numerous ecology-minded charities vied with each other to condemn the crimes as well. It was an opportunity to solicit donations for the mainstream groups, to promulgate a voice, the compromise, of *'reason'*. One of the oldest pro-animal lobbies in the nation reminded its more than a million members that there were better ways to attack inhumanity, and their newsletter cited that organisation's critical support of the landmark *'Humane Methods of Slaughter Act'*. According to this legislation, livestock and poultry – which enjoy absolutely no rights under the congressional *Animal Welfare Act* – would nevertheless be entitled to the benefit of certain pre-slaughter 'recommendations'. Owners of egg farms, for example, would be asked to cram no more than five adult hens into the customary one foot square wire cages. Such hens usually spent their whole lives in metal crates that allowed all of five square inches per animal.

Those hens, it must be admitted, were the lucky ones: half-a-million male chicks were simply killed every day upon birth, considered useless to the market, while four billion older chickens were chopped up, vacuum wrapped and delivered to grocery stores every year.

These disturbing facts were presented in a positive light and meant to persuade members that action on behalf of animals – however plodding and incremental – was possible without recourse to violence. Executive directors of several organisations around the country expressed outrage at the tainting by a few sick people of a venerable two hundred year old tradition of animal rights.

In spite of all this, Jerrasi dispatched undercover operatives into many of those environmental hot beds in the hopes of finding any leads. But it was soon apparent that such groups were indeed coming forth independently to reprove the maniacs at work, while expressing some sympathy for the murderer's apparent goals of drawing attention to the tragedy of animal abuse.

That latter suggestion irked Jerrasi and Madrid. For them, there was nothing tragic about animal abuse, as interpreted by ecologists; because animal abuse was rare in their estimations. Sure, people sometimes maltreated a pet, and they were assholes. If Jerrasi ever saw a man whipping a horse, he'd more than likely say something. But he didn't count research animals, or strays, or cattle, or sheep, or birds, or the whole vast gamut of game, let alone lesser life forms, among those worthy of consideration. Attributing rights or feelings or intelligence to such creatures was bound to cause problems – that's how he summed up the situation, 'bound to cause problems' (he was thinking that problems of *conscience* were better left alone. In his mind, Nature had conferred the right to kill, the right to eat, the Biblical right to make all other life-forms flesh for our dinner table. Meat-eating was ordained by all of the Apostles! Popes ate meat. The Tibetan Dalai Lama, Martin Luther, Calvin, most or all of the great theologians, hell, even God, ate meat).

And so, in the end, he simply declared to himself, or to his partners on the job, or to anybody who cared to inquire, that the attribution of human qualities to animals was just about as nonsensical as claiming Divine Right for trees or bushes or flowers.

To reverse this tendency in man, as the killer was advocating by his actions, was to threaten – in Jerrasi's mind – the bedrock of civilization.

The man needed to be eliminated, and fast.

But so far, Jerrasi's team had no evidence to support even the claim of a serial killer, or killers. Not a single clue. Whoever had committed these murders, was massively expert. No message was ever left behind. The murderers stole animals, but no one knew where those animals were released, if in fact they ever were. No one who might have had contact with the culprits ever knew about it, or lived to mention it. Not a ruffle, not a single item. No wake. No manifestation. Not a single source off the street. Weapons came from nowhere, went nowhere. Not even a hint. As far as traditional evidence, fibres, DNA, fingerprints, forget it.

But at least, it was now apparent to both Jerrasi and Madrid that this was no animal liberation *movement*, but the monstrous vision of one or more men. A woman was not capable of such things, he had decided.

Jerrasi began to suspect a Vietnam vet, someone – or some group – of possible commandos, special forces, men with the kind of skills it would take to pull off a beheading like that, high atop a skyscraper in noonday Manhattan, without ever being seen, or leaving any trace. It was incredibly well orchestrated.

He ordered up several hundred boxes of files, but the FBI was not in a position to manage so much data assimilation. Jerrasi, Madrid and a team of eight others spent months working through the reams, with no additional insight.

They tracked down half-a-dozen veterans who were likely candidates; vegetarians in special forces units, who had demonstrated wavering allegiance to their posts, one who had been dishonourably discharged after three months in the jungle. But he had gone on to kill himself, and the others proved to be dead-ends as well. It was a pity: Jerrasi, at one point, really thought he was on to something. One of the greatest marksmen in the history of any military academy in the U.S., easily Delta Force style of hitting a bull's-eye, a brilliant student to boot, but a cheat, namely, one Brian Laffont. But Laffont apparently disappeared in South America after being thrown out of the Air Force Academy in the late 1960's and a police file showed that he was involved with druglords, and killed. In the meantime, the killer continued to act.

Three weeks after the severed head business, the most successful furrier in Aspen, Colorado, was found skinned alive in her Ajax Mountain Chalet. The hideously tortured flesh of the fifty-five year old business woman from Scarsdale was scattered in pieces atop the fox, mink, sable and snow leopard pelts that covered the inside of her pricey domicile. It was clear from Jerrasi's follow-up investigation that she had been stripped naked, obviously at gunpoint, gagged, her hands and gold-polished nails smashed in the steel jaws of a Conibear trap produced for the occasion, and her pampered feet crushed by the murderous clenches of a leghold used most commonly for lynxes, beavers and fox.

Then some sort of large butcher knife was applied to the still conscious victim. Her skin peeled off as finely as if it had been a honeyed Danish ham.

I will get him Jerrasi was quoted as stating in the *Aspen Town Crier*.

Locals had only recently been engulfed in a nationally followed vote over the issue of banning furs from that town. The ban had not been ratified. Now somebody was getting even and townsfolk were horrified. It was one month before ski season, and the expected tens-of-millions of tourist dollars.

Jerrasi ruminated, dreamt, mulled over nothing but the case. It consumed him with intermittent chills and fevers. He'd doodle details of it in his pizza. One night he saw the killer. A hundred yards of motionless fur separated him from the sudden darting mass beyond. It was no bear, no moose, but the barrel of a gun, aimed at Jerrasi. There was an interminable pause, the air making ready to detonate; a flock of birds flew up out of the high limbs, a moon's crescent rose just slightly above the horizon. Jerrasi shouted "NO!" and pushed his son, Tom, out of the way, as the charge came ripping through the chilled stillness.

Jerrasi lunged upwards from his pillows, hitting his left eye with his right fist which had punched forward in a desperate maneuver.

He lay awake, breathing furiously remembering the imperceptible. Birds, and the rebound of a thunderous discharge still trembled inside. And continued to tremble on the Metro into work. At the newsstand. In traffic. Before the computer. In conversation with Madrid, or Muldoon, with Ned, Tulsi or Shelley, or any of the others on his team. Birds squawking.

This was no philosophical after-tremor, but a cosmic similitude which served to repeat the trauma of his son's death at every inch along the way of the investigation.

An investigation which superseded all else in his life. His demands upon the staff assigned to it had become – in the eyes of some – excessive. Madrid, the last to complain, was the first to notice it. But he also understood his partner's dilemma: Jerrasi was obsessed because he had nothing else. A compact little townhouse just off East Pennsylvania Avenue, walking distance from the White House, a stone's throw from that part of the ghetto not yet yuppied over with health food stores, and used bric-a-brac from Ethiopia or Afghanistan. He had his jeep and his guns. He kept no picture of his former affiliations, neither his son nor wife. No memento mori of any kind, but rather, a clean slate of the day. The fireplace was fake, throwing up the flames of a gas jet. In his bathroom, a shower massage. In the kitchen, all the recent gadgets. He enjoyed his wok, his fondu machine and garlic press; his bread and pasta maker and his electric potato peeler. He had a 48-inch screen on which he watched *NYPD Blues* and football. In the summer, sometimes, he'd go to the racetrack, or to adult movie theatres, in search of something.

He believed vigorously in the letter of the law, and had made an example of himself that was military, stolid, perfect. He could not conceal his indefatigability, the persistence by which he followed the scent, with none of the charm of a Columbo. In his own way, Jerrasi was a killer. Neither tears nor fear could divert him. Neither the squeals of a human being, nor of an animal, could shake him.

One day a member of Jerrasi's staff, a bright young woman named Shelley Pendergras from the Justice Department, who was in the process of making a slight career move over to the Bureau, brought an item to his attention.

"Remember that one from the Air Force Academy?"

"Brain Laffont."

"Good memory."

"Who died in a drug-related manner."

"Wrong."

And she pointed out how their original information was incomplete. According to more reliable sources that she obtained from a friend over at the Office of General Counsel for Treasury, a man meeting Laffont's description – early twenties, Portuguese-speaking American – was part of a Brazilian police raid, in 1970 or 1971, on a poachers' camp along some river in the southern part of the country. The money from the skins was making its way into the hands of customs officials in Arizona.

"He was an informant?"

"For the Secret Service, we think."

"You think?"

"Nobody's sure. Files are unclear. The whole thing is roundabout. But it's a lead. Maybe a good one. I attended this conference at the Smithsonian on wildlife conservation last week. There was a specialist on anti-poaching among the group. I asked him if he had heard of any vigilantes in that area during the last twenty years."

"And had he?"

"A movie producer in Kenya, various tribal sorts in Sumatra, Borneo, eastern Siberia, Tibet, and this fat fellow in Brazil, the American."

"What was his name?"

"Brian."

"Who was the guy's contact with the Brazilian police?"

"He's dead."

"See what you can find out. But don't waste time."

A week later, Jerrasi and Madrid were having lunch over at the National Gallery. They'd long ago tired of the cafeteria at headquarters. And there was an exhibition of cowboy artists – mostly Remington – which interested Madrid. He thought it might be a good distraction for Jerrasi.

"Do you know he also wrote about a hundred books?" Madrid said, while hastily devouring his curried victuals.

"Who the hell is Remington?" asked Jerrasi.

"You're reading Dostoevsky and you don't know Remington?"

"What the fuck are you givin' me here?"

"That bronze horse, with the cowboy. Everybody knows it."

"Oh. That one. Sure. I know Remington."

Madrid finished his ice tea, looked up, saw Shelley, and motioned her over to the table. "She said she might have something interesting coming in," Madrid explained, on sighting the pretty young woman.

Shelley placed a folder on the table before Jerrasi. Inside it was a single sheet of paper, a fax.

It described how, in 1980, a Brian Laffont was brought in by police in Tokyo, in connection with the killing of a security guard at a circus. They'd rounded him up in a net that encompassed literally hundreds of Caucasians. Laffont, police concluded, was merely a witness to the crime, which involved not only a murder, but the theft of several large mammals. He was released without further questioning after all of an hour at the station.

In 1981, a man meeting Laffont's description was charged with obstructing the entrance to a biomedical research laboratory in Wisconsin, along with dozens of other protesters. He was released on his own recognizance.

"There must be video of that protest?" Jerrasi at once stated.

"Unfortunately, not," Shelley informed him. "Or not that we know of."

"And that's it?"

"For now."

Both Jerrasi and Madrid silently thought about the information. Finally, Jerrasi agreed that it was interesting. "And if we ever catch up with this fat fuck – pardon the expression – I'm sure it will fit the pattern. Sorry Shelley. I don't mean to belittle your fine efforts. It's just not there, or not yet." He knew they needed more, not that he had more to offer. He turned to Madrid, "Let's see our Remingtons."

Jerrasi was beginning to fall apart. Madrid could see it. Not only the persistent nightmares, but the alimony. It was draining him. Everything seemed to be working against the high ranking agent. He'd let his phone bill go, even rent on his townhouse. Jerrasi played the maverick only so well, but the fact was, he was alone. Madrid and his wife would have him for dinner on occasional Sundays, but they had a ten year old girl, Alice, who made him uncomfortable. Or they'd take in a hockey match together, but Jerrasi was increasingly weird, sullen, pissed off. He wasn't acting as part of a team. This had become his own battleground. Like some cross to bear. He didn't want competition from amateurs like Shelley.

Five months had passed. There was no case. Nothing. Shelley's inroads had dried up, the others had spun countless wheels, dithered, dragged, gone nowhere. Except for one salient discovery, by Madrid: two dishwashers, or whatever they were, in the Manhattan kitchen that catered the board meeting lunch, where the CEO was butchered. Hadn't they mentioned a fat man? Bingo, sort of. Jerrasi had written up his report and delivered it to his departmental head, Raymond Kinesey.

Kinesey was a retiring sort, very cautious, never excitable. He enjoyed the respect of everyone, the animosity of no one. Kinesey was one of those bureaucrats who could be personable without being personal. He had no grief to settle, it seemed, with anyone. He'd come up through the ranks, not a bad looking man. Two of his daughters were also in the FBI, very unusual. A career family that sought no medals, no glory. Just competence.

At the same time, Kinesey – who was eight years older than Jerrasi – seemed incapable of understanding or accepting passion in others. It was not professional, he believed.

Jerrasi sat before him. Kinesey had the file in his hands.

"Two cartridges, more than likely belonging to any one of seventy hunters. A dossier on a Portuguese or French or American soldier of fortune that peters out nearly fifteen years ago. I'd say of no interest to this case. Nearly three thousand hours of – from what I can decipher by the summary – irrelevant interviews. You've got nothing at all on the lobster business. Not a thing on that dismal Aspen murder. Except, I suppose, you could say that both the lobster thing and the Aspen thing involved the murder of women. And really nothing on the hunting fiasco that Maine's State troopers haven't themselves figured out. And that's squat. What do you have here ... Two nervous New York Italians working ignominiously in the rear of a kitchen who think they remember seeing a fat man, and a tall lean swarthy skinned guy like themselves, with a moustache, who 'seemed maybe nervous'. Great! And that's it."

"There's nothing ignominious; they were employees."

"Fine. Employees. So?"

"A fat man," Jerrasi emphasized. He was desperate and he knew it. Kinesey just stared at him.

"They said, a fat man. Both of them said they saw a fat man, also Caucasian, who was dressed in the chef's clothes."

"I see it. *Uomo da molto.* A fat man, or a man of weight. That could be ambiguous."

"They described him as a sort of Ralph Goodman or Pavarotti sort, but with more of the football player, or foreign legion type body."

"That's swell."

"We checked with the caterers. No such fat man. He was an impostor. That soldier of fortune was also a fat man. I want to take it to the next level."

But Kinesey had already gone beyond this chit-chat. He'd prejudged the file.

"We have a situation here in Washington, Bob, requiring someone with your kind of background in drug enforcement. It involves diplomats, immunity, and what we know to be ongoing shipments from the Far East."

Jerrasi remained still, beyond the hectic flush of his pores and jangled nerves. He had better come up with an ingenious rebuttal or it would be over. He might as well quit the force. That's how much this meant to him.

Kinesey continued, "You know damn well you're too close to this case, Bob."

Raymond, by his soft, flat, immoveable stare, knew all the details of Jerrasi's son's death, coming immediately in the wake of Bob's divorce, his having to move out of his house; how he'd lost half of his $44,000 a year salary to Cloris, who herself was probably unemployable for years to come, because of Tom and her breakdown; and how he was now living in a drab apartment in downtown Washington, obsessed with finding a phantom perpetrator.

"I know how to separate personal feelings from professional duty. I know better than most."

"I think it needs a fresh perspective."

"There's ten of us on this, Ray. Not just me. We're doing it by the book. Turning every stone."

"I'm sure you are."

There was a standoff. Jerrasi hesitated to plead or bring up past skeletons. But then Raymond restated his decision. Jerrasi had no choice.

He began, "You probably remember about three years ago, when your daughter found herself in over her head."

"You saved my Julie's life. Don't think I'm not forever indebted. Because I am," Kinesey volunteered.

Jerrasi remembered how she'd been wired at a luncheon, with two of his own former FBI classmates suspected of high-level involvement in an extortion ring. Jerrasi and others were monitoring the situation out of a hidden truck around the corner from the restaurant. Jerrasi was the one who went in and saved a desperate situation. By nailing his two former buddies, his reputation did cartwheels among the rank and file, before it got better. It got Kinesey his present appointment and saved his daughter's ass.

"I'm thinking of your long term career," Kinesey went on. "Maybe I'm just a little concerned about your personal well being, Bob. You've been through a lot."

"And don't think I'm not grateful to you for those concerns. But believe me, the only thing that's going to keep me sane – I know that's what you meant – is doing this right. Finishing what I started. You know that's how I operate. We got a lunatic on the run, or a couple of them. Maybe a whole conspiracy. Now I think I've got the scent. Yes, I have a personal motivation, I can't deny it, though I'm not saying he killed my son. The facts do not support that, yet." He had to admit that, at least before Kinesey, though he didn't believe it for a moment. But it might reassure Kinesey that he was thinking straight, doing it by the book. "I want him, Ray. I need him. You can understand that."

Kinesey thought it over for a day or two. It was the money thing that was weighing him down. The cost of the operation was eating up other areas of the division. But finally he caved in. There was no denying his debt on account of Julie. And he felt sorry for Robert Jerrasi. For the lawman who, like so many others in the system, had equated their destiny with the capture of another man. Kinesey had managed to transcend so small a picture of himself, by sitting above the grimy minutiae of everyday. His mental universe had become social, to the extent that he was considered one of the FBI heavies, a high-ranking administrator, a man who had lunch with the Director of the FBI at least twice a week; who knew Congressmen, officials in the White House; who went to those parties on the side of the Washington official track, evenings that a Robert Jerrasi might only hear about, but would never know first-hand. Jerrasi's parties were the yearly barbecue kind, division picnics, or ballgames along the Potomac. But he stopped going to those, as well, on account of there being so many young boys Tom's age playing ball.

Two months after Kinesey's decision to permit Jerrasi's team to continue their quest, a perfume manufacturer in Paris was abducted, tied down, his eyes burned out by the same potpourri of chemicals and agents his company had been pouring over the retinas of small mammals and rodents for years – nail polish removers, hair-sprays and deodorants. The fellow essentially cried to death.

French police were left with not one clue. Same with DGSE, the French foreign intelligence. No sighting of the intruder, or intruders, for they had no sense of the singularity, or plurality of the crime. They only knew during which hours the event had taken place and that whoever had done it had studied the comings and goings of the chief executive very carefully, probably for many months. The culprit knew when he returned from the country villa, where his limousine remained parked, his code of access, the placement of video cameras, and so on. They had spent six weeks pursuing a money angle before Jerrasi heard about the crime. Money had been shifted from a Caribbean account, traced, and then discovered to have simply been legally transferred, within the company portfolio – to the Isle of Jersey. No money, in other words, had been stolen. Another curve ball. Jerrasi went to Paris for two days to survey the record of details surrounding the Parisian inquiry. But by that time, the details were soft. And since there had been no evidence to speak of, the trip was essentially a waste. But what bothered Jerrasi was the possibility that *The Animal*, as the FBI now designated him, had colleagues in France, or lived himself in France. If that were the case, he'd have limited jurisdiction in the continued pursuit. And he might not even get a shot at extradition since there were so many international contenders.

But all of these tribulations lost their punch in the face of a continued string of murders in other countries. In all, Jerrasi knew of over one hundred deaths thus far which, he was convinced, had been committed by the same conspirators. And still nothing. A file as lacklustre and impotent as any in his career. The erratic nature of the 'events' yielded no semblance of continuity, either geographically, or in time. Never a trace. It was uncanny.

Never once did *The Animal* make a mistake, or leave behind a message. Nor was he predictable. At least somebody like the fifteenth century French satanic murderer and sodomizer, Gilles de Rais, was predictable. It was the pretty little boys he went after. Same for the Texas electrician Dean Corll: little boys, whom he tortured, killing nearly thirty. Same for Albert DeSalvo, David Berkowitz, Angelo Buono, John Gacy ('*The Clown Killer*'), Albert Fish, and Ted Bundy – they all left deliberate clues, the shape of knife slashes, foreign objects stuffed in orifices. They wanted to get caught, to have a relationship with a cop who would never quite be up to their level. To bury that cop's face in his inferiority. They all perpetrated crimes within a narrow confine. Buried bodies in crawl spaces under their house, or out back. Were vagina, or cock, or anus crazed. Or hated homosexuals. Went after the same type of victim, within a limited region and a limited amount of time. But none of these invariants seemed applicable to this *Animal*. Jerrasi was stunned by the difficulties.

The conspirators could strike anywhere. In New South Wales, Australia, a large ranch, preparing to destroy four million surplus sheep rather than allow its prices for mutton and wool to plummet, was stalked and attacked. The government decision to allow the slaughter had occurred only six days before, which meant that whoever executed the attack, was well up on the machinations of the ranch, had people in place ready to go. Jerrasi had to believe, by that point, that he was dealing with some sort of international gang of terrorists, enormously mobile, well-funded, thorough – not just two conspirators. The German and British Secret Service cooperated; even the new ministry to supplant the KGB offered files, but none of it amounted to more than misleading assumptions, all of which complicated Jerrasi's private sense of a vendetta. Meanwhile, his team's inroads into the animal liberation front proved fruitless. These were essentially well-meaning, temperate individuals, followers of Mahatma Gandhi, they claimed, whose idea of a radical assault went no further than a noisy protest march in front of a university Board of Regents office, the occasional theft or destruction of laboratory equipment, and the symbolic liberation of an animal or two inside. A few million dollars damage. No big deal.

At a huge indoor fish market in Osaka, the three leaders of the local cartel – caught out touring their facilities – were killed, served up like one more elaborate meal of California roll and yakitori shish kebab. The Japanese police stumbled around in total perplexity. They had no inkling of such crimes. No fish, no money, had been stolen. The competitors were clean. There had been no underworld involvement. No protest launched. Whoever did it could not have been Japanese, in their opinion. But this hope was not substantiated, because there were no witnesses. There never were any witnesses. But their embarrassment prevented them from encouraging much more of an investigation. Nor were they prepared to reopen that old file on one Brian Laffont.

Jerrasi spent the night with a meiko, a young Geisha, in the Pontocho district of Kyoto, thirty minutes by train from the scene of the crime in Osaka. He spent two thousand dollars of American taxpayers' money on the girl. A large preying mantis hung from the screen shutters overlooking the river in their room. Elegant neon lights rippled and fed the waters below with whispers of oblivion. Jerrasi sank his face into her chest, sucking the nipples until they were hard as rock candy. The sound of passing trains and overhead jets and crowds of people outside made him sick. He was getting nowhere. In any sense of the word. There was a pressure on him to win that had nothing to do with the morality of it. He was beyond morality.

One week back in Washington and Jerrasi was roused in the middle of the night by a phone call, alerting him to a rather large-scale massacre at a

Hamburger Palace in southern California. There was that *meat* connection, of course. But the assailant was dead, Jerrasi examined his corpse in some detail, visited his relatives, his leased condo and by all that could be determined, this was not *The Animal*. Had he been part of their terrorist team? Nobody would ever know. Jerrasi wasn't sure. But he hoped not.

Three weeks later, during a Federally-ordained bison shoot in Montana, six young hunters were blown away. Madrid was at the scene within hours. Jerrasi could not handle it. The landscape and particulars were too close to home. Yet the cartridge size bore no resemblance to the events in Maine years before. Moreover, different cartridge sizes – different weapons – were involved. There had to be two culprits, at the very least, in that there had been no engineered domino effect: the victims had been shot at close range. It lent additional credence to Shelley's theory regarding Laffont, and the hearsay of Madrid's two Italians in the Manhattan kitchen.

At a donkey-diving circus playing in Elko, small potatoes by contrast to sheep farming in Australia, the organiser was drowned, fifteen donkeys freed. But this time, Jerrasi had a crucial piece of evidence: a man saw the donkeys being loaded into the back of truck, which headed south on Interstate 80 towards the Ruby Mountains.

"Did you see who loaded them?" Jerrasi asked.

"No. Sure didn't," the old man replied.

And that was that.

Jerrasi and Madrid followed the road into the Rubies. They reached a dead-end after some twenty-five miles. They searched for donkey tracks and found none. They headed back towards Elko. About eighteen miles from town, searching carefully for dirt turnouts or any signs of donkey activity, Madrid – wise in these matters – caught the scent of fresh donkey shit.

He was on to it. With binoculars, the two men spotted the herd, wild and free, foraging on the fresh sprigs against the low-lying hills of the mountains. All fifteen were accounted for.

"Tyres!" Madrid exclaimed.

"Brilliant," said Jerrasi.

Madrid was kneeling down over the gravel turnout where he had detected the tyre prints. They photographed the prints, followed them thirty feet out into the sage, Jerrasi recording his observations on his little hand tape recorder. Then they drove out in their rental car across the semi-arid stretch in an attempt to reach the donkeys. The animals were skittish and in no mood to be recaptured. But Madrid tried. On foot he stalked them, raced across familiar terrain, while Jerrasi watched with binoculars, maintaining a vantage point over any unexpected intruders. Madrid came close, only to spook the animals. They kicked at him, and then – in complete authority – ran a hundred yards and stopped. Madrid tried again, with the same silly results.

Then he saw something on one of the animals. It was a piece of paper taped to the butt. He knew it was for him.

Madrid started over again. Stalking quietly, circling, playing their game. Donkeys are by nature difficult to catch, when in number. And dangerous. But Madrid knew all about that.

He closed in, whispering donkey tunes, extending his hand with a clump of grass. He got close to the one in question.

Now he reached out: it was a message, the first, handwritten in ink. But he couldn't read it from twenty feet. He came closer. The donkey kicked at him with a force equal to a head-on. Madrid dove, filling his right shin with cactus needles. The animal, meanwhile, zig-zagged away with ferocious zeal and dexterity, leaving Madrid hurting in the sand.

Suddenly, one of the other mules ripped the paper off the side of its companion – the timing, as Jerrasi witnessed through his binoculars, could not have been more humiliating – and proceeded to consume it, masticating vigorously, while moving away from Madrid.

Madrid gave up.

"Some cowboy," Jerrasi barked.

"Mules are tough," argued Madrid in his own defence. "I want it captured and its stomach pumped."

"You're crazy."

"I'm telling you."

"Which one? They all look alike," Madrid pointed out.

"We'll pump all their stomachs if we have to."

"It'll take helicopters and nets to catch those mules."

"So be it."

"And by that time the one in question will have taken half-a-dozen shits. The message is gone. It's history. I love the desert."

Jerrasi knew that Madrid was right; and that *The Animal* had planned it just this way. *That* was his message. The donkey's ridicule. Shit in the dust.

They returned to town, without anything more. The truck which carried the animals had been the owner's truck, and it was missing.

"I want you to track down every show in this State that uses animals. I want that information by tonight," Madrid delegated to Shelley by phone.

They stayed over two days in Elko, working with local police to track down the stolen truck. There were roadblocks and aerial surveillance, but the truck had already left the State, or been ditched under cover.

Not twenty-four hours later, a stage performer in Utah was murdered, his orangutans stolen. Jerrasi and Madrid – only four hours away – had missed their chance. Shelley had not been quick enough. By the time they reached the scene, there was no scene.

Today, there were three more bodies. Jerrasi did not feel hopeful. Only glad to be in Los Angeles. To take in some movies while he was at it.

Somewhere out there, amid thirteen million other southern Californians, was an *Animal*. He envisioned the eyes, like those of a weak and hairy Tasmanian echidna, that's how he thought of him. He'd seen one at the Sydney zoo. Black and spiny, grovelling, hungry. Deranged.

Just thirty-six hours away. Where could he go in thirty six hours?

Around the world, Madrid had reminded him when he drove Jerrasi to Dulles.

Sutton escorted Robert Jerrasi out of the pathology lab, emanating animosity. Nothing stated. Only the reciprocal impatience which came from entirely separate agendas that day. Sutton was in no mood to hear Jerrasi's foul mouthed litanies. This FBI cracker was not happy with the way the quarantine station had been dusted for prints, or checked for signs. Well that was too fucking bad, thought Sutton.

"I guess that's it then," Jerrasi concluded, before turning towards Sutton's front office door where Ms. Armstrong was busy being tight-assed.

"People from my staff'll be following up on this. There may be other questions for the officers who were at the scene."

"Anything we can do to help," Sutton remarked pleasantly enough. "And I trust the rest of your vacation goes well."

It was an understated dig that irked Jerrasi. He removed his sunglasses, placed them in the vest pocket of his suit, smiled and said, "Me too. I like Los Angeles, and a few of the people. Not many, though." Then he turned and headed out.

"Oh, by the way," Sutton called to him before Jerrasi was lost down the corridor, by way of the most disinterested and parodying afterthought; a piece of information that would normally have come to Jerrasi while still in Washington, but he had not even bothered asking, that's how rich his vein of cynicism ran.

"There was a witness."

Jerrasi did an about face with a dumfounded wrath, and was then propelled downstairs two floors by a sprinter's craze, to an office where the blond was sitting smoking a cigarette on the police psychiatrist's couch. She'd already been through an hour of questioning, which greatly annoyed Jerrasi. He examined the notes taken by the presiding officer, then dismissed him.

Jerrasi introduced himself to the woman with a cordial and empathetic regard, a policy of many years having run polygraph, then slowly began, the notes of her previous statement in his hand.

"You've had a hard night, I imagine?"

"Yes"

"Are you all right?"

"Not really."

"Did he hurt you?"

"No."

"But it was a *he*?"

"I think so."

"Usually there's one thing about a person we never forget, and are never unsure about and that's whether it was a male, or female."

"What about transvestites?" she said.

"Well, of course, in that instance, one never knows for sure. Why, do you think the assailant was a transvestite?"

"He, or she, wore a mask," she replied.

"I see that from these notes. A black mask."

"Uh-huh."

"You heard a male's voice, I understand?"

"That's right."

"So more than likely it was a male."

"Yes."

"Did you did get a look at the person behind the mask?"

"Sort of." Jerrasi's heart skipped several beats, it seemed.

"Eye colour?"

"I don't remember." She wiped stray hairs off her forehead that had separated from her pony tail and come out of her plastic barret.

"You couldn't see the eyes, huh?"

"I did. But they didn't register."

"Why not?"

"What do you mean, why not?"

"Do you think they could have been dark or light?"

"I really don't know."

"Okay. What about the size of this guy?"

"Large."

"How large, six feet, six-four, what are we talking?"

"I already said."

"Oh yes, I see you've already stated that. But just tell me. It helps me to try and picture this individual."

"How long are you going to question me? I didn't sleep all night," she said with irritation and the jitters.

"Not long. Just a few important details. Do you drink?"

"Alcohol?"

"Yes."

"Why do you wanna know that?"

"Were you drinking last night?"

"I had a few beers before going into work."

"But in your estimation, your judgment was not impaired?"

"You're gonna give me a driving ticket?"

"No."

"Well that's good, 'cause I probably couldn't pay for it the way things are going."

"I'm just trying to get to know you a little bit better; to understand where you were at, you know, mentally, when this terrible thing happened to you."

"You married?" she suddenly asked.

"I was married for many years. Now I'm divorced."

"She divorced you, right?"

"It's hard living with an officer of the law."

"What was the question?"

"His size." Jerrasi was not put off. He'd conducted hundreds, maybe a thousand interviews. Though none like this. There was too big a rainbow sitting before him, nearly the gold itself, if only he could win her confidence.

She took a drag on her cigarette. "He was bigger than my husband."

"Go on? I obviously don't know your husband."

"Maybe six-five, or a little less."

"Six-five is this tall – he held up his hand. That's very high. You've said six-three in these notes, but you think he might have been taller, then?"

"This tall?"

"No, he wasn't that tall."

"Six-four?" He lowered his hands an inch.

"Does an inch really matter?"

"It could."

"Keep it at six-three, then."

"Muscular?"

"Yes."

"Like a weightlifter type?"

"No." She was hesitant. "Like an athlete. I think probably very handsome. Strong chin."

Jerrasi adjusted his bolo. His right eye, the slanted one, quivered.

"His voice?"

"It was very nice."

"How was his voice nice?"

"He spoke like a caring person."

"Was that before or after he killed three innocent people?"

"Before, and after, I mean, well do you really want me to tell the whole thing over again?"

"Yes, if you don't mind."

"Of course I mind."

"You don't have to."

"I know that."

Jerrasi could hardly hold back his excitement, his relief: here was the first tangible link, in nearly a decade, to the murderer of Tom. This woman still had *The Animal's* aura about her person, the patina of more than eight years of the chasm. She carried his handprints somewhere on her body, had been spoken to.

"First, he shouted," she began, drearily.

"You said he shouted 'Stop, Now,' and you looked right at him." Jerrasi's heart was pounding.

"Yes. No. I mean, I looked down. I was afraid. I don't know."

"Do you think his voice and the eyes you can't remember – and the way he moved, and so on – were the characteristics of an Oriental, or a coloured person, or a White man?"

"Possibly a Negro," she said.

Jerrasi was on the edge of his chair. He'd always stared at *The Animal* in his mind as something White, upper crust.

"What makes you say so?"

"I don't know. Just things you sort of pick up."

"He walked with rhythm?" Jerrasi asked.

"Maybe that was it. Maybe so," she said. "Black people do tend to have rhythm."

"Did you ever once date a black man?" asked Jerrasi.

"Yes. I did," she replied.

"So that's how you'd know. Or is your husband black, excuse me?"

"No, he isn't. Sometimes I wish he was."

"Why's that, if you don't mind?"

"Maybe he'd loosen up. Maybe he'd be more agile– " Her voice started to shake. Jerrasi sensed that she might start to sniffle or cry. She was a strange one, unstable, not smart, but capable of leading him on. And he didn't know why she'd want to do that. And she'd used the word agile which definitely did not fit her profile.

"Okay. Just between us. Forget what you said earlier to the officer. Clear your mind. Tell me plain and simple. I'm not taking notes, as you can see. There's no tape recording going on here, either."

"Nothing hidden? Like those wires you see cops wearing on their bodies, or a candid camera?"

"Nothing like that."

"Do I need a lawyer or anything?"

That took Jerrasi by surprise.

"You're a witness to a crime, ma'am. Ordinarily, that does not necessitate your needing a lawyer's services, since you're not under any kind of suspicion. Unless, of course, that is, unless there's something you're not telling us, me, I mean?"

"I just didn't see that much."

"But you did not know the assailant prior to the crime?"

"No, 'course not. I still don't know him."

She was smart, alright. "Whatever you can tell me will be very helpful. Let's just keep on moving. I want to get out of here as fast as you do. Nice day like this."

"Okay, okay." She thought about the events before speaking. Jerrasi was puzzled by the extent of her nervousness. Only a polygraph could read it right, and there were no grounds for even asking her to go through that. Unless enough discrepancies emerged to warrant a more solid suspicion of insider complicity.

"Joanne was tending the birds. I was getting ready to mop the floor. The two security guards noticed something. They went to the side door, which is kept locked, I guess."

"You guess? You don't know?"

"I just started working there. I really don't know the lay of the land quite yet."

Right there his complicity theory fell apart, he knew. The timing, the coincidence, it didn't jive with any insider know-how or reliability. But for that matter, he thought, neither did the physical and mental wreck that sat before him. "So go on?"

"Well, they stepped outside. We heard– "

"Who's we?"

"Me and Joanne, we heard some groans and then these faint sounds, like thug-thug, but real soft; he must have had his hand over the gun barrel – no, no. I guess– " She was rethinking that part of it. "Obviously."

"Obviously," Jerrasi said, rubbing his eyes, nodding.

"Whatever quieted the gun. But we didn't know it was gunfire or nothing like that. Just something going on."

"But you knew they were security guards, carrying guns, so that there was something to be protected, and thus the possibility of robbery, or whatever – of danger, I mean?"

"Oh sure. Those birds are pretty valuable."

"So you knew you heard a thug-thug but you didn't know it was gunfire?"

"Maybe we knew. I don't know. You don't expect that sort of thing with birds. At a bank, sure. But not with birds. Although I guess the feathers are especially valuable."

"I suppose they are. And how many thugs?"

"Two, I think."

"I believe you're correct on that."

"Really?" She evidenced pride in herself.

"Did you see the bodies lying there after the police arrived?"

"Yes, I did. There was a lot of blood. Horrible."

"You know how head wounds are. In fact, each of the two security guards received a single bullet in the head. One of them also took a hit to the throat."

"He did that?"

"That's right, ma'am."

Jerrasi wanted her to know that this was a calculating murderer she was reporting on, not some soft spoken caring individual. Feelings in the aftermath tend to change one's perception, Jerrasi knew. He'd once obtained a confession from a young man who had murdered his father. The boy would have gone free except for that confession, which resulted from Jerrasi's emotional entrapment of the kid, who had set fire to the upstairs of his family home. The kid had sneaked out, waited for the flames to engulf the house, then rushed back in to save his father and thus be a hero in his father's eyes. But he was too late. The man had already sustained massive third degree burns. He died a few days later, with his son by his side. Police would never have suspected the nineteen year old boy. But Jerrasi did, during a sympathy call, which turned into veiled interrogation beside the body of the father at the hospital, just minutes after his life support had been turned off. What do you suppose an emptied gasoline can was doing behind the neighbour's shed? Jerrasi had mused out loud. The boy had no idea. Just emptied, too. And within minutes Jerrasi had the boy begging his dead father for forgiveness.

Interrogation was like chess. Or sexual seduction. He'd ensnared a male nurse who was raping paraplegic girls by confusing him on the legal definition of 'penetration'. The young man had finally owned up to the fact that he'd only touched it to the girl's lips, maybe stuck it half an inch in, but no more, believing Jerrasi to be a good guy, to have come over to his way of thinking; that the FBI shared the young man's frustration at being arrested for something he didn't really do, or at least not completely. "I never even came," he'd protested.

One used one's opponents' weaknesses. One preyed upon weakness, lavished weakness with support, gained sympathy for oneself, so much so that the opponent was lost in a maze of feelings, an outpouring of sympathy that no longer could recall its original plan; that had lost its compass reading. Those quirks and kinks showed up in polygraph as nervous twitches. The opponent – as Jerrasi had to think of his subjects – struggled with all the cleverness of lay persons. They were like un-equipped campers flailing through the woods, tripping on vines, freaked out by the slightest screech overhead, on guard for snakes and bears. They had no chance against a rigorous interrogation. Sooner or later they would betray themselves, break down. And if break down was not in the cards, something else would give them away. The process never failed. And though confessions by themselves were not admissible in court, the slightest corroborating evidence made them so. In the case of the young man, it was the empty gasoline can. And a set of his footprints leading from his backyard to the neighbours' yard. In the case of the rapist, they recovered semen stains from one of the victim's bed sheets.

What was so ironic about it all was the fact that silence could never convict a man. Short of that confession – in cases lacking material witnesses or other evidence – Jerrasi and his kind were forever out of luck.

"And then?" he continued, looking directly at the blond.

She squirmed a little more, as if the severity of her circumstances – the night before – had only just dawned upon her.

"And then Joanne called to them, and when they didn't answer, she walked to the door, and he grabbed her. He pushed her inside, holding the gun."

"What kind of gun was it?"

"It looked like a military gun, or rifle, or something in between."

"Do you know much about guns?"

"No."

"Go on?"

"He shouted not to look at him. I looked down at the floor. And then she said "I can help you!"

"Joanne said she could help?"

"Yes. I think she was trying to make him calm down. I thought it was pretty smart myself. I guess it wasn't so smart."

"Why's that?"

"Well damn, she's dead ain't she!" Her hand was shaking and she put out the cigarette. "So then he told me to get into the back room."

"How did he get you into the room, did he push you?"

She raised her voice in sudden agitation. "I don't know!"

"Is something wrong?"

"It's just all pretty troubling. Think if it was you."

"I quite commiserate. I can't imagine if it were me. Being held hostage, my God! With the threat of my life being squandered just like that, for mere birds. In fact, I'd say you're one hell of a brave woman."

"Thank you." She quieted down.

Jerrasi asked her if she wanted something to drink. She asked for some Scotch. Jerrasi had a Pepsi brought in, instead. The psychiatrist's phone rang. Jerrasi picked up the receiver.

"Yes? Fine. Have him wait."

The local FBI contact had arrived. The LA office would handle looking into such details as any tax evasion, Federal officers that had come on site to check the facility, any previous problems at the location, and so on. But Jerrasi did not want to spoil the atmosphere in the room, the level of intimacy he had achieved. He continued.

"I just want to go home," she pleaded.

"I know you do. So do I. So he was large, you think he might have been black. He wore a mask. It was skin tight?"

"Yes."

"Covering his neck?"

"Maybe."

"And being black, that means he probably did have dark eyes?"

"You could assume somethin' like that."

"He got you – either by pushing you or simply ordering you, you don't recall which – into the back room, where he had Joanne tie you up."

"That's correct."

"There was nothing sexual about all this, I don't suppose?"

"Not really."

"Huh?" Ooooh ... A pulse was riding his brain.

"He did touch me."

"Where?"

"On my shoulders."

"Did he unzip his pants?"

"I'd remember that if he did."

"Or try to touch you– "

"No."

"He didn't look at you funny?"

"The way you are?"

Jerrasi blinked. "No, I mean sexually?"

"Yes. No. Maybe," she said with the vaguest hint of a smirk. Jerrasi had seen this sort of thing before; the victim's sense of being special, or vindictive, when asked.

"Did he have any body odour?"

"It was nice."

"A nice odour? Like sweet, or what? What's nice mean? Some sort of cologne? Which?"

"I don't know."

"How old was he, do you reckon?"

"Had to be young by the way he held himself and all."

"Thirty?"

"I'd say so." She was thinking quite a bit older than that, anyway, but checked herself with last minute restraint. It seemed to her that whoever he was, he had a cause and she was not adverse to it. The streaks of thought that gave her over to this sudden impression were elusive ones, and she had no trouble subsuming them, amongst the folds of her haphazard speech and petty annoyances and womanly mannerisms. Jerrasi continued to sense her disquiet, or some contradictory thread keeping her separated from his line of questioning. Yet not enough to warrant outright alarm.

"Then what happened?"

"He ordered her into the other room. She said the names Alfred, and prime rate, and he said she was crazy."

"Prime rate?" Jerrasi was confused. "Prime rate? What about the prime rate? Did she mention a particular bank or anything? Was any money exchanged?"

"It could have been. I heard all kinds of shuffling. I don't know. Prime rate, and then, I think something about the law. I didn't hear anything more for a while. Then he said, 'Clean up the mud. And don't brag'."

Jerrasi was baffled. "Do you know an Alfred associated with that facility?"

"I sure don't. Like I said, I just started."

"Then what?"

"So there was the sound of cleaning. Then the sound of dragging bodies into the room. And then I didn't hear anything for about ten minutes. I tried to get free. I couldn't. And then I heard this big truck backing to the entrance. I heard Joanne yell 'Okay'."

"She yelled Okay?"

"Yeah."

"What do you think that meant?"

"I don't know."

"Do you think Joanne was in on it? And that she got double-crossed?"

"In on stealing birds? I guess it's possible."

"And then what?"

"Then there was some whispering. I couldn't make it out."

"You're sure of that?"

"Absolutely."

"As if she really were in on it?" Jerrasi asked.

"You don't really think that, do you?" the blond asked, frowning and stumped.

"That's what we're here to find out, ma'am."

She drank from her Pepsi.

"So then?"

"Then the birds were squawking real loud because they were dragging – both of them that is – dragging the cages into the truck. The phone rang. Joanne said they were out having coffee."

"You're sure they were both dragging cages?"

"Oh yes."

"How do you know that for a fact?"

"Well, because I heard them. I mean, more than one cage at a time."

"I haven't been to the scene of the crime so I haven't yet seen the marks of the cages – most of them are not there now, of course; they were all stolen – so I don't know how big they were. But I assume you know and therefore you believe that one large, possibly black man, could not have dragged two at the same time, is that correct?"

"You're talking too fast."

"The cages were large, I gather; too large for one man to drag several at the same time?"

"They were large. Too large."

"So again we have a scenario in which your friend Joanne could have been in on it from the beginning?"

"I suppose. But we weren't really friends. I mean, I hardly knew her."

"What did you know about her? Tell me. Then we'll get back to the phone call."

"Well, she was pretty and young, I think she was part-time in school."

"Where?"

"Isn't that all in the report?"

"No, it isn't. There's nothing about her going to school."

"Her parents would know, I'd think. Have you talked to them?"

"Not yet. Have you met them?"

"No. To be honest with you, I don't even know if her parents live in

California, or are even alive. I mean, we never talked much, at least not yet."

"What school do you think she attended?"

"Could have been Loyola. That's close by."

"But she never said which?"

"No."

"And what do you think she studied part-time?"

"Veterinary care."

"Yes?"

"Definitely. She knew what she was doing. The sort of stuff – medical, I mean – you wouldn't pick up just on the job. Or I wouldn't."

"Was she very close to her employers?"

"I really couldn't say."

"And you never went to her house or anything? Or knew if she had a boyfriend. Maybe he called during work hours? Or came to see her?"

"No, nothing like that. And as I said, I'd only just started. You're asking me the wrong questions."

"Just trying to be thorough. You know how cops are."

"No, how are they?" she livened.

"They're under stress, and underpaid," Jerrasi said with a grin.

"Like everybody else," she seconded.

"So you never picked up a phone call for her that might have been personal?"

"No."

"The phone rang. You indicated earlier that Joanne said that 'they were out having coffee'. She was referring, I presume, to the two security guards?"

"I guess so."

"Strange. Why do you think she said that if they were dead?"

"He had a gun, for God's sake."

"Of course. Now it says in these notes that you said that the phone rang again, maybe five minutes later. And that's when he shot her. You heard the gunfire?"

"One bullet. I heard one loud crashing bullet. And then I heard the phone fall, and then Joanne fall."

"No other bullets?"

"I might have heard some scuffling sounds."

"Ma'am, did Joanne have a gun?"

"I don't think so."

"But you only remember definitely the one bullet?"

"Yes."

"You're sure?"

"Yes."

Jerrasi was slightly perplexed by that one, given the eighteen bullets that penetrated Joanne's body and the fact that it was known Joanne carried a gun and had managed to discharge several shots. Was this dame lying? Was she part of it? Was she just in lingering shock? Or manipulating him expertly. The word agile was bothering him. Or maybe she really didn't hear.

"And then what?"

"Well, he came back in and apologized for the knots being tied so tightly around my wrists. My back was to him. And he told me I should quit my job because I was working for gangsters and didn't even know it. And he pulled out the phone."

"You started the job two nights ago?"

"That's right."

"Are you going to quit?"

She started to cry.

"Here." He offered her some yellow Kleenex that was in a dispenser adjoining the couch.

"I need a job," she finally said. "I've got two kids and an unemployed husband with no legs."

"No legs?"

"That's right. But I don't need what I saw in there. Is that legal the way they were keeping those birds?"

"It's being looked into."

"I wouldn't be surprised one bit if they were gangsters."

"It's possible ... How did your husband lose his legs?"

"A heavy piece of metal shielding for a Titan – you know, those missiles – fell off its crane, or conveyor belt, I'm not sure how it happened, but it cut him in half. Good thing there was a surgeon on duty around the corner at the local hospital."

Jerrasi itched the back of his head. His hair was thick, curly and dark, rimmed with silver. It accentuated his lean build and relentless manner. One might think he was a New York attorney.

"I assume the company has a generous medical plan?"

"We'll see. We're suing for twenty million dollars."

Jerrasi wasn't surprised. It was this woman who was agile.

"And when he suggested you quit your job, what was his voice like?"

She squished the tears out of her eyes. "I told you. He had a nice voice. I could tell he was sincere. And then he walked out and I heard a truck pull away. And that's when all the Thailand people came running in, I mean, maybe ten minutes after that."

"How many of them?"

"At least, let's see– " she starting figuring, "eight. The man and his wife, my boss, and five young men. They all had guns. And they left within minutes. Everyone was yelling in Oriental. You can see why they was mad, with all their birds gone."

"You don't speak Oriental, I take it?"

"No, I don't."

"And then what?"

"And then the lady called the cops and she screamed at me and she slapped me while I was still tied up. Can you believe that? She blamed me, that bitch!"

"Did the officer ask you if you wished to make a complaint, a formal complaint about being slapped?"

"No way. I told you. They were all carrying guns. You bet they were gangsters. Who else would act like that? I just want to disappear. Next time, I'm working for Dunkin' Donut. I used to work for them and figured I could do better in life. Hey – I'll take a doughnut any day."

"I like doughnuts, too."

"What's your favourite?"

"The glazed twists."

"Yeah, they're really good."

"Is there anything else you can remember to tell me?"

"I don't think so. Oh, my hearing's not too good at distances. That might have, well, who knows."

Jerrasi scratched his neck. It was too much.

"So that what you heard in the other room between them might have been off?"

"Yes."

"Well, that's all right. Not your fault, I suppose. You've been very cooperative. I'm going to call the Doctor, who just wants to advise you about certain matters."

"Like what?" she asked, a little freaked out. She was wanting to be through with all of this.

"Should you have any headaches or psychological stress pertaining to this incident, he'll tell you your options."

"That's funny," she said. "Thirty milligrams of valium'll do."

Jerrasi's eyebrows jerked slightly upwards. "I'm also going to leave you with my– " he took out his card and a pen and circled his direct line at the office, as well as at home. "You call me any time if you remember anything else, or if anything should happen. You can tell me, or anyone on my staff."

"Like what?" she asked, starting to act definitely pissed off.

"Nothing's going to happen. Should something come to you."

"I would like to forget this incident, forever."

"And you will. These things take a little time."

Jerrasi thanked her and walked out. Funny woman, he thought. A little like Cloris.

Now he at least had confirmation of several points that he had belaboured in his sleep, wanted so badly: a black mask, possibly a black man. Large. Suave. Has a calming effect on his victims. The perfect criminal. Even able to evoke a tinge of sympathy, sexual desire, from those he had tied up. He emended that, appreciating that she was the only known victim to have ever survived his presence. For Jerrasi to make him out to be the perfect criminal made Jerrasi the perfect sleuth. He relished that kind of relationship, the way a taxidermist gingerly reveres the creature he stuffs.

He believed the stirrings of a showdown were familiar, born of the hunt, not merely imagined. The witness had given him what he perceived to be perfect mortar, water and sand; had brought together pieces of a puzzle that had frustrated him until this moment. The picture was not yet there, entirely, in his mind, though a composite would be generated, with her help. She was not finished. A polygraph was in order. But that didn't matter to him now. In his bones and atoms he knew that the clock had begun to tick.

My brother also knew, you can be sure.

ESCALATIONS

Bumbling and indecisive, I was not ready for this. The words fail to convey their implicit terror, the insistent, the raw and ungiving burden of introspection that being his brother caused me.

Few were my hours of immunity from a recognition that all our ways were in vain, against the greater likelihood that sooner or later the family name of Felham would be splashed across the media. Iyura, not one to take kindly to sudden upset, the invasion of privacy, a revolution in the household – I know this from our many temperamental squalls – would likely give Bart a new, Japanese name out of pride, or spite, or some abstruse, indefinable Oriental solemnity. Our marriage would have the wind permanently knocked out of it.

It was all so unfair, that I should have to live in the shadow of coming events; should bear the indignity of premonition, anticipating the horrible prospects of ruin, in the midst of a young and happy career. The way some people might be haunted by the IRS, or the fear of cervical cancer.

I feared going to jail, losing everything, on account of half-deeds which I could not quite decipher according to my own juridical presence of mind. Had I, in fact, equivocated? Done something wrong? Wrong? A doublespeak that berates my present contagion of ethical ambivalence. That sneers and jousts with former stability, kicks up the dust before me, urges me forward, murmurs hallucinations behind me, stalking every certainty I had once relied on. By holding my tongue? By not turning in my only brother? Was that so illegal? I could not ask a lawyer. That was unthinkable. One could not trust a lawyer, anyone, not even one's wife in these matters, whose brother was a lawyer.

That Felham had trusted in me necessarily invoked my reciprocal silence, by oaths ancient and abusive. Right or wrong, there was something epic about two brothers locked unhappily in loyalty; it had proportions, allegorical precedent. It had me cornered.

Two brothers need not take on epic dimensions. Once they've outgrown adolescent rivalries and griefs, most are probably just friends, allies, or, conversely vague antagonists. And others are merely indifferent to one another. Muppet and his own brothers, for example. Sometimes, though it is probably rare, confined only to history, they end up on opposite sides of a battlefield, wearing different colours, beating different drums. Yet this was the weight of circumstance that enshrouded me. A stress leading, one might consider, to fratricide. Let me call myself 'he', for the moment, in as much as my projections – born of that oath – were part of the escalating problem. My irresolution, call it hypersensitivity, hidden and angry.

The darkness. The incessant wince, like a blood clot, a pernicious muddle in the upper respiratory tract, something palpable, phlegm-driven, out of breath and odious; a monster that never stopped hammering the chords of his undoing, or that's how he reasons to himself; that was the reality of this great tragedy which had so usurped his previous Eden of mind and made both of us a synonymous shadow figure, subject to a single psychological profile. One voice. One set of hands. One heart. Equipped with that advantage, I could divine his every glimmer of hope and phoneme and unreason.

Neurons connecting as if history had ordained them to meet, not on any written page, or in any liquid solution; not by any logic or organic root system, or family phenotype. But in the very nature of police work and the inevitability of our bad luck. The pronouns hasten their confusion, like a schizophrenia lock-jawed in one instant, judicious in another. Surrounded by foes, by those who would end this nightmare of eight years, who even now are circling, reforming, preparing for a final assault, I'm sure. As I am preparing; as I have dreamt and prayed for my own deliverance. Does one walk out with one's hands raised shouting "I SURRENDER!" or hold up a white flag, stammering forth; or, besieged, in a final defence that is tantamount to suicide, fight to the finish? He's hiding under cover of my life. I am an accomplice, no matter how I cut it. What do I do? What was I supposed to do? Shore up like a man, in isolation, with no one to talk to? Talk to him, my conscience declared.

Just love me Felham had implored, during the worst of his confiding. It was a word I could not remember him ever having used. A word that engendered universal affection, not merely one brother's feelings for another. It sounded so effeminate the way he said it, inveigling, unreal, skewed – *love me* ... But its obvious desperation went right to the Memorial Wall of my heart, etched in truth. My conscience was hooked on that love, almost worth defending. My older brother needed my sanctuary. That sonofabitch! Entrapped by a consanguinity I detested and alternately cherished.

Forget Jason. What was there for Felham? There was nothing. No prize. No graceful retirement. Escape, only; exile, damnation. The electric chair. What was there in my love that could remedy a ruined existence? The belief by one other that what he was doing was right? With only Muppet in the world, he must have needed that, in his solitary hell, with no feedback whatsoever. Not a single statement in the newspapers or magazines that I am aware of ever came out in support of what he was doing. The condemnation from animal groups was unanimous. Felham was nothing more than a terrorist. So how could he continue to believe in his war, against such universal condemnation?

It seemed plausible to me at the time, after I'd reflected on the situation, that he was continuing to engage in his terrorist activities for more or less criminologically predictable reasons; because there was no way out, and to cease doing so would be to admit that he'd been wrong, and that he was finished. It could never happen that way. The desperado, the serial killer, cannot stop, I've read. His voluntary muscles and involuntary philosophy are in control of the triggers. He can never give up. Every victim is a step on a ladder which is leading to ultimate purification. Which is why I had become so necessary to him, and eventually, he to me.

And there are other bright lights in the deranged psyche. The mass murderer perhaps hopes to be lost in the tidal surge of an opponent, or of a humanity that can no longer hurt him because it can not find him, or because he is already dead. Dead so many times as to make death pleasurable. He has so stirred up the indignation against him, that his final going down, his capture or execution is like one of those fanfares beneath the Bastille. His crimes should be large enough, in his mind, to make them volcanic. So large, in fact, that he no longer exists. Only the crimes, the Napoleonic Wars, the Hundred Years War. A single individual with a purpose.

Perhaps you recall that incredible avalanche off 22,000 foot Mount Huascaran, in the Peruvian Andes, back in the early 1970's? I read about it. About the one lone survivor who – watching the oncoming mountain, that rumbled twenty five miles towards the town of Yungay at 300 miles per hour, exceeding terminal velocity by some metaphysics – ran to the highest point in the immediate vicinity, which happened to be the town cemetery, clung to the highest cross, and prayed. The avalanche must have been deafening. One small piece of it hit a rise, flipped into the air and came crashing down in some valley, displacing an entire lake. But the trillions of tons of granite and ice, friction transforming the weight into fire, lava, mud, energy, came grinding to an uncanny, God-decreed halt, inches from where the one survivor hung on. How is that possible? After covering miles and miles and the entire village below him, with all his family, relatives, friends, possessions, everything in his world, destroyed? I mention this anecdote for one reason: there were moments when I saw my brother clinging to that cross, saved by his Lord. At other times, I willed myself atop that cemetery. Which of us would survive this ordeal? Who would be the victor?

His voice surfaces ... It was to be our last conversation for some time, conducted in the utmost privacy. "How many have you killed?" I ask, resigned to the impossible reality of Felham.

"I have no idea," he mulls resistingly. We shared a similar stubbornness that way.

"No idea?"

"Maybe fifty, or a hundred."

"Or two hundred?"

"Perhaps."

Ralph, my father, apparently killed numerous men during World War II and admittedly both Felham and I always marvelled at that fact. My father was not robust or physically built-up, like my brother; he wore oversized trousers and always looked like a tourist. Mom constantly ordered him to buy new, modish jackets, for he was a good-looking man who needlessly ignored himself, a product of Depression thinking. To imagine that rather gentle soul killing men – dozens of men – was mythic and wondrous, a mysterious ode to righteousness that welled up in the inexplicable, ultimately undiscussed truth of my father's own mission in life.

"Just like Dad," I said.

"Yes."

"Except that he was acting within the scope of the law, national security, national defence." With that comparison, one we'd knocked about before, I had drawn myself into a battle that would leave me mortally wounded. The argument escalated like a Cuban missile crisis of theory and assertion, placing my brother and me at polar opposites. Between us, we held the whole world hostage.

"You really believe that adding the word 'national' to a cause of deep conviction makes it right, or wrong?" he said.

"No. I don't necessarily believe it. Certainly not in the case of the Third Reich, for example."

"Or Vietnam," he furthered. "Or Chile. Or Iran. Or Guatemala. Or the whole damned Cold War."

"So you've killed maybe a few hundred. Maybe even more than that?"

"Possibly. You never know in a gun battle."

"And you've fought lots of them, I suppose?"

"Quite a few."

"Good god, Dirk."

I was mesmerized by the image, slowly turning like a kaleidoscope.

"Even if I've killed five thousand brutal bastards, what's it to the world? A few less mouths to feed," he went on, having grown frankly irritated by my evident lack of instant recognition of the higher truth, in whose destiny-piercing light he preferred to stand unambiguously.

"Five thousand, you say. And you really think that's a possibility?" Such numbers were astronomical, beyond meaning.

"Yes. I would hope so."

Hope so ... My brother was too reasonable to be commonly crazy, which made any indictment on my part that much more delicate. Yet the more he explained, the more reasonable his actions appeared. This was my undoing. Forgiveness became less and less relevant. A logical world bathed in the blood of revenge surfaced instead. Not Mafia revenge, clan or tribal justice, but the vision of just him, striking down those who had struck down His creation. There was a primordiality to its coherence that could not be assailed or countered. Did he believe that all of God's creatures were equal? That even a killer deserved to live? Clearly not. So adamantine was his wrath that he would not have hesitated, I think, to eliminate every meat eater on Earth. Should his enthusiastic capital punishment include tigers? "No," he said assuredly. "*They* are not overpopulated. We are."

"So *that's* what's really bugging you, overpopulation?" I couldn't exactly call it a childish obsession, since I too believed the human population bomb to be the greatest danger on earth. I mean, obviously. At the same time, that he should view his numerically insignificant killings as any kind of antidote, was simply insanity.

But that wasn't all of it.

"There are far more than five thousand murdering evil bastards in the world," he went on. "If I can get rid of my share of them, I will have done my duty."

"Duty? Duty to whom?"

"To you, Jason. To me. To the memory of Mom and Dad. To the collective unconsciousness, any hope for dignity, of our species. But more importantly, to the animals that those five thousand are killing everyday, in exponential degrees."

"Those are awfully convinced words." I was actually thinking *preachy*. He'd found his pulpit.

"I'm not here to argue my belief."

"I know you're not. I wouldn't try to argue with you, not at this point. Maybe before you first spilled blood. Maybe then. But now it's too late."

"Just accept it. It's fact. It's my life. I'm doing what I know is right."

"Why didn't you kill Saddam Hussein?"

"Too well guarded. It wasn't worth the risk. If I'd known what was to happen with the spilling of oil in the Gulf – all those fish and marine mammals – I don't know ... Perhaps I'd have tried something."

To have to think about them; to see the bullets detonating the faces, disintegrating throats, rupturing bowels, fragmenting bone. To have to make the connection with my brother. And to have to decide, feeling the pressure all around me, the hair standing up, the tempest descending. *Decide*! My heart was racing.

"If you read that five thousand Indonesian islanders died in a typhoon," he said, "you wouldn't give it more than a passing thought. I mean, shit, 300,000 Bengalis died in typhoons. Did you trouble to find out even one of their names?"

"Of course I didn't."

"Or inquire as to whether anybody needed some free food over there, my rich little brother? Don't try my patience with this yuppie caring crap. The world's overpopulated. Fact. The more people that die, the better off the rest of the planet. Fact."

"That's not a philosophy anybody can or should live by."

"I agree," Felham declared with a sudden glimmer, in my eye, of rationality. "Nevertheless, for every average human being that lives, that uses pharmaceuticals, and soap and perfume, that eats meat and chicken and fish, and drives an automobile, or flies by plane, and heats his house, and buys his children presents in fancy-wrapped containers, and purchases real estate and goes on and on, not counting the ones that deliberately take part in hunting or ranching or animal by-product industries, well, I would guess that an average person in a high-consuming country like this one is responsible for killing on the order of one million animals during his or her lifetime. That's right."

"And isn't it also true that white blood cells in an innocent child, and in an innocent adult, are dying and being reborn every second in the millions? And that every second, chickens are dying, cattle are dying, bugs are dying, but other chickens and cattle and bugs are being born?" And I was also reminded of that fact that my brother was one to talk about flying in planes and driving automobiles. He probably consumed more per capita jet fuel than most, in his globe-trotting vigilantism. Not to mention his obscenely pricey automobile.

"Yeah. That's all true," he nodded compliantly. "And 300,000 other Bengalis and Indonesian islanders are also being born anew."

"So where's the justification for deliberate killing?" I pressed him. If nature has its own bylaws, who are we to interfere? I was also concerned about whether the innocent and the guilty die differently. Did the Aztec priests who lustfully ripped the wombs and hearts out of living young women feel more pain at death than, say, Helen Keller, or Mark Twain? How would Nero stack up against Buddha at the moment of physical decomposition?

"The human heart, little brother."

I said nothing. The heart ... What did he mean? What was I feeling?

It had really never dawned on me up until then that Felham might actually think he could change the system. That he could reverse a million years of man's carnivorous appetite. All over the world, in a matter of years. Could he be that ... naive? Brave?

Whatever he meant, whatever I felt, the agony could only be protracted. No psychology could touch him. He needed love, support, but no analysis. I loved him in spite of my despair; but when such love is troubled, must think about itself to that extent – am I doing him *more* harm? – it is no longer spontaneous or genuine. It begins to doubt itself, as mine did, and must put on a face, manifest veneers and airs and try doubly hard to pretend the love is pure, real. It becomes false and dangerous. Infected with all the bitterness such filial ties will bring. I was tied in knots. Stumped on the image of my brother altering evolution, because his heart bade him to do so.

There is a long-standing theory which holds that love, contrite love – the grieving for someone else that had become, heroically, modestly, the grieving for oneself – is the only way to convert sinners. An acceptance from one's insides that there is a petite, gleaming nugget of Goebbels or Genghis Khan in each of us, so that no man may freely cast the first stone at the harlot. I don't know where that theory comes from. The Old Testament, I presume. But whatever the spiritual glories and neuralgias of contrite love, in the case of the brothers Felham, nothing but catastrophe could result. Any appeal or self-effacement or full disclosure – that he should give himself up to the system – would merely result in Death Row and the final mumbling ministrations of a Father. What else was there for him?

And for me? Temptation. To turn him in while I still had a chance. Freedom. Mom and Dad were dead. Iyura did not know. Who was there to judge me?

Accept Felham ...

My fist, squeezed tightly around the contrite love which burns up inside me. I am powerless to do anything. I have always been powerless and even this apperception does nothing to alter that.

I look at him, whose physical presence suggests the value of faith. A strong, good-looking, principled man. He's never touched coffee. Who has, remarkably, risen above his tragedy, one would have to conclude; not by raving like a lunatic, which I would surely have preferred – for then there was at least a clear shot at the insanity plea – *that word*, but rather through his deeply held convictions. Right or wrong.

I hear him speaking on through the haze of my self-interest and miasmas ... *Where is the justice? You know, little brother, justice? If there's veal, there's no justice. If there's a traditional Thanksgiving dinner, there's no justice.* He had his own conspiracy theory about hamburger. And it made the Kennedy assassination look like a sunny afternoon on the putting green.

And he would cite that ghastly image from Nadine Gordimer's *July's People*. It was characteristic of him to do so. How some 'piglet was hit in the body and (lay there) kicking in a tantrum of pain; or thought its waving legs were carrying it after the big safe bodies of the adults', an image that palpitates agonizingly in Felham's whole representation of himself. I can't just pass over that image; I continue to see the poor prostrate piglet, believing itself to still have a chance, to be running away with others, a salvation in the final second. Felham had become an interspecial psychobiologist who'd gotten inside the brain, the fragility, of other animals. And dies with them, dreams, hopes with them, and is plunged into their ever-sensing despair. I think he just wanted to die for all of our sins, wanted to die with the animals and let people know that he had died with them. That was the whole point of my brother, I think; the basis for his ethical being. The actual murders must have been afterthoughts, follow-throughs. The emotions were much deeper and lasting.

If there's a single chicken sandwich in this whole world, then there's no justice, and there's no way I'm going to sleep at night ... A sentiment which had catapulted him from being just another 'guy', to suspecting his whole species of conspiring against him ... *Un passo, un detto – un mezzo, un fior – lo mettono in sospetto* ... as Puccini's great librettists, Giuseppe Giacosa and Luigi Illica had written in *La Boheme*. 'A step, a phrase – a glance, a flower – everything makes him suspicious'. He'd personalized the words as a child. When we were a happy family, I had assumed.

"Here, read this," he said, shoving four pages into my hands, which he had evidently brought out of some file long suppressed. "It's an editorial," he went on.

"You wrote it?" I was surprised. My brother had never even written me a letter. He had always been notoriously guarded with a pen.

"Please just read it," he repeated. "Maybe it will help you understand me."

It had been written in response to a popular nature monthly that had infuriated him by politely referring to, but craftily skirting, the topic of meat eating and environmentalism, an unforgivable contradiction in his mind. I sat down and peered into my brother's words, enthralled by a document that actually tended to articulate the present dilemma. The paper was yellowed, not entirely legible – it had been scrawled in evident anger – and sent anonymously. It was not dated, though Felham recalled having written it sometime in the early – 1970's. It was apparently the only time he had ever tried to organise such thoughts on paper.

"Go ahead, read it out loud," he insisted, as if the paper was evidence, a barometer of reliability, or truth. Maybe he thought that in my mind this credo, as it were, would lend some authority to his views.

So I began.

"Your magazine recently published opinions from around the U.S. on the issue of environmentalism and vegetarianism. Of those sampled, not one individual referred to the moral indefensibility of killing animals. Not one voice demanded an end to the suffering of animals. Not a single person called for a popular uprising against the age-old trend of killing animals. What kind of assholes subscribe to your magazine?"

I stopped right there. "You expected them to publish this?"

"Well I thought, oh hell, I didn't care. It was the editors' chat which pissed me off. Keep on– "

"Instead, we read statistics, writers baiting one another, the conveyance of apologies and excuses as inane as the overall tone of dismissal which characterized this futile piece of shit."

"That's the way to convince people," I interrupted.

"Fuck you," he said.

"You call your opinion page 'Last Thoughts'. How come nobody uttered 'Last Rites' or final prayers, for those whom mankind – and editors – find it easier to ignore and consume, than cherish and love?"

"This strikes me as an appalling throwback to Homo Erectus one million years ago," the editorial went on, "when approximately twenty percent of the male audience prided itself on massacre, and licked the gravy off its fingers, while young women (80% of the food producing audience) gathered pulses and grains, tubers, roots and berries, or – later – began planting."

I looked at him. "You studied that stuff at the Air Force Academy? Roots and berries?"

"Hardly."

"But are you suggesting that we are not meat eaters by definition?"

"Correct."

"I don't believe it. Higher mammals eat meat. It was fundamental to the growth of Homo Sapiens. Our erect posture. Our bipedalism. Our larger brains. We're addicted to meat for a very good reason."

Felham stared at me with the self-evident twist I'd gotten myself into: something in me had poured out, and it was not the real me – a vegetarian! – but some other redneck antiquarian anger. I couldn't believe it. Was I simply trying to belittle a mass murderer? Or myself?

"Meat eating is primitive. For humans, it has nothing to do with evolution, and nearly every credible physical anthropologist and evolutionary biologist has said so.

"You cited persuasive statistics to support the conclusion that destructive land use, greenhouse gasses, energy and water loss, ground water pollution, and the perpetuation of unwanted chemical adulterants, all result from the meat industry. But where was the ethical component in this litany of resource- oriented thinking? Furthermore, you presented a much stronger outcry from those meat eaters who insisted that, 'Predation was natural' and that the whole environment would topple if we ceased partaking of our allegedly rightful, carnivorous legacy. Which is just so much garbage! Still others put forth eloquently stated scientific mumbo-jumbo to verify that you can have your environment and eat it too. That after all, the killing of oats, or seaweed, or wheat, is perhaps just as obnoxious and painful to the organism, as the slaughter of a cow. And therefore, vegetarians have no right to moralize.

"The illogic, rancour and futility of such diatribe dulls the mind, taunts the heart. People who have been killing animals all their life, when questioned about it, suddenly rise up with a clamour to defend tomatoes.

"To pretend to speak about environmentalism without positing and acting upon our commitment to humanity's ethical obligations, would be akin to whining during World War II about an 'environmentally suspect Third Reich', without any mention, or effort to save, the victims of the Holocaust. To gloss over the greatest tragedy ever perpetrated by one species in the biological history of Earth, namely, mankind's arrogant and unchallenged obliteration of most other life forms – meat eating being the most sustained, calculating, widespread, and heartless form of such violence – strikes this reader as monstrously ignorant, and self-serving.

"Ignorance that masks its intolerance, self-interest, and callousness with the tired logic of abusive millennia; a logic now appropriated by those among you who would dare to call yourselves environmentalists.

"There can be no environmental consciousness, no lasting solution to the ecological mayhem all around us, without an ethical core of intention."

This is what kept burning in me as I read on. His *ethical intention*. I knew he was right. At the same time, I wanted to turn him in to the police so badly, just to see him read this editorial before a jury in his self-defence; simply to observe how the system might grapple to absorb it, in the light of what he had done. It was the perfect acid test ... Why had he wasted it on a lousy editorial that predictably sank into oblivion?

"There is no disputing the fact that species are vanishing at an incalculable rate; that animals universally are under siege, the human motives for such carnage too numerous to diagnose. Given what we know about the declining numbers of most animal species, how can any thinking, feeling person subscribe to meat eating?

"It all boils down to greed, stupidity, and laziness on the part of those of you who would argue that meat eating and environmentalism are compatible impulses. They are not. Meat eating is a function of the taste buds, which can be controlled. Evolution does not condemn us. Our choices condemn us. There is no residual biology in our gut that compels us to kill the neighbourhood grocer for our meal, any more than it demands the slaughter of the innocent. Meat is not an addicting chemical. We have the power to rise above it, even if a few other species do not. But keep in mind that 98% of all energy transfer on Earth comes about as the result of herbivorous appetites, not meat eating.

"Once you are truly aware of this, you will remain aware, because it has become your self-awareness, your ethical uniqueness in a world of tumultuous change. You do not forget how to ride a bicycle. You do not forget that the destruction of the rain forest, the coral reefs and estuaries, the bat, is a calamity; or that nuclear war is the end.

"To argue that bunches of cauliflower are just as helpless and sensitive to pain as a turkey may or may not be true. There's no question that every living organism feels pain. But the argument – with all of its yet to be learned revelations – has been perverted by those who would use it to invalidate all distinctions between plants and animals, so as to justify the killing of EVERYTHING! If we are to survive, we must minimize violence: taking concerted steps, day by day, like alcoholics on the mend, to reverse the murderer in man. There is no other way."

I glared at him, or grinned, stupefied – as was he, I think – by the terrible irony. He had – by his look – evidently evolved beyond that absurd contradiction. "Keep reading," he advised me.

"Meat eaters do not acknowledge that murderer in man, this planetary calamity, because no law exists, no legislative or juridical opinion has ever been set down in this country that would tamper with their daily bullying of animals, or prejudice those men against killing for their dinner. America – and most cultures – look with pride to the hunter, exult in his efficiency and resourcefulness. Goaded by popular opinion, uncurtailed in his bloodlust, the meat eater had every bulwark, the sheer magnitude of other meat eaters, to support him; to go on and on defending the butchery, in blissful ignorance of the billions of animals who suffer and perish continually, every second of every day and night. Those men, and women, and young persons who kill are the most inhuman of all animals. To suggest that because other animals kill, humans can do so with a free conscience, is to deny the magical purpose and *raison d'etre* of conscience in the first place. We are shepherds, we know better; some would even argue that we are the front-runners of animal evolution. If that is true, then we are responsible for setting a pattern on Earth that is tempered and wise and gentle. Meat eating is utterly unrestrained; an ecological, medical, and spiritual disaster for everyone. It was in recognition of this once too obvious credo, that the Bible clearly stated, 'Thou Shalt Not Kill'. Period. No ifs, ands, or buts." Felham winced. I guess he'd forgotten about that part of his essay, as well. I looked at him. "Interesting," I said. Both the Bible and his theory of minimizing violence, were postulated before my brother started killing, I assumed.

"The Bible also says 'An eye for an eye'," he at once marshalled.

"An eye for an eye and the whole world goes blind, remember? Gandhi."

"A perfect but inapplicable aphorism," he retorted.

"Maybe it's not a good idea to use the Bible as a source when it comes to killing people," I suggested.

Then he started to get hot under the collar. "This ring a bell, little brother? 'And I will make your cities waste, and bring your sanctuaries unto desolation ...' *Leviticus*, verse thirty-one."

"Allegory," I begged.

"He that killeth an ox is as if he slew a man."

"You're sure it says that? I never heard that."

"Isaiah, sixty-six, verses two and three."

I wasn't in a position just then to dispute his memory. But he wasn't finished.

"Ecclesiastes: '... a man hath no pre-eminence above a beast'. That's the true covenant, Jason. Even the lowliest critters. Book of Proverbs, 6:68: 'Go to the ant, thou sluggard, Consider her ways, and be wise ...' God warned mankind, 'Fuck with the beasts and you die'."

"He didn't put it quite like that."

"That's what he meant. 'Desolation'. That's the exact word God used. Vengeance. God knew that people have a deep craving for revenge, when they feel that His Kingdom has been deliberately abused. And he supported it."

"I thought he spared the world for even one decent person? And when did you get religion anyway?" I also knew that Felham was the one in the family who always went to Church. But it was for the music, the Ave Marias, and recitativos of Monteverdi. We all knew that: older brother loved the choir. I never thought for a moment he was actually *observing* the lyrics.

"I didn't. I'm not."

"Sure as hell sounds like it."

"I'm just citing facts. Every religion, nearly every myth, folklore, deification, has a similar Bible, or song cycle. A self-defence that's built into its self-righteousness. It's no longer religion, but rather, the psychology of survival."

"I thought God was love?" I meant to contest his methods, now that I felt more certain we were speaking the same language, or at least wielding a similar syntax and grammar.

"God *is* love. I don't believe in God, per se. I believe in that capacity we call – that you just knowingly called – love. I love. Mom and Dad loved. I know you love. It's because I love so much. You must understand me. Get it right. Since you've come at least as far as you have– "

"That's big of you– "

Impatiently, he sped on, " We're the same blood. We're the same– "

"We were the same. Now, we're as different as day is to night." I couldn't accede so easily. What was I doing? Was he finally getting to me?

"You're just afraid."

"Afraid? Try harrowed, repulsed, queasy. You are my worst nightmare."

"Your worst nightmare?"

"How would you react if you were me?" I asked him.

"I'd stop *reacting*, and start *doing*."

"I didn't mean to have the centre of my universe thrown topsy turvy."

"Galactic catastrophes are common enough."

"That's fine. I'll keep my galaxy the way it was."

"Not on your lucky stars ... Because you can't. It's not that simple."

"It was that simple. A wife. A job. A child. A good life."

"For you."

"All right, for me," I protested. "That's who I am. That's all I am. I'm not the Messiah, like you seem to think you are."

"No Messiah. No. It's only because I want so much ... for so many. Ahh, shit. You dumb brat. The world could be perfect!"

Brat ... He used to call me that. And I detected what could have become a tear.

"And what if God – the God you and I were raised to treasure, as Roman Catholics – in fact planned all of these animal sacrifices?" I posed.

"He didn't."

"But what if he did? What if the galactic cataclysm was preordained and it spelled the eventual demise of most other species. I mean, let's face a few facts, Felham. Those tigers you referred to. The lions, vultures, ants, even birds and other primates cannibalize flesh to survive. It's no accident ... Well?"

"Obviously, if there is a God, he's no different than any other egomaniacal tyrant, and he should stand trial."

"And the happiness in this world? He's guilty of that, too, you know?"

I had to laugh at the thought of God guilty on how many counts? Innocent on how many counts? How could a jury stack it all up? The achievement of the Himalaya, or Bora Bora, or Yosemite, versus a little Saturday afternoon game of tag on the Serengetti. Some spilled drops of blood, an instant of pain, the gazelle collapsing in seconds, its neck broken, its air passage checked, impulses to its brain flooded with carbon dioxide, blistering eyes, terror-racing heart, all stopped with the oblivion of a mercifully quick death, and subsequent feeding of feline cubs which by most aesthetic standards, are at the top of the beauty charts. A hung jury, in other words.

I held up the editorial to further scrutiny, with a gentler eye.

"Meat eating is about killing animals, not simply eating meat; killing in proportions that no one can begin to gauge or comprehend. The killing of docile innocent animals whose throats are sliced open in matter-of-fact assembly lines, while their bodies dangle and writhe from steel snares and claws, and the weight of their terrified lungs and hearts asphyxiate them, as the butchers, swaying to the heavy metal melodies of their headsets, slice and pulverize and gore, puncture and boil them alive, often missing with their hatchets and hacksaws before finally doing in the animals with lumberjack hydroclippers of every size and shape and razor sharpness. The unimaginable conditions, the putrid lakes of deep and despondent blood, wasted life, the mountains of hideous pain and wretched brutality, disappear at the air-conditioned grocery stores and hygienically preserved meat counters; and vanish within the elegant bottles and fancy containers. So that America, the beleaguered, prides itself on environmental protocols, and Earth Days and ecological hand-wringing, and scientific bandstanding, while suffering souls all around us are cast cruelly to an oblivion that makes Hell seem more agreeable.

"You think the above killing grounds are justified so as to continue the habit of meat? Then prove it; do what the poet Percy Shelley recommended, and then, only then, may you judge yourself on the level of other, non-human predators:

" 'Let the advocate of animal food force himself to a decisive experiment on its fitness ... tear a living lamb with his teeth, and plunging his head into its vitals, slake his thirst with the steaming blood; when fresh from the deed of horror let him revert to the irresistible instincts of nature that would rise in judgment against it, and say, Nature formed me for such work as this. Then, and then only, would he be consistent.'*

"There can be no environmentalism without a thoroughly unambiguous belief in the preciousness, the importance, the fragility of life on Earth," my brother's essay went on. Hard to believe that it was written by one who now set out to murder thousands of people.

"Meat eating spits in the face of that belief system, countering caution and self-restraint with gluttony, and a mockery of all that the life force has achieved, in four and a half billion years of biological aspiration.

"As children of nature, endowed with a heart, a conscience and a brain, we ought to know better; we cannot continue the charade of supposedly caring about the planet, while turning our back on an estimated seven billion mammals and avians condemned to being eaten every year, in the United States alone. The numbers on an international scale have never been calculated but they surely amount to tens of billions of animals. Just one fast food chain, among many, boasts, on its billboards, of having sold nearly thirty billion hamburger patties. And it goes on."

I figured he was probably referring to Hamburger Palace, which by now, many years later, was getting close to the one hundred billion hamburgers mark, or more than sixteen burgers for every human being on the planet.

"For these, and many, many, other reasons, I will never take an environmentalist – or any human being for that matter – seriously, who, knowing all this continues to eat meat."

He concluded his rambling affront with a quote from Milton's *Paradise Lost*:

> 'No light, but rather darkness visible, served only to discover
> sights of woe,
> Regions of sorrow, doleful shades, where peace and rest can
> never dwell, hope never comes
> That comes to all; but torture without end ...'

And he signed his sermon, 'Anonymous'.

I knew that it was hopeless. He had to be out of his mind to think the editors of a magazine would pay attention to this kind of evangelical tirade. Clearly they didn't. It was never published. He and his cult of the children of nature were left to seethe in solitude. Maybe if it had been published, none of the subsequent events would ever have happened, I reasoned. Of course, that's what they also say about Hitler being rejected from art school.

* *A Vindication of Natural Diet* in Percy Shelley, *Selected Poetry, Prose and Letters* (ed., A. S. B. Glover), [Nonesuch : London, 1951] pages 900-913.

"They must have thought you one arrogant sonofabitch."

"I don't know. They never sent the piece back. I never heard a word from them."

"You're not surprised, are you?"

"At the time, sure I was."

But I was relieved, I must say, by the fact of so forceful and consistent a logical position, rambling or not. Nearly two decades of the same beliefs. It gave me some respect for a murderer. A man capable, in anger, of dashing off so articulate a manifesto. It also countered that virulent bacterium, that queasy antipathy in my gut, which I'd been carrying inside me every day to work, every night to bed. Felham's declaration somehow helped to free me of it. At least I now had an explanation, something to work with, a way to explain my brother's quest to myself. It could only end in the tragedy he had long ago set into motion. But at least it carried some classical weight.

Felham was not unaware of that tragedy. Contrite love, the traditional, God-fearing love, the love of a Father who takes confession, was not the love Felham needed or wanted. He simply hoped for the love of our growing up together; the trust of two brothers, who had only one another in this world. If I were to turn my back on him, I would be guilty of having denied our past, which was filled with so many good things; but also of ignoring the fact of a little Hitler in my midst. No, I don't really call him that, or think that. He's Dirk. Older brother. But that animal inside him, he's the one I point the finger at. If I sympathized with *that* to any extent, I would have to go all the way; harbouring the one inside of him.

I had already chosen to permit him to maintain a cover at the restaurant. My decision was essentially a non-decision. I volunteered nothing, kept my peace, prayed for him. Prayed for all of us. I tried to keep it in line, to maintain. To never yield to that lurking heaviness on the cusp of the everyday; to give no sign, stare in no cracked mirror, avoid crossing the path of black cats, or skipping under ladders. No slip-up. Like one who's had too much to drink, but drives the straight and narrow path towards home, defiantly holding onto the wheel, maintaining the proper speed, not too fast, not too slow, keeping it together.

When the risk of being hit, caught out, is everywhere paramount. That was my love. Holding the wheel of myself, not giving up, nor giving away his whereabouts or identity; but still undecided, day after day, refusing to jump off, incapable of joining him. Had I made my choice, granting me the freedom to ignore his predicament, or sympathize? Had I become complicit on account of being a good listener? Guilt, before God, is the beginning of a long road, I was always informed; the path to redemption and righteousness. But how does guilt of my sort acquit itself? Where does philosophy end and collusion begin? Where do action and idea go their separate ways, or commingle? And what does the law say about it? Hell if I knew.

Was I, after all, really guilty? Yes. I must have convinced myself so. Or else why did I suffer? Why did my hands tremble, and my trigger fingers close up tight at night, so that I had to unclench them as if opening the palm of a dead man in the morning? And how did I know that this week would be different? That the storm was coming. I don't know. But I knew.

Fight for what you believe in, father used to tell us kids. Did fighting mean being willing to die? It did for him, though he wouldn't have wished that upon his two boys, I don't think. To stand up for another was different than declaring that you also partook of his crime. Otherwise every dignified lawyer would send himself to jail as well. It does not happen that way because each of us wants to survive. We can not be expected to carry the cross for another. Or few of us will. And those who do are not long for this world. Their message remains. But such messages are only remains.

There are always to be expected a few martyrs who make a difference, who sacrifice themselves, lead others towards the cause of freedom. Garibaldi. Joan of Arc. They happened to be on the right side of public opinion, ultimately. Unlike, say, the leader of the Taiping Rebellion, who only succeeded in having all his followers commit suicide, after storming much of China and leaving millions dead from hunger and war. All in the name of a good cause. And then there was Castro betting on the Soviet coup. How can one predict which bets, which history books, which public opinion, will turn out to be good ones, and which bad? Play the odds, I suppose.

An article in the morning paper catches my attention. A certain court must determine whether five environmental radicals charged with conspiring to thwart the operations of a nuclear power plant are in fact guilty. The judge was not overly impressed with one long dead poet from Massachusetts, cited in the proceedings. Easy for him to say, asserts the judge; sitting all day beside Walden. But a pond, and the human sentiments that may attach to it, is not a nuclear power plant, quoth the judge from his written statement. So it's never simply a question of odds, or precedent, or fame, or even the eloquence of a well-argued manifesto, like Felham's. It comes down to the judge. What he had for breakfast – meat and potatoes, or vegetables? Whether the State legislature had approved of his pay hike the month before. Whether his son had lettered on the high school football team, or whether his daughter was still seeing that longhair. Perhaps the judge disliked longhairs and therefore civil disobedience. Or perhaps he had stock in a utility company that supplied inexpensive power via nuclear.

Whatever the reason, Thoreau cut no favour with that judge on the day he sent the radicals to jail. History, the validation of personal ethics, of a whole life, could easily come down to what side of the bed our judge and executioner woke up on. Whether he was a meat eater, or a vegetarian. That stinks, of course.

I was at sea. Trying without any measure of resolvability to recast my brother's dilemma in such a manner as to absolve the both of us from guilt. Now I was in it with him, simply by thinking. Without even sensing the extent of his guilt, the damage he had done, the innumerable bodies he had dispatched. Every thinking moment presented me with an opportunity to see his crimes in a new light. But the same shadow kept emerging, the same morbid turmoil. My mind was thick with the agitation of my brother's life; his presence in my being tripled my cholesterol count. I suffered from headaches, which was something new; I had a minor car accident, from pressure in my colon. I got caught doodling at traffic school, then got locked out for being ten minutes late after the coffee break. That meant I had to go through a whole eight hour course another day. My sleeping was eruptive. My lovemaking distracted. Yet I had to keep it together. What was I going to do? Jump off the roof, confess? Confess what? That my family had produced a madman? Genes. Remember the genes. We're all guilty, in a family. And I no longer considered him mad. That's the point I wish to stress.

Neither God nor faith nor even reason can hide my nakedness. I cannot kill my brother, as Cain killed Abel, or turn him in. I would not suffer upon myself such unknown consequences – wandering in exile through the land of Nod, seeking vengeance sevenfold, according ill to all other tribes, a marked man. What does it even mean?

And therefore, I must accept the fact that I have, in essence, joined him. But in truth I was not prepared. To think is not to act – our great dilemma is not even to *know* how to act. Thinking makes children of us all. Like debate, it commits us to standing still. To say so is to reinforce one's exposure, vulnerability. I was a sitting duck.

Magda, the restaurant's office manager, had been notified that we were to receive a State health inspector on a routine visit. "They want to be sure of these new tofu brands," she told me. "Tofu's all right, isn't it?"

"I assume so," she said, parting her eyes, surprised I should even ask, since I was always the one who chose the manufacturer up in the Santa Cruz area after very carefully studying the matter. I had already forgotten, lost track. "*Are you all right?*" she suddenly inquired.

"Yeah," I stumbled. "Why, what is it?"

"I don't know. You were mumbling to yourself."

"I was?" *About what?* I wanted to ask, but didn't.

"And it wasn't the first time." She eyed me tenderly, but with certain doubts. I could see her mind was working, suspicious. "I think you need to take some time away."

"Magda, I'm fine. Bart hasn't been sleeping. I haven't been sleeping." She was leading two others down to the back dock to receive a shipment and transfer the goods into the refrigerators. I then had to check that the soy milk and pasta noodles, the creams and perishables, were being properly disposed of at the right time. I kept notes of everything according to State regulations. Organically grown soy beans, filtered in water, wheat gluten, magnesium chloride, soy protein isolate, canola oil, wheat starch, gums, rice syrup, beans and dried figs, the day's vegetables and fruits and other dairy products, those sorts of combinations at the heart of my business. And that supplies were in good order, inventories up-to-date and logged into the computer. It was my job to oversee all ledgers, and make certain that tips were being properly allocated, written down for tax purposes, the paperwork then handed over to Felham for his scrutiny. That *had* been our system for years, though Felham's time in the restaurant usually amounted to no more than one day a week, on average. I had a meeting planned with a banker regarding a loan I wished to secure, for a new product we wanted to produce, a canned gazpacho according to my mother's own recipe. With cashews and pimentos and two dozen other ingredients, laced with parmesan. There were numerous hurdles inherent to the business of canning and distributing food, especially across borders, that needed to be addressed. State approvals at various mundane levels. That was my week. Was I born for this? Yes.

Jessie day dreams. Clyde Maybe should be back by now, she figured. She'd go over to the restaurant and surprise him. Should she, really? Was it too forward of her? *Clyde, Clyde ...* she'd practised to herself.

She thinks: *I'm already going ahead with this thing, thinking seriously. Of course if he wanted to see me, don't you think he would have called? NO. He's a shy one. You figured that out already, girl. The way he was at the Gymboree, hapless, ungainly. And the same could be said for the aborted dinner, his questionable candour. That too was part of his pardonable manner of taking the light out of his face.* He was new to the singles' scene, somehow, she reckoned. *That's good.* She hated experienced men ...

She left her office, met a female friend for an hour of yoga class, skipped lunch, and got into her car. There was a parking ticket. Twenty-eight dollars. Her fury lasted a few seconds, then she stuffed it into her glove compartment and drove off.

Like an electrical storm. Every ounce of moisture, every scud of cloud, the barometer dropping, a feeling in the air – converging threat. Guilt, like a magnet, bringing in the filings. There were many hours that separate the commission of his deed, from his return. Not quite a day. But in that time, the filings had landed, were accumulating, like some exotic crystal with perfect facets. The opponent was coming into place.

During the night, while Jerrasi was being driven to the airport, Shelley Pendergras was still at the office trying to get more of a fix on Brian Laffont. Her boyfriend was in a band, and was on the road, so she had no particular incentive to go home to their apartment just yet. What's more, something interesting had come in over the wires: a mass murder in Bangkok. There were few details. Just now she was faxing the FBI's contact at the Thai National Police Office for more information. Shelley knew that the owners of the bird sanctuary in Los Angeles were also Thai. Could there be a connection, she wondered? Her team was trying anything.

The information she'd requested came back within half an hour. She read the report and picked up her phone and placed a call to Madrid.

"Hi. What's up? Where are you?" he said.

"The office. Listen to this ..." and she read him the summary that had been faxed from Bangkok.

"Gotta be the same people," he replied.

"Here's the kicker," she went on.

"I'm listening."

"Last night a Thai, male, name as yet withheld – we're not sure why – was found dead in his car in the Bay Area."

"There's a large Thai population there."

"Wes, it's in this same report from Bangkok. He was one of them."

"How come they're faster than we are?"

"Interesting? They found him burned up in his Porsche that had gone off the road at high speed on some mountain. There were skid marks. It suggests a chase. It seems to me – with Robert in LA – that somebody– "

"Right. A sign of three. Three conspirators, I mean. Unless ..."

"It's a one hour flight from Los Angeles. It would have been simple," she said. Shelley had instincts about those two Italian dishwashers in New York. But there was also the evidence from the Australian hit, suggesting even more numerous links. Still, they had this sign of three.

Madrid had begun to yawn, but nervous energy cut it short, leaving his voice stifled.

"Who is it?" Shelley heard Madrid's wife ask in the background.

"I gotta go back to the airport," he groaned. He and his high school sweetheart, Cissie, made love first, perfunctorily, like rapid transit. They played bucking bronco. She brought herself to an orgasm with her second and third fingers and went back to sleep. Alice, their daughter, had an early morning appointment at the orthodontist.

Jerrasi was helping himself to the salad bar at the Los Angeles Hilton, having resigned himself to one *fucking* caesura. The quarantine station was dry, not a thing to go on, typical; the blond witness had checked out on polygraph, and as for the Thai operation itself, there were no existing conditions, per se, no birds, by which to determine whether any infractions had been committed, not that it was relevant. His pocket phone summoned him away from a final dollop of Ranch-style dressing. It was Madrid speaking from Lieutenant Baggot's back office at the San Francisco Police Station south of Market Street. Baggot was a very congenial cop, with a squirrelly moustache, a pleasantly tanned complexion, wiry hair, and a relaxed build. He looked much like Terry Thomas and had spent years doing DNA follow-ups on rape cases, as well as other sundry forensics. He wore his gun like someone who had never seriously considered using it. And his easy grin suggested an optimist who loved the city, its natives, even the bad guys, and especially the new mayor, a cop like himself. There was another reason for that Gomez Adams grin: his after hour visits to Broadway, where his girlfriend of seven years worked as a stripper. Instant communication. From the soul. She had coconut breasts and a brain like a jukebox, and life was perfect for them.

Baggot had gotten a partial ID on a set of tyre skid marks on a hairpin curb on Mount Tam adjacent to the point at which the Porsche '89 Turbo sailed into oblivion. It was a lightweight, probably Italian or British sports car. Baggot ran his fingers over the tracings in the gravel like an Indian tracker; fondled the curves and subtlety of purpose, diagnosed from the road-skewed course an urgency, which he interpolated like some Shakespearian motive; and all amplified by the record at the Department of Motor Vehicles.

"You're sure about this?" Madrid pressed him before calling his partner.

"I don't have a whole lot of doubt."

"That's a contradiction."

"A small one," Baggot urged. He knew skid marks. Weight, tyre shape, any number of parameters that tyre dealers themselves hesitated to declare. Baggot drove a '73 Jag. He had his hobby horse down pat.

He ran a computer multiple cross-reference search for any tall, possibly black, male owners of exotic sports cars in Marin Country.

At the same time, an intensive undercover manhunt was initiated.

"What does that mean, out here?" Madrid inquired.

"It means we send, in this case, nearly fifty men and women out into Marin County – that's a large region, you know – and they look. They look everywhere."

Jerrasi took the last United shuttle up to San Francisco, rented an Alamo Mitsubishi compact and missed the post-earthquake exit downtown. That forced him east over the Bay Bridge and he found himself on Treasure Island, looking back admiringly at the skyline over half the bay. At that same moment, Madrid and Baggot were sitting in a wealthy, retired architect's home, above Stinson Beach, questioning a man who'd been walking his two setters around midnight of the night in question, and had noticed the passing blue or black or burgundy Aston-Martin, though not its occupant, or occupants. He was certain it was an Aston-Martin, because he used to drive one.

"What year?" Baggot asked.

"Pretty new," the fellow said.

Within ten minutes, Baggot was able to establish that the DMV in Sacramento showed no licensed Aston-Martin in the region. Jerrasi had called in. He was at the station downtown.

"Tell him to get dinner. We'll be there in less than an hour," Baggot relayed. "I have this hunch, see," Madrid came right out with.

Baggot smiled. "Registered in another State."

Madrid nodded. "A very careful driver."

In the morning, the SFPD distributed hundreds of photographs of the generic vehicle in question while beefing up their manhunt. Jerrasi and Madrid stayed in a room of the China Town Holiday Inn, up on the twelfth floor, where they could overlook much of the city, all the way to the Golden Gate Bridge. Across the street, tai chi, and mah-jongg games occupied the motley crowds. A day of heat, potentially of fire; dried hills and wind-cured seascapes. The ever-present tension, something undercutting and dour – one of those too perfect days, if you were only a tourist. Jerrasi was pacing the void out on a sheltered balcony, phone to Bangkok in hand, validating pieces of information that had come in by fax from Shelley in DC. The calibre of bullet used in the massacre, the style of the hit, a record of every foreigner who passed through customs that day, and the day after.

Just before noon they had their break. And a big one.

"Marin County. The Amidha Center." Baggot was on the phone with Jerrasi. "An Aston-Martin has been seen entering from the main road, on more than one occasion."

"Who saw it? What colour? When was the last time?"

There were no answers. An anonymous phone caller. But that was enough.

"This may be it," Jerrasi said, kicking into his loafers, grabbing his things, re-checking his gun harness, then out the door. *Why anonymous?* he vaguely pondered. *Disenchanted confederate? An enemy? Or the man himself? A challenge?* He'd seen stranger things.

Madrid wolfed down the remains of a burger and fries, threw on his jacket and jolted towards the door.

After eight years, and every dead-end, Jerrasi sensed that he had struck a manhunter's Klondike. Madrid, disappointed by the lack of forward motion in Los Angeles, where an eye witness had actually spoken with *The Animal*, was less exuberant about their chances. They'd been closer in the past, and gotten nowhere.

"Two points of a triangle," Jerrasi aired.

"We've been four hours away, Bob, if you recall. And zilch."

"I got a feeling, this time."

"You said that last time."

Baggot had his whole team on the ready, choppers, upwards of fifty patrolmen in as many unmarked vehicles, all heading towards a stakeout of the Amidha Center. Jerrasi had his own legion of local bureau investigators closing in.

"You never did Zen, did you?" Madrid toyed with his partner, as they circled up the hill past a torrential shade of eucalyptus groves.

"Sure I did. Every time I jerk off."

"Maybe it would be good for you," Madrid grinned.

"Fuck you. D'you load up?" referring to Madrid's gun.

"Just let's talk gentle with them. That's their thing."

Jerrasi contemplated the caution. Madrid checked his piece and made a phone call.

"Baggot, Madrid here. We're approaching the centre. Where are you?"

"Five minutes away, overhead."

"Tell him to stay out of earshot," Jerrasi added.

"You hear that?"

"We'll circle out over the water. We'll be one minute away if you need us. The others are coming from everywhere. They've all got orders to keep a distance." They were all tuned to a scrambled signal.

The Amidha Center complex comprised a number of greenhouses, small courtyards, tea rooms, meditation chambers, private living quarters. The exclusive haunt of the fancy and free. There was no gate. Jerrasi came to a stop fifty yards from the unguarded entrance, and probed the exterior with binoculars. No sign of the vehicle, or of any unusual movement. Madrid already had the sense of the place. It was no Waco, Texas.

"Where's the fellow in charge?" Jerrasi asked the first person they crossed, a gardener who was turning soil in a patch of lettuce, or rhubarb, or whatever it was.

The worker was not altogether forthcoming and pointed unanimatedly towards a cluster of rear structures.

"What are you planting, anyway?" Jerrasi asked.

"Leek."

"Leek ..." He turned to Madrid. "You ever eat a leek?"

"Never even heard of a leek."

"Asshole," Jerrasi blurted out the window. He reckoned he'd been fucked with.

They drove towards the rear. Madrid hopped out and moved towards an area of parked cars.

"Watch me," Jerrasi advised. "Follow me at some distance. I got the keys."

They moved in tandem, normal browsing, like they lived there, or had come to sign up, careful as cops can be not to arouse any suspicions.

From inside a distant window, framed in bamboo, Kano Suzuki Roshi was practising with his sword. In an hour he had a seminar to teach. He could make out Jerrasi ambling his way.

There was a knock at an outer door. A student, dressed in blue silken trousers and an effeminate matching blouse, billowy sleeves and sporting a slightly perverse twinkle in his eye, greeted them in Americanized Japanese.

"I'm looking for the fellow in charge," Jerrasi replied, pointedly unimpressed.

"Is Sensei expecting you?"

"Who?" *Gentle ... gentle ...* The words crept up on him as Madrid staked out a position in the rear of the house. Jerrasi flashed his badge. He didn't like diddling.

"Please wait here," the flimsy disciple pattered. But Jerrasi stayed right with him. "Excuse me??" the watchdog remonstrated.

"You got a problem," Jerrasi said matter-of-factly.

"Your shoes. We don't allow shoes."

"You do now."

Beyond the adjoining room, in a courtyard of ceramic tiles and chrysanthemums, the Sensei was wielding his glint-edged katana, steel sinuosity, slowly unfurling the philosophical cuts of his craft, as if he were wielding a tea ladle, and all to the low murmured words, *This very moment, Into heaven I throw high ...*

In spite of his preoccupation just then, the Sensei heard all of the exchange, had seen Jerrasi flip open his wallet, and now awaited the encounter with undetectable resolve.

The Sensei, or Master, was bald, thick-throated, weighted down in clustering Asiatic brocades, embossed dragons of silk, and surrounded by paraphernalia that indicated opposition, the ascetic and the lavish, simple design, ornate decoration, unity of space and multiplicity of symbols. A compression of contradiction that Jerrasi noticed, and smelled in the heavy-set man moving suspiciously before him.

"That's some sword," Jerrasi said, dodging a motion that might have hurt had the Sensei so intended. "It's called Kendo," the Sensei harkened. "It relaxes me."

He ran through a number of dance steps, choreography fashioned after red leaves, the void, a rock, an ox's neck. His movements were graceful though asymmetrical, applied with a light and toying touch, that suggested hatred and restraint, both.

"That weapon registered?" asked Jerrasi.

"Not a weapon. Poetry in steel," the Sensei answered demurely, lowering the sword and placing it in a velvet lined wooden container, that lay upon a spartan altar at the entrance to his study.

Jerrasi withdrew a photograph of an Aston-Martin from his pocket.

"You ever see a car like this?" he asked the Master. "We had a report that somebody who comes here frequently, drives such a vehicle. It's called an Aston-Martin."

"Very nice car," the Sensei said, studying the picture, then studying Jerrasi. Then he shook his head with what Jerrasi at once took to be a sly unregister. "Have never seen this car."

"We got a call from one of your students. Said it was here a few days ago."

"Could be. Why not ask student. I have never seen."

Jerrasi was fuming, shaking his head with the hostile grin of incredulity, of *Why are you protecting a monster you hypocritical piece of Zen Shit!* He stepped back indoors, and lifted his eyes to the woodwork on the ceiling. It was a soft and elliptical panelling, like balsa, or teak, and finely done, patterned, Oriental. "Who's your carpenter?" Jerrasi asked.

The Sensei calmly referred to a "Mr. Goro. From Kyoto."

"What would he charge someone like me to do a little house of woodwork in this manner? With a similar courtyard. I mean what would you guess, just ... ballpark, doesn't have to be exact?"

"Around one million dollar." He smiled.

"Yeah. I figured ... Well, let me show you this picture one more time. Now look real close." Jerrasi was furious. One fucking million, for that faggot artsy schmartsy?

The Sensei examined the image, with a desire, pent up and nervous and un-Buddha-like, to buy that very car.

"Nothing rings a bell?"

"I am so sorry."

"Why do I get the impression that you're not telling me something?"

"Nothing to tell."

Kani Roshi knew very well whose car the picture resembled. The man he had initiated in the tea ceremony, and the art of bushido. He had taken the equivalent of Felham's confession.

There was a time when both men had fought with swords in the surrounding redwood forest. Roshi caught that he was dealing with a fighter, a mercenary, a man of secrets. Roshi had his own clandestine Pacific theatre, where his Rinsai Zen, the not terribly trouble-free centuries of cumulative introspection, had been put to the test. He had taught Felham when to yield, when to egress. The two shared silence and ambiguity. From the beginning, they knew about one another, somehow; divined that the surface sobriety held back a lethal web of unstated demons and designs. Roshi had quietly entered Felham's orbit, surreptitiously gaining the man's trust, not needing to ask, not wanting to know. He liked this warrior. Ethically, he was bound to say nothing.

In Jerrasi, the Sensei had instantly recognized an unfriendly and evasive redneck, and had no compunction about lying to him.

"The man we're looking for is a mass murderer. I'm sure they have an expression for it in Japanese. In this country, harbouring that kind of criminal is a very serious crime."

"In Japan, such a felony is unthinkable."

"Well, there you go." The two men looked at each other.

"You think of anything, here's my card."

Jerrasi then showed the photograph to the meditating mantis who'd remained standing before the door. He too indicated absolutely no knowledge of such a vehicle.

Jerrasi asked him if there was anybody staying at the centre who had a particular thing about animals.

"We all love animals here, of course."

Jerrasi walked out and relocated the gardener.

"You ever see a car like this?" he asked the barefooted Oriental.

The gardener shrugged his shoulders.

"Bunch'a fuckheads," Jerrasi mumbled to Madrid.

The two FBI men walked across the grounds of the centre, stopping everyone they saw. No one knew of an Aston-Martin. Within minutes, a gong rebounded throughout the twenty manicured acres, and residents moved in to congregate in the communal lecture hall.

Jerrasi shoved his fists against the side of his vehicle. "That cocksucker knows."

They started up towards the lecture hall.

"I'm going to show this photograph to every one of those fags. I sense anyone of them obstructing justice, we're taking him in," he thought out loud to Madrid, "and we're gonna leave a stakeout here."

Madrid's phone rang, the quiet jingle of a sistrum.

"Yeah? What? Well, damn!" It was difficult hearing over the din of the chopper.

"We got another lead," he informed Jerrasi. "It's Baggot," Madrid said. "They got something."

"Give it to me. Jerrasi, here. I hope you've got something better than this shit?"

"Write this down."

Jerrasi took the name and address of a restaurant in Sausalito.

"When did they last spot it?"

"Four nights ago. Some car enthusiast and his wife saw it. It was in the valet lot," Baggot shouted.

"Three points, triangle closed," Jerrasi pounced, out loud.

Muppet was driving up the same hill, on his way back to the farmhouse, when half-a-dozen unmarked cars, all carrying portable flashing lights, passed him and everybody else on the road, coming from the direction of Amidha Center. A low-flying chopper swept by as well. He could see the occupants of the vehicles. His eyes caught Jerrasi's.

From a phone booth at the depot in town he'd placed a call; from a gas station another; and from a small specialty shop leasing seeing-eye dogs, yet a third. Appointments, contacts, schedules. A furtive darkness of details. Now, he went straight for another phone at the Muir Woods Inn. All familiar points. He knew what time Felham's plane was expected, could rightly make out his buddy's itinerary across town, noting time of day and likely traffic, and rang up his beeper.

At that moment, Felham – who knew it was Muppet calling (Muppet being the only one with his number, of course) – was in a taxi crossing the Golden Gate Bridge, ten minutes away from Ralph's.

"You don't have a car phone?" Felham asked the driver.

"No, sir."

"That's alright." He was thinking back to the blond, and how her face disintegrated as the bullets did their work; of the little bird on his shoulder, Feather, and of the birds that probably wouldn't make it. He was wondering about the other woman, the one he'd spoken to; would she talk? What could she say? How had he behaved? Good! Like a gentleman, under the circumstances.

There was no remorse. Felham thought about Maryland. He was anxious to get on with it.

My name? What's my name? a panic suddenly gripped him.

"Turn off there," he blurted out, not wanting to miss the first Sausalito exit.

Maybe, Clyde Maybe, he at last remembered ... *Shit!* ... he sat back. Muppet waited in the phone booth.

Jerrasi and Madrid entered the parking lot of Ralph's. Jerrasi spoke with the head valet, showing him the photograph. Three dozen armed police were already taking up inconspicuous positions surrounding the establishment, all speaking with hand phones. The parking attendant on duty had no idea who owned the restaurant – Felham didn't advertise his role – but he had seen, once or twice, a similar car to the photograph in question. On the other hand, he could be mistaken, he said.

"You get a lot of cars in valet parking. Probably every make there is, after a while."

Jerrasi strode defensively inside, swept the lowdown downhome decor, with a mild but all-seeing glance, Madrid taking an unpronounced backup – he always backed up with a toothpick between two teeth, boot heels leaning out, elbow on the edge of a door, real cool, real easy going, you'd never know, whether in a Chinese ganghall or the rodeo, his eyes arranged like a Catscan; but he could draw his weapon and unload a dozen cartridges in a dozen foreheads faster than ... as Jerrasi spoke affectionately with the hostess.

Asked her questions. "So tell me, sweetheart, this car mean anything to you?"

The crossing of swords is inevitable, the Sensei had once told Felham. *First crossing*, it is practice. *Second crossing*, it is warning. *Third crossing*, there is no return. The words were laden with melodrama. Japan, and the Zen swordsmen particularly, had a fondness for aphorisms, for solemnifying koans, which they countered with an essentially subtle humour, that ranged across the whole gamut of unrevealable human fallibility.

Two times this day, though no one person knew it as yet, swords had crossed. For at that very moment, Jessie was on her way out of the restaurant. She had been in the area, and wanted to surprise the man who had been on her mind incessantly since their date. She had no idea if he was back in town but she had decided to leave a note and flowers for him regardless. Jessie's impulses didn't worry her. Either he chimed to her restlessness, or he did not. Concord or nullity. The odds were nothing new.

Muppet waited. Usually, Felham would pull over without delay and find the first phone. *He must be on the bridge, or in traffic* he sized up. Muppet was a superb study in patience. There was a heavy hit ahead for them, untoward timings, split-second matters, even an unknown or two – how he might wing a conversation, and what number of employees might be on duty. Questions that simply were not answerable for certain. He had his squirrels, insiders, but he'd not exactly squared with them, trusting no one, while acquitting himself of any doubt, since weapons were involved. He could only really trust in the Glen, a preserve where they intended to release as many animals as they could get. The rest of their plans were vulnerable: the neurosurgeon with whom he'd arranged an appointment, and his secretary, who was to leave word at the desk; a confidence in timetables, faith in the friend of the brother of the refuse collector who brought in the large bins, one to be camouflaged with a backup weapons stash if the in-house cabinets failed them. Too many strangers in all, reliance upon the waiting vehicles, a truck of the right size, the dependability of the detonator and the magnitude of the incendiary devices. Mostly, belief in a stolen diary which, allegedly, detailed the labs in question, the grim variety of cages, the precise way cats' tails were taped to electric prods, Rhesus monkeys to restraining chairs, dogs – victims of so-called 'learned helplessness' – to their kennels, rats to their mazes and bone-crushing cylinders, rabbits to their outmoded Draize racks, pigs in their burn-testing cauldrons. All these things and many, many more. Allegations, unproven. But Muppet had seen enough to recognize a distinct and sickening verisimilitude.

Why don't you pick up a goddamned phone?

Muppet was never the one to squirm. Painless. Fear, in a big man, sweats before it quakes.

Fear, not the fear of unknown, but the anticipation of premature destiny. Muppet was one of those unfortunate intellects who could count individual faces in a crowd, empathize with too many sets of eyes, recognize one mouse amid a thousand, ten thousand.

He had come by this effusive and humane penchant quite naturally – watching all his siblings eat while growing up. He was always big, and thus always served last as a kid – his parents' futile attempt at discipline. So Muppet never knew for certain whether there'd be food enough for him. They were not poor but he did go to bed hungry on occasion. He'd stare down his leaner clansmen, down to baby sister, their mealy portions, the consumption in their eyes, the feints and thrusts of finger and fork and salivation, all those markings of dinner time on the human animal. And this acumen, brought about by his overweight and a large family, never ceased in other domains as well. From junior high tug-a-war, to the shooting range in college, and finally into the Brazilian outback, he was ever the acute observer. Aggressive, defensive, yearning, counter-strategising. Concerned with survival. Muppet had somehow magically come to cherish life. He ate, calculated, risked everything, remained a solitaire by and large, a man without hope, in order to continue to love the world that had been so good to him. Muppet – Brian Laffont to some – had become a circumference of filial vows, God the Father, Christ and Holy Ghost, wanting only that every one of God's little creatures should equally relish the day; should have the freedom to be themselves, to fly if they have wings, to swim if they have fins, to run if they have hooves, to make love, to rear young 'uns, to do all those things that God intended.

And for the most part, Muppet had done those things. Cops or no cops. He was the freest of the free. Because he knew how much he enjoyed. Because the cage of his discipline, his ethic, had truly liberated him. Nobody could touch him. He planned on going out with a bang, instantly. But if they should catch him alive, why he'd just stick a flower up their ass, and mark his days in prison – he loved bread (granted, the hot sourdough kind smothered in melted sweet soy butter, not likely behind bars), he constantly craved water (it had to have ice, though, also unlikely) – until such time as he might stand trial. And when he did, he had one hell of a speech prepared. The speech alone would make it all worth it.

So, for Muppet, the thought of premature extinction was simply unacceptable. He never accompanied Felham to see Sensei, but had his own technique, and it worked, and it seemed sufficient. All that was required was time, time enough to figure out the solutions to each aggrieved little creature. To say that men might listen to them was ridiculous, an insult to grammar and possibility. Perhaps someone else would carry the torch, but probably not. They would not effect a changed world. But Muppet did believe that they could make at least a small difference, and that was worth everything. Forgetting the few minor elements of his renunciation – women, friends, never a tranquil second without the deep disquiet of being an outlaw – he was nevertheless content to be making an *effort*. That was what drove him. The knowledge, in his mind, that he'd been responsible. That he'd taken the gift of his life and acted according to conscience. Nothing more. Nothing less. And it was not so much *Muppet* that mattered, he reasoned; but the *flame* that burned within Muppet.

And the closer the opposition got – the tyre tracks, he knew it had to be the tyre tracks, or some fuck up in Los Angeles (*but Felham would have called, he would have let me know?*) – the more frantic his craving to seize additional time. There were so many plans ahead, elaborate expeditions already worked out with care and tenderness. Time translated into a few more lives saved.

The panic button. *Why hasn't he called in?*

Jessie had described Maybe. The young hostess had blinked twice and frowned. "His brother owns the place," Jessie went on. "A lawyer."

"You probably mean Dirkson. But Jason's no lawyer, I don't think," the hostess conjectured.

"It's Clyde, I think."

"Ma'am, Jason Felham owns Ralph's and his brother's name is Dirkson. You wanna leave a message or what?"

Jessie thought to leave the mylar-wrapped riot of blue gentians and yellow jonquils that were in her hands, then reconsidered.

"No. Thanks."

She turned and had started out, remembering why it was not a good idea to force the luck of strangeness, or the time bomb of frustration between idea and completion. He'd lied. He'd obviously been scared off, or never really wanted anything. He'd lied to her. She'd again played the fool.

And as she passed the man with his boots crossed and the tooth pick held so cocksure, a frame of mind more than a tool, she glanced at him. And he, passing his look across the largely empty restaurant, it being around four in the afternoon, was seeking any weapon holder, anyone who might suggest complicity or threat. She heard his apparent companion, whom she'd not seen, mumbling something to the same hostess. Nothing audible. Madrid finally looked square at her, an eyeful she was, and Jessie turned away and walked out.

Down the eight wooden half-steps beside the pier, moving briskly towards her car, which she'd parked herself. When suddenly a taxi cut her off, at a slow speed.

"Stop right there," Felham told the driver, pointing at the curb where Jessie was walking. He'd seen a man with a waist walkie-talkie, and probably gun, standing fixed in a doorway. And then he'd seen Jessie. Several other vehicles were entering and leaving the parking lot at the same time. The taxi had entered the flow.

Was she a setup?

There is no return ... not at the third crossing.

"Where's your car?" he said quietly, knowing that they might well be his last words as a free man – what insipid words, if that were the case – his windows down, right beside her as she strode. Then, addressing the driver, "Keep moving, follow her."

"You lied to me."

"I what?"

"You could at least have told me your real name, Dirkson!"

It would be hard for the taxi to pull out again. Felham was torn now, dealing with an overload. He'd just spotted two other stakeouts. There'd be others. They'd have scopes. They'd be watching. He mustn't slump down. She mustn't raise her voice, or make any kind of scene. Her tone implied that she didn't know what was happening. Were they onto her, or his brother? Or the car? The compression of reality, so sudden, so unexpected, and at his own restaurant. The odds were desperately against him just then. He could lean down in the taxi and just keep driving, driving away for ever and ever, perhaps. But then, just possibly, one of the stakeouts might be on to the taxi, or they might follow it as a matter of course. He made his decision.

"Where's your car?" he implored.

"What's it to you?" She resented his manner just then, was repelled by everything about him, and felt doubly stupid carrying flowers.

"Where is it?" he said more heatedly. "And don't toss the flowers ... Please!"

"There," she pointed. She could not mistake his tensed voice for anything other than fear.

"Okay," speaking to the driver, "pull up along side. Nice and easy."

"Something wrong?" the driver asked.

"Yeah. My love life. *Comprenez?*"

Felham got out on the side opposite the restaurant, closest to the water, where no stakeouts could be.

"Open it. I need you. Open it. Don't look around. Act natural. Please."

"All right." She did as she was told.

"That'll be thirty three dollars plus a two dollar airport tax, that's thirty five dollars." Felham left him a fifty in the passenger seat. "Your door's locked," he informed her. She turned on the ignition.

"Don't go away yet," he ordered the taxi. "Don't move."

"Get in," Jessie said, putting the flowers in the back and unlocking the door after a moment's hesitation.

Felham slid in low and put on shades. "Now pull out nice and easy. Don't look at anybody. Watch what you're doing. Make no error."

"Will you please tell me what the hell is going on?"

"Just ... just go. Go. Get out a'here. But not too fast. Don't squeal the tyres."

She steered around the taxi. Felham took a careful look at the man in the door. He counted six unmarked vehicles, with occupants watching. His heart pounded furiously.

They reached Highway 101. He studied the rear-view. The taxi had pulled away, along with two others, a Toyota and a BMW, luncheon-goers. No stakeouts seemed to follow.

"You have a car phone!" Felham declared.

"Have to, in my work. Which is where I'm headed."

"Fine."

"Not fine."

"Look, I'm sorry about the name. I can explain."

"You don't have to."

"But I will. I've been thinking about you. But I've got to make a phone call. Do you mind if I?" He'd already picked up the phone, and dialled the Muir Woods Inn.

Muppet's thick voice was right there, deploring his long wait with a breath of dire mulling. "Nice of you to finally call. What happened?"

"It's beginning," Felham said.

"I know. I tried to warn you. Horde of 'em, chopper included, just left your cosy little commune not fifteen minutes ago. Where are you?"

"I was at Ralph's. They're everywhere."

"Where are you now?"

"I'm ... remember that woman I had dinner with– "

Jessie eyed him, bewildered and saddened. Saddened by what already appeared to be complex and troublesome; saddened by the ruse, which she had known at other times; disappointed that this magnet of her thoughts for several days, had turned into a conniving man on the obvious run, a criminal of some sort, keeping secrets which she had no interest in hearing. And now, true to form, she was stuck, driving a liar on the lam. *Why do I always fall for losers*, she was thinking. *Trouble. Trouble ...*

"Stay away from the farm."

"Agreed. I'll call you from a hotel in the city at six."

"Check your watch."

"I read four-seventeen."

"We're in the Bethesda Hyatt tomorrow evening. Name of Striker. Party of two. There's an early morning United. Striker, reservation for one in first class. Got it?" Muppet asked.

"Everything in order?"

"Naturally."

"You feeling all right?" Felham went on.

"Jitters. Usual. Maybe a few more, this time."

"I know."

"What happened?"

"Everything went okay. A little messy. Bad info."

"The guards?"

"I'll tell you later."

"You can't talk."

"Right."

"Just tell me if you got the birds out."

"Yeah. It was really beautiful. Most of them made it, I think. You taking the same aerial?"

"You mean airline?'

"Yeah."

"No. A Delta. Twenty minutes later. Check the rent-a-car, Hertz, for your vehicle at Dulles. I've got an Avis, which I'm leaving off at a truck stop on the way in. Changing to the truck. It'll be waiting. We'll meet at the hotel. I'll fill you in at six. Dirk– "

"What?"

"You think the Sensei told them?"

"Never. It's the car. Someone saw it that night."

"That's what I figured. What about your brother?"

"I don't know. I really don't. I have no doubt they'll scare him, maybe follow him, work his phone. Poor kid. But he won't– " he meant to say 'talk' but checked himself " –won't say anything. We've already been through that."

"I'm sorry."

"I better go."

Muppet hung up, sat down at a private booth and ordered some heated yellow squash soup and a cold Bud.

"Are you going to tell me what's going on?" Jessie demanded, as they headed up the hill towards the tunnel, which would momentarily spill out in one graceful descent towards the Golden Gate. Fog was pouring over the ridges, amassing in an unlikely arc above the freeway. She was attracted to him, she didn't know why, exactly; handsome, dangerous, foreign – not a foreigner, but alien – and he needed her. She was needed, not by a woman in labour, but by a man. Simple ingredients, however much layered in doubts and circumstances that did not bode of the perfect relationship.

"Can I help you?" Jason Felham said.

"And you are?"

"I own Ralph's. Who may I have the pleasure– "

Jerrasi flashed his badge. The flash of illumination. Jason's heavenly nemesis come home to roost. Jason's last breath. His final moment.

"You ever see a car parked in your valet lot of this make?" Jerrasi showed him the picture.

"What is it?"

"Just please answer the question."

"I don't ... I don't know. I don't recognize it. Whose is it?"

"It's called an Aston-Martin. Do you know anybody who drives an Aston-Martin?"

"I have to think, to think about it, that ... an Aston-Martin ..."

Jerrasi couldn't help but take in the man's nervous manner. Madrid, meanwhile, held his ground. Jason saw him, sensed the bulge at his hip, then noticed a similar bulge along side the chest of the man before him.

He's hiding something. Just like that sonofabitch Samurai was hiding something. Or maybe it's just me? Jerrasi thought to himself: can't be just me. Fuckin' A.

"No, no."

"No what?" Jerrasi asked the stuttering amateur.

"I don't know the car."

Hold in your anger, goddammit ... "Well we have two witnesses who say they've seen this very car, maybe a different colour, on numerous occasions, at this establishment of yours."

"Look," Jason went on boldly – he was now getting the hang of it, now that the inevitable had begun, now that his untested being had surged from lassitudinous depths and sluggish fear into the limelight, "I'm no car buff. It's not my thing. I run a clean vegetarian restaurant."

Clean. The word struck Jerrasi queerly. As queerly as agile. And Jason, too. Why did I say that word? How utterly inane and uncalled for. What did it mean? Where did it come from? A gangster's word. A word that means you're trying to hide something, or defending someone!

Vegetarian, alright, Jerrasi thought. He didn't want to end the little tryst. It was too exhilarating, nearly vindictive, too close to the picture he'd contemplated for all these years.

"Mind if we sit down? There's a few more questions I want to ask you."

"No. No problem." Jason's knees were giving way. He watched the FBI man pick up his little portable phone and tell someone to hang tight. Poor Jason, in his normal panic, thought he heard a chopper circling overhead, or nearby, and imagined the entire place damn near surrounded.

Madrid kept his spot at the door, though now his concentration was rather focused on the hostess, who returned the look.

"You a cowboy?" she asked.

"What makes you say that?" Madrid responded.

"Nice boots."

Madrid left his post to chat more intimately. It wasn't the time or place to be talking loud across a distance of twenty odd feet.

"What's your name, darlin?" Madrid gobbled up the sweet young thing with his big dark eyes, tucking in a nibble or two of wrinkled shirt beneath his silver-studded belt buckle.

"You sure are a cowboy," the hostess commented almost ethnologically. "Nobody ever called me that one before. You a cop, too?"

"FBI. Used to ride broncos, though."

"Somehow those two professions don't deserve each other in my mind."

"What do you mean?"

"I don't know. They don't flow. There's something missing in between."

"A few teeth, some broken bones, and the age of thirty."

She smiled. "You from Wyoming?"

"DC."

"What'd he do?" She looked over at her boss, Jason, who was seated in a corner talking to the other FBI man.

"Nothing. We're just looking for the owner of that make of car."

She'd already been showed the photograph by Jerrasi, which led to her calling Jason from the back in the first place.

"What did the owner of that car do?"

"That's what we're trying to find out."

"Then how do you know he did anything at all, if you don't already know?"

"That's what we're trying to find out."

"You already said that."

"I know." He grinned.

She twisted her head with an ironic look of 'you a misogynist, or just stupid, or are you really as Wyoming as all that?' – smiling, finally, at the realization that the FBI's the FBI and nobody should expect more than that from them.

"I wouldn't guess it had anything to do with unpaid parking tickets? You being FBI and all."

"I wouldn't think so."

" 'Cause I've got one or two and I'll tell you something right now – you might have figured this out already about California girls, or maybe not: but if anybody is gonna arrest me, I sure hope it's you!"

"What a neat thing to say," Madrid carried on.

"Neat ..." She chuckled. "That's alright. I can see you're married. Otherwise, I might not be so bold."

"Me neither," he said, admiring her brilliant long black hair, defiant sneer, gossamer white skin, a twisted nose that added appreciably to her sexiness. She turned to do something and he noted with all the observing powers of the FBI, her shapely buttocks, like you see on those Grecian urns, set spectacularly beneath her tight denims and Balinese blouse, with its green splashes of verdure, hand-painted. She turned back around and smiled at him. Her azure bright eyes gave loft to the entire room.

"You're the sole owner here?" Jerrasi asked Jason with a routine edge, taking down details in a small, metal-covered three-by-five note pad. His pen had Holiday Inn written on it.

"Yes," Jason stammered.

"That's a yes, is it? Merely routine, mind you. If I don't make up at least one or two questions, my younger partner over there'd think I'm slipping in my old age, and he'd just love to become the big cheese, higher salary, that sort of thing."

Jason counted the seconds, while counting his options, while puzzling through the hot fire of reckoning, each word out of Jerrasi's mouth, giving him an added word of stalling time, but the concentration on the word did not help him one bit in the formulation of a plan, a strategy, a response. *Lie. Don't lie. Lie. It's routine. He just said so. They could ask half a dozen employees who'd know. Who'd know his name. But they won't. They have no reason to ask. They'll be outta here, forever. Don't stumble on an insignificant detail, don't do it, Jason.*

"Yes. No. What was the question?"

"I asked you if you were the sole owner?"

Now Jerrasi put down his note pad, not wanting to further upset the young man. He, too, looked puzzled, awaiting a response to a straightforward query.

"Yes. Oh sure, there's some outside investors, that's what I was thinking about. But I'm the one who's here each day, nearly, keeping it afloat. Restaurants are not easy businesses, especially vegetarian ones."

"Oh, why's that?"

"You know."

"I do?"

"Most people aren't in to vegetarian cuisine."

"I know I'm not. But California's famous for it, isn't it?"

"I suppose so."

"In fact, isn't it *tres chic* in these parts?"

"Some might think so. Our menu's fairly sophisticated."

"Mind if I– "

"No." Jason handed him a menu. It was bamboo paper, handwritten calligraphic style choices (Iyura's stamp).

"But there's no prices?"

"That's right. We think it's offensive to put a price tag on nature."

"Well ain't that a kicker. It's got charm. A little contrived. But I like it.

But how do you know what to order, if you're not one of those tres chic types with lots of money?"

"That's easy." He pointed to a sign over the door, where Madrid had been standing.

PAY WHATEVER YOU THINK HEALTHY, CRUELTY-FREE FOOD
IS WORTH!

"Oh you gotta be kidding?" Jerrasi laughed with a scornful East Coast disbelief.

"I'm not kidding. Since there's no meat or fish or any of those high cost consumables, we've got a secure safety net, in terms of not over-extending ourselves on the foodstocks. A steady clientele, superb reputation, if I might say so. Low cooking and service costs."

"Pretty daring, I'd say. You make a good living, do you?"

"It's all relative." *Why is he asking me this? What if my brother – don't think his name, he'll detect the thinking – but what if he has been doing something wrong with the books. Yes! That must be it! My god, he's been holding back taxes to cover his expenses. Those expenses ... But I looked over the taxes. But if he's seen the tax forms, then he knows I'm telling the truth, it's only me. Of course! Oh, if I hadn't have had the presence of mind, the calm expertise under fire, if I had slipped a 'No' instead of a 'Yes'! To catch my own self, when it wouldn't have been necessary! How dreadful. But that's exactly what people probably do in my shoes ...*

"How much, if you don't mind my asking? I only wonder, see, because in the FBI, well, frankly, the salaries suck. I'd just be curious what a decent person like yourself could make by leaving the payment up to people. Understand that in my line of work, people are not predictable, no sir. Not one iota. And they tend to be utterly self-interested, stingy is what I mean."

"I'll bet that's true."

"So, how much?"

"Well, net, or gross?"

"Gross. I don't mean to pry."

Jason calculated in his head for a second. "We probably did two million last year."

It sounded desperately evil to Jason just then. That kind of money. Jerrasi whistled. "J-e-s-u-S!"

And the whistle furthered Jason's sense of isolation, wrongdoing, before a civil servant who *so* obviously felt twinges of ... *of what*?

"But keep in mind that's before costs, overhead, taxes, all that."

"Of course. Still, lot of turn over."

"Not really. Not compared with the fast food chains or– " *I shouldn't have mentioned that. That was a mistake.*

"Anyway, I've kept you. A busy man like you. Making that kind of money."

"Most of it doesn't go to me– "

"Oh, I know it doesn't. Here's my card. If you should happen to see or hear of anyone driving an Aston-Martin, you will call me?"

"Certainly. Certainly, officer." He was holding back the shaking in his hands. Or he thought they were shaking. Maybe they weren't. Maybe it was all a head trip, from the very beginning.

Jerrasi got up and started towards the cosy twosome that had developed at the hostess' stand, when he turned back to Jason, something on his mind.

"There was one other thing. You, uh, don't know of anybody who might drive such a car, and might also be affiliated with the principles espoused on that sign there?"

"What sort of person?" Jason, nearly off his guard, was thrown back into the whirlwind. *Why, why is he asking that? What does he suspect? I already told him I don't know anybody who drives my brother's car, shit, don't even think the fucking name–*

"A fanatical sort. The kind of person who might take that 'cruelty-free' business, or that 'healthy' business to heart. And commit a crime."

"No. I really don't. Like I said, I've never even seen that kind of car. And the only people who come in here, well, they're very decent types."

"And I wasn't suggesting that they weren't. Just thought you might think of someone, somebody in particular, who– " he put up a hand as if to contemplate physically the exception to the rule, for Jerrasi, in truth, had a hunch, and the hunch was taunting him with scratch, with nada, mocking the possibility that had now, on two occasions, and merely miles apart, slipped right out of his fingers, " –who might have confided in you, or someone you know."

"Confided what?"

"I don't know. That's what we're trying to find out."

"Well if I hear of anyone like that– "

"Good. That's swell. FBI'll appreciate anything you can tell us. And I don't suppose you mind our talking to all of your employees? In case somebody saw that car?"

"No. Of course not. And I'll ask around all the vegetarian restaurants – we have an association, you know – and let'um know that the FBI is looking for this person."

Jerrasi did not respond to the suggestion.

"How many people do you employ?"

'Well, let's see, counting the part-time, and the ones in parking, I'd say, well there's four in the back and– "

Madrid stepped up to Jerrasi with his hand phone extended. "It's Baggot."

"Robert, the office says you just got a call from Florida. Here's the number." Jerrasi didn't have to write it down.

"Give me a few minutes," Jerrasi said to Madrid. Jason was left calculating his employee count, attempting to fathom a hidden significance in each face. The car? Who has seen it?

When Jerrasi returned the call, to Tarpon Springs, it was to learn from a Minister who was at the time conversing most sympathetically with others in a brightly-lit living room, that Jerrasi's mother had died earlier that morning of a stroke.

"You must be that one with the chin she always spoke of in her last years," the man of God exclaimed. "My! How she doted on you. I feel as if I know you."

"Did she suffer?" he asked, not with any suggested grief.

"No, I don't reckon so. She pretty much made tracks ... just tore up that road."

There was a certain embarrassment in her death, which Jerrasi had not counted on. The California foray had so far proven disastrous, he even sensed himself falling into wish-fulfilment, blurring the dismal truth – Kinesey would be watching all – and now he'd have to go to Florida for the funeral, wasting valuable time. Losing the scent. He burned inside. Perhaps it was meant this way; Jerrasi's excuse for escaping failure.

"An eyewitness, she even talked with him; tyre tracks, three accounts of the probable vehicle, we're in his territory, people are possibly lying on his behalf – and still nothing!" Madrid aired, beside Jerrasi, on their way out the restaurant door. They would leave stakeouts at both the Amidha Center and Ralph's, as well as dispatching tails on the Sensei and Jason Felham, just to be sure. But all of ten minutes had revealed that none of the other employees knew anything about an Aston-Martin.

"See if you can give it a week," Jerrasi asked Baggot, knowing there were costs. Madrid, who would stay in the city a few more days, drove Jerrasi back to the SF airport.

"We're nowhere," Jerrasi sighed, weighed down by the conflicting news of his mother, and the realization that investigative work was shot through with a kind of unaccountable amateurism. "We can find a computer part in eight hundred square miles of Scotland, and trace it to two Libyan creeps, and we can't find this piece'a squirrel shit when he's right under our nose."

"We'll find him." Madrid's heart wasn't really convinced, however. It was true that after eight years they were closer than ever. But it was as if my brother were watching them all along, toying with them – as with the mules. He was in charge. And furthermore, this was essentially Jerrasi's cross to bear. Madrid had been brought in without the same level of motivation. Of course, he'd like to see them brought to justice, drawn and quartered, fed to jackals. He had his own idea of who they were and felt the powerful impulses associated with winning, staring in their eyes, seeing them in chains, spitting in the air. Just the supreme pleasure of saying to his face, "I'm gonna watch you *fry*, motherfucker!"

But he also knew an obsession that had virtually taken a good investigator out of active duty. Jerrasi was good for nothing else. In a sense, though still young and vital, *The Animal* was Jerrasi's retirement. Sort of like fishing in New Zealand. Shelley Pendergras, and half a dozen others, had been forced into that same morbid hallucination with him. Now, granted, the FBI wanted the case resolved. But there were other cases, too few investigators, a stretched department. Shelley had recently figured that the taxpayer had contributed several million dollars to the eight-year investigation and so far there was nothing, absolutely nothing, to show for it. The game was boring.

Madrid was frustrated. *The Animal* represented something like a Nobel Prize. But there were so many other more accessible trophies and Pulitzers out there – the Jeffrey L. Dahmer-types; killers, rapists, bank robbers, every imaginable fraud for the picking. He wanted to track down foreign terrorists – would love to get his hands on a Middle Eastern swarthy sucker, twist him down like a roped steer and make him eat his own shit – but instead, he was condemned to following Jerrasi, whose *reactionary* temperament turned him off. Madrid knew himself to be relatively liberal. He was one of the few men in his agency who had voted repeatedly for Clinton. He instinctively hated Republicans, *despised* them's a better word. He suspected all rich people of butt-fucking little boys. That's because he caught one, once, at a country club. He wanted more wilderness areas, an end to oil wells; tarmac banned from National Parks, chlorofluorocarbons curtailed in the upper atmosphere, and barbed wire forbidden; he even felt outrage at rancher friends who took it as their right to go off shooting wolves and coyotes and grizzly bears. Madrid never said so to Jerrasi, but, in truth, he felt a twinge uneasy about *The Animal*. Maybe he even went in mental circles on the subject, preferring to let Jerrasi take the lead. Perhaps he even looked with some anticipation at the next outbreak of violence.

Jerrasi caught the first plane out to Tampa/St. Pete. Madrid checked in at the Kyoto Inn, and called that hostess over at Ralph's, to see about getting together for dinner. Madrid was married, but he didn't see that as a sufficient reason to prevent his enjoying some pretty dinner conversation. Cowboys had genetic license, he always figured; so at least he should be permitted to enjoy the scent of a new perfume on a young bosom, and the secret juice of untamed eyes and restless thighs beside him, at a dinner table in North Beach.

Done. She was as game as a hot chocolate sauce confronted a la mode.

"Did my boss tell you about his brother?" she asked.

"No, why?" Madrid said, coolly.

He had been describing some of the grosser times of his rodeo days, growing up in the wild west, twenty-foot snow storms in Montana in the fifties and what they did for fun in Billings on Saturday nights. "He's also into the outdoors, I imagine," she went on. "Doesn't say much, but my impression is, he spends a lot of time around animals."

"What makes you think so?" Madrid queried, scooping up his portion of a Caesar salad.

"I've smelled it on him."

"I hear that. I've stepped in my share."

She grinned. "I grew up around animals, sort of."

"How's that?"

"My father was a zoo technician in upper New York. Dietary adviser. I came to know dozens of little beasties by the stink he took away with him. There are certain odours you can't just shower off. I've smelled big cats on that man. Also ungulates."

"You ever ask him about it?"

"Yeah, once. He said it was a German cologne, and that sort of ended the conversation." She shook her head. "If he didn't own a vegetarian restaurant, one might think that he was into some kind of no good."

"What's his name?"

"Dirk's his first name. Nobody calls him that, though. Jason just calls him Felham. We all do. He's not there but a few days a month."

"You're sure he owns the place?"

"No. I just always figured. The two of them are brothers. I mean they're both the boss as far as I'm concerned, if I screw up, that is, though Jason's the one who really knows what's going on. I think it's more of a hobby for the other one."

"But you don't happen to remember what kind of car this Felham drives?"

"I never saw him outside. Are you investigating him?"

"Maybe. That's strictly confidential. You understand?"

"Right." She took a sip of her Swiss Altima pear juice. "I will say this, he's rather mysterious. Keeps to himself, that is. Doesn't hardly talk to anyone. But when he does, it's very sweet and decent. Never seems nervous. Just a real regular guy. Probably rich. Probably been around, too."

"How old is he?"

"I'd say he's in his late thirties, early forties. Probably felt some pain. You can tell that about some men."

Madrid's brain raced with the implications as he took a fuller description, solicited casually. He did not want a mere breakthrough to interfere with other priorities and pheromones. But it was clear that this Dirk fellow met the description of the suspect in Los Angeles in nearly every way. Though he wasn't black.

He excused himself to use the men's room and, from there, placed two calls on his portable phone, one to Baggot, and one to Shelley Pendergras.

Suddenly, the game had picked up. Just like that. And it was his ace, not old Jerrasi's. He'd be pissed.

Jessie was prepared to drop Felham off at the Huntingdon, where he had opted to stay. But their conversation evened out by the time they'd reached Lombard and Van Ness, so that he had volunteered coming to her office, and she'd agreed. Their dance must have been preordained. Vulnerability forms its own cult by natural laws as specific as watering holes. He'd spoken on her car phone to Muppet, unabashedly, because he had already decided to let her in, at least part way. By the time they reached the birthing clinic, where two births were expected that evening, he'd confided in her, wanting to kiss her, to hold her, contradicting the unfeeling austerity of years with what was, though he wasn't about to admit it to himself, a premonition of the end. She played some abstruse part in his deliverance. There was virginity in their haste and bravado and desperation, all in the course of a five mile traffic-ridden itinerary, eyes dredging for truth, trust toying with peril, peril with trust.

In the excitement, both felt the bone marrow, a bond of panic, the need to confess something, the fact that only one other human being can provide such comfort, at the exquisite moment of his or her nakedness. *Stay with me forever, don't let go of me. Please believe me. Love me. Guide me. You are my salvation. My dread. My nipple. My man. Forgive me ...* Emotional eternities compressed into a practical cause and effect.

He unloaded what was needing to be told. "They killed the jaguar. I'd rescued her from previous poachers. They skinned it, probably alive, then roasted its flesh. They certainly didn't need the food. Even if they did ... "

"What did you do?" Jessie asked.

"I killed them."

"You murdered men?"

"Yes. They were operating a poaching ring in the jungle. Killing hundreds, thousands of animals. No one was about to stop them. No one even knew. Do you know what it means to nab a large parrot from its flock, to hunt down a jaguar, or steal baby anteaters from their mother?"

"I don't want to know. You killed men?"

He remembered the harpy eagle gliding elegantly above the primordial trellis of liana. Giant otters patrolling their riverine kingdoms, while anacondas slept away the dripping hours in the original branches of creation. Immense turtles would throw themselves in and out of the shadows, as every imaginable fish darted luminescent through the hundreds of hidden tributaries. More species of fish in the Amazon River than in the entire Atlantic. He had seen white-lipped peccaries foraging along the seeping varzea forest floor in search of fruit, whole communities working together, soft, silent, cooing creatures, that had been at perfect biological peace in their garden, for millions of years; munching on the acai, the tucuma and orange caja. Delicacies that just grew without the slightest prompting. Evolutionary shades, humidity, green. Felham had luxuriated in that Eden, for a time.

But that was before the *Seringalistas* and *caboclo* – appropriators, venders, descendents of the Portuguese *conquistadores* – coveted that paradise, going after the so-called 'resources', like manatee, and jaguar skins, and the *seringal* or rubber-producing regions. Burning their calling cards into the world's environmental movement, giving definition to the concept of endangered species. The very corporation whose chief executives Felham had unwittingly agreed to protect.

How could he explain those feelings to her, or the schism wreaked in his heart at that moment of turbulent horror; of that late night, in the rain and mud, surrounded by ignorant hatred, and the charred ruins of magnificent creatures that hung pitifully by their hooves and necks, from crude gallows fashioned in the haste of avarice, in the secrecy of evil?

When he forced his way beyond the tent and recognized the remains of his own pet, blackened, crisped, that had become one more nauseating victim of the same greed which was wiping out not just hundreds, not just thousands, but tens-of-millions of animals in the Amazon.

She only heard that he'd killed men. Which was so typical, he thought.

"They were not men. They were butchers."

"And the police?"

"They're still after me, twenty years later. Enough sirens in my sleep to make a philharmonic of pursuit."

"My god. That's what's going on?"

"Yes."

"Which makes me an accomplice?"

"Not yet. That's up to you. I don't mean– "

"Don't say another word."

Nor could he say another word. He had not intended to tell her as much as he had. He certainly was not prepared to tell her the rest. That the jaguar was only the beginning. That he had spent twenty years trying to bring that poor innocent beauty, Coocoo, back to life.

She was thinking on her feet, parking in the back, entering the office with one hand to her heart, which she could hear beating. *We're being watched* she feared. Gunsights were narrowing down on her every footstep. She moved, frozen inside. Alive to possibilities. She could claim that he'd kidnapped her, made her drive him away. Would he deny it? Did he carry a gun? Would he use it? As repellent as these notions were, assailing her one by one, each image also held out the prospect of a frenzied, passionate love affair, the best time of her life, love, rendered more and more agonized by each increasingly inconceivable pitfall.

"How are they?" she said, managing somehow to greet her two assistants, one of whom had seen and remembered the gentleman beside her and nodded affably.

"They're both close," Jessie was informed.

"I'll be back," Jessie advised Felham. "I've got to check on the women." She never used the term 'patient'.

Felham went and sat on a couch in Jessie's office, away from the activities. He was feeling the slack in his muscles for not having worked out for two days and set about to do a few hundred pushups and situps on her floor. He normally did a thousand of each, everyday.

Marsha's legs were wide apart, the midwife's hands grappling for the newborn, when Jessie thought she heard the cries of a baby jaguar.

Blood. Fluids. The woman was having a difficult time of it but had steadfastly refused a doctor to be present. "I'll be fine, I'll be fine, oh God ..." she kept vowing, like a mantra, animal injunctions from her heaving depths, arms and hands all around her, assisting the arrival of the unfathomable seed, mythic journeyer from her gut – whatever you want to call it – which cramped down and twisted so that her insides felt iron and lead and freedom-less; the pain pushing her into explosive corners of the room, a body she did not know, hated, would have rebuked if only possible.

Jessie watched, cringing with the fear of forces moving in. That might check her own impulses to go all the way with him, into flight, exile, whatever was required.

But the agony subsided at once, with the emergence of a perfect replica, the woman's own, creation ad infinitum, closed eyes, scrunched-up cries subsiding as her breast was given to its pursed and purple lips. As helpless as a newborn jaguar, Jessie again registered.

Over four hundred born at her centre. She had been the one to make it feasible, to push for grants, investors, to enhance the climate for natural childbirth in the Bay Area, to the extent that even the hospitals now boasted of homelike surroundings for a more natural birthing experience. Whereas before, everything was dulled to the point of non-sensation. To get it over with, quickly, efficiently, painlessly. To feel nothing. The woman was, for her brief duration in the conventional delivery room, a birth canal that groaned and squirrelled and had to be injected and put out of its misery.

Jessie admired the infant, whose Jack Frost skull of fuzz and cobalt blue eyes, semiquavering grovels after milk, dust-like avoirdupois, softly gloaming, gave her a chill. Potent proximity. A man in her office. A killer. That she was falling for. A child she always wanted. The contraries of the moment closing in with so unexpected a force as to sit her down, where she stared, smiling, at the happy mother.

"Good work, Marsha," Jessie and her colleagues congratulated her, whooping it up with merriment. "You did great."

"I did, didn't I?" she beamed, bewildered and wan.

There was a second mother, Jenina, Haitian, a dancer, in perfect shape, down the hall. Some time this night, she too would deliver new life. The grammar was entangled in the febrile nature of a process that Jessie could not claim except as surrogate manager; onlooker for nearly a decade. Maybe that realization was the very frenzy now pounding in her heart. Or was it him? She walked down the hall, hearing a new round of groans coming forth from Jenina's room.

Her own mother had nearly given up. Jessie, she vowed, had another mission, and it was to care for the remainder of the world. Why that should preclude her having her own was one of God's mysteries which Mrs. Moran was not eager, or even entitled, to call into question. She accepted it. If God had a plan, so be it. So be Jessie. Yet her mother never stopped wondering, passively suggesting, then insinuating.

Then passively aggressively.

Then just plain aggressively, when father wasn't standing right there, usually, at the phone. Never run an Irishman's patience too thin ... *When the heck are you gonna settle down and make a baby, you stubborn girl?*

"I'm a failure if I don't make a baby, even if it's with a man I don't love, is that it?" Jessie had tossed back at her too many times.

"A baby'll bring love."

"No, Mom. It doesn't work that way."

"It did with me and your father. Your sister– "

"I don't want to hear. You're not dependent on your children, Mom."

"Family is important."

"Yes, I know. I know."

"How difficult would it be to get pregnant? Maybe you're not able? There are doctors– "

They'd had the conversation a hundred times. Always, the phone calling, and a less than perfect marriage, confounded her mother's incessant will-to-grandchildren, which had become her salvation, from about the age of fifty-five. And that was odd considering her utter lack of patience. While her parents always fantasized about taking care of the grandchildren, they had shown little interest in ever baby-sitting their own six nieces and nephews, hated the noise, hated the utter chaos of Aunt Molly's kids in Ithaca; the house, the pets, the constant shouting, all the talk and obsession with offspring. Yet that's all they could think to address, in Jessie's case. That without such chaos she was nothing, ruined. Every family on earth, the same rude wonderful skewing of genetical argument and demand.

And yet, however one might attempt to ignore it, the heart of that universal plaint was as true as the day it began. Her parents stabbed her with their simple, feeble cry for immortality. To have their name, their strong jaws, jacamar green eyes, claret-coloured skin and particle-red hair carry on; patience or no patience, the line, the matrilineal descent of highland clan and two hundred years of Dublin, and more recently of Idahoan lineage. What a contradiction, her parentage, fighters and pacifists in the same bed. Lucky for Mom, she was the fighter. More painful to Jessie was her knowledge that it was not even the immortality that mattered. *What would we have if not you and your sister?* Mom would say, and Dad would nod. Brenda was younger, also single, studying architecture. *We just don't want you to be lonely when you're our age. I can't bear the thought of you not having the same joy in a child that you've given to us.* Jessie would hurt. And Mom would cap off with, *You're such a great kid. You deserve such happiness.*

Well, there was no disputing THAT. Which tended to nullify Jessie's best defences. There was no other focus in her relation with her parents now. They always claimed that she was defensive on the subject of her own pregnancy, projecting unfulfilled longings on others. Of course she was defensive, with the two of them always leaping into the discussion of fertility pills, singles' bars, even some Chinese quack in Boise who prescribed a teaspoon of Robitussin daily. Said it opened up the vagina, made everything more receptive in there. Terrible thing was, every woman in that clinic got pregnant. Which just went to validate, in Jessie's parents' minds, their wisdom and claim against their daughter.

Jessie thought about her trip to visit Mom's ancestral roots in Dublin. About their nights in the pubs, where Mom could consume three pints of stout, pulled just like the Dubliners know best, and attract men like fleas to her daughter. The conviviality of stout. That's what she was thinking, when Felham stepped in the door, out-of-breath.

There were enormous cries echoing now.

"Congratulations!" he said.

Jessie held out a towel to Jenina, standing beside a midwife, her thoughts rearing away from Mulligan's, a pub in Dublin where Joyce used to sit and write his *Ulysses*, and where her own mother first got uproariously drunk.

The baby was silenced against the Haitian woman's breast.

"I really need to tell you something," Felham said to Jessie. Jessie had utterly lost track of time. She'd been with the two women for nearly an hour.

"Excuse me ..." Jenina was in good hands. Jessie and Felham returned to her office.

"You're the first woman I've had dinner with – I mean almost dinner – in many years. You wouldn't know that, or necessarily believe it, or ever think anything of it, but it's true. And to me it was rather, well, important."

"We didn't eat anything."

"We will, I hope."

"Will what, eat dinner?"

He paused, biting his thumb. He never bit his thumb, he reflected.

"Like I said, I'm on the run."

"You confided in me for a reason. Why?"

She still did not know how to address him, given that concept. She thought: *You didn't act like a man on the run sitting there leisurely in your own restaurant: your own employees knowing you. I didn't see sweat building up along the temples, or a cloud hovering over your brow.* The reality of it had still not reached her, not really.

"It's complicated. I've led a double life, until now."

"Why now?"

"They're on to me."

"After twenty years? This very day. Just as I'm walking away from your restaurant?"

"There's more to it than one jaguar."

She studied him very carefully. Then, "How much more?"

"Much."

She considered her move, touching a cuticle. "What do you want from me?"

He wanted everything, wanted nothing. He wanted to breathe freely and easily, like other men, men that could comfortably court a woman such as Jessie without hell stalking their every move, condemning every hope.

"Take me to a hotel, drop me off, and never say a word to anyone about me. You never met me. You never heard of me." Those were the words he said, almost as if to torture himself. Because what he said to himself, *Stay the night with me, make love to me, put digitalis in my coffee,* were choked back.

"Why should I bother, if that's all– " sincere frustration, even scorn, animating her casuistry.

And still he abused himself by stating the opposite. "Don't bother. I'll get a taxi." He was coming back to the reality. Had he been merely using her? If she had not happened to show up at the restaurant when she did, would he have gone to her? He would have gotten away, but would he have pursued Jessie?

Yes.

He must have said something out loud, words from the silent opposition inside him, which his very thinking had drowned out, leaving him stranded, not knowing.

Maybe he said that he'd been thinking about nothing but her, since that evening together, that he had wanted to call, wanted to be near her. Or perhaps he simply stated the obvious, that she was incredibly beautiful, that he was probably falling in love with her, just like that. Whatever it was that he said ...

Suddenly, he heard her say, "Stay with me."

And they stared terribly at one another, beholden to enchantment. She noticed his lips tremble. They were dry, and he feared to wet them.

She came to him on the couch. She sat down. She threw her arms around him. He buried his head.

She cried.

Muppet finished his dinner, then placed a call to his favourite sibling, the little one with flaxen locks, who always needed his special protection from the local older boys. It had been over a year since he'd called. She was the only one in his family to whom he felt compelled – not so much to say goodbye, but to favour a hello. That was life.

"Clio? It's me."

"Mup?"

Amish quilts. Her knees straddling his opening hips. *We are so naked beneath the stars* she realized. *The wind picking up countless leaves and hurtling them through the dark neighbourhood beyond. Does he love me? Does it matter?* The cries of two newborns in her ears ...

HIPPOCRATIC OATHS

habemus confitentem reum – *we have before us an*
accused person who pleads guilty

a malas lenguas, tijeras – *for evil tongues, scissors*

Once the motive is sound and the will in place, then the act of killing is hardly physical at all, he'd explained to her, sometime after making love. Or that's the ideal, he thought to himself, considering Earth, air, fire and water, birth and death, this ceaseless stream of embodiment and disembodiment, love and hate, words countering other words.

The scars, the pleasure-giving thickness of his ambling fingers, all took on new import in Jessie's mind, diagonalling across the bed where she lay in listless suspension, incapable of moving out of the way of his verbal expiations.

"How many have there been?" she inquired, unable after a night together to put the man beside the murders.

"I don't know. Quite a few."

"How many would you guess?" Her query had no basis in a real desire to know. Her repulsion at the idea of murder, of violence, was incompatible with the pleasures that this man had unleashed in her body. Incompatible with everything decent people like her were universally devoted to, took for granted, understood from the basis of their being. She expected no answer, or none that could mean anything. It was simply scared incredulity speaking.

"No idea." He was not about to tell her of the five thousand evil bastards in the world. That was his good breeding, or chivalry.

"How can you not know something like that?"

"You want vivid details? Why talk about it?" He still held the glowing candle in his palms, a George de la Tour of waning happiness, nurturing whatever attenuated light was left between them. Rare and privileged.

"What else is there to talk about? If you've really killed someone, what life, I mean how can you, how can you expect–" she turned away, enthralled, outraged, disappointment verging on its own fatality. "How can you go on? Or expect another person to stand by you, near you, to touch you?"

"You just have."

"I don't know what I did." She turned away. "You murdered somebody, more than one?"

"It's done in war all the time."

"You're not in a war."

"It's all in the point of view."

"Are you prepared to tell that to the jury?"

"There'll be no jury."

"No. I suppose you plan to die on the battlefield?"

"Maybe."

"You're crazy." She threw on her bathrobe and went to pee, closing the door behind her.

What am I doing? her mind whispered, staring in the mirror. *I'm afraid. I'm really afraid.* He was no terrorist from a refugee camp. No volatile or repressed sadist; there was nothing about his manner to indicate a mild-mannered psychopath. Not that she had ever met, or knew anything remotely about such people. But she had a sense and it did not convey in the slightest a man who would kill people. It was simply not credible. On the other hand, she thought, why would he say he had, if he hadn't? To sabotage a passion? Pretty stupid; and he was not stupid. Were those policemen at the restaurant? Or had he invented them, too? She readily admitted to herself that a lot of people, intelligent men and women, committed suicide, every day.

And if his story was true, or what she'd heard of it, then *he* was committing suicide. *I'm not worried about getting away so much as getting in, doing the deed, avenging the unspeakable wrongdoings* he'd told her. But it did not ring of truth, of human behavioural truth. She'd seen no police cars, no guns, nothing to indicate that Felham wasn't suffering from some bizarre persecution complex. A sense of vainglorious importance, and corresponding paranoia. She just didn't know. She'd made love to a mystery and he was there, in the other room, lying naked on her bed. There was a phone adjoining her toilet. She stared at it, and her mother's number riddled her head. Then her hairdresser's, Torrance Bader, a sculpted, bald New Yorker, shimmying fingers, who'd worked on the best heads in show business and who proffered a smile that would comfort any woman trapped in her bathroom. The world was going to be all right, he'd tell her, yet it was not enough to keep her from sudden and overwhelming nausea. That the one man she had slept with in over a year, that might have interested her, really stirred her insides, should be one of two things, an outlaw, or totally insane. She didn't know which was preferable. He carried no gun.

No knife. Would such a man design to hold her hostage? It would be so easy. 911. Three digits. *Call, Jessie! Call for help, you idiot!*

"You're really one warped human being," she cried out, returning to the bedroom. Then she threw her hair brush in his general direction, more dead on than she expected.

He dodged the object with an understanding compliance, and nothing that he could say, exactly, in defence of himself.

"Why did we have to ever meet?" she questioned with a near sob of futile anguish.

"I don't know."

"You don't know. You don't know. You don't know anything. Of all the days for me to go to that one Gymboree. Stupid imbecilic fate!"

"I'll leave. This was a bad idea." Felham rolled over and began scooting into his pants. He was stinging inside.

"There was no idea," she spat, bleary eyed, "bad or good. It just happened. One night. That's all, it's finished. Just as well," she continued, wanting to at least resurrect something of the experience they'd shared, but fronting a sounding board for its cancellation, less by way of strategy than hurt. The pang of no obvious solution. Analogies brimming in her. Every criminal. The world's woes. The bad timing of it all. Throw in some homeless, all those rare diseases common to babies – she'd seen a few – and maybe the Congo or Somalia. Just her luck, all right. No centre had ever held, no record of their having ever kissed. No romantic handwritten letters. No hope. She was utterly stymied by her situation.

"Really," he asked, doubting her embittered veneer.

"Really," she said almost snidely, courting ruination because there seemed, just then, in the anger and futility of the moment, to be no other way.

"Yeah. Okay." He was as desolate. "Then I'll be seeing you. I'm sorry for this." It was as if there were a bomb in the room.

She looked at him and felt only desire. Impossible, heaven-help-me estrus.

"And where will you go? Where can you go?" she inquired, noncommittal but frantic that he might actually leave.

"I don't think you want to know."

"But I do know. The world is not an option for you." Did she think that would grab him? Give him to understand that he ought to reconsider walking out that door? She felt utterly helpless.

"What a generous way of putting it."

"You obviously believe in capital punishment." The frank facts, the implications, she reckoned.

"Is that a question?"

"It is a fitting subject for reflection."

"I can see it really hurts you to contemplate– "

"Felham." After their evening together she was comfortable addressing him by his last name. Perhaps it was an inherently necessary disassociation from the real person, or drift in that direction, her protection. "What do you expect?"

"I don't expect anything from you. I'm grateful for this one night."

"That's just dandy. Well it's not, not for me. I'm not some– " she stopped herself. Then, " –me too. I'm sorry about just now." *Tell him the truth, girl!* her insides beckoned. "Do you have any idea how many men I have turned my back on? The restraint, oh shit, call it dignity – 'cause that's what it was, that's exactly how I intended it to be, my life, my beliefs, what do you think I'm doing bringing babies into this world? I have got to have something– " and he heard a fragmented pleading in her spin on the word, and it plummeted to his innermost heart. She put her head towards his side, yearning to impede the action of his exodus. "I really like you. It's not possible, not in a sane world; but this is not a sane world. Please ..." and she trailed off, utterly confounded, going nowhere. Not having a clue what to do. "I'm also deeply sorry." She didn't even know for what, exactly.

They both remained quiet for a while. He walked back to the bed and they touched restrainedly, held back by the intrusion of obvious impediments to any talked-about future. Until finally, she countered the sombre mood: "Will I ever see you again?" It was the feeble fighting back in her, against mammoth odds, Felham's weight, an unwillingness to declare its intentions, the ghastly implacable image of the man beside her.

"I hope so."

"Do you really?"

"Yes."

"But what's it supposed to mean? What possible meaning can it have?" She realized just how she was grasping, and re-grasping, at his words.

"Only my feelings. I can't tell you that everything outside those feelings, the world around us, is not going to change, or is likely to pardon what I've done, and what I must do. But now, here, HERE– " he placed some fingers ever so gently to her cheek, " –that's real, that's what I feel, that's all there is."

"Why do you have to go?" she finally queried. "What do you still have to do?"

"Can't you fathom what I'm up against? You just said it. I have no options. Certainly not a girlfriend." He realized at once how stupid the word sounded. Girl friend. How teenage. What remorse must have motivated it. Beyond the remorse, tenderly rising, the pride and the need that a woman should understand him. That his efforts be appreciated by a feeling, thinking human being, other than Muppet. By a woman.

"I have certain duties," he concluded, not about to tell her. "Animals that will die horrible, horrible deaths if I don't intercede on their behalf."

"There are laws to protect them."

He didn't mean to get wound up. But it couldn't wait. "Jessie, there are laws to protect scientists. There are laws and tax loopholes to protect fast food chains. There are laws to protect zoos, and circuses, and the medical and fur and cosmetic industries. There are laws to safeguard ranchers, and farmers, and American agriculture. Laws that guarantee a continued supply of pets, of dead turkeys on Thanksgiving, and chicken and fish and meat, seven nights a week. Laws are for people. There are no laws to protect animals. And there never will be. Not in this or the next generation. Not as long as there are– " and he stopped himself, suddenly very depressed by his own outline of human destiny with its unanswerable conditional. He had meant to refer to guns and corrupted taste buds and bank accounts, thinking of the American, the Oriental, the European, the Middle Eastern, the Asiatic, the Latin American, the Scandinavian, the Australasian diet – had he left out anybody? Thinking of poachers, and animal products and medicine, of industry and real estate and machine culture usurping animal culture. But even that broad sphere of human invasiveness failed to encompass the syndrome.

"Not as long as there are what?" she pressed him, her hand gingerly scratching the back of his scalp.

"People," he blurted out finally.

"People can change laws." She mouthed the empty words without having any interest in them, and she knew it. So did Felham.

"You ever heard of a guy named Noam Chomsky?"

"The famous linguist." *A murderer is asking me about Chomsky* she thought.

"That's right. Something of a political maverick. Very savvy. Very radical,"

"Everybody's heard of him. So?"

"He once said something to the effect that by even entering into the whole realm of debate, of argument, pro and con and con and pro, details and tactics, feasibility and footnotes; by even acceding to the legitimacy of debate – that was the catch phrase he used, 'the legitimacy of debate' – one might already have lost his humanity. Well that's pretty much how I see it. You don't stand around the classroom, debating laws, when the whales are being slaughtered, right now, this very minute. Obviously people were social beasts before they were human beings. You've got to prove your humanity out there alone, apart from the blunt and huddled masses. One has to think for himself, independent of all that. Never take humanity for granted. People cannot be counted on to change laws, that's what I mean."

And their conversation drifted, like two lovers shipwrecked in the open sea ... "You've got it all worked out, haven't you?" she charged. "I think so," he returned. "No compromises?" "Hope not." "A real fatalist." "I love animals. That's all I'm saying."

They both appeared doomed.

She didn't know anything about this desperado, not really. Whatever he said, however penetrating, was more or less cancelled in her mind by the very tone of his voice, which left no elbow room, provided no cue for rebuttal. What was the point? He was as unflexing and self-sure as the notion of murder itself. How could she fathom his righteousness against the context of his alleged deeds, horrible, hideous deeds? There was no turning back. Whatever influence her feelings might have on him were personal matters, heartbeats the law would ignore. He'd go to the electric chair with a passion for one Jessie Moran flaring in his nostrils. Nobody would care. Why should they? Empathy? Would her commiserations return to her, by all that is popular and fabulist about the theory of karma? Or catapult him with greater odds into an after-life? Did the spirit count for anything any more? None of these academic pursuits, the product of a belaboured and hard-breathing self-pity, were worth a damn. He was leaving, he was condemned, she was infuriated to the point of that condition, temporary insanity, which has so left its imprint on the twentieth century, or that's how she interpreted it at that moment. Jessie was a veteran of that condition just then and whatever hopes and visitations she had experienced in the previous few hours were now about to stifle the dream of love with asphyxiating abruptness. No ephemera could be any more brutish and short and given to the psychosis of separation.

"We'll work it out." He meant that. It was ridiculous but he meant it. She had brought him back to a human temperature. The physical intimacy had given him, for a few hours, his old self again, with its andantes and respites. Though he did not see how the combination could work, not in America, at any rate. He was a dead man. He knew this in the bottom of his lungs, where most surety and faith respire, give vent, hold out against, or turn their face away, or simply collapse, like a collapsed lung. He held out, knowing there could be no you and me, no just-the-two-of-us; staring down at a distant untouchable horizon in her many-textured patinas, female form, innocence. At least he had seen it, had witnessed the greatest sunset in his life. He hated to do it to her; was tormented by everything the night had meant, because it could not last, whether he wanted it to or not. Simple. End of story. *I'm sorry*, he was thinking. *God, I am so sorry.* "I don't want it to end, not here, not anywhere, do you understand?"

She was thinking how easy it was to be brave with mere words, to appoint love to the highest court in the land and let it stand in judgment upon all other items of human experience. In her Sanhedrin universe, just then, she could well perpetuate their mutual desperation and nobody could touch it. Because it was pure and free and recognized by that highest truth. She brushed back her shoulder-length hair, that shone almost gold in the early morning hours, reflecting chips of magenta and russet off the stained glass oval, leaded and bevelled, that was the eastern window of her bedroom.

"You'll call," asked she, also ridiculous, but the motion, the asking, the sentiment, was so easy. She could not have been more depressed by the ambivalence of the moment. The penumbra of exile shadowed her curved figure, drama detailing every essence of pore, fingertip, eyelash, bone. It was so sour, fateful, as to be exciting. Wrenching. Everything she'd ever wanted. She had never been at an execution. Now she found herself dressing the prisoner. And now, one more time, she touched every part of the murderer's body, mouthing the person, receiving his ardour, exalting knowingly in the poison. It might have been a bedroom in Verona.

"I'll try," he replied, realizing, dreamily, as he left her sitting in her car at long-term parking – he did not think it was a good idea for her to take him all the way to curbside – that she was no sunset, no parting shot, but sunrise, the real thing. He knew she was not asking questions, or not yet, or not persistently, and that she would put up a fight, but that everything would be all right.

"It only costs twenty cents," she said.

She drove off, following one of those searing twofold countenances, the look of fate, of haggard supplication, that two people, banished from each other, one marooned, the other a sudden émigré in her own land, proverbially exchange on the gangplank of love. Fabled romances in wartime.

How much did he really tell me? she thought. *And what if... She'd used no diaphragm. And coincidentally, it had been sixteen days since her period.*

I don't care what I've done he remonstrated.

Felham never ordered vegetarian on airlines. Just one more caution. He picked clean some hash browns from the sausage and tried to sleep. He had planned to have returned to the farm so as to retrieve a document that Muppet had gotten his hand on, reading material for on board. Now it was just as well that he could doze. His nerves were aching.

Dulles was grey. Drizzling. Felham picked up his rental car, drove to the Hyatt, and checked in under the existing reservation for Striker. His first impulse upon lying down and flipping on the television, was to call her. He stopped short of the folly, noting that events could have escalated during the day.

They were on to Jason, whose wife observed an odd vehicle sitting catty-corner to their home on Fernwood Drive at six in the morning, when she was already up with Bart, who'd had a bad night. There were numerous cars parked along the side, but none with figures in them eating a sandwich. Iyura watched, then suddenly turned away when she saw the man put down his napkined meal, take up a pair of binoculars and study their house without the slightest compunction.

"My god, Jason. Wake up! There's someone spying on us," she said.

Jason stood erect alongside the fringe of the cement-hued Levellors, in their Japanese Bauhaus bedroom, peering past the crannied edge, confirming for himself. Now his head reeled. He groaned with an explosion of inner bedlam, bad dreams of the apocalypse.

"Who is it?" she insisted.

"They're looking for someone who works at Ralph's," he confessed, figuring out the connection easily enough, not knowing how else to say it.

"Who?" she enunciated with haphazard alarm, somehow relieved that it was not them the stranger was after. "Somebody part-time, a bit of a drifter. You don't know him. They probably think he'll come here looking for a pay cheque."

"A pay cheque?" She had always evidenced a heightened fear of authority in this country, which had gotten worse in many ways. Her perennial dread hit an all-time high just then.

"The fellow may be in a little trouble. There was a policeman asking me some questions yesterday at work."

"Why didn't you say something?"

"It's not our problem."

"And they think he's going to come here at six in the morning and they're going to catch him in our front yard, where everybody in the whole neighbourhood can see? I'd call that our problem. What did he do?"

For his part, Jason was burning up, aware of being implicated by a brother who was, at least theoretically, changing the world.

"Go out and ask him what he wants!" she decreed.

"Are you crazy?"

She started towards the door. "Then I'll do it." Jason grabbed her wrists.

"Don't. They'll think that maybe we're ..."

"We're what?"

"I don't know, facilitating ..." There was a pleading in his voice which Iyura took as a sign of serious trouble.

"It needn't involve us," Jason concluded.

"Jason, you're scaring me."

Iyura took Bart to her breast and sat down with a look of non-comprehending anger. "So how long is he going to sit out there?"

"I have no idea." Jason could tell that were he to divulge any more than he already had, she'd flip out. She had this unpredictable proclivity. Japanese temperament, given to mood swings both berzerk and sublime, concentrated like a readable haiku. In Iyura it might also turn to wrath. He had ample reason to suspect in her an utter inability to control the unknowable. Their arguments had always hinged upon his turning back from total confrontation, for fear of not exactly knowing how crazy she might become. Their marriage was held – if not precisely captive, then certainly on edge – by this difference in reactions to even small annoyances. Her excesses could be embarassing, her silences protracted; her lovemaking unabashed, solicitous and free, her dander slow burning, malicious, or given to epidemic and outbreak. For all of her PhD, Iyura was unbalanced. Jason had married a minor time bomb. These were mere personality quirks he could accept, nothing serious.

But Felham's secret, with which he'd been entrusted, was another matter. It threatened, somehow, the child. And Jason was not about to test the limits of Iyura's quirkiness on that score. He'd seen too many subtitled black and white films in which the faithful Japanese housewife took a knife and killed her husband, or avenged someone in exasperation, some Buddhist suppression of centuries suddenly released in the stream of woman, before taking her own life.

She picked up the phone and started to dial.

"What are you doing?"

"I'm calling my brother. He'll know what to do." Her brother the lawyer.

Jason grabbed the phone from her and set it back down. "I wouldn't do that. You call a lawyer and the police will know we're afraid."

"Are you saying they're tapping our phone?" Now she was greatly sobered.

"Anything's possible."

Robert Jerrasi did not expect the death of his mother to bring back any flood of pent-up memories. He was certain of his inoculation against such plebeian and self-destructive sentiments. But his malice towards that woman had mysteriously softened; it must have been the years, for he hadn't seen her in three, though he used to call her every couple of weeks, to the point where he found himself now playing the dutiful son, holding up decently amid well-wishers whom he did not know, and should not have had the slightest interest in. But he did. He schmoozed, wanting to find out everything. Did she talk about her deceased grandson, Tom? Did she ever mention how the boy died? There was a minister, the black man who'd first called him, and whom Jerrasi found surprisingly evocative at the burial, which starred two-dozen of his mother's bridge partners, and was filled with heartwarming Ay-mens and Hallelujahs.

"And the Lord Giveth, the Lord Taketh, but always the Lord Giveth Back ... a wink, a grimace, and another wink!"

The earth was soft and warm, crawling with ants. Fragments of beach grass, ferruginous and dusty. The wind buffeting the ceremony, sniffles, doilies, hot clouds foraging overhead. Jerrasi tossed a clod onto the casket.

Little sandwiches had been prepared by his mother's closest bridge-playing partners. Green olives, toothpicks, rather stale white bread cut up into miniature isosceles triangles, smeared with mayonnaise just this side, Jerrasi detected, of turning yellow, and covered with jots of ham and cheese and tomatoes. There was a cake, dolorous and bitter, meant to be unenjoyed, he supposed, for that's what it was, though the party talk was party-like, not a murmur about his Mom, really; but rather, the next day's game, mentholatum bandages, special heels, hurricane weather.

It hurt, he realized. It hurt that she should be so subsumed, so instantly snuffed out in the NOTHING of it all. No reminder. Not even any interest in himself.

He had details to work out concerning her estate that would take a day. No more. She had $17,000 in her money market, bringing her 4%. She'd been slipping way behind inflation. There would have been no way to cover extended hospitalization, or nurses, or a nursing home. She was lucky, Jerrasi contemplated, remembering times throughout her life, his legs propped up in bed, a football game on the tube.

The death was a relief. He felt only that the Lord had been merciful.

The minister and his wife came to call on Jerrasi in his hotel room unannounced. Jerrasi slipped into a shirt and put down his shot of brandy.

"I could see you were suffering, son, and all alone," the black man proclaimed at the door. It was room number 18. Three locks and a deadbolt. "My wife, Esther, made you a dessert I think you'll appreciate."

"Hello. I'm real sorry about your Momma. Here, try this." And she gave him a rich Devil's Food chocolate cake. "Home baked."

Jerrasi surprised even himself when he invited the couple in. He was a touch lonely, after all.

When Felham got out of the shower, Muppet was already in the room, watching the evening news. Felham asked about the truck.

Muppet pointed to the window. Felham lifted back the doubled-vinyl drape and glanced down at the large fifteen thousand pound vehicle that took up a whole line of spaces under the parking lights, in the shadows of over-hanging linden trees and rainy twilight. It was a Pac & Value produce truck, sixteen wheels, the kind that kept Americans supplied with heads of lettuce and bananas.

"Document's on the bed," he said. "It's not pretty. The fellow's definitely kindred. He's drawn up a whole diagram of the room numbers, hallways, given us a thread through the maze, including the way out down in the furnace room. It's all at the back. See you later."

"You trust him?"

"Read it. If you can't trust that, who can you trust?"

Muppet went out to finish some calls and last minute arrangements from a pay phone, and pick up some dinner for the two of them. Underground connections in Baltimore were to provide Felham and Muppet with an arsenal of plastic, undetectable weapons and explosives (the whole exterior of the building was wired like one massive magnetometer), very sophisticated incendiary devices, timers, electric wire clippers, an infrared deactivator, stuff bought in public auction from the Drug Enforcement Agency.

Felham stayed in the hotel room studying the report.

It was a meticulously documented diary, notes of a lab employee who had assisted numerous researchers for over a year at the Association of Biological Animal Research Units (ABARU) in Maryland. The material had never surfaced before. Muppet had been placed in contact with the fellow through a computer billboard on the EcoLog software. Calling up the 'Conferences' directory, unread files, long hand communiqués, 'General Anarchy' subject matter, they'd felt around each other very carefully until, through one mutual connection, they established mutual grounds. Muppet, remaining unidentified as he always did, had received a xerox of the twenty pages by overnight mail in care of a hotel in San Francisco, while Felham had been preoccupied in Los Angeles.

Posing as a graduate student, Muppet had then solicited an interview with one of the key academic chairpersons at the ABARU. Muppet knew that this man who figured so prominently in the diary, Q. Bernhardt was his name, was in charge of the committee on grants. Together with his colleagues, particularly one Dr. Claudius, Bernhardt dispensed more Federal money for animal research at hospitals, universities and the 129 medical schools throughout America, than was forthcoming from any other funding source in the world. He was the Fort Knox of misery, a man above judgment, of impeccable credentials, like all of his colleagues, a man of science, beyond good or evil (in his mind), beyond censure, a darling of the government, of big business and of big universities.

Bernhardt, according to the dossier, had a second wife, Nancy (his first had died of cancer of the uterus); he had three teenage children, a fish tank, a big shaggy dog, and several rabbits at home. He belonged to a country club, loved contemporary art, voted Republican but was not known for being conservative in any way. He was a regular churchgoer, professing peace on earth most Sundays. He gave generously to charities, and even volunteered two hours a month – and twenty-four hundred non-deductible dollars a year – to feed the homeless at a centre in downtown DC.

Bernhardt did not waste time speaking before conferences at expensive hotels in Hawaii or Sri Lanka. He was too busy in the lab, doing what he did best. He had become one of the youngest members of the American Academy, because of his relentless research, his prolific article publishing, and his stellar ability to sift through grant applications and make decisive, ground-breaking choices. He was generous with his friends, always the first one to praise others' work, and optimistic about life, despite his profession having failed his first wife, and a growing complaint from some specialists that animal experiments were wasting good dollars on dead-ends; were actually hampering innovation and insight; and that a cure for cancer might have evolved years ago if animals had never been deemed appropriate grounds for cancer research. After all, what causes cancer, or the hiccups for that matter, in a kangaroo rat or a pygmy goat, may have no bearing whatsoever on a human being, or vice versa. But what those outside the medical profession might view as self-evident, was by no means the majority opinion among doctors, or was a subtlety so little appreciated by the scientific mind, the bunker mentality, as to invite scorn and hostility and tens of millions of dollars worth of counter PR. The biomedical establishment would do anything to squelch dissension – marshalling thousands of angry letters to persuade most major encyclopedias to delete each and every sentence that even suggested of 'misery' among research animals; mobilizing vicious campaigns to block the broadcast of network dramas that attempted to explore the issues; negating any public forum that presumed there was a so-called issue in the first place. Animal researchers had become classic paranoid schizophrenics, Jeckylls and Hydes.

There was a picture of the tall, well put-together figure with his greying sideburns and tanned complexion stapled to the opening of the dossier. For someone who supposedly spent all his time in research labs, he looked amazingly healthy. That was on account of his tennis. He was a killer on the courts.

But it was his behaviour in the laboratory, and that of his many colleagues – not dozens, not hundreds, not even thousands of men and women and fresh bright brains just out of medical school or doctoral programs, but tens of thousands of them around the country, generation after generation, century after century – that was truly the killer, relentless, currying every Congressional favour, every tax paying public's approbation, the homage of Nobel Prize committees, the honour of school children, of all of society, on the grounds that research on animals was absolutely necessary for the continuation of human existence. That every major human affliction – heart attacks, AIDS, third degree burns, radiation exposure, mental depression, human violence, all the myriad diseases resulting from the consumption of meat or alcohol or sugar or fried foods or drugs – could not be adequately under- stood, without recourse to a scalpel and a bunny rabbit.

That's what Bernhardt and his friends obviously believed when they first pledged themselves to the Hippocratic Oath and to the age-old Cartesian edict that animals are merely machines, their inordinate expressions of pain nothing more than the grinding and squeaking and unfeeling friction of metallic-like parts. Thus, the biologist who testified in 1963 before the U.S. House of Representatives, insisting that 'science had not yet proved that animals suffer', offered remarkable insight into the way such men truly think.*

Propped up in bed, Felham read the typewritten diary:

'The following observations represent the compressed highlights of my fourteen month employment at the Association of Biological Animal Research Units complex hidden outside the Beltway. I do not claim by any means that ALL of this behaviour took place every day. Rather, I present the summary of what I saw, heard, and experienced, the net accumulation, in my capacity as animal undertaker, disposer of corpses. There are no doubt some ambiguities here, the product of a little hearsay, and maybe some accent marks in my psyche, the inevitable grammar and punctuation of a damaged human being and of a memory I'd like to erase. If anything, I've probably understated my impressions, if not the facts.

'These notes have been altered only for the sake of expediting a summary; they were beleaguered at the time of their writing, highly secretive, the product of a painful immersion in the Inferno that America prefers to ignore.

* Documented in J. Vyvyan, *The Dark Face of Science* and Stephen Clarke, *The Moral Status of Animals.*

'I was paid nine dollars an hour. I worked in two dozen different labs, all part of the same complex, which – if you've never been inside it – is about as large and bewildering and protected by armed guards as the Pentagon.

'Prior to my employment in Dr. Bernhardt and Dr. Claudius' labs, I was a student at American University majoring in Biology. As an undergrad, I had seriously considered a career in medical research, which is what brought me to the ABARU job (it was called a paying internship). I was very excited by the opportunity to work – however menially – in the company of famous scientists. Bernhardt was once nominated for a Nobel Prize. My parents always wanted me to be a doctor and I always thought it might be a most rewarding career. That's finished. I'd sooner starve.

'*January 11th:* It's snowing, high winds across Maryland, yet the sun is piercing through the gale, turning the ice blue, the trees prismatic. A magnificent morning. Inside, another story. I take off my galoshes, hang up my coat, and there is Bernhardt, his surgical gown resembling a butcher's smock, smeared in blood and yellow ooze, pieces of monkey fur sticking to it. He says good morning and asks me to help out in the electric shock lab. Normally, I was assigned to bagging bodies – cats and dogs, mostly, as well as scores of rodents – in the radiation and amputation rooms. But Bernhardt's managed to get hundreds of monkeys in here with a staff of less than fifty to deal with them. They're overwhelmed with their windfall of live subject matter. Middlemen in India, Africa and Southeast Asia must have killed twenty, thirty, forty thousand in the wild to come up with these live ones. Chimps, gibbons, baboons, Sagnius Marmosets, Owl Monkeys, African Greens, Cynomogus, the omnipresent Rhesus.

'They've been shaved, spring-clip electroded for subsequent shocks, locked in to pillory neckplate restraining chairs and left, for weeks at a time. They can't move any part of their bodies. They howl all night from the arthritis, edema, psoriasis and ulcers that have engulfed all their joints. Sixty Herz shock intensities were delivered every three, or six, or sixty seconds, day after day after day, until they died. In the meantime, the investigators here watched, took notes, popped open beers, ate pizza, made some videos, and congratulated themselves on gaining valuable insight into the stimulus response mechanisms of primates subjected to extreme shock. The animals' escape tendencies, and the time it took to reduce these beings to trembling, whimpering, inert, brain-dead balls of fur, no longer able even to blink.

'The monkeys typically burst their abdominal walls, lost their teeth and lips from frantic gnawing at their own appendages, at metal, at anything within grasp, and ruptured their own stomachs from the sheer agony. There were other physiological factors taken account of. But in the end, after four weeks, all but one had died.

'I called her Meg, after my Grandmother, who I watched suffer in a nursing home, in pain, unable to speak, or read, or hear; the victim of forces she could not control, until she weighed a mere eighty pounds, and death was her only salvation. This little Meg, weighing nine pounds, who'd been yanked from the lowlands of the eastern Himalaya one spring morning, drugged, stuffed into a crate and shipped ten thousand miles to Baltimore (I had made a point of tracking down a xerox of the transit bill of lading), after having seen her family wiped out by poachers acting in accord with the U.S-Indian agreements on scientific cooperation, died three days after her month-long ordeal.

'I found her in her cage, curled up, paralysed, eyes wipe open and in terror, and I was the one who got to dispose of her and all the other corpses. There's a furnace down in the basement. At night, in winter, the smoke can be seen rising above the complex; a thin line of dark ash, like the plume from a power plant, except that, these are the combustible remains of some of the most magnificent and sensitive creatures I'd ever seen. I can't say they were loving, because by the time they got to the lab, they'd been transformed into psychotic, desperate beings who knew they were doomed, that no one was out there listening. One might be tempted in a more maudlin frame of mind to compare this situation with that of the human condition; alone in a dark universe, with no God to hear our pain. That sort of thing. But I don't think the comparison holds up. No Sir. This was deliberate damnation. Not Left Bank existentialism.

'Bernhardt was pleased, and ordered more monkeys. He still had money under that particular two million dollar grant, and figured he better spend it while he had it. I should note that no pain-relieving substances were ever used during the experiments in this lab. No postoperative analgesics were employed either, because, in Bernhardt's words (as described in his routine reports to the U.S. Department of Agriculture), such relief would interfere with test results. Always the same excuse.

'*February 20th:* Certainly the same excuse with Dr. Claudius and his research associates, Dr. Jed Masters, Brooker LeRue, Sarah James Headford, Nason Higgins et al, members of the neurophysiology team at ABARU. Their brazen idea of good research consisted of mutilation, burning, bashing, and amputation. Their alleged rationale: how the human – I repeat, human – body functions, following severe trauma, trauma of all kinds. But trauma to animals, not humans! Trauma was their buzzword and they seemed to compete with one another in the formulation of ever more ingenious types of trauma, which they automatically assumed could be fully extrapolated to Homo Sapiens. I couldn't help but marvel at the extent of their cruelty, which I'm sure they took to be splendid creativity, with its own growth curves and moments of particular genius.

'I was attached to this group for two months. I know that they each came recommended with extensive pedigrees, fancy resumés, honours, doctorates, heads of important-sounding committees. Each had a knack for raising lots of grant money and assuring their own steady pay cheques. When the President assured America that several more billions would be channelled for AIDS research, these were the sorts who got their hands on the dough. Dolores, Bernhardt's personal secretary, showed me the monthly memos. Dolores, let me point out, was not one of them. She had a heart that had been breaking for years. The average research salaries were fifty-five thousand dollars. Some made considerably more than that. Not bad, since all they did was torture defenceless animals.

'Guinea pigs were favourite subjects of this team. On Valentine's Day, they burned fifty of the animals over approximately seventy percent of their bodies. No pain relief was administered, not even whiffs. They all died within twenty four hours. Why that should have been significant, I do not know. I was not there to question the scientific importance. I was merely a lowly cleanup worker. But it seemed to me that burning guinea pigs was bull. If I'd been able to sneak a video camera in, I certainly would have filmed this because it seemed so monstrously unnecessary.

'LeRue and Higgins burned rats, more rats than you've ever seen. They not only burned them, trying to keep then just short of dying, so as to then inject some organism called P. aeruginosa, the source of infection for human burn victims, into the wounds. Something about serum albumin, and the protein that forms around the place of trauma. All the rats were subsequently put out of their misery. The scientists seemed very pleased with the results.

'Dogs. They'd toss the pound-seized mutts into boiling water. Hundreds of them. They were apparently interested in the effects on canine blood flow, on the lungs, the whole cardiovascular system. Thing is, I never once saw a scientist take any notes. They just watched the animals, then put them on the steel operating tables, opening them up still alive, some of them unanaesthetized, in some cases removing still beating hearts. It was exactly what you'd imagine of the Middle Ages.

'After a time, I could no longer watch, which I suppose some in the Establishment might use as a case against the veracity of what I'm reporting. But I saw enough, believe me; a boiled dog is a sorrowful sight, needless to say. Taxpayers contributed over a million dollars to having those dogs boiled. I know this because once again I was frequently privy to the secretary's memos. All of them had been pets. You could see the way their tails wagged when they were first brought in. The scientists in charge ordered them starved, so as to avoid dealing with any vomit during surgery. Their water bowls were often dry, covered in scum, their cages caked in excrement because we were too few to keep up with it all. Only once did a government inspector come around. I wasn't on duty, but I was told that he basically looked the other way, helped himself to some coffee, and signed his report to the effect that the lab was a model of well-run biomedicine, spotless, humane, caring. Good coffee. UN-real! Keep in mind that dogs, (especially the purpose-bred beagle) are the favoured victims of science. It is said that eleven Noble Prizes have been awarded for research on these animals, the most commonly used defence, by the Establishment, for continuing the murder. Prizes. Blood money. Fame. Glory. Pretty secretaries giving them blow-jobs.

'Throughout the spring, Claudius' team performed countless experiments in the hopes of devising new forms of trauma. They always had the trappings of high-mindedness. Science with a capital S. They'd insert femoral arterial catheters to measure blood pressure and monitor the heart. They'd scrutinize the rate of blood clotting, of glucose intolerance, you name it. And these indicators justified doing anything, absolutely ANYTHING!

'Claudius clearly wanted to impress Bernhardt, since Bernhardt was supervising the committee that examined grant applications from all over the country. Claudius knew he had to keep coming up with ever more convincing experiments.

'The hopelessly insignificant effects of repeated shocks on the grooming behaviour of parrots (a Scarlet Macaw that must have once been gorgeous and used to remark to all the cats in the lab, 'Don't even think about it!' and which kept frantically screaming 'HELLO!' the more it was tortured); 'giving up reactions' in kittens following brain lesions; chemically-induced writhing in fox terriers; pain thresholds in dobermans; response to complete appendage amputation in pit-bulls; Rhesus monkey reaction curves under varying irradiation regimes; airway response and tracheal trauma in guinea pig suffocation experiments; rabbit, horse, cow, goat, and Rhesus reaction to poisoning, blinding, amputation, mutilation, laceration, scouring, boiling, electric shock, prodding, and induced psychosis.

'Every form of aggressive behaviour, tail-biting, cannibalism, even suicide was studied during my stay at the laboratories. Protein metabolism following comprehensive burn tests was a big one. Also popular was the implanting of bipolar electrodes in upper canine teeth. I think they got that idea from the film 'The Marathon Man', which of course was utterly amateurish compared with what I witnessed. These were professional torturers. Men and women who had gone in some cases fifteen years to medical school, to become connoisseurs of pain infliction.

'In times past, these little Hitlers were seeking a confession, or the incrimination of an accomplice; spoiled wrath, demonic curiosity, blood-thirst. Their tools encompassed every known machine, barbed hooks, racks, leaden balls, the crucifix, steam, needles, nails, the hot iron boot, a stretching device that tore off limbs, thumbscrews, the refining furnace, horses, boiling oil, the so-called parrot's beam for stretching a body into oblivion, and varieties of iron gauntlets. Nowadays, only the rationalization has changed. The medieval methods are the same. There is no consolation in the fact that every injury inflicted on an animal has at some time or another been tried on a prisoner of war, a thief, an intellect, a heretic, a witch, or an adulteress. Hitler bitches and Hitler disciples and Hitler secretaries and guards and comptrollers and managers, and Hitler computer specialists and Hitler hypocrites and frauds, and civil servant Hitlers. So many Hitlers under one roof that the name itself become a parody of the human universe in my mind.

'And of course for sheer numbers of corpses, Germany's Holocaust – six-to-eight million Jews slaughtered – barely got off the ground compared with this place, if you add up all the dead animals around the nation – experiments funded by the ABARU – one has to conclude that God, such as He is, is losing the battle.

'In the radiation experiments, a few of the investigators sought to replicate tests conducted back in the mid-1970's at the United States Air Force School of Aeronautic Pathology in Montana. In those original undertakings, something like five hundred Rhesus monkeys had been exposed to heavy doses of proton irradiation. The dying animals were then studied. Causes of death – ranging from thyroid fibrosis and gangrenous skin necrosis to acute leukaemia and spinal osteo-arthritis – were much reported on at the time. ('Mortality and epidemiology in proton-exposed primate subjects', Radiation Annals, Vol. 17, No. 5). Researchers at ABARU confirmed, for something like the hundredth go-around, the same findings. How many times the monkeys vomited, following 2000, then 3000, finally 4000 rads; who died first, females, or males; at what point they'd lose consciousness, or muscle coordination, and so on. Now what the hell does such redundancy mean, I kept asking myself? And why study it on live monkeys when it's been proven that the data can be mathematically derived using computer simulations? Or cell culture in vitro?

'The redundancy was explained to one assistant as being necessary because every death is different. Again, logic dictates: what the hell differences does it make? Of course every death is different. They'd drown the animals, stuff toxins down their throats, in their eyes, or drugs, implant things in their brains, mostly the ventral midbrain. Or inflict electrolytic lesions in the brainstem.

'One investigator figured out, by accident, how to change a cat's sexual preference, by electrocuting the amygdala of the brain's limbic region. He was thrilled, and I was told that he called his fiancé with the news – made a big joke about it – immediately after the previously heterosexual Persian tried to copulate with another male cat. The brain implants were all done under the guise of supposedly studying basal ganglia and the cerebral motor cortex with its associated muscle control, and the ability to flee from injury, which the scientists had already effectively cut off. Autopsies often revealed that death had resulted from cardiac necrosis. Those that didn't die were put away, with overdoses of sodium pentobarbitol. We didn't have the battering rams that have been used on baboons at various Ivy League universities. But we did have other means, an arsenal as vindictive as any in the history of torture, I'm sure of that.

'They'd force animals that were already weakened by unimaginable stress, or tuberculosis, or shigellosis, diseases picked up from people during their capture and transport to the lab from the wild, to kill each other – including parents and children; they'd study the effects of induced anaphylactic shock, break bones, teach them the fine art of helplessness, force corrosives, like sodium hydroxide (i.e., lye) down their throats. They'd inject rabies or tetanus; they'd set out deliberately to punish them. "Punishment" was one of the popular buzzwords in the laboratory. Punish them for what, I once asked? (Bad report card? Wrong religious belief? Political radicalism?) Just punishment, I was told. Like the animals had done something wrong. Maybe they hadn't bled enough, or screamed loud enough to satisfy the hypothesis of the investigator. I saw two instances in which a researcher hacked off a leg and an arm of an animal, just from sudden rage.

' "That'll show him," the scientist had literally boasted. It was one of the rare instances when an animal was ever given a pronoun. Usually it was just 'it'.

'Once, a graduate student had the ill-grace to question Claudius about such patently grievous behaviour. I heard Claudius' answer.

' "It's a propaedeutic," he said.

' "What's that?" the grad student asked.

' "Look it up."

'She did, and so did I. It meant needed for preparation or learning. A word used frequently in those labs. Claudius' point, I suppose, was that mutilated nervous systems and limbs grew back, or did not grow back, and that information was relevant.

'Amazing. Moreover, it was as if the researchers were on some kind of killing high and needed daily fixes. They couldn't stop themselves. Surely a single experiment, performed twenty years ago, and written up in countless volumes and encyclopedias, sufficed; the way the definition of a word in a dictionary suffices. Why go on killing, if not for this drug-like addiction?

'And there was no 'downer', no law, no reason to come off that high, because the supply of the 'drug' was a constant: the money, and therefore the animals, kept flowing in. The scientific/industrial Establishment in every country has an investment in keeping it all going. Hundreds of billions of dollars being made.

'Muricide, the use of rats to kill mice, seemed to be a form of entertainment for the scientists, when they wearied of the other forms of torture. They would tie the mice up, introduce genetically-altered super-aggressive, starved and dehydrated rats into the cage, and watch as those rats viciously attacked the unprotected mice, finally devouring them. To watch an animal being eaten alive, any animal, is enough to destroy your insides. To know that this was the invention of married men who pride themselves on their humanism, was ... how can I put it? The death of God? The total loss of faith in our species? Unspeakable?

'Prolonged thirst and hunger were favourite 'experiments'. I suppose the researchers figured that they could learn how starving Africans ought to behave. That's it. That's it exactly.

'The same thing goes for induced seizures, sleep deprivation, prolonged exposure to radiation, noise, threats. Researchers were good at threatening, jabbing with sticks, kicking cages, screaming at the animals, spitting at them, throwing wads of shit at them. One female investigator took her own shit in a ladle and smeared it on the face of a monkey held down in a stereotaxic head holder. The animal had peed all over itself that morning, messing up the woman's electrical experiment. The monkey (a male) hated this woman to such an extent, and was so helpless to do anything about his predicament, that he just started eating himself alive. I actually saw him take a chunk out of his own arm. Sarah said it served him right.

'Sarah. Somewhere out there a man probably would like to fuck this whore. Imagine this young woman scooping up her own feces from out of the toilet, calculating all the while, trundling her load back into the laboratory and proceeding directly to her victim. And then delighting in smearing it all over the primate's face. This woman deserves to die. To be gang-banged by bull elephants.

'Graduate students assisting the researchers would frequently tease the nearly dead monkeys, which were held in restraining chairs. The animals' eyes were glazed over, their hair standing on end, their little hands frozen in the pain they'd suffered, and they'd just sit there catatonically while the students pushed their heads this way and that, trying to see if there was any life left in them, which there wasn't. Once or twice a monkey would slowly try to turn its grossly purpuric face towards the student, to gain eye contact, but didn't have the energy or the remaining muscle coordination. Again, the air around these animals was doomed. It was as if these students were going out of their way to prove to the Creator that Homo Sapiens were insane and should be eradicated at all costs.

'Surgeries were performed – lung transplants, open-heart, kidney transplants, gastrectomies, bowel anastomoses – and no pain relievers were ever administered. Again the analogy to the medieval torture chambers is the only apt one. There's no way to describe it. Had I attempted to do something, I would have been arrested and that would have been the end of my documentation. So I watched. I'll never forget it as long as I live. It makes me sick to be part of the human race.

'Often curariform agents were administered to paralyse the victims. Oh this is cute. The investigators loved doing this to frogs, injecting the paralysing liquid into their dorsal lymph sacs. Something hideous and gross about the immobilized frog, with its enormous eyes frozen in place on the scientist. Curare does not work to curtail pain whatsoever, only the muscle response. In fact, it may well increase the pain.'

My brother underlined that fact.

'And it means that one can do anything to an animal and it can't fight back. So obviously, when restraints got in the way, and they wanted to be able to fully manhandle the animal, curare was the preferred mode of operation, whether for frog or monkey.

'I figured, after a few months in there, that I'd seen it all. That is, until I was introduced first hand to the so-called battering drum. They didn't just use the traditional mice and rats, guinea pigs and frogs in this contraption. They saved it for dogs and cats and sheep. Even monkeys. You cannot believe it until you've pulled them out, like I had to do.

'The drum, you may not know, was devised by two fellows during World War II, Coble and Nollip. It's this big metal jerry can (originally it was created for smallish creatures) but today anybody can engineer refinements. The one in our lab was large enough to contain a few standing people.'

Felham circled this point with a red pen, then continued reading.

'There are metal triangular projections welded on the inside at irregular intervals. The drum is fitted into a revolving motor-driven harness that holds it and spins it, up to forty times a minute. The animal is placed inside.

That's it. After a few minutes – and hundreds of collisions with the sides and the triangular projections – the animal is removed. It's usually dead, but not always. Every part of its body is broken and ruptured. They say it's useful for studying auto accidents, plane crashes, and the like. Many of the major auto manufacturers routinely kill tens-of-thousands of animals in this fashion every year. Buy a car and you're buying into that. The government demands it. That's right. The U.S. Consumer Product Safety Commission requires testing of everything that the public is to be exposed to. Whether it be an air bag or an electric toothbrush or a Walkman. Although I must confess, in our lab, there was never any music, or the brushing of teeth, or use of airbags.

'Jed Masters was the real heavy when it came to inducing blindness. He was an expert at it. If it were up to him, all animals would be blind. I know that sounds childish but if you'd seen him perform, you'd know that the guy loves to inflict pain. That's who he is. It doesn't take a psychiatrist to recognize the signs. Lucky for Jed, the rabbit's cornea is not by nature blessed with effective tear glands, and this makes it all the more vulnerable to experimental blindness or eye irritation, or pain – you've seen how the cosmetic companies tape open the rabbit's eyes and then inundate them with perfumes and shampoos and chemicals. A few companies have wised up. It's gone out of fashion. But most still do it. Once again, it's part of the Consumer Product Safety Commission's legalized torture, found in the U.S. Code of Federal Regulations (in this instance, US Laws, Stats., 1979, CFR, Title 16, 11, 1500. 42). And it was a big part of Jed's life. His happiness. His wife's happiness. Their BMW and Mercedes 300. The tuition for his boy's Ivy League education. Their summer house in Nova Scotia. If God were ever to enforce his own legislation, 'an eye for an eye' and that sort of thing, Jed, Jed's family, Jed's friends, Jed's professional colleagues, and their families and friends, would have a real problem.

'The same barbarism was condoned and perpetuated with respect to the forcing of toxins down the animals' throats and eyes, which is apparently mandated by the *Federal Hazardous Substances Act*. All kinds of Acts, and rulings, and special exemptions. And it was all bullshit because nobody gave a damn or even came round to see what was going on, and the money kept piling in, and the scientists kept receiving awards and accolades and invitations to speak at conferences and at universities.

'And I kept wondering – having done my own undergraduate work in biology – if what kills an animal really kills a man. That's what the textbooks allege. But it's all confused, of course, if one recalls that big chemical company, the developer of thalidomide, which inflicted such widespread damage upon mothers and fetuses, and resulted in that huge class action suit, was let off the hook back in 1970 following an extensive trial because all the scientists called in to testify, insisted that animal tests could not – I repeat, NOT – be legitimately used to extrapolate for human beings. Which pretty much reverses the conventional wisdom of the AMA and biomedical community and everything we were taught in college. In a single, celebrated trial, the whole basis upon which all these animals are tortured and executed and 'punished' was tossed out the window. Except that no one was listening. That was merely a single expedient which shows you how powerful scientific bias in a court of law really is. They've got it all on their side. The arguments, the money, the elected officials, an ignorant citizenry, a greedy marketplace. Nations, Presidents, Congress, the consumer – all eating out of their palms. It goes on and on and on. Hundreds of millions of animals in labs just like these.

'With the exception of occasional – I repeat, occasional (it was actually rare) – whiffs of two percent halothane in one hundred percent oxygen, a relatively useless anaesthetic, administered haphazardly, without the slightest consistency or interest in whether it actually sedated the animals – these investigators succeeded, by my count, in killing six thousand seven hundred and eighty-three animals during the period of my documentation. I counted them as I bagged them, night after night. Morning after morning. On average, nearly one hundred per night, twelve an hour, nearly one every five minutes. There were a few of us doing the bagging. I was the only one counting.

'Now, if you happen to glance at the Animal Enforcement Report of the Secretary of Agriculture to the President of the Senate and the Speaker of the House of Representatives, you'll see statistics that don't quite do justice to what I believe I have observed. For example, they'll tell you that in one recent year, only seven percent of all animal experiments involved deliberate pain, approximately 2 million animals in all, and that of those there were some 120,000 animals suffering pain that were given absolutely no drugs to curb such agony. In the State of Maryland for one year, however, it is stated that a mere 1,012 animals fit that pain/no-drug category. Well, if that's true, then for fourteen months my vision must have been obscured by the tears I shed each day. I suppose that's possible.

'To trust those figures, you'd have to trust the records and diaries and official forms filled out by the murderers themselves. And when did you last put your trust in anything a murderer said or did? What's more, as far as I can tell, the documentation ignores all the rodents. They're not telling you about the millions of rats and mice and squirrels and hamsters, et cetera. They're saying that the bulk of those animals were guinea pigs. In many of the States, including this one, they're stating that no primates whatsoever

– zero – were experimented on. I'm just an intern. I can't take on the 'authority' of a whole State. I don't know anyone who can, or would.

'What's more, to give you some idea of the shoddy state of enforcement of even minimal animal welfare laws in the U.S., in one recent year, with tens of millions of animals being subjected to the sorts of experimentation I witnessed, there were a mere 11,056 compliance-with-the-law inspections carried out by officials; and of that meagre number (figure one check for every ten-to-twenty thousand animal experiments – an absurd and woefully inadequate ratio) only 122 violations of the law were ever submitted, and of those, a mere 15 violation cases ever actually reached any kind of decision, for or against. It's the worst sham imaginable.

'I always wondered whether neighbours in the area didn't smell the putrid odour from the plumes at night. Claudius certainly smelt it, because I'll never forget one of his remarks. It had to do with the Nazis and the killing of the Jews and the smoke from the gas chambers. He said that, he had to admire the Nazi doctors, however misguided their politics and racial theories, because he was certain that by doing medical experiments on the Jews – on live subjects, in other words – that science owed the Third Reich a real debt of gratitude. He mentioned various physiological syndromes that would never have come to light had there not been the thousands of Jews who sacrificed themselves to science. That's how he characterized it. Jews sacrificing (as if to say, volunteering) themselves for the advancement of scientific wisdom. Without those Jews, we'd know less about the human being, he said.

'It was this kind of talk that convinced me of the sickness of our species, the fascism, the evil, of science, which justifies anything, everything. This scientific God syndrome has left me utterly isolated. I find myself bereft of all biological links to family and friends, preferring the company of animals, to men.

'Claudius, by the way, is one of the big cheeses in the Academy. Both he and Bernhardt received bigwig medals of honour, from the White House, or the Academy, I can't remember which, for their courageous work in these labs. That really got to me: these fascists, these monsters who had built their reputations on the torture and re-torture of little animals. Keep in mind that they don't usually kill the animals outright, following an experiment. They prefer to use them over and over again, to extract as much pain as possible from any one creature, every last ounce, also keeping in mind that they don't ever acknowledge the fact that animals feel any pain.

'I remember one bobcat they had in here – now bobcats are an endangered species in this neck of the woods – they'd caught it somewhere and they must have put that cat through a dozen rounds of burn experiments before they finally determined that it was utterly useless to them. Like an empty beer can. And then you know what they did to it? Claudius was late for a lunch date so rather than put the destroyed, but still breathing animal to sleep, he picked it up by its hind legs and simply smashed its head against a wall repeatedly until it was dead. How can I forget it: I was the one told to clean up the mess. The head dented in. The eyes slowly closing. The once proud claws hanging down, stunned and lifeless, the utter senselessness of it all, and the hate, a hatred that was consummated in me which is as dangerous a hormone, or chemical, or portion of the brain, as any neutron bomb. Except that I didn't know how to explode. I was like a computer without a keyboard, a bird without wings. Roaring inside. I wanted to kill that man. To do unto others what they had done unto me. I was that bobcat, you better believe it. And I'd seen enough killing. I remember that day for another reason – it was when some big tobacco litigation was going on at the same time as a sexual harassment suit against the President. I kept thinking how outrageous that Americans should be concerned about the details of an encounter in a hotel room, however humilitating for the victim, a woman, yet killers like Claudius can massacre a beautiful bobcat, God's creature, rare and elegant, before half-a-dozen male and female employees, and THAT'S not construed as harassment.

'You might wonder whether such behaviour, in so fortified and concealed a laboratory, might not be an isolated example of transgression within the greater medical research community. Definitely not. It goes on at numerous universities and corporations around the country. I should mention that according to Dolores, and the memos that I managed to see, often at personal risk (Dolores was getting ready to retire, she was fifty and was weary of hearing all the screaming animals – she rarely saw them from her plush office just outside Bernhardt's, but there was no way anybody in that facility could be insulated from that perpetual, dreadful din), that damned near every government agency had a hand in the research, and would send visiting dignitaries to look in at the goings-on. Never groups – Bernhardt worried about groups – but individuals with special passes, from corporations and from government and universities. All were involved in similar experiments, in one way or another. Swooping up money from taxpayers, from alumni; non-profit donations to hospitals, which in turn divided out the money to their on-staff researchers. That's called 'charitable giving'.

'This whole orgy of killing was totally justified in the minds of the many perpetrators. They saw it in a perspective which for them was very clear: either you are prepared to experiment on live Homo Sapiens (Claudius would prefer Jews, or Communists, or any members of the overpopulated Third World, or mentally incapacitated individuals, or babies with incurable diseases, or fetuses that the mothers have promised to abort after the experiment was concluded) or you experiment on animals. It's that simple.

'I'm certainly not so sure it's that simple and by the end of the following Winter I was ready to kill myself. I went to New Zealand, instead, hoping to find solace on the South Island, do some skiing, and exorcise the horror from my insides. They tried to induce me to sign a confidentiality statement – I guess they figured I was pissed – and I told them to screw themselves. Unfortunately, what I found throughout the South Pacific were cultures nearly as brutal as what I'd run away from. In New Zealand, they kill animals not for bogus research funds but for meat, which they consume and export in vast and unrelenting quantities. Both islands stink of slaughterhouses. I found Australia even worse.

'I went to Tahiti. Same deal. There, it's pigs. Intelligent, sensitive beings. They keep them in these shit-hole cages and seem to delight in tormenting them. Children especially. They kill pigs in front of other pigs. The people roar with laughter when the pigs squeal in pain and futility. They kill them slowly, essentially skinning them alive. The pigs lie on the ground convulsing, white foam pouring out of their nostrils. The Tahitians have these big parties for the tourists on the beach and everybody fucks everybody else and poets romance the moon.

'I'm back in the Washington area. I work. Having to do with children's books, part-time. My nightmares are recurrent, however, and I find myself needing more and more uppers and tranquillizers and sleeping pills of every sort to get through the night, to get through the day. I don't know what the answer is. Or how long I can handle this. I heard something about a religion in India that forbids all animal research, that effectively boycotts any by-products of an animal. They are supposedly total vegetarians, believe in no god, keep no pets, harness no cattle, are strict environmentalists – something like ten million of them – and they've been like that for millennia. I was told that they cherish all living things as if even an ant, or a rat, had the same rights, the same evolutionary individuality and soul, as a person. It all sounds too good to be true. But I plan to check it out because I've got to do something, otherwise I'm going to go extinct. I'm already insane.

'So much for my personal story. Anyway, enclosed is a detailed diagram of ABARU where all the skeletons were buried as of 11/97, quick exits, secret entrances, which key scientists are where, their offices, the guard stations, the hidden infrareds, the hidden surveillance cameras, where the phone lines go, where extra-on-site security weapons are stored, whole caches, even grenades. They're prepared for the worst. They must know that what they're doing, what they're abetting, is deeply, undeniably wrong. The guards, by the way, are everywhere, as you might expect. Some are even paramilitary. They are equipped with AK-47s, I'm told, even attack dogs. They know that there are protesters all around them.

'The police respond very quickly from the outside whenever protest marches or animal liberators try to block employees from entering the front door. They've got like a special 'ALERT' bell, a direct line to the police. It's real scary. Much like a penitentiary. I should note that no protester to my knowledge has ever gotten through these doors. I've never seen the paramilitary go to work. I wouldn't want to.

'The guards are not any more sympathetic than the researchers and administrators. It's not just a job for them. When they check in on the labs which they do nearly every hour, twenty-four hours a day - they stare with a dumb conspiratorial willingness at what's going on. Everybody in that complex knows exactly what's happening. Maybe some, like Dolores, are unfamiliar with the sordid details, but they know the general scheme of things, all right. It's the conspiracy of science. And the weird thing is, nobody, nobody EVER talks about the animals outside of the lab. It's as if they don't exist, when in fact that's ALL that exists, or I should say, once existed.

'It is a Federal system of sadistic torture, vivisection, and animal genocide, which has been carried on for decades under the fraudulent guise of respectable medical research. And nobody on the outside knows, or wants to know, or is willing to find out. My parents, my friends, my teachers, wouldn't listen to me, or suggested that if it was bothering me that much, I should just quit the job. Just like that. As if that would have solved anything. As if I could ever live with such cowardice. You can't imagine, or maybe you can, how many people are convinced – without knowing the first thing about it – that animal research is essential. Americans have been hopelessly brainwashed on this issue. The animal rights people, by and large, acknowledge the essential futility of trying to change the system. So they address the smaller issues, fighting for legislation that would provide one extra visit per week to the labs by a custodian of the U.S. Department of Agriculture. Or demanding that a squirrel monkey be given an extra twelve-square inches in his holding pen, before being led to the slaughter. That sort of thing.

'For whomever, and for whatever it's worth, I hope my little write-up is clear. I don't have the guts to do what's necessary. I pray there's someone out there who does. God help all of us.'

It was signed, 'A Concerned Citizen'.

Muppet returned with large foam ozone-consuming drinking containers, a pound each, filled with the rummagings of a salad bar. He went heavy on the lima beans, a staple Felham had detested since childhood.

"You get through it?"

"I just finished. Everything on your end checked out?"

"Seems to. It's a big place. Lot to do."

"A lot to do," Felham added gloomily. It was the biggest hit of their career.

"Nice to find a soul in distress once in a while," Muppet remarked, nodding towards the dossier.

"He must be what, twenty-one, twenty-two?"

"Certainly old before his time," Muppet suggested. "We were that age, once."

"Nobody should ever get that old," Felham said.

"Made me pretty ill just reading it," Muppet went on.

"We are going to stop it," Felham stated clearly.

They shared a look which seemed to both of them to be new, though neither acknowledged it. It was the look of fear that had mutually resolved itself to whatever had to be. Not fear of death – for they had come to terms with that years before, and had lived death repeatedly since then – but the angst, the real world, of not completing what they knew needed so absolutely to be done. To not finish. It was a concept infinitely more hideous than, say, the human condition, which had invented such outrages in the first place. As far as Felham was concerned, you could take the human condition and shove it. It was the animals – the remaining species on Earth – that mattered. The odds were heartbreaking.

"We'll just do it, that's all," Felham repeated. He was at the zenith of his reasoning faculties.

Muppet was not ordinarily one to reflect on these matters – he acted, he didn't talk about it – nor did his good old boy weight and lack of pain sensation and easy stride and huge fashion, simple smile, tender mannerism, southern accent, soft and mild – an enormity of mildness – ever betray the inferno underneath. To be killed by Muppet was to be put to sleep, almost kindly, I would think. He was a piece of nature that flowed as assuredly as the wind, or circulatory system, indefatigable, like a tank across the North African desert or the implacable descent of the Brahmaputra.

They seemed ... thrilled is not the word ... gratified, that's it, nearly light-humoured, that they'd already impacted so appreciably towards a cause, *His great day*, which both men so fervently trusted in.

And it was that upbeat stride which saw them past security at four-thirty in the afternoon next day, at ABARU's front door. They carried dozens of plastic explosives, enough to do the job, very clever ones – the size of pages of a book, actually glued inside medical textbooks with printing on them, pertaining to the female physiology, totally undetectable weapons, and they'd had the whole morning to apply their respective make-up, so that video cameras routinely recording the entrance of every individual past the magnetometers, would have no record of the real Muppet and Felham. Passes were waiting for them, compliments of Dr. Bernhardt and Dr. Claudius, both of whom had granted brief interviews to the aspiring researchers.

How had Muppet managed that, I wondered? He obviously had read enough to talk his way to Bernhardt, had absorbed enough facts and sense of the material to persuade Bernhardt that he was a serious graduate student, that he had followed Bernhardt's work, just as Felham (aka Striker) had followed Claudius'. That both men were considering their options – whether to work in neurophysiology at some American college, to take a position offered in Brussels, or to work for the military. Obviously, Bernhardt's defences were down, and he more than likely fell swoon to Muppet's extraordinarily disarming accent and flattery.

As for Claudius, Bernhardt set it up, having never spoken with Felham but having heard of him through Muppet. The Claudius interview was to take place thirty minutes after the Bernhardt, which would give Felham time to identify weapons caches, the mainframe computer room, the telephone routing system and the brain centre for all of ABARU's surveillance. The whole interview thing baffles me, given how important, how utterly consumed by meetings and 'research' these two men were. Perhaps it was Muppet's intimate knowledge of Bernhardt's early papers, published in such magazines as the *National Journal of Physiological Engineering, The Annals of the New York Science Web*, the *Journal of Toxics, Drugs and Higher Pharmacology*, and so on. I can imagine Muppet discussing the minutiae, impressing Bernhardt with his willingness to become part of the conspiracy.

They could have made it easy on themselves, paying visits to the two scientists at their homes, instead of walking into one of the largest, most tightly secured facilities in the United States. But their vision was not simply confined to taking out two principal researchers. They intended to hurt the ABARU ... to hurt it bad.

Numbers of combatants they were up against meant little to them, in terms of mowing men down; just more zeroes added to the calculation.

At four forty-five sharp, just as Dolores was notifying Dr. Bernhardt that Edgar Lewis, PhD, (Muppet), was waiting to see him, Felham was walking briskly towards the ABARU electronic brain cache, which made a whole lot of sense on one hand, and no sense at all on the other. It was the other, the senselessness, which Felham was counting on.

There were half-a-dozen women (women plagued him), monitoring three walls of video. Every lab was constantly swept by panning cameras. The slightest irregularity prompted an armed response. It was everything he expected. The cache was expertly concealed. Without the insider knowledge of the 'Concerned Citizen', Felham would have never found it. He knew that to simply blow up surveillance would be to set off every alarm in the complex. He had to destroy the mainframe computer, plant his own plastic explosives, get hold of stations, one by one, on his way to Claudius' lab. Once surveillance was down – which Muppet would know, because he was wearing a two-way radio collar with a lavalier mike perfectly situated beneath his chin, under his shirt, so that both he and Felham were 'live' – he too was to go to work, destroying all of Bernhardt's files, and then Bernhardt and his associates, armed with two plastic handguns, and enough ammo to take out forty-eight people, and then get to the nearest cache. Felham and Muppet planned to have made their peace with the researchers by 6 p.m. At which time, they then intended to systematically liberate all the animals. Every last one. They had to get them all, because of the fire they planned to light. Rodents were easy. They would simply disperse them in hordes out the back doors, out windows into the trees, out blown-up walls. An avalanche of pissed-off rats, unleashed on the nation's capital. Rabid dogs, AIDS-infected monkeys, drugged sheep, eviscerated goats, cats attached to shock experiment devices, animals in restraining contraptions, or hooked up to IV apparatuses, or incapable of moving for the reasons they had read about, or maimed beyond recognition, these and any number of other complications were likely to confound the two men, however. I do not know what they actually counted on. Any marine creatures, like fish or dolphins, would be impossible. And there was certainly not going to be the time to unhook every mouse from every experiment, or escort every wounded skunk or delirious parakeet to the back door. They'd do whatever was humanly possible. It was far more than any other human on the face of the Earth was doing.

Standing to the side of the locked entrance to the glassed-in surveillance room, Felham quickly withdrew his plastic .45 calibre silencer weapon, shot through the door, and unloaded his round, killing all six guards instantly. He then severed all wires and plugs and disabled the entire video monitoring system of the complex, a prelude to his opening the cache, slinging two fully loaded AK-47 assault rifles and dozens of rounds of ammo over his shoulder, filling his satchel with grenades and placing his first plastic explosive in the surveillance room, timed to go off in one general radio emission, which he and Muppet had agreed to wait on until everything was in place at once. They needed at all costs to avoid alerting outside police and had studied their insider intelligence to the extent that they felt it was possible, assuming the mainframe could be destroyed and the telephone circuit boards with it.

Two nurses were running away from the area, having seen the goings on. Felham shot both of them. There was a scream down the hall. Felham ran, sliding around the corner, where security guards were running past a group of young people, their guns and walkie-talkies drawn, in his direction. Felham opened fire with one of his machine guns, cutting down everyone, every last person. But, of course, that meant that the whole bloody place was now attuned.

"It's happening," Felham muttered into his own lavalier. "Surveillance is dead. Killing has started. I'm on the run. Your turn. I love you, man!"

Felham had memorized the map of the joint. Now he ran, killing wildly en route – anybody, everybody. He was not interested in minor ethical delineations at this point. If they were inside, they died. Several hundred thousand animals had to be rescued. A few hundred dead humans was a small sacrifice to pay. That was their reasoning. That had been their decision.

The killing felt good. Savoury and warm and revengeful. Full of the needs and desires and lost hopes that those animals deserved. Seen from space, such carnage as my brother inflicted that night would appear trivial. Dust motes colliding in the interstellar chaos. Hardly noticeable.

I feel like a Walter Mitty, trying to imagine their *Mission Impossible*, those glorious pyrotechnics, impossible timing, their own horror at seeing the wasteland inside there, these two men whose hearts were crying out with love, as they proceeded to kill scores of human beings; the kind of massacre you read about in Croatia, or South Africa, or Assam, but not Maryland.

"What was that?" Dr. Bernhardt asked, when Muppet paused to listen to Felham's message in his earplug receiver.

"What was that? Why, Doctor, that was a message from God. It's time to die!" And he pulled forth his handgun and put a bullet squarely through Bernhardt's heart, and between his eyes. The body grabbed backwards against the wall. Muppet then called to Dolores.

She stood at the door.

"Shut it," Muppet ordered, his gun aimed at her.

"What's your name?"

"Dolores Sanchez," she said. "Where's Doctor– "

"Shhh!" Muppet whispered, motioning with a finger to his lips. "You remember that kid you showed the memos to last year?"

"I had to do something," she began, quaveringly. "I couldn't stand it." She then saw Bernhardt lying on the floor behind his desk. She'd missed him until now.

"My God. You shot him!"

"That's right," Muppet said matter-of-factly. "Now you did a good thing, Dolores. A good thing indeed. You're not going to get hurt if you do exactly what I tell you. Okay?"

Her knees started to give out. "What do you want?"

"We're here to save the animals."

"We?"

"There are others on their way."

"I can't believe it," she cried, staring dumbfounded at the pool of blood which was drifting away from the wall. It was a revelatory moment for her, Muppet noted. "You shot Dr. Bernhardt?" And then she declared, "Thank the Lord!"

"He is dead, ma'am. He's not going to hurt any more animals, ever again."

"What do you want me to do?"

"I want you to unlock every cage in every laboratory in this wing that you can. Don't worry about pissing off the researchers." He wasn't about to divulge what was really going to happen. It was moments away. Everything needed to be done precisely, efficiently.

"They'll bite."

"The animals? Just be careful," Muppet cautioned her.

"Do the ones you can. Now hurry!"

"What are you going to do? There's more animals than you can imagine."

"We're going to set them free."

"How did you get in, How ..."

"Time to move, Dolores."

Muppet went ahead of her, taking out a good twenty lab technicians in a surreality of bullet spray and exploding bodies. It happened so fast that screams had no time to form. Reactions were obliterated. Dolores fainted.

DAMMIT! Muppet's mind pinched, springing feverishly back at her. There was going to be a fire and he did not deem her an appropriate victim. It had already been decided, between he and Felham. Animals were frantically resisting, cowering, fearing the worst, that their time had come. Muppet rapidly deployed a nearby hose and sprayed Dolores with water. Seeing that he'd roused her, he carried forth to the business at hand.

Running for the cache, securing the machine guns, planting plastic explosives at the far end of the corridor, then joining Dolores who was up, unsteadily, trying now to do what she'd been ordered, her dress all wet.

Monkeys were loose, running insanely towards the open corridor, growling and hooping, leaping over the tables. Scientists were arriving, and falling, as the bullets took them with precision. Muppet was now fully armed.

The sound of an explosion ripped through his lavalier.

Felham dove down a hall, as the computer room, equipped with two Fujitsu supercomputers and hundreds of accompanying machines, convulsed in a mighty series of detonations. Dozens of technicians disappeared in the fulmination of glass and flame and billowing smoke. Both B and C corridors were now on fire. Felham had already taken out the main phone routing boxes, as well as the hapless switchboard operators. There was no way for a phone call, a police or fire alarm to get out.

"We've got it to ourselves now, bud," Felham said. "How's it going?"

"Little resistance. Hurry it up, man!"

Felham heard the guards running. He kneeled, aimed, and waited. Suddenly, fifty yards away, a mob of armed men, some in paramilitary fatigue, others in blue officer uniforms, slid across the vinyl-covered floor – terrible for running – in a riot of panic-mode aversion. Felham tossed two grenades and opened fire with one of his machine guns, mowing down the horizon of the hall. He whipped around and mowed the opposite direction, which was wise, as he was a microsecond away from the receiving end of others, too numerous to count. He slapped two more magazines into his weapons.

People were running everywhere, though no alarm bells sounded, having been perfectly shot out. Fire was raging in two sectors, as Felham moved from room to room now, killing whatever humans he could find, bashing out windows, opening cages, releasing animals. Fast, faster, furiously. Incredible strength. A sense of mission.

He'd been through enough releases, wearing thick gloves, to know what to look out for. But he'd never encountered so much animal psychosis, reactions that were startling: birds barking, monkeys tweeting, pigs growling, dogs vomiting with fear.

And there – a two headed lemur, and a dog with two dicks, the second one having been surgically applied to its head. And a ... *what the fuck is it??* A rat the size of a watermelon, strapped down, dead, in a pool of not red, but blue blood. The genetics lab.

What are these people? his mind reeled.

He was himself the psychosis, releasing, pulling the trigger, releasing, pulling the trigger. He'd wiped out the B and C corridors. There was still A corridor, the front entrance. Felham and Muppet met at the main doors, a huge lobby area with photographs of several past Presidents all warmly commending the brave work of this country's medical researchers. Felham aimed and disintegrated the pictures and the plaque.

"Now!" Felham said.

They began killing, dozens and dozens of people. It was a terrible, flawed massacre. I say flawed in recognition of the fact that killing is wrong. Terribly wrong. Yet there seemed, in their minds, to be no other way. Remarkably, they were fast enough, and well-armed enough – compliments of the ABARU weapons caches, and one Concerned Citizen – to be able to make a clean slate of it. The blood ran deep. Animals were slipping in it. A horse, bewildered, skid through a front wall of glass, exploding into a bed of gladioli and continuing across grass towards a parking lot.

Flawed in another sense: people in the parking lot, dozens, possibly hundreds, of workers, on their way in for night shifts. Felham took out ten minutes worth, but he had more important matters to contend with. It meant, at best, that someone, soon, was going to alert authorities. People running at a distance. Too far away to deal with. Time, now, was surely limited.

The two of them ran furiously towards the main neurophysiology lab on C corridor, where Felham had already left Dr. Claudius and his associates, Sarah and Jed Masters, in the man-sized trauma drum, with the motor drive at full throttle. He'd dragged Sarah from under a table, ripping open her blouse, spitting on her exposed breasts – a tribute to her by now famous femininity. Claudius and Masters had refused to move. Felham had annihilated their knees with a short burst of fire power, then shoved all three of them inside. By now the cosy *ménage-à-trois* would have attained the consistency of Mom's Gazpacho.

Twenty thousand rats, alive; eleven hundred rabbits, many blind; countless mice, dead and alive.

'The monkeys. Get the monkeys," Muppet shouted, as they continued planting detonators, not wasting a second, killing other guards who came round to defend the bastions, smashing windows, setting fires in those labs that had been emptied, reloading, tossing grenades like they were bread crumbs for pigeons.

How I now envy such guts, verve, how my heart is seized with a deep-seated sense of belonging to their magic bullet club. I forever wanted to fly. The Peter Pan or Cyril Tourneur in me, I guess. I always craved this purebred, Elizabethan-like revenge. I admit to the fascination.

A colossal comeuppance that carried them towards the rear of C corridor – they had memorized the entire floor-plan – where the big Pac & Value truck awaited them in the dock, its rear doors open.

Now they chased monkeys, hundreds of them, towards the end of the linoleum and neon-lit passageway. Out of the harsh, moribund glare, into the soft, awaiting moonlight. Those that were crippled, amputees, or brain dead, Felham put of their misery.

By now it was nearly ten in the evening. One human had been spared, Dolores. The killing of the others had taken on so enormous a dimension that neither of them had any idea how many they'd actually felled. It had to have been into the hundreds.

They were far more concerned about getting the animals out before the detonation. And they were scrupulous about it.

The truck filled up quickly. It was an ark on wheels and as they pulled away, it was only the detonation – sending acres of red brick and 1950's glass and steel high into the air with a rumble and a series of lightning-like flashes that lit up miles of town – it was this unexpected armageddon that threw the waiting multitude of police into a frenzy as the truck, under the guidance and adrenaline of Muppet, came crashing through a makeshift barricade of patrol cars that had squealed into place five minutes before.

The enormous truck broke through one other barricade as well, getting onto the Beltway. DC, Virginia and Maryland SWAT teams had already had forty minutes to prepare, having been cued in from the first cruising policeman who'd noticed the fleeing workers on their way in from various parking lots at ABARU. But the opposition had no idea what kind of hostage situation might be unfolding inside, and was therefore haltingly mobilized. The explosion, and escaping truck, caught them totally by surprise. "Jesus!" was the one and only solemn rebuttal.

"You wanna drive?" Muppet asked, not with any unbecoming levity or pertness, just amazed to be alive.

"You're doing fine," answered Felham.

What the police didn't anticipate was that the truck – mistaken for one of several similar-looking service vehicles at the docks – was also equipped with the latest in shoulder-held bazooka-type anti-aircraft weaponry, Pakistani contraband left over from the Afghani rebels trade. As Felham took out a chopper and cleaned the rear view, so to speak, of assailants, he felt sublime impulses, the religion of settling scores, leaving no enemy alive, obedient only to nature. The chopper exploded on a city street.

Into the very darkness, having actually done it. At eighty miles an hour, all the way to the forty-acre Glen Sanctuary eleven miles away, operated by a local animal group, which had, through other concerned citizens, agreed to receive any animals that were in limbo.

And that's where the truck was left, while two other vehicles were picked up that had been prearranged.

"What are you feeling?" Felham asked as he and Muppet prepared to make their way to the Baltimore airport before the FBI managed to teletype descriptions of them.

"I couldn't believe a dog with two dicks."

"Did we save it?"

"He's out there roaming the city streets, Georgetown, probably. Looking for action. His dicks'll have the last laugh."

"We were lucky."

"Fuck. Those were serious bastards."

"I feel good," Felham said. He missed Jessie.

"Me too."

"We were seen. In the front. Had to be a few survivors in that mess." Felham was so high, so lofty and head-spinning in the sweat of success, that he contemplated, just for a ridiculous instant, retirement with that woman, somewhere.

"Here," Muppet applied cold cream to Felham's face, in that way dissipating the flesh-tight facial cover-up.

Felham did the same for Muppet. They cleaned themselves up to look respectable. They had last planes out to catch.

"Now they don't know what the hell we look like," Muppet presumed.

"I liked you prognathic," Felham needled, managing a grin. It was, in fact, a pleasure even rarer; a pleasure I have wracked my brain trying to imagine; plumbing depths of risk in him, that would nevertheless explain the death-wish behaviour of a man still relatively young, staring at his whole life before him, for the sake of animals, to rout evil.

But where does that action begin, and inaction cease? Where does evil become relevant to the person? In one's bedroom, certainly, when a stranger breaks through the window and threatens to kill one's children. But what about one's neighbour's children? Or children a mile away?

And what about a goose in the backyard, a goose you've raised from a hatchling? Along comes a homeless person whom you catch strangling it for his dinner. You try to stop him and you find that he's got this piano wire, see, he's come prepared, and the only way you can stop him is to hurt him, hurt him bad, perhaps. Do you do it? Does the blood mingle, from goose to child? Are the associations relevant? My mind says they are, based upon what I've sensed of my brother's own dilemma in the last twenty-four hours. That evil exists somewhere between the bedroom and a few miles away; that barbarism, the flow of blood, be it a bird's or a child's, is the by-product of the same brute, and he's got to be stopped. He's got to be ...

I realize that DNA dictates that we survive as individuals and are thus not anxious to risk ourselves, certainly not in defending a bird. And yet at the same time, there is a psychological blending of evils which must occur – I'm certain that's what's happened to my brother – a blending as complete as the elements in water, or air, or blood chemistry; that renders all victims universally the same victim; all blood the same blood; cells, cells; molecules, molecules. That in the ethical universe there is no separate identity, but rather a principle, a life force, whose priorities cannot be disputed.

And as I see my brother, standing around beside his car out there on the dark road at night, having just done unprecedented injury to a Federal institution and its hundreds of employees, discussing as casually as the fine points of a Lakers' game, the evening's moments, I also feel the astronomer's perplexity, which is our smallness against overwhelming forces. What is a bonfire, some smashed windows, and the rat-tat-tat of a few machine guns in a corner of North America, against the greater importance of that nearly five billion year old life force, whose origins are of the galaxies?

We are all one. The FBI and my brother. The homeless vagrant out to strangle the goose, and the goose herself. Which tells me two things: first, that amid such ethical and biological unity, a lot of people are going to go crazy trying to avoid unpleasantnesses, compromises and choices (who should live, the goose or the homeless person?) and second, those who have the strength to hold back the black humour or insanity of it, are going to have to actually *make* choices. Many of which will be cruel, and painful, and insane ones. Those who refuse to make insane choices – as novelist William Styron so grippingly contemplated (who will the Nazis take, your daughter, or your son, for example) – will have to do something else. Like Felham. So that to be human, one will have to prove it to fully experience the insanity (not revel in it, but know it), and then manage to go beyond. How to transcend that feeble throb, every cry in the dark, which is biochemically rooted, they say, in the hypothalamus, or pineal, or the pituitary, or the heart, or the soul – wherever the hell it is. There's just no way around it. But getting beyond it is nothing more or less than a call to action. The imagination can contend with the insanity, can even convince itself of having made the important leap forward. But imaginative leaps will not statistically curb the ABARUs of the world. I now see no other choice but that of an older brother.

There's no doubting the doublespeak of all this. The sluggishness in our nerves that accounted for, what, seventy thousand nuclear warheads on a small green planet? The fear in our throats that has perpetuated, I was once told, two hundred and fifty thousand battles just since the time of the Renaissance? Two hundred million people murdered in the twentieth century alone? Over fifty thousand in the United States in 1997? If those aren't insane choices, then certainly my brother's actions are not insane, either. Eighty 'Allied' soldiers died in the Persian Gulf to liberate a small, dusty country called Kuwait, whose leadership was anything but Democratic. Millions of fish, birds and aquatic animals also died as a result of that war. The burning oil wells will more than likely account for yet other long-term cancers all the way to India. I would consider what Felham and Muppet did this night – the liberation of tens-of-thousands of animals, otherwise fated to horrible death by tyrants far more ingenious and evil than one foppish dictator in Iraq – to be far less offensive and destructive than the Persian Gulf War. You may agree, or not. It doesn't matter, now. Muppet and Felham pulled it off.

Astronomy allows for such comparisons, up among the moons of Saturn, or the distant nebulae, even if the Circuit Courts and the general reader do not.

Where does that leave all of us who've asked at least once in our lives, Am I not my brother's keeper? Or a dog that's had a second penis transplanted on to its head, and is nevertheless supposed to remain man's best friend? Such thoughts are inevitable. I'm changing, alright. Suffering more, suffering less. I eat a pretzel and watch CNN. Their cameras are panning the devastation in Maryland. They say that police and FBI have got two suspects, neither one in custody at this time, and whom they can not as yet name.

"You got enough cash?" Felham asked.

Muppet counted out forty-eight one hundred dollar bills and some change. Felham had that much plus some. He'd stashed a substantial donation for the Sanctuary in an envelope in the glove compartment of the truck, which had been left at the far end of the estate, where the gate was ajar. Nobody greeted them. Muppet had worked all that out in advance. This way, when and if the animals were traced to the Glen, the heads of the organisation could claim that they had simply received an anonymous phone call stating that animals would be delivered. No point of origin given. It would eliminate any legal entanglements for them.

The two men had backed the huge truck up just flush with the high forested gate, opened the rear doors of the vehicle and gotten the chaos of life out into the protected open air. There were going to be problems, dogs chasing cats, cats chasing birds, monkeys chasing one another. Others were already dead. But at least they were free.

As it turned out, exhaustion, illness and trauma precluded predictable animal aggressions. Muppet and Felham stuck around long enough to witness a miracle in evolution: lions and lambs proverbially lying down beside one another in the moist and merciful sward.

"Wow," Felham murmured.

"I hate to part with these," Muppet later said, stashing the machine guns in a nearby bush. They'd driven a half-mile away from the Sanctuary in their two borrowed jeeps and had stopped on a semi-rural side road to finalize the next phase. It was a clear night. There was next to no traffic. Up the road a bit were the dimmed lights of a dance tavern adjoining a gas station. They could still hear the distant shrill of sirens converging from not a few States.

"That was nice of them to provide ammo and everything," Felham said.

"It was the least they could do."

"I couldn't think in there."

"I just went with my rush. This energy. It's going to keep flowing, or it's going to die. I was free of any ambiguity about what was what, and what was left to do. I just did. I don't think I really looked. How could you look at that?"

"We must have killed quite a few animals. I hate contradictions."

"Had to do it," Muppet rationalized.

"We better get going. What's the name this time?"

"Cavendish. John."

"Right. Hail, brother."

I, too, no longer had the luxury of thinking of it as a contradiction, their compassion for animals, hatred of mankind, the inevitable winners and losers and accidents, because now I was also part of their quixotic misadventure (some might take umbrage at that characterization, but that's not my problem). Felham and Brian Laffont were the only two suspects, and that inescapable fact was amplified by two eyewitnesses, though cloudy and based upon the blurred motion at night, amid fireworks, and taking into account that both Muppet and my brother were in disguise. Yet the physiognomies rang true, our phone was tapped, our movements followed. It may not yet have been made public but the name, Felham, was marked forever.

Now it was only a matter of time, of growing imprecision. As it was, I'm sure that plenty of animals had been left, missed, lost – had to be so – and plenty that got caught in crossfire, or were killed in the explosions. The news showed the remains of the ABARU's many buildings. Some had not been touched at all. But the central sectors were demolished and most of the animals had been 'stolen', as commentators put it, though there was no way to know how many, since most of the files had been burned and all the computers – with all the grant and research information – destroyed.

That might have contrary implications for the future, I initially suspected. What if all the experiments that had been done, the supposed 'information' lost forever, were now done all over again? Also destroyed on those computers were invaluable medical data: case histories, millions of pieces of information relevant to this nation's practice of medicine, I imagine. We may all be back to herbal remedies, for a few weeks. Sure.

Around midnight, Kinesey informed Jerrasi in Tarpon Springs.

"You missed all the excitement."

"Huh?" Jerrasi had been sleeping off a taxing dosage of vodka, a tribute to his mother which he had allowed himself, following a most pleasant evening with the minister and his wife and her chocolate cake.

"Your boy – your boys, I should say – have just messed up a large portion of southern Maryland." Jerrasi lunged up and forward from his pillows. "What are you talking about?"

"*The Animal's* in town, Bob. You missed him," Kinesey explained. "We all did. Sorry about your mother. Now you better get up here."

It was more or less like that. Jerrasi took Delta at five in the morning and was on the site by eight-thirty. Madrid, Shelley Pendergras and others were there to meet him.

One local reporter likened the look of it to the aftermath of a midair collision – say, two 747s – over a populated urban region. That about summed it up, both in terms of body count and charred wreckage.

"This is who we think we're dealing with," Madrid said, handing Jerrasi a photograph of Dirkson Felham. "We still cannot locate an image or reliable ID on the other one. But we know there are two, and Brian Laffont seems to be our man. Or at least he fits the description we've been working with."

Two survivors, speaking from stretchers, described the two men they saw shooting at the front door. Jerrasi, ferret-nosed, studied the photograph, which he held while standing amid a rubble that defied reason, that certainly contradicted the machinations of just two men, he didn't care how well-armed they were.

It was a picture of Dirkson Felham from his wallet-sized license. Ungainly, big-necked, longish-haired, little to indicate a mindset, a naked eye, a temper that could be divined or predicted. Jerrasi was disappointed. He'd hoped for a connection, something to place the face in the dark forest of that long ago day; a recognizable spectre. Instead, it was a roughly collegiate, unforthcoming aspect, neither sombre nor menacing, no sense of discipline (which once again contradicted the obvious truth of the man) nor of particular credo. Yet the murders had been as specified and deliberate as any in the FBI's history of serial killers. More often than not, a killer's countenance could be read, in spite of the context in which the photograph was taken. You just knew the psychopath lurking beneath the furrows, swarthy eyes, or pursed lips; an aura of off-centering self that was diseased and controlling. Jerrasi had his own theories about killers. It was their sheer love of killing that distinguished them from the one-time murderer, a passion for seeing suffering played out, over and over, that addicted them to the habit, forming its own rules of the game which they adhered to no matter what. And those rules, like their faces, could be read, once the cipher was worked out. But there was always a cipher.

This Felham, however, operated on different principles and that's what was so annoying to Jerrasi. The man claimed, by his actions, to be himself principled, in support of a cause. So that the cause – which had universal ramifications – became the suspect, open for debate, while people were dying and the real suspect became invisible. In that respect, he was a secret agent working for a government. He was his own island, with its unique laws, morality and public opinion. Only once before had Jerrasi encountered this especially infuriating dilemma, and that was on an Indian reservation, where the laws and obligations and ethical choices were entirely different, in some cases, from those of the white intruders, regardless of their Federal Bureau badges.

Come to think of it, Felham looked a little like an Indian, Jerrasi thought, peering at the wise-ass, don't-fuck-with-me face.

"I want this photograph in every post office, grocery store, police station, court house, in every town ... Print thousands of them. I want roadblocks. Airport security checks. Buses. Train depots. I want him. I want this sonafabitch!" he ordered to the heavens, Shelley Pendergras and Madrid at his side.

"Yes'sir," Shelley replied. "Does that include the press?"

"He is only a suspect, wanted for questioning," Madrid butted in. "We have no evidence to build on, not yet anyway. Wouldn't be proper."

"You can take 'proper' and stuff it up his cock-sucking ass!" Jerrasi railed.

"I mean 'legal'," Madrid clarified. "We disseminate that photograph to the press, and his lawyers first thing out'll be screaming to the district attorney's office, about the undue process, the gross miscarriage. He'd be right back out on the street."

"You wanna bet?" Madrid caught the vigilante drift. "Fuck legal," Jerrasi went on, a tumbling, dire eumenides. "Fuck logic. They used insider weapons. There's no trace possible. They wore gloves. No fibre. No mistakes. So far we got nothing. NOTHING!! They're outta here. We got nothing but this pieceashit photograph, and that background check and we're gonna GO with it. Do you understand?" Then calming down, Jerrasi fixed his tie and grumbled, "Run it by Kinesey. Never mind, I'll tell him myself. SHIT!" And he kicked the front tyre of his vehicle, then nervously placed the call.

"No," Kinesey, agitating from his carphone, resolved, "absolutely not." "It's him, goddammit. Two survivors here recognize him. He fits the account of that dame in LA. What's more, we now know that under an alias, DMV shows ownership of an Aston-Martin."

"That's good. That's very good. But I still can't do it, Bob. Think about it."

"I'm thinking real clearly, Raymond. You hear those sirens in the background? You have any idea how many bodies we're talking about? We're into Jim Jones numbers here. And we have absolutely no clue, after eight years. That looks real bad for the Bureau."

No, that looks real bad for you, Kinesey wanted to say, but didn't. There was no point. "I'm putting two hundred more men on the case."

"That won't even do it. Don't you see the way these guys operate? We're talking about terrorism, Raymond. Random terrorism within the United States."

"Catch them in the act, Bob. See who they're working with. Because they sure as hell aren't working alone. There's got to be more of them. Recruits. A breakdown somewhere. Someone's got to talk."

"I wanna haul in the brother." Jerrasi went on.

"On what charge?"

"No charge. We just want to talk to him in more depth, now that his brother is the likely candidate."

"Fine. And while you're at it, I'd like to see us place our people at every animal rights meeting, at every environmental meeting and conference coming up. There can't be that many of them. Who's teaching this stuff on college campuses?" And he rattled off a dozen names of organizations. "What about the Nature Club? The World Ecology whatever you call it? Hell, maybe there's even insiders over at EPA, or Interior. Some berserk Ranger Rick."

"We already positioned ATU people [that was the Bureau's Anti-Terrorist unit] six months ago. Nothing."

"Do it again. They didn't waltz into ABARU without help. Probably inside help. They didn't just come by that truck. There's a team and they're absolute pros. And the only way these sick fucks are ever going down is if we catch them in the act, Bob."

"The photograph, Raymond. I need it out there." Kinesey thought about that.

"Don't make me repeat myself, Ray ..."

"There's absolutely nothing the Bureau can do to prevent leaks," his boss finally capitulated. There was no reason to thank him. Jerrasi hung up.

By eleven that morning, both Felham and Muppet had quietly checked in to separate hotels in a moderately-sized town in northern Texas, just about the time a reasonable likeness of Felham, many years dated but nonetheless him, as well as a lead graphite composite picture of Muppet began filtering down to many of the nation's noon hour television news briefs, and rolled off countless printers for afternoon and evening newspaper editions around the country.

In his room alone, Felham stared at the phone, debating whether or not to call Jessie. The television set was on, and to his astonishment he saw his earlier self, a double, back from the unexpected instant that stared uncomprehendingly into space, toward the cheap bright light of an Alaskan DMV office in Anchorage, years before. Yet even back then he might have known that such photographs will haunt us. That he was on a path with no return. That every shortness of breath is leading somewhere; the most minuscule detail, gesture, word, will be used against us; a flurry of cant, or a slow latitude of idleness, no meaning intended, may be easily turned into an aftermath of despair, until there is cause for the most venomous and self-aggravating superstition. Until every action, no, each thought – the tyranny of it!– becomes accountable to a judge and jury.

That's where the both of us were left, pondering the recurring caveat in Kierkegaard, where he invokes a *thorn in the flesh [that] gnaws so profoundly that he cannot abstract it – no matter whether this is actually so or his passion makes it true for him ...* *

And now it is truly too late. For how many people must have seen the images? A young man named Tom in crocodile shoes, the janitor at Jessie's clinic? A dozen employees at the restaurant? A Haitian woman who'd just given birth? Women who'd been at the Gymboree the week before? All it took was one recognition, one phone call.

Felham looked into the mirror, weighing the possibilities of further disguise, or full exposure, and I knew, I knew without a doubt, that he must have been feeling what is commonly called in these parts of Texas, rapture, the rapture of what might be his last night on Earth.

The light, enemy forces, glanced the corner of my eye, mirroring the unglued desiderata, what I might have done with my life, besides business school and cowardice and the easy way out ... I might have, I might have,

* Soren Kierkegaard, *Fear and Trembling,* and, *The Sickness unto Death* (trans. Walter Lowrie), [Doubleday : New York, 1954] page 204.

helped a stray, a foundling, a defenceless someone, anyone, just one precious ... Would it have been so difficult, is it so hard? Right here, in these hands, and then, as a just reward, to be reborn an albatross, a rare blue butterfly, a Himalayan mountain goat ... a soul worthy of the dream. To have done something decent with myself ... Done something ... Did something ...

"DO SOMETHING!" my throat rasped.

"WHAT?? What did you MEAN by that?" she cried out, shaking me.

"What? WHAT?" I jolted upwards. "What was I ... I was saying something?"

"You don't know?" The unreality, the nightly visitation of it leaving her so completely in the dark. She pleaded, "Come out, come out, wherever you are," holding me like a mother, for the last time. "Where are you, Jason? What's happening to you? TALK TO ME, PLEASE!" And she just closed her eyes, having felt the spectre, but having no name for it, yet. It was so sad. She turned away. I'm sorry, Iyura, my head pulsed. Turned away, now angrily, disappointed, convinced her husband had totally ... "I'm sorry," I half uttered. "It'll get better." *Better? Better what? What was I doing? How long could she put up with this? How long had I been in this way? Who am I? What am I thinking, planning ...*

Until my little scene, my dark and ugly secret. Pitiful penumbra between man and wife, shattered for good, as two uniformed State troopers, I guess they were, carrying weapons – they knew all right, somehow they'd found out, had made all the connections necessary – accompanied by two plainclothes men sporting sunglasses, their suit jackets open, *Day of the Jackal* urgency, egressed cautiously from patrol vehicles that had just advanced onto our street, slid through the front gate and stalking heavily, letting no precaution escape them – I recognized the burnt sinister silhouettes, had mentally prepared for every step – came up towards the redwood-shingled house where I stood waiting for them behind the closed drapes. I'd been waiting all morning. Longer than that, even. The troopers were staking positions to either side, their guns raised, while the two others prepared to walk up on to the porch and ring the bell ... A plangent pause.

What are they waiting for?

You bastards!

TONGUE AND IDEA

During which time I saw it all. Or at least as much as one brother can imagine, and can have been moved to action, albeit far less satisfactory, or completely, by another. In a brief span, after years of muddling along, a wave of clarity had swept over me in my brother's name. And the web of life which would logically have entangled him – with all of its players, assailants, love triangles, combatants and victims – rose up in choral dimensions. I had strength, now; the world's woes were heightened, my own duty, or possibilities, made spectacularly apparent.

Some people, thus afflicted in past times, built bombshelters, or disappeared into trailers out in the desert where no one could hear their mad ravings. Or, closer to home, slid into homelessness and screamed at passers-by. Still others chalked it up to grotesquely over-written feelings, distortion of fact, obfuscation of reality. Dramatic 'purple'. Well ... Let them!

For whatever faults bedraggled me, I was coming swiftly to closure on an elaborate blueprint for action. Whatever its shortcomings, this scheme provided me an inner counterbalance, my only survival, in the face of a battle no one else around me seemed able, or willing, to recognize. If you doubt my word, keep an eye out in your local newspaper during the coming months, or years. You'll see.

It would be easy to declare that those who ignore the way in which they live are condemned to a future in which they have no hand. Expect that *having no hand,* casting no vote, making no choices, remaining mute, is the most libellous form of complicity with the status quo. Those who are silent – and I don't necessarily mean *literally* – are guilty.

And so it begins for me ...

That fast-skipping bitch in her designer pumps and closely-bound knees and little time to spare, a frizzy blond, bow-legged, as oblivious as the pavement, but vindictive, all right; a young-to-middle-aged, self-important person, perhaps a salesgirl aggressively on the up and up, maybe a lawyer, after all, given the salary range and her now living in this upper middle-class neighbourhood; perhaps a recent divorcee living high off her alimony. I have been watching her. I have observed her dragging an old, nearly feeble low-to-the-ground dachshund by a metal leash and constricting collar up to the same tree every morning where, to get him to do his business, she'd literally kick at him, more precisely, she'd kick at the region of the dog's bowels in order to move *them* more quickly. And I figured out that this poor dog probably shat uncontrollably on her precious white mohair rug and so now, before going to work, she was determined to get him to go ... her wench-tongued gutturals, that grating face ... In all her impatience, not even considering that perhaps her dog was sick, in pain.

And at the same time, ineluctably, a power surge had shocked all of my senses into alignment; I am under water struggling with dozens of lobsters, our claws are taped, our eyes are waxy and forlorn, imprisoned behind glass at the grocer's, just waiting to be ... not to be ... boiled alive, more precisely; while *Homo Sapiens* saunter by, pushing oh so civilized grocery carts, some turning their faces from the sight of *live* animals! dreaming, instead, of their *dead* snails, rabbits, deer, frogs, bear, salmon, eel, squid, quail, geese, pony, cat, hen, halibut, crab, tuna, lamb, penguin, egret, hippo, wildebeest, and muskrat and on and on, and paean after paean, and aeon after aeon, my insignificant voice, my losing breath, of turkeys and porcines, and corned beef hash and veal, these latter items whose sheer magnitude, I eulogize, I beg forgiveness ... The cows.

And consequently scream, I pray, I scheme, I root for Him ... down there, in my very own agonizing Texas, that most central State of the world, or state*ment*: of all that's wrong and has been killing me, please, Stop! That dachshund, those lobsters, or as Mussolini put it, help me *translate other people's pious and worthy intentions into concrete achievement.* I don't care that it was a Mussolini who said it. It's the only hope, the veritable metamorphosis that means anything. A dream of reason ... escaping from stupor into motion from the *idée fixe,* into action.

I knew I'd be looking at assault with intent to kill, what – two hundred thousand dollars bail? Three years in jail on good behaviour, prior to the possibility of parole? To skip out on the bail would send me to the slammer – if they caught me – for easily twenty, twenty-five years.

A bell, eviscerating my insides, a raging at the door, they'll kick it in, demons, detectives; Let them. Any time now, Father ... Just me and ... and ...

You. Go on, get going. Make your calls and get a bite to eat. There won't be time later. The familiar comfort of simply chewing. Out into that vast, hot, windjamming sky that blows clean and liberated across the grasslands, from as far north as the arctic, and there's only barbed wire to deflect it in these parts. But he'll be collecting wire clippers, soon, I imagine.

He turns on the rental car radio, heading north on the main boulevards, past a string of furious fast-food joints and one church after another, and he picks up an old Jimmy Dean hit, typical, and then turns the channel only to hear that week's USDA livestock report, in proper Hill southern dialect, as it's known in West Texas:

... With a heavy demand, trading on beef variety meats was brisk; cheek meat pressured prices two dollars higher. Hearts and lips finished the week firm, while the balance of variety meats closed off at generally steady price levels. Export demand was adequate on continued light supplies of tongues. Supported by good export demand, hearts finished the period at higher price levels. As with beef, trading on pork variety meats was steady to firm. Feet and salivary glands finished a dollar higher, while trading on inedible tallow and greases was slow on light offerings. Protein feed supplements trading was moderate to steady, though there appeared to be a lower undertone on packer hide offerings ...

Felham stopped in a line of traffic beneath the flashing red light adjoining the railroad crossing.

... Slaughter steer and heifer ranged fifty cents-to-two dollars higher, while slaughter bulls moved steady to nearly three dollars higher. Feeder cattle were uneven this week. The carcass equivalent index value of A Choice one-to-three was five hundred fifty-to-seven hundred pounds. Carcass was up at a dollar sixty-nine, at a hundred at seventy-six cents for the week. Boxed beef demand and offerings were mostly moderate. The estimate composite of boxed beef cutout values for A Choice one-through-three ...

And suddenly felt the wind rattle his Mazda as the long-stretching locomotive with its bright and cheery multicoloured boxcars, travelling through the juncture at some thirty-five miles an hour, carried more than a hundred completed hydrogen bombs off towards the rest of the nation, while twining beneath the rumble was more of that radio data regarding barrows and gilts and feeder pigs, spareribs and skinned hams, ears and chitterlings, neck bones and sweetbreads and scalded tripe, packer bleachable tallow and yellow grease; butt-branded steers, eighty-five percent Panhandle area blood meal and bone meal and selected livers and unscalded lips. The daily vernacular of Business As Usual viscera.

They were in one of the very best bastions of redneck America to do damage, to convey His higher callings. There were, of course, dozens of other nearly-as-grim locations in the U.S. they might have selected: Kansas City, Oklahoma City, Dodge City, Sioux City, Sioux Falls, South St. Joseph,

South St. Paul, Omaha and Denver. Easily half-a-million slaughter sites throughout the world, factories churning out animal food twenty-four hours a day. Sacrificial lambs lining up in a distance comparable to the moon and back. My brother and Muppet's war might not persuade the Congress to impose vegetarianism throughout the land – which had always been the straightforward goal – but it would certainly make some people look twice at their own diet, their soul, their strength of character, before tearing into their next veal chop. Then again, it might not.

Thinking positively, it might even scare up some serious talk in the red meat epicentre of a country that Felham's data showed was busy slaughtering some sixty billion pounds worth of live animals every year – sixty billion living pounds, tortured to death; let's see, the Holocaust, figure an average of one-hundred twenty pounds per Jew, times six or seven million of them – we're speaking of a scarcely imaginable calamity, that inflicts seventy of those Holocausts EVERY YEAR. And it's legal, it's celebrated, every community in America, the world over, praises it. The only difference, of course, is that the Nazis intended (and nearly accomplished) the total extinction of all Jews, whereas Texans, Americans, most of the world, do everything in their power to *perpetuate* the genes, the bulk, the meat, to multiply cows ad infinitum, for the slaughter. An industry grossing nearly forty billion dollars annually. Six billion pounds of murdered flesh in Texas alone, a State with approximately 15,400 cattle farms, as well as the largest and most efficient slaughtering houses in the entire world. A State where nearly 400,000 cattle and even more pigs are butchered every week. Twenty-five thousand a day in just one sprawling plant, the mournful object of Felham's present expedition. Nearly a million throats slit every week, while the animals are still alive. Every week, a million sets of eyes beholding man's infernal handiwork. And just right up the street. No way to miss the smell of all that blood and blood money in the air, the true scent of American culture. Blood pits.

It was no longer the animal numbers that figured in his plans; numbers that had overwhelmed him, left him powerless and without hope years before. It was the human numbers that mattered to him. How many he could kill.

For Felham, the only decent thing to accomplish in this current man-made world was point-blank revenge. Thank god for the gun, for bullets, for full automatics. Given the condition of our human genes, my brother would have liked to have murdered every murderer, to have wiped out most of the population of the United States, as far as I could deduce, given the numbers of meat-eaters (collaborators with the enemy, as he likened them). He would have spared minors, I imagine, especially since high school biology could work so remedial an impact on certain sensitives, as it had on Muppet and Felham, Indeed, if every child were forced to spend an entire day and night, weary and beleaguered, in a slaughterhouse, vomiting with grief, there's little likelihood they'd permit their parents and older siblings and schoolmates to force them, to shame them, into eating meat ever again. For that matter, if every slaughterhouse were exposed to the outside world, constructed, say, of glass walls, so that pedestrians passing by would have to peer in, meatpackers might well go out of business overnight. Fuck'um!

Then again, pedestrians might just walk by and look the other way. Fuck'um!

The killer rage – that incommunicable scream, that NO ... that universal pain – could only find relief in the weapon, in his hand, in the trigger, against the finger, not blind but unforgiving. Rape. Massacre. Slow torture. Destruction. Obliteration. Monstrous revenge. If there were a way to become a life-preserving benevolent tyrant, buoyed along on the shoulders of – not Communist, not Khmer, not Aryan – but vegetarian masses, sending young biology patriots out on missions to smash windows and burn all the butcher shops, he would gladly have done so, instead of resorting to the gun.

At the same time, how could he ever acquit his soul, the insane onrush of suffering in his head, hideous, indelible images, of all the past atrocities? The aching was like a vice squeezing unrelentingly. He would happily have shouldered all their pain, become every one of those cows. There is nothing so pitiful and helpless in the whole world, as a one thousand pound, bewildered cow strung upside down by a shackle on its ankle, bellowing, clawing clumsily for life, trying by all of its unpractised instincts to find its friends, to ward off the death he knows is coming. A blood splattered wall to his right, a little human killer with an unreachable mind, unreachable heart, to his left; surrounded by bayonets, knives, shotguns, air guns, electric captive bolt applicators. How to become that cow? Frightened, in agony, no one to hear it, the cruciate ligaments of its knees rupturing, the fetlock and hip joints dislocating, the skin being peeled off while he still clings to every final breath, blood pouring out of his nostrils, covering his eyes, pain burning like the fires of the sun until darkness descends with a quick splutter of weakening surmise. And the lights have gone out forever. Who can ever answer to the feeble ferocity of a cow's final bellowing query: *Why?*

My brother could have suffered with more knowledge, and that would have made it in some mystical way more tolerable, he reasoned. The knowledge that cows were saints and human beings devils. And that God would rectify the balance sheet in the end.

That is the eternal dilemma which separates conscience from the rest of the brute creation in man. But Felham would never escape the terrible, terrible fact that he, too, was a human, a devil, who had lost faith in balance sheets, save for whatever rogues he could pick off in the cosmic struggle. And yet, I envied him his desperate tactics, which must have provided at least the sense of a lifted burden. I envied him with so haunted a desire that my envy now made it my fatality to live.

He and Muppet were a nation, the two of them. Who else could they talk to? They clung together. With the emergence of Jessie, you have my brother struggling to become three-dimensional, to somehow integrate the love of a woman with that hormonal maelstrom of genetic androgen, which made him a hyena among cowards on the plains of darkness.

The darkness turns into sunrise, sentiments of hate are confused with forgiveness. Waves in his ears. He can't hear himself think, his anger, his thoughts, poised on that trigger, while his heart had not dimmed since the first moment he suckled Mom's nipples. What's it going to be, I ask him?

Fuck'um.

There was, of course, the hydrogen bomb, manufactured in mass numbers over at the factory. Sprawling silently underground just down the road a piece, evil ensconced in the loveliness of Christianity, for this was a largely Christian community, a metaphor of the highest good. He and Muppet had thought about that factory, long and hard. Who wouldn't have considered it? And I assure you, had there been a bomb that could be dropped, shall we say, *selectively,* without harming innocents, they would surely have gone for it, would have figured out how to get their hands on it, deliver it, and they would have blown that sucker across the Panhandle, across every diseased corner of the United States, Europe, the Third World – wherever the animals were being tortured. Everywhere, in other words. Call it a metaphor too perfect for action. The phrase 'all or nothing' no longer applicable in this century.

The nuclear weapons train passed out of sight. Felham continued on his way into Ragtown, as it was once known; this Spanish yellow rose blossoming in the heart of short-grass cattle country. The illimitable Texas Panhandle, *Llanos Estacados,* or staked plains, thought worthless and uninhabitable a century before, when a whole cow could be had for two dollars, the value of its hide. The animal itself was considered valueless. Like Yellowstone. At best, in those days, philosophy was cheap, life was cheap, cows were for leather and for shortening. The buzzards got the rest. Texas. Rack and pang and retribution. Tophet and Avichi. Fire and brimstone. Perdition and pandemonium. But as far as American history was concerned, this was the breeding group of *real men:* cowboys, cattle ranchers. The backbone of American idealism. The Wild West. Well fuck it! That was Felham's reaction.

He stops at a Toot'n'Totom payphone to call her, but then checks the impulse and buys some M&Ms instead and picks up a local paper. His picture's not in it but he knows they've got tonight, and tonight only.

He puts down the paper, resolved now. What was going through his head, I wonder? To bring her into this was mad, he must have known that. And yet he could not shake her from his visions. Maybe it was love. Maybe being held by her. He dreamt, just then, of a life together; a life free of turmoil and pursuit and fuck'ums ... A life that had forgiven him his sins. Felham believed in non-violence. He venerated Gandhi, St. Francis, Buddha. What he had done by killing people he did not consider wrong. He knew that Gandhi subscribed to so-called 'just' war. Christianity, even Franciscans, sanctioned *just war.* Buddhists had fought their own just wars for centuries. And so would my brother. Worrying about the morality of it was like debating the proper usage of a fork and knife and tea server among Neanderthal. Morality, etiquette, civilized behaviour, didn't enter into it, in his estimation. Justice did. The world was overpopulated by angry, indecent, murderous people, oblivious people, and the animals were dying out as a result. Nobody was doing anything because, by and large, the world was asleep; and Felham was not about to waste his life ignoring the problem. He tried to do his best to stop it. That's all this was about. Those who'd been killed were guilty. He, too, had paid a price, and suddenly, at that phone booth, Jessie seemed to him to be his right, his worked-for blessing, the one consolation of total self-sacrifice.

Having changed his mind, finally, he dials her direct line at work. Heat in his throat. Felham is afraid of the consequences. It is 1:50 in the afternoon her time.

"Yes?" she says in what Felham picks up on as a hushed and distraught way.

He pauses, last chance to abort, and then says, "It's me. Clyde."

"Jesus," her voice exhausted with fear.

"No, Clyde," he repeats, coddling, wanting to grin. *Had she seen the news?*

"Where are you?"

"What does it matter," he airs protectively. That she readily accepts the pseudonym, which once had caused her such consternation, tells a lot. And might keep her out of trouble, just in the event ...

"Are you – I saw the news ..."

"You did ..." he says resignedly, cutting off any reference to specifics.

"Yes."

"Then you understand."

"I think so. I'm trying real hard." She knew, more or less, let's say less, what the ABARUs were all about. And she'd already heard the first radio debate in her office, prompted by the massacre, in which some of the realities were described by a pro-animal group spokesperson. The factions were heating up. There was no question that this loner – whom she'd essentially *picked up* in a grocery store – had stoked the beginnings of something; not quite a national reappraisal, but at least the spark of dialogue, however overwhelming the odds. But she also figured out that such actions might only give added cause to those in power, a renewed urgency to carry out their heinous mandates, to conduct their research, to spend the taxpayers' money, to fortify their interests. She had thought about it all. Nothing good could come of killing people. Of that she had always been convinced. But nothing good could come of killing animals, either. Her head was burning with the impossible ambivalence. She was no vegetarian, never had been; or, described more sympathetically, she was one of those vegetarians who ate fish and chicken and occasional meat.

And suddenly her own contradictions meant something to her. His every breath was filled with her own needs. Perhaps, in so few words, he detected it, because now, their meagre semblances of thought, desire, terror, were like heat-seeking missiles at odds, looking for warmth, asymptotes wanting feverishly to connect, that had every reason to do so, but not knowing, either of them, what the other was really feeling, hoping for. Or what, in this world, was possible, after all.

"I've become a vegetarian," she suddenly said, surprising even herself. A statement not yet of fact, but transforming. She could never go backwards again.

"Thank you," he replied, no intonation possible.

And at that moment, cruising up the street from a big-time cattle auction in the centre of town, were several horse-drawn wagons running tourists out towards breakfast along a nearby canyon rim where they'd cook up buffalo steaks on mesquite open fires, and the cowboys would probably show off their branding and rope handling. Suddenly the lead wagoner raised his pistol and fired into the air with a boisterous *hee-hah!*

"What's that noise I hear?" she asked.

"Cowboys and Indians." Even that was too much, he immediately realized.

"I have to see you," she decreed.

"Even knowing?"

"Especially."

"There's not much of a future."

"We've been through that. It's *now* I'm speaking of."

"Maybe you're in over your head?" he warned.

"Maybe I am. A woman sometimes knows the moment she's impregnated. I've seen it happen."

Felham's grip on the phone went weak. He nearly dropped it. "You're kidding??" he blurted with electricity.

"I don't think so."

"That's ... that's FANTASTIC!" he nearly cried out, restraining the timbre only slightly, so that it sounded like a painful realization, or the first hint of tears in my brother's life.

"I'll call you tomorrow," he finally converged in haste, reassembling himself. "We'll figure something out."

"I love you," she stated clearly. "I love you madly."

"Bingo!" Landford White gleamed officiously, looking at Robert Jerrasi, Wes Madrid and Shelley Pendergras, taking off his headset and rewinding the reel-to-reel. They all had the young man in the crocodile shoes to thank.

White, a surveillance expert with the Bureau, had overseen the rapid deployment in Menlo Park of the wiretap with court orders sent down by facsimile and marked 'Top Priority'.

Jerrasi looked anxiously at his watch, then said aloud, "Shit! We've got to stop the SFPD from questioning that brother."

They all knew it: one phone call from him – me – or my wife, a single tip, and they could lose Felham.

They were guessing, of course, but logic dictated that Felham and I were somehow co-conspirators; that I'd have Iyura, or her lawyer brother call down to Texas and warn him.

Their timing could not have been more precious. Baggot was getting ready to proceed up the stairs, off the grass, to the door, when the little mobile phone he wore on his belt summoned his ear.

"What?"

"This is Jerrasi. What's your situation ... Okay, this is very, very important, listen to me: we're asking you to BACK OFF, NOW. BAGGOT, GET THE HELL OUTTA THERE! MOVE IT!"

Felham must have felt extraordinary, the way I did when I first heard about Bart, whose Eurasian skin and eyes and Buddha body – all his Japanese components – were going to ensure that future bliss which no adversity, not even the executioner's ground, can nullify. But, of course, back then, I had had far more confidence that life for me would unfold in such and such a manner, more or less normally, decisions taken carefully, slowly with the trepidation of a younger brother who knew nothing about weapons, and had no intention – then – of ever finding out; whereas he had no such stability of mind, no foreknowledge, no reason to believe, or hope for anything. Anything. Until now, at the moment which he'd already set into motion ...

Felham continued driving, having not eaten since before the hit in Maryland. It was flat, as flat as any place in North America. Cheap apartments, rundown houses, the gaudy churches, a plethora of billboards, more than one commending sausage, a few higher rising buildings of steel and glass, and some normal middle American neighbourhoods, sweet, pretty, even cosy, were all that held back the implacable laws of form governing the Panhandle all around him.

Felham could see thirty miles up the road, it seemed to him. Thirty miles of oat grass and monotonous dirt. The clouds, the sun, were bigger than life.

And there was history here; these folks had their own Alamo, of sorts, and Pueblo Indian habitation dating back twelve hundred years. It wasn't until the 1870's that the white man made his debut, funded by British and Scottish banking investors. He rounded up the then resident Comanches, wiping out their buffalo and introducing longhorns. There was this fellow by the name of J. F. Glidden, an easterner, who began mass producing barbed wire and he dispatched his son-in-law to the Panhandle with instructions to fence it all in, the whole damned West, which is nearly what the lad did. In the late 1800's, forty percent of all steel smelted in the U.S. went towards barbed wire, for use by the emerging dynasties of cattle barons. Gigantic cattle hotels (feedlots) were introduced, along with the railroad, which, of course, expedited the selling and shipping of wholesale herds en masse.

In the early twenties, the cowhands came up with electric prods for moving the cattle into the *corridas,* where they could be easily got at, auctioned off, or slaughtered on site, part of the hotel concept, which now adjoined the killing areas. This meant, of course, that the cattle knew they were going to die for days, or weeks, or even months in advance.

In the meantime, the grasslands themselves were being steadily denuded of any remaining forest, for the same purpose – to open every last piece of terrain to the Johnson grass and Turkestan bluestem and Indian and switch and Stipa needlegrass and gramma and any of the hundreds of other varieties of Texan seed that four-bellied ruminants liked so much to devour, so that calculating human carnivores – darling daughters, First Ladies, exquisite sounding poets and sober MDs, school teachers and heroes and billions of supposedly evolved *Homo Sapiens* – could stuff their mouths, fill their stomachs and then defecate their piles of high cholesterol, agony-ridden innards-of-cow, the simple truth ringing in Felham's head, continuing through town.

By the middle of the century, hundred-ton machines with steel blades were mowing over the last cedarbrakes and skin-oak glades, leaving only the scrag and bee brush, the black persimmon and large stalks of Spanish dagger, to stand in the way of horizon after horizon of grass. Grass. GRASS.

The grass made the ranch. And the ranch made for one third of all U.S. consumption, the cow, its final expression in the form of human shit.

This cow who once made for 'romantic' employment, jobs for the *vaceros* – the Spanish cowboys; and the cheap labour types like the *volteadores* who shouted at the animals to help round them up; and the *tumbadores* who specialized in throwing calves in preparation for the branding. Throwing was not exactly the right term, for in essence it was crashing into them on their flanks, football style, and relying upon one's body weight to bring them down. The *marcadores* actually placed the brand, burning it in to the hide so as to make it last, forever.

But the real cowboy brought down his animals with a throw of the rope – big loops, overhand throws, the *piale* which caught the animals by their two hind feet, snapping ankles, crushing jaws as they slammed into the dirt; or the *media cabeza* which went for the jaw straight away; and dozens of other high-sounding Spanish techniques mastered by the *vaqueros*. They'd sometimes go after bobcat and coyote with the same polish, tie the captured animals down to the back of their horse, and drag them through prickly pear country for miles. A slow way of killing the said varmints.

There were plenty of such varmints in Texas. And it was, of course, legal as hell to aim shotguns at any of them, be they friendly Hispid Pocket mice or Thirteen-lined Ground Squirrel, Golden Eagles or mountain lions. If it moved, why, then it was worth shooting. Not everything had been shot. There were still a few Cave Bats (not many) and Eastern Moles and Ringtail Cats inhabiting the Panhandle, even the occasional Barbary Sheep and Badger. And now and then a Black-footed Ferret (one or two, literally) would dart across a road in the midnight. But largely, the survivors were confined to the Whitetail Deer and Roof Rat variety. Lots of jack rabbits and cotton-tails; multitudes of gophers and Spotted Skunks. Sometimes, Grey Fox or Pronghorn Antelope. And countless birds. Now and then they might be spotted in someone's food, but mostly it was the cattle that were eaten and the Armadillo Grill, where Felham now waited for Muppet, gave every indication of this diet designed by, and for, the locals.

The tongue of man. The tongue which, in most people, had conquered the idea. The idea of restraint, of pantheism, of compassion. What is that tongue but the taste buds which it comprises. Taste buds that have been described in one textbook as '... pale, oval bodies in the darker-staining epithelium, beneath a hole ... spindle shaped supporting cells, the ends of which surrounded an inner taste pore ... Nerve fibres from a subepithelial plexus (that) penetrate the epithelium ...' * But such anatomical prose hardly accounts for the diverse penchant in man, the ephemeral gratifications, say, of calf's heart dipped in paprika sauce, or any of the countless blood puddings, or Indonesian *Sate bumbu dendeng* (coconut cream-marinated dog served on skewers), or *Mokh* (Algerian parboiled sheep brain casserole), or for that matter *Vulvulae botelli,* the ancient Roman pig uterus, a real delicacy that was apparently stuffed with pine nuts, dill and cumin. **

Felham, who had never given the time of day to his taste buds, not since Brazil, anyway, stared balefully at the menu, with its predominant barbecue briskets and beef stews, chicken fried and rattlesnake steaks, dozens of different hamburgers and steak sandwiches. As well as a vast inventory of Mexican meat dishes, Trochos de Pollo Pibil, Chorizos Mexicanos, grilled bistec and Albondigon para Playa – Mexican meat loaf. He sat in the least conspicuous corner. This was a town with more than its share of security people, on account of the controversial nuclear weapons plant a few miles away. The security had been a consideration, but not a deciding factor, when it came time to single out a slaughterhouse. In fact, all that security suggested an unlikely cover. Where antinuclear protesters had been coming for fifteen years to save the world from destruction, who could ever have cause to worry over two cantankerous cow sympathizers, in dun-coloured mail-order local clothes, the pointy boots and three and a half inch brim hats, the snap shirts with pointed yokes, the sloppy Levi jeans, shirt hanging out, all gotten first thing past the airport at a nearby convenience store on the way in? Working livestockmen. Mussed hair. Loose fitting garb. Cigarette smoking. Two days of stubble. Could've been millionaires with copper or oil or helium, or certainly ten thousand acres or so. Then again they might have been mere yard boys. It often looked the same down here.

"Mornin'. Coffee?" the aged but spunky waitress plied agreeably on her way round.

"Please. No cream."

She poured a cup and asked what it would be.

"I'll have some of your Ranch Style beans, Miss. Skip the fried ham – my cholesterol – but go heavy on the onions and hot sauce," he said.

* I. Friedmann, ed., *The Ultrastructure of Sensory Organs* [North-Holland American Elsevier : 1973] page 3.

** Calvin W. Schwabe, *Unmentionable Cuisine* [Virginia University Press : Charlottesville, 1979] pages 117, 132 and 174.

"You want some cornbread with that, it's fresh?"

"Why sure. No, give me a grilled tomato sandwich instead. Lots of mustard." Felham loved mustard.

"Mustard's on the table."

Muppet, meanwhile, was on his way back from a certain gas station on the road into town from the local airport. There, out around back, out of view, standing side by side at the urinal, he had met their old Air Force Academy buddy Mickey, who'd just flown in some businessmen from Cannon Air Force Base outside Clovis, New Mexico, twenty-five minutes away by air. The jet he'd commanded was a sleek and pretty Grumman G-5 with intercontinental range. It could take you from Texas all the way to the jungles of South America. All the way to China, if needs be. Mickey was no longer flying the Swing Wing F-111D tactical fighters for which the Cannon 27th Tactical Fighter wing division was famed. That was for the younger generation of hot shit Desert Storm vets. Mickey was a middle aged has-been in their eyes. And he was; living out his days amid sustained bouts of depression and discreet pill popping. His wife had left him from sheer boredom and the bitterness of never having had kids. His savings were nearly spent, but at least he had a job which maintained his pilot's rating – a flying lackey for visiting government top brass and corporate types. He owed Muppet and Felham a big one, dating back to Academy days, and there was now nothing in his life which prevented him from fulfilling that obligation.

The businessmen had come for two days to visit the nuclear weapons facility, to step through those two-ton explosion-proof doors, and stroll along blast-absorbing corridors, and finally stare in wonder at the concrete and steel gerties that are programmed to cave in, containing the plutonium contamination in the event of any high explosive mishap, and all the employees with it. A courtesy tour.

Muppet had worked out the details of this little gas station tryst weeks before. He was still operating under the illusion of anonymity. He did not know – and neither did Mickey – that his and Felham's pictures were already out there.

"You put on a little weight!" Mickey noted, his fly open, slapping the Missouri giant on the back.

"Aim straight, you amateur." Muppet ridiculed him. "I see you're still touting that same crewcut, though it's gotten pretty grey, boy. Good to see you."

"Damn, it's good to see you too. How's Dirk?"

"Dirk's been better. Listen, Mickey: did you bring the stuff?"

"Well what do you think we're peeing here for, asshole! It's out in the

trunk in two crates. You better back your car around. I suppose I shouldn't
ask."

"Better for you if you didn't."

"Lotta fire power. I guess you know what you're doing."

"Not really ... So how'd you manage it?"

"Are you kidding? They've got thirty-four hundred enlistees at the base,
but only one supply sergeant on duty at the Armoury between midnight
and five and he likes to get stoned. Anyway, they got so much junk, nobody's
gonna miss anything."

"Here's the keys to my trunk. You'll find my old Flak jacket. Take it."

"I can't—"

"No, I want you to."

"Okay, thanks Mickey."

"Yeah sure. What the hell. I've left some goodies on board the jet."

"Like what?"

"Flame-thrower, two MP-5 machines, and some more rocket propelled
gadgets. You sure you two haven't been recruited by intelligence? I mean
who are you after? Fuck it, never mind."

They'd agreed that Mickey would check into his hotel sometime after
his confreres arrived – he would have needed time to log his arrival on
board and deal with the local gate maintenance and airport tower. He'd
leave word at the front desk that he'd be out late for dinner and to hold any
incoming messages, not that he was expecting any. But, in fact, he'd never
return from that dinner, the victim, instead, of an abduction by two armed
and dangerous outlaws. Neither Felham nor Muppet had flown a large craft
in years. They needed Mickey. They'd need a full load of jet fuel, if they
made it that far. Muppet did not question 'ifs'. Mickey would be their
'hostage', so as to keep him out of trouble. He'd spend the night back at
the jet waiting, and start up the turbos as soon as he received a call from
Muppet that they were on their way. The moment the two of them reached
the airfield, they'd be ready to fly away.

Muppet made the switch from one car to the other. The bullet hole that
an eleven year old girl, a Viet Cong, had put into Mickey's breastbone was
still visible in the jacket. NATO Round, 7.62 millimetre, your basic AK-
47. Your basic impulse: hesitate, she's only a kid. He had the drop on her.
But hesitate and you're dead. Mickey was lucky. Their mutual friend,
Stilling, was less lucky. He got it in what they called a Heidi Hole over
there. It came as no surprise. The tunnel rats were crazy, opting to crawl
through enemy bunkers which had been booby-trapped with grenades or
vipers. Stilling's widow and son lived in Clovis. Mickey, who was himself
a casualty, sterile, sort of looked after the boy once in a while.

He felt the handles on the two M-60s, worn, salubrious to the touch, and noted a couple thousand Glasser rounds, the sort that explode inside a person at a firing rate of about 700 a minute, an updated M-16 as well, equipped with a second RPG barrel for shooting half-a-dozen grenades. There was also a good deal of Czech plastic, similar to what they'd used in Maryland, just less concealed. Night camouflage, a scanning radio, additional boxes of ammo, two hunting knives and two bolt-action rifles with laser sights thrown in for good measure since the operation was to be at night. Mickey had admittedly gone overboard. He was a generous soul and of course had no idea what it was all for.

"You're a gem, Mickey," Muppet hailed, with a tender nudge against his face.

"I'll see you dudes later," he replied. "We'll party."

"Hell yes!"

Muppet's Missouri was all around him as he headed towards the cafe to meet Felham, an upbringing around cows, whose universal lowing was as tranquilly ingrained in Muppet's sensibilities as the bovine weight he carried in his own gut and muscle and thighs, in the multiple stomachs his parents always inferred, given the enormity of their son's appetite. Cattle beside the roads, drifting along fences where the wildest grasses bloomed, immune to cutting.

He slowed down to take a good hard look at them. Muppet had grown up around the Brown Swiss and Guernsey sorts. Milking cows that mosied through life, and through most people's consciousness, without exerting much emphasis. Cows were taken for granted – parts of the landscape, the oldest domesticated creature, older than dogs, according to some Turkish fossils. At least ten thousand years of slavery to *Homo Sapiens*. What did it mean? When did the sacred oxen, whose horns were once symbols of fertility to the Stone Age and throughout the Near East, become chattel, and then food? How could the human soul have plummeted so disingenuously?

Muppet was keenly attuned to what it all boded. He felt himself to be the cow, in much the same manner that ancient Sanskrit texts gazed upon the creature as upon eternity and likened it to the whole world. Muppet had not merely admired cows. He'd studied them with that scholarly curiosity to learn, for example, about the first century AD *Ordinances of Manu,* which had proclaimed the unprecedented sanctity of the cow, a line of logic which Gandhi himself adopted in this century when he recognized in cattle the ultimate icon of ahimsa, or nonviolence; a *poem of pity,* he called them.

Muppet had read how, throughout Asian and African literature and lore, the cow was sacred. Indian saints became cows at the moment of death and to this day Hindu India worships the animal in countless rituals generically termed *Go-puja* – from bowing before images of cows, to purifying themselves in boiled milk. Krishna himself was a cowherder god, though the term 'herder' does not quite serve the real meaning, which was Krishna's *companionship* with the animals. Regardless of the iconography, or manner of obeisance, the cattle in India were always left alone, free to wander. To this day, there are everywhere scattered these sacred herds and buffalo cults and elaborate mythologies, closely guarded truths about the human psyche which can only be explained by the cow, the buffalo, and the zebu – an estimated two hundred million of them roaming the fields and roads and back alleys of the Indian subcontinent. The common belief, of course, is that the cow is a reincarnated spirit of a person. 'To kill a cow in India is thus unthinkable. And so legends of poetic justice abound, like that of the famous King whose own metaphysical compunctions bade him have his own son executed for killing a calf'.* But today, most Indians eat meat.

A situation not unlike that of Missouri, where Muppet had been raised having to imbibe the milk and meat of utter trauma. A culture that kept cattle slaves. Missouri in the 1950's was not quite up to the mass factory farming of the present day but it was bad enough, the techniques of slaughter as sloppy and ghastly as they continue to be.

There had been two unforgettable events which had turned his mind around, a casual observer of cows transformed into their champion, passive acceptance of a system becoming adamant hatred and defiance. Instants of contact that were indelible and telling, and against which he could never again turn his back. The first was a moment of communication, a precursor of things to come.

More recently, what Muppet had found unbelievable throughout his extensive investigations was the fact that in all vastly assorted literature – literally tens-of-thousands of so called scientific publications – there was not a single research paper on the subject of intelligence in cows. No genocide of one species – the complete denial of an animal's existence – has ever been so thorough, he realized.

This is merely one more reflection on the stupidity of farmers and ranchers. Muppet grew up with these farmers, admired many of their finer qualities – their earnestness, their good humour, their hard working mettle. But he did not admire their stupidity, which was nothing more than an insensitivity born of greed, compliance with a dogma passed down from earlier generations, that demanded expediency in all things. A short-cut to

* See Gabriel la Eichinger Ferro-Luzzi, *The Self-milking Cow And The Bleeding Lingam – Criss-cross Of Motifs In Indian Temple Legends* [Otto Harrassowitz : Wiesbaden, 1987].

profit, a technique for dealing with the too obvious reality of slaughter and bullying and manhandling and despair. The *bona fide* existential angst that might have gripped at the adults, during brief moments of agricultural lucidity, but surely assailed the children once in a while. There's nothing quite like the charred remains of a rooster on the dinner table, a rooster one used to play with, to stoke introspection. Adult farmers might think they're schooling their young darlings in the art of life, preparing them to carry on the family operations, to withstand the proverbial onslaught of hard times and fluctuating markets and subsidies, dry seasons, leaf rot, foreclosures and illness. But, in fact, the children of those farmers who exploit animals are simply being educated to kill, desensitized to all that the farm should connote. The young ones grow up in this milieu and take pride in their abilities to milk those four tits on the udders and to put the horses out to pasture and eventually will think nothing of beheaded roosters and pet hogs destined for their dinner table. Every fleece is a golden fleece; every cow a commodity. But not in the beginning, when the children know they'd better keep their counsel, maintaining a conspiracy of silence about their strange existence and the tacit acceptance, universally subscribed to, of animal drudgery and their parent's complicity in it.

The constant demonstration of such parental authority over all other creatures seemed appalling to the young Muppet, a callousness that did not equate with his idea of family, of farm. Even at the age of seven years. The romance of the cowboy was simply untrue. How well Muppet remembered.

His parents were not stretched, like some of their neighbours, on account of an inheritance from a grandfather who'd been a big success in horse trading. But even as gentlemen farmers with a large family, they had to work and Muppet was always around cows. Some were milk, some were beef. They were not animals. They were hardly alive. Those eight hundred pound bulks of ambling quiescence were seen by Muppet's dad and mom to be nothing more than money.

But life contradicted that appraisal. Muppet recalled how he'd been playing on his favourite hillside and a group of milk cows had strolled up to him demanding to be scratched – he was their fence. And how he ended up spending a delirious afternoon scratching their backs, their ears, their jowls, and watching mothers and calves play – play as furiously, with as many skips and jumps into the air, as puppies. And the cows smiled and they spoke and groaned in joy and to the child's eye this was more true and more important then the Red Scare, or Kennedy's assassination, or the night the Beatles appeared on Ed Sullivan. And it was altogether incompatible in Muppet's mind with the fact of his parent's and his community's addiction to red meat.

How could he love his parents when his parents were part of the syndrome which subscribed to the murdering of cows? When they murdered those particular cows? How could he fight in a war (Vietnam) when he'd be fighting on behalf of people who killed cows?

He couldn't. When he went off to the Air Force Academy on scholarship, it was for a free education, more than any kind of conviction, for his heart was up on that hillock of green, cow-ambling Impressionism, and he had already made up his mind about the war. There was no way he was going to fight. He lived forever in that afternoon, remembering the sensation of big cow lips sucking on his tennis shoes, pulling off the socks and absorbing his toes. To have cows sucking on your toes ...

Who, what, are cows? Why do they so pull on the universal heartstrings? And why do they not pull enough, in most countries, to be spared? Muppet devoted much time to the contemplation of cows.

Muppet's acquired insights into the cow's diet, sensory capabilities, social behaviour, flair for communication, erotic passions and subsequent embryology, were analogous to the highest mammals. Cows can make love at any time during the year, just like people. And like people, their love is explicit, their eyes all expressive. Their eyes are BIGGER than ours; THEIR BRAINS TOO! You only had to look once at them to figure that out! Cow gestation takes between nine and eleven months. They are strict vegetarians – which make them God's chosen ones to begin with. Their hearing and vision and olfactory nerves are superbly evolved. They can see the primary colours with vibrant clarity, which means that the colour of blood is not unknown to them and the fact they must wallow in it in the slaughterhouse adds immeasurably to their hysteria. To Muppet's hysteria.

Muppet had seen cows speaking to one another. That's a given. As a child, he had sat beside a family of cows, the bull nearby, for hours at a time, and had witnessed literally hundreds of ethological signs, words and gestures expressly conveyed. Every zoosemiotic verb, desire, nuance, tense, colour, mood, confidence, innuendo, admission and joy came across, not just in the ordinary grunts the world thinks it knows, but in subtler tones, flips of an ear, pawing and rubbing, licking, pushing and itching, the orientation of horns and rumps and shoulders and, mostly, in the particular *look* of the animal. Their curiosity is legendary.

When cows speak, it is music. It was to the cave painters who clearly worshipped the animals. And it was music to Van Gogh who sat near cows in the fields where he painted, day after day, outside of Paris. Cows were the embodiment of philosophy to the Venetians, who worked them into nearly every canvas and literary epistle. Sannazaro's *Arcadia,* perhaps the most profoundly poetic evocation of pastoral tradition during the Italian

Renaissance, was about the landscape of cows, cows themselves, and the troubadour shepherds who pined away their days beneath mulberry and olive trees. The cow became the ideal of amity, the passive and restrained, their meadows and hillsides transformed into the classical setting for great dreams, always a Parthenon of unblemished marble on a distant escarpment.

The history of painting, both eastern and western, is encompassed by the steadfastness and dignity of cattle. In northern Indian miniatures, they are always seen accompanying the Gopis, the dancing girls, the Rajasthani tribal people, the ascetics, and the great Gods Siva and Krishna. They nurture the Christ child in the West, and lend substance and credibility to every human habitation.

But by 1855, in the French painter Constant Troyon's *'Boeufs allant au labour, effet du matin'*, the cows stare out at us in horror asking, How could we have forsaken them? Every fable, religious allegory and commercial label – Swiss chocolates included – fails to account for the unending torture to which cows, *Bos primigenius taurus,* have been subjected, despite their many artistic champions of the past.

Cows acknowledge no exclusive territory but share their grazing and resting and watering holes without the slightest friction.* As a family, consisting of the invariable old one, numerous adults, as many adolescents, and a few calves, there is evident respect for seniority, and a generous care taken with the young. But among the buffalo, there is no acknowledged leader of the herd. They all take care of each other.

The cows and buffaloes know something. Muppet intuited that as a child, but as an adult – staring at them off the side of the road in northern Texas – those cows possessed all the wisdom of the world. A secret slang, or tremor, that could only be explained in terms of touch and wind and the scent of prairie. Their consumption of the Earth's herbs and moss and verdure puts them at the very apex of photosynthesis, mammals in touch directly with the energy of stars and the transfixing capacity of soil. Such processes are not diluted. Their souls speak directly to these effects. Their weight is pure, their flatus pure. Every cow eye is a crystal ball, and Muppet had stared countless times into them.

But cows are not augurs: they cannot read palms; their genes have been skewed to the extent that their escape reflexes have been severed. Cows are easily unnerved, but against the rancher they are powerless.

Once, long, long ago, they had less to fear. For all domestic cattle descended from the now extinct race of aurochs, whose noble and graceful

---

* For much of this material on bovines, see Heinz-Georg Klos and Arnfried Wunschmann, *The Wild and Domestic Oxen* in *Grzimek's Animal Life Encyclopedia*, Volume 13, Mammals IV [Van Nostrand Reinhold Co.] pages 331-398.

images remain on the cave walls at Lascaux, in southern France.

All the other bovines in the world (outside of India) have been domesticated, enslaved, genetically altered, doomed to milk factories or slaughter, to grocery stores, under such appetizing names as Simmental Piebalds, Aberdeen Angus, Jersey and Ayrshire, Hereford, and Holstein-Fresian. But in Texas, it is the big beef breeds that have made big Texans, big Americans, and guaranteed that the slaughtering business would always be profitable: Charolais, American Brahman, Santa Gertrudis, Brangus and Charbray. Deceptively-ringing brands evoking the litany of red meat for ever and ever.

It was that same monied allure which galvanized high school students looking for vocational alternatives to college back in Missouri. Muppet had known his share of them. They'd go into town and hear a retired school teacher from the big city, using the one and only textbook on meat from the late 1930's, proclaiming the wonders of today's slaughterhouses with the kind of poetic license better suited to an analysis of Walt Whitman.

And he'd expound to these young boys and girls, kids coming into full bloom, one of Muppet's brothers among them, about back and loin fat, half inch to three quarters of an inch, the marbling evenly distributed, to give it that special finish and conformation, typically known as A Choice. And like a biology lab, except it was all cooked and eaten after class, the students would kill their own cow, their own calf, along with a pig, and countless squab broilers, pullets, capons, slips and stag chickens.

"Thirty boys and girls chasing down a hog with long-knives, like it were a Sunday picnic after Church," Muppet had once described that day for Felham. "Ganging up on the concerned thing – to hear it screaming out in defiance, pleading – as they converged on it, swinging their weapons, the animal's body bouncing, writhing, kicking, as they overwhelmed it. And soon it was dismembered. And the instructor then felt comfortable enough, the job having been done, to step forward and expatiate on the still quivering remains. It was so primitive."

And they'd all compare notes and cuts while hearing about America's darling, William Pynchon of Springfield, Massachusetts, the first official meatpacker, of hogs, in 1662; and a fellow named Perkins who evidently invented the original ice-making apparatus, an indispensable component of any of the slaughtering trades; or G. H. Hammond, the real genius behind refrigerated railroad cars for hauling meat. And old Mrs. Wilmer Steele who, back in Delaware in the twenties, managed with the help of vitamins, to breed broiler chickens indoors all winter with artificial lights. A new and artificial nature. The next exalted phase in mankind's manipulation of all other animals, just one step away from mass assembly lines and bioengineering. A modest little married gal doing all that, imagine!

They'd see an old film, the only one available of the so-called 'disassembly lines', the term given to the killing rooms with their overhead conveyor belts and hooks. They'd lose, invariably, a few of the vocational students at that point, the same way a few young doctors characteristically fell out of the profession at the first real sight of blood. But then these were tough farm people, after all, comfortable with the down and dirty ways – helping animals to give birth on warm spring nights, burying their dead, choosing which chickens would be chopped up, and going after them whilst murmuring those deceitful, becalmed nothings in the animals' ears. Young contradictory men, and gals, who'd obviously made it past any discomfitures at home, and were now agreed upon a career in killing.

And they were apt to vocalize like, *I'd sooner shoot a human intruder in my family's house than I would a defenceless deer* (except they'd kill raccoons and squirrels without blinking), or, *I feel no violence towards animals, only assholes.* And many of them would turn right around and go off to spend their summer vacations dispatching and sticking, scalding and picking, finishing and dressing, chilling and packing; America's premiere participles, the stuff of slaughterhouses. And many of those would stay on, the ones good with knives, as most of the boys in Missouri were. That's always the question you'd get asked by packing house personnel, *How are you with knives?* And if the answer was 'not bad', then there was always a job opening. Used to be three, four dollars an hour, but these days it was up to thirteen.

It's not an easy job providing Americans with their most loved diet, namely meat. A pound a day for the really forward-thinking individual... The meat eating races have always advanced mankind. Meat eating means progress, civilization, the endless struggle to go beyond the dumb animals who are our friends. And so it's up to you kids, the hard working livestock executives of tomorrow, and the industrious meatpackers, and the feedlot owners, even the sales girls, who must ensure that America remains strong. And that means, on occasion, holding in your gut like a man, gritting your teeth and swinging that knife ... And that's almost exactly how Muppet's brother was indoctrinated at the local Vocational Meat School just outside of Poplar Bluff. By that time, the scientific community was already intent upon pushing the technology well beyond the mere knife in a man's hand. Big corporations were getting into it. It was widely assumed that one day a perfect animal would be genetically engineered specifically for a chicken sandwich, or a double chilliburger, without wasting a single corpuscle or piece of bone marrow or minute of human labour. Intimations of Dolley.

Then one day, Calvin, his brother, invited Muppet to check out the *scene,* a plant where they killed anything that moved, except the workers, of course. As much as the sight of a murdered jaguar in Brazil can change a man's life, an hour's tour of a Missouri slaughterhouse was enough to have altered Muppet's entire universe. He knew from that day on that he would never acquit himself for having gone and seen and done nothing. As a human being. As a feeling animal. As a man who had waited millions of years to speak his peace. What could he have done? There were a hundred employees, including his own goddamned brother. In a diction that was determined to transform the inertia of habit, he would become the Babe Ruth among these sluggards.

His anger had grown up like a stout oak that begins as an innocent seedling. Yet nothing could have prepared him for that malignancy of images and sensations, that tabernacle of death, top-heavy with an exposition of the unending torment. In no other sphere are mere *words* to oneself so separated by other, unbearable and unappeasable facts of life. My connection to Muppet's experience becomes mute and naive at this juncture. I cannot attest or relate. Only re-invent.

Even outside the plant, the harbingers were manifestly speaking to him. He could see the streams of manure. An adult pig shits and pisses about seventeen pounds worth every day and all that concentrated nitrogen and phosphorous kills streams and lakes and earthworms and trees and ends up in aquifers where it destroys people's drinking water. Parts of Holland have been wiped out as a result of the slaughterhouses. You might catch the total catastrophe all at once, the way a Vermont maple without leaves in summertime has got to tell you something about acid rain. But the shit piles have something else to say to you, as well: that much of it is going back into the factory, as Muppet soon discovered.

The flies swarmed over him as he approached the main entrance. Once inside, it was the conveyor belts that Muppet first beheld, moving fast with writhing chickens dangling by their talons and being moved at the rate of something like thirty a minute. The process of disassembling them was systematic. Workers hit them with baseball hats – this was like spring training – and then tossed them into vats of boiling blood, ripped off the feathers, cut off their heads, drained as much blood out of them as they could in the shortest time, and then sent them down to where the majority of the women worked with cleavers, chopping them up into packaged parts. Nearly every American in those days was consuming roughly six hundred pounds of such packaged parts and dairy products per year.

It was long understood by nutritionists that the vast majority of plant energy and nutrition was irretrievably lost in its low-efficiency conversion over to meat. It was also recognized that land was being over-farmed to keep up with meat production which in turn had introduced a host of new pariahs into the human body, namely saturated fat and cholesterol. Cancer and heart disease, America's two primary killers, were directly the result of eating meat, or at least that's what Muppet came to believe.

But such information was not eagerly disseminated by the meat industry back in the 1950's. Later on, the meat conglomerates and medical establishment learned how to 'calm' the public by avoiding certain phrases or words. Cage and gestation crates in which animals were actually restrained with chains around their appendages became known as 'maternity beds'. Feedlots and battery cages became 'cattle hotels'. And the meat processing industry launched expensive campaigns to convince consumers that in the absence of animal protein your body would stop working. Countering the first wave of medical concerns, Choice A cuts were described by industry spokesmen as essentially fat and chemical free. Lies. New concessions were made, the so-called 'free range' systems. But these, too, were essentially bogus designations, in that the slaughter, and the process of slaughter, had become economic invariants. Meanwhile, vegetarians were characterized as fanatics, communists, marxists, Cuban revolutionaries. The only slur that didn't hold was in calling them Jews, since everybody knew that kosher food was one of the meat industry's most reliable (and disgusting) markets.

Muppet stared at the chick-pullers – low-wage workers who were busy tossing unwanted male newborns into grinding machines that turned the still living babes into instant protein gruel. Already, in those days, several billion chickens a year were being instantly snuffed out in the United States. And since an individual wire mesh cage was worth more money than a bird, the cages were done away with and the chickens were cramped into cheaper, total-confinement sheds. Calvin's particular job was to help chase down the chickens and then attach the weeping birds to the waiting hooks on the conveyor lines. Just like in the Pogroms in Russia.

The birds knew, all right. Muppet saw a few of them actually break their own necks struggling towards the light, or the upper atmospheres, which might have been intimated by a sudden fume-free breeze through the factory from outside. Chickens, forced to live atop metal wire, had within days developed dangerously inflamed joints and sores. And often they'd get their legs caught in the wire meshing of the shed and die within hours for lack of food or water. Or be crushed in place, by other panic-wracked birds, when the catchers came to take them to the disassembly line. Every animal knew everything that was going on.

There were pigs waiting to be killed. Pigs brought in day and night by local small-time farmers. That's usually how it worked. And those pigs that did not drop dead from anxiety, or pneumonia, were crowded into cages that frequently gave rise to cannibalism. The boredom and stress and sheer pig terror induced all kinds of pitiful behaviour, the kinds of things logic should anticipate, whether in Missouri or Dachau. Pigs would try to eat their way out of the wire meshing. Pigs without hope. To have no hope. To see the living, larger humans shuffling among them, without even a single empathetic eye, even a murmur of understanding. Black women cutting out the glands between the pig toes. Cutting gall bladders off livers, young boys emptying the contents of stomachs, skinning kidneys, tramping through offal. The pulling of guts ... wet, vile, membranes of fat, humidity, steam, pools everywhere, slippery, gravity, drainage, open trenches, no windows, darkness, bibs, low and dirty ceilings, heavy shoes, burns and scalds, incised wounds and screaming, constant screaming. What man could vouchsafe this kinesthesia of God-murder? Horridness? Eternal damnation?

Captive bolts burning their brains at point blank range; cane-shaped prods smashed into the animal's throats. The animals frantically throwing their heads down into the rear flesh of the terrified animal right before them, hoping to dodge the inevitable – why Mohammed called this the equivalent of killing an animal twice, since he or she knew it was about to die. And had to stare at it, smell it, hear it, in advance.

Men wore earplugs to protect their inner ears from all the animal screaming.

Later on, the government would pass a *Humane Slaughter Act* which required [9 C.F.R. 313.2 (f)] that animals be rendered unconscious prior to shacking, hoisting, sticking and bleeding. And which warned against 'excessive' prodding. Words like 'excessive', 'minimize', 'discomfort', 'excitement', 'rendered', 'equivalent of' ... words and laws open to ghoulish misinterpretation. Meaningless caveats. The verbiage itself, an atrocity against any hope of human redemption.

Muppet, the pig in him, heard the bullets, bullets to the head, which were the normal method of execution. The bullets stood out beyond the blur of atrocities, a blur as word-lost and verbose as any desensitizing. Nothing could account for the sensation of seeing a murdered animal, nothing!

Though officially corn-fed, in fact, the animals were fed anything – from wood shavings to rat turds. Whatever was on the floor, or in the waste troughs. There was not much consideration for the renderers in those days (they were the men who came in to take away diseased animals), or not in Muppet's region of the State, because more than likely all the animals were diseased. What with their eating their own recycled wastes.

Meat School had not prepared its students for such conditions, but once on the job it was easy to accept since it wasn't so different from the local farms where many of the young students grew up. This was business, after all.

There was always a Federal inspector who'd sniff around, and whose presence was tantamount to codification. His just being there made everything right. He was a trained veterinarian who knew what to look for. But he was by himself, among men who worked hard for a living, and carried knives, or guns, or electric prods and weren't to be fucked with, especially the managers and bosses. This poor underling had tens-of-thousands of carcasses to be concerned about, and knew that if he for one moment upset the efficiency or economic prospects of the plant, his name was Mud. In small town Missouri, mud was quite serious. So he was not likely to play hero, or exercise any of the carcass condemnation or retention regulations during his weekly random sample taking.

And furthermore, local consumption of meat and poultry was exempt from some of the inter-State commerce laws. It didn't matter if the animal suffered from melanosis, or tuberculosis reactor, or eosinophilic myositis, or any of the other dozens of degenerative, infectious, or inflammatory diseases and disorders that were so common in the factories. Marek's disease, otherwise known as cancer among chickens, was the biggest killer of all.

But, again, it didn't matter much. The meat got processed and shipped out all the same. Families all over America routinely came down with Salmonella enteriditis, a form of food poisoning endemic among livestock and poultry. On average, something like five million Americans catch the bacterial illness every year, and some ten thousand folks suffer from associated kidney problems and blood in their loose stools. But there were no consumer groups to speak out against the abuses of the meat trade in those days. Even today, the Federal Drug Administration has looked at few of the chemicals going into the meat, many of which are suspected to be carcinogens.

The industry has always been the biggest around; bigger than automobiles, bigger than oil and gas, and so much more endearing since it conveys its *blessings* in the privacy of one's home, with family, over the dinner table, just after the Lord's Prayer, against the indisputable intimacies of the tongue – the one freedom no man will ever cede; in the hot-dogs served up at baseball and football games, at wedding barbecues and company picnics, every morning, lunch time, evening, throughout all of American life.

One could argue disease until kingdom come, but what ultimately mattered was the taste. Maybe it wasn't even the taste at all, but the inner knowledge that it was an animal one was eating. The self-loathing, the domination of another creature, and the sickly sweet pleasures such dominion carried with it. Maybe this was the modern day equivalent of cannibalism, alleged to have been normal at one time in human evolution. Whether most people had, in fact, surpassed such odious biological characteristics was doubtful, given how they obviously retained some powerful sense of it in their predatory appetites. But neither anthropologists nor psychiatry paid much attention to such aspects of modern diet. Probably because most anthropologists are meat eaters.

Sometimes, the Federal agent would administer a quick fix to the animal, in the guise of an injection, or a pill. But in those days, most of the animal drugs were untested. All kinds of amino acid solutions, sulphates and chloramphenicols, even phenylbutazone stress pills. The stuff of human stomach cancer or degenerative diseases. The whole system compounded itself. It just got worse and worse.

Muppet stared in unrelieved commiseration, not having a clue what to do. It was the genesis of the Napoleon in him. For why should all those animals have to suffer, when Muppet – who felt virtually no physical pain – was allowed to walk out of there and enjoy his day? Why? Why was it so? If only there had been a way, some cosmic miracle, that would have allowed him to transfer his own physiological problem – his inability to feel pain, that is – to those animals.

As far as walking out of there, it would not happen. The animals stayed with him. And what had been a congenital deliverance from the normal hurts of life, was now a monumental hell that Muppet would never shake.

"So what do you think? You want a job?" the manager asked him, impressed by Muppet's size.

And then he got the idea to deck the bastard. He was most certainly prepared at that moment to beat the shit out of that wrinkled money-grubbing asshole.

"Well? Do you want it or don't ya?"

But he withheld his fury, knowing that he would have had to fight them all off; and he was unarmed, and furthermore, he still had to live in Missouri, at least for another year.

Bullets and squeals and sudden convulsions, drowned in blood, until the body simmered down and was still; silent uncelebrated prelude to the cutters and choppers and packagers. There was Muppet and his brother standing ankle deep in blood and guts and flying feathers, and the boys shouting and having what looked to be a pretty decent time in there, aprons smeared with the colours of a painter's palette, one late afternoon, long ago, in the midst of metal cages and metal-slatted floors and dead corpses and struggling animals on all sides. Slaughtered hogs, decapitated chicks, birthlings that could have loved, could have made a child happy or kept an old and lonely person company; kindred spirits that belonged to this Earth as much as anyone, reduced in a minute to insensate body parts, these are what paid witness in his own heart to the atrocious hubris all around him. No human damnation could be more justified than that which slaughterhouses assured. But when? How long did Muppet have to wait to feel the sweet pangs of his revenge? To effect the imperatives of release that gripped his insides, wrenched his confidence in the nature of things, made him as unstable and psychotic as any patient in any ward in any time. On behalf of the animals ... Who are still there, every day. Every night. Every minute. The picture that continued to plague him. The diatribe that won't diminish. The black and white nightmare of himself in the faint light of massacre from some twenty-five years ago. He was in there for just about an hour.

Muppet's eyes quavered against the intense sunlight as he drove into the parking lot of the cafe, and noticed at once a State patrol car. Inside, two rangers were having coffee and reading the paper. At that same moment, Felham left a twenty dollar bill and walked nondescriptly out the door. Muppet had not yet rolled to a stop. The two men shared a look and proceeded to follow each other half-a-block apart, past the slaughterhouse, which they eyed carefully, and just beyond the sprawling far outskirts of the city, where they slowed down some, looked, and then proceeded several miles towards a littler Austrian-American farming town. There, at a local Catholic church, they sat alone beneath the statue of the Madonna, Our Lady of the Crops, as she's known, and quietly discussed their evening plans.

Kinesey unlocked a drawer on his desk and withdrew a memo, which he handed to Jerrasi. "For your eyes only."

It was coded SI, or Special Intelligence, the highest level of classification, not in the FBI, but CIA. Jerrasi read the two paragraph document, then looked up at Kinesey. "You gotta be shittin me?"

"You make plutonium with a high explosive, and you have what's commonly called power. That power is very concentrated in northern Texas, Bob, your *Animal* may or may not be up to it. The intel is inconclusive. But I assure you, nobody in this town is prepared to be wrong on that one," Kinesey intoned quietly with the same rooted confidence of his professorial days out at the FBI Academy in Quantico, Virginia. That's where he and Jerrasi first clashed on strategy. Then, as now, Kinesey was the boss.

"But why?" Jerrasi railed. "Give me one clue of the pattern that would point to that?"

"Subversion," Kinesey cited.

Jerrasi rolled his eyes. "You keep calling it that."

"You bet."

"Every event, every goddamned one of them, has been about animals. We have absolutely nothing that says he's political, or even desperate, in the conventional sense. And we know of only the two of them."

"The girl?"

"They just met. That's been verified by four sources. Look, Ray, I know this bastard. Eight years. I've been on him for eight years."

"You know him so well I'm really hurt you've never introduced me."

"Shit."

"Don't give me this eight years crap, Bob. I've got this other problem, you see," Kinesey added. It was the point all along.

"So what does this mean?" Jerrasi said, standing awkwardly. Kinesey again rose forward from his leather recliner, reached across his black granite desk and retrieved the memo from Jerrasi's suddenly weakened fingers.

"There are three divisions of the National Guard which have already been dispatched to add additional protection to the plant. Army tanks, the works. Over a thousand men. CIA's got people on their way as well. I want the best part of your team working with them."

"That's a crock!"

"Goddammit, are you listening to me? I do not relish the idea of those bastards getting their hands on a nuclear weapon, do you? There's the potential for considerable extortion in that."

"They have no way to deliver the explosion."

"That is a technical debate. But what is no debate, Bob, is the profound embarrassment. Let me put it differently, the career demolition that would result, were it learned that the FBI was off protecting cows, when just up the road, nuclear terrorism was unfolding. Do I make myself absolutely clear?"

"And if we're all wrong?"

"We won't be. You see, there's plenty of backup now. The local police are on top of it and they have no problem with some of our boys working with them at the other location. If that's where you want to be, I'll respect that. You always impressed me with your gut instincts."

"Instincts? It's simple logic, Bob." Jerrasi was incredulous. "How many? How many do I have?"

"Thirty good men."

"Thirty is BULLSHIT! Are you out of your mind? And you're telling me the other team gets a thousand? After all I've been through?"

"There you go personalizing this thing. Just what I was afraid of." Jerrasi looked up at the polyurethane lavender-coloured heavens, with their long neon lights, stalling for time, quelling any and all defeatism. He then fixed his sardonic gaze at his boss, nothing left to say.

"Bob," Kinesey went on, "the packing company has agreed to a twenty four hour hiatus. They were not eager to do that. It means a lot of money to them. But they've been convinced. And it was done very quietly. We'd like to eliminate any bloodshed this time. You'll have the place to yourself."

It was an infernal dig, but Jerrasi let it go. It was the first time Kinesey had gotten directly involved with the case, even overstepping Jerrasi's investigation by dealing directly with the cops in Texas, where Jerrasi was now headed. He'd be flown in on a special bureau jet with Madrid. It was like retirement. Except for one salient fact that swam upstream in his brain, like an irate sperm with one thought only: *You want to leave me out there with thirty men, fine. He's going down, one way or another.*

"I must say, I was glad to see that you'd requested the local police to keep a wide berth – that is, until they actually *do* something," Kinesey concluded, by way of conciliation.

My brother was not a religious person, as I think I've indicated. At least not in the common sense of the word. And certainly less so than myself. Nor could he fail to appreciate the irony of his Catholic upbringing, in view of the way of life he had chosen. Yet, for obvious reasons, the Church of the Lady of the Crops, was not at all repellent to either him or Muppet, and provided a useful safehouse until dark.

There were nearly three hundred churches in these parts, dozens of denominations. It was truly a final frontier of faith; faith in the Messiah, trust in the special destiny that God had in store for hydrogen-bomb loving cattle ranchers. Not only were these law-abiding believers feeding Americans with the much touted protein of conquerors, but they were protecting America, as well. The signs all over town commended this double-edged sword. Ecclesiastical ambiguity showed up in department stores, hamburger stands, used car dealerships. Every other radio station smarmed the listener with forebodings, trumpet blasts and the four horsemen. Armageddon was near at hand, but those Texans loyal to the message of Christ could rest confident in the knowledge that they were the chosen ones; children of the coming rapture, just like David Koresh. To their credit, the local Catholics had supported the U.S. Catholic bishops when, in 1983, they'd collectively issued a pastoral letter outlining their stance on war and peace. In that decree, the *sword,* so frequently mentioned

* A.G.Mojtabai, *Blessed Assurance* [Houghton Mifflin Co. : Boston, 1986] page 120.

in the New Testament, was interpreted to mean *decisiveness,* not murder.*
But in fact, the predominantly Christian (though not Catholic) local citizenry
had enthusiastically *endorsed* the presence of the nuclear weapons factory,
and of the slaughterhouse. Somehow, these two industries appealed to Bible
thumpers, fit in comfortably with teleologic destiny. Christ, in all his
compassion and wisdom, was understood to have approved of making
world-threatening bombs, and this oddity of religion cast a tangible pall
over the entire Panhandle, as inexplicable as the human heart.

... *Help us to understand more fully the dignity of our toil and the merit
it acquires when offered through thee to thy divine son, Jesus Christ. Amen*
read the inscription on the Madonna.* Directly below, on a hard wooden
bench, Felham and Muppet sat discussing their plans.

Felham had his own one-liner of prayer, coined right out of The Book
of Matthew, where it says, simply, 'Blessed are the merciful for- they shall
obtain mercy'. For my brother's part, that mercy would never be extended
to men who abused animals. For, unlike Matthew, or St. Francis, Felham
was convinced that the Prince of Peace could never have laid down his
sword until the sinners had been driven out. He who sheds blood shall see
his own blood shed. Jesus would come in the night, like a thief. And, by
morning, all would witness the great day of his wrath, the wrath of the
Lamb, and a new Earth would be born. And Felham would intervene to
'bring to ruin those ruining the earth'. That was Revelations (11:18) and
that was history, still repeating a passion play, in his person, of good versus
evil, precisely because evil persisted; and while it really didn't matter to
him, Felham knew that there was ample textual support elsewhere, indeed,
throughout the whole Bible, to justify his and Muppet's own claims of
revenge: Isaiah, Ezekial, Jeremiah and Micah all rallied their clansmen to
fight on behalf of God. 'The Lord is a man of war'. Moses had said in
Exodus, 'mighty in battle'. The Apostle Paul similarly exploited the military
metaphors – helmets, breastplates of faith – and in his *Epistle To The
Ephesians* advised every Christian to don the armour of God and be a 'good
soldier of Jesus Christ'. Augustine repeated that pledge, in his enormously
influential *Contra Faustum,* by recommending that every good Christian
be willing to die, in military uniform, if need be. It was that argument –
and the merging of spiritual and legalistic jargon – which essentially
schooled the later Crusades.

I was a groundswell of nostalgia and relevance, Catholic and rebelling,
stoked by the metaphors, the apparent justifications, yet repulsed by the
hypocrisy. I stood wondering and hidden, seeing the silhouettes of those
policemen suddenly and unexpectedly retreating from my porch, getting

* A.G.Mojtabai, *Blessed Assurance* [Houghton Mifflin Co. : Boston, 1986] page 65.

in their police cars and quietly driving away. What had happened?

And I imagined my brother going over the fine details of what they must have known to be their last hurrah. I had seen my brother's image on the television. As the hours passed, I was seeing it everywhere, closing in with a zeal, or claustrophobia, like a form of punishment. I had to choose and my brother was my very own anger, like Cary Grant in *The Bishop's Wife,* guiding me.

Mine is the blast of the thundered word by which all things were made. I permeate all things that they may not die. I am life ... his person echoed. It was St. Hildegard's vision, but Felham's battle cry. The whole world was his parish. That whole world – or nearly so – was guilty.

Muppet had found it difficult to unearth much of anything about the company. It was privately held, which meant that it did not have to divulge information to the Securities and Exchange Commission. The secrecy around slaughterhouses had long been state-of-the-art. But Muppet had managed to find the name of the company's private brokerage firm, whose annual summaries were published on microfiche, and these he could obtain through a Bay Area business school library.

Muppet had not yet told Felham the most pressing of all such data, I think because he might have considered this the end of the road. You wouldn't have known it to look at him. I'm simply reading into the situation. Felham prompted the information by asking how many rounds Mickey had left them.

"We're looking at 1400 night-time employees, if that's any indication," Muppet replied.

Felham didn't react. He didn't dare.

"Men and women who make about twenty-five thousand a year, thirteen dollars an hour," Muppet quickly went on, changing the weight and balance of such quanta. "Company's overall revenues were something like six billion last year, one hundred million of that cited as profit."

"Fuck it," Felham said, exhaling. "I don't care about that."

My brother had already figured on a full scale battle as big, or bigger, than the one in Maryland. He knew how many animals were in there, and he must have surmised how many pairs of hands were necessary to process that burden of meat – 170,000 cows and 300,000 pigs – that were allegedly killed each week.

"They're an angry bunch," Muppet said. "The union's waged eight violent strikes in recent years."

"How violent?"

"Don't know, in terms of any casualties. All kinds of violations, though."

"Violations, huh? That's funny." The very concept of trucking, or hygiene or 'humane' violations was really a joke, considering the bigger picture.

"A few Democratic presidential candidates got into the fray. OSHA slapped the company with the largest fine in the government's history, 2.6 million."

"For what?"

"For failing to report something like a thousand job-related illnesses and injuries."

"Guess that means among workers, not cows."

"Guess it does," Muppet nodded.

None of it mattered to Felham. What mattered was the fact that this company was one of the largest slaughterhouses in America, probably in the world, hidden neatly away, ripe for the taking.

And fortunately, there had been a defector from the plant, that Muppet had located through Ecolog, and she, in turn, had anonymously provided a full accounting of the security systems, guard posts, weapons stockades, and locking codes on the confinement pens. This woman had had herself committed to an asylum, following four years on the job. She could no longer smell anything, after all the scent of blood in her nostrils. She could no longer taste anything, either. The stench of corpses lay heavily upon her body, seemed to infect her lymphatic system, her hormones, her dreams. She'd wake up hearing the screams, seeing the glint of knives, the laughter of big men, big-bellied meat eaters. Her husband was one of them. A bigshot in the firm. They were divorced now. He decided she was crazy. So did the Judge in the 186th District, who awarded custody of the two children to him.

But she was lucid, all right. And mad as a rattlesnake. Now she lived in Freedom, California, near Watsonville, where she discovered a whole new life for herself. And people she could talk to, and eat with. She was trying to get her olfactory senses back together in the redwoods, in the rain, eating salads comprised of flowers – nasturtiums and hibiscus – and taking long solitary walks along the coast. Her confession on Ecolog had been her parting shot. One woman's small step for mankind, as she had put it. In her heart, she sincerely believed – she knew – that the slaughterers didn't mean what they did, that they too had been totally dehumanized by their work and just didn't have a clue how to break out of the vicious syndrome. Too much money in it. Too much pressure during hard times. The Catholics in town had created a special fund for workers at the weapons plant, who wanted to renounce their job and seek alternative, peaceful employment. But the fund was only for those at the bomb plant, not the slaughterhouse, and anyway, it was only worth about twenty thousand or so. So it was no alternative. The only real alternative could come from within. And Lucy, as she dubbed herself – perhaps in homage to the archaeological Lucy, the oldest known female mystery in all of human evolution – was a lone voice crying out in the wilderness.

At eight p.m., darkness nearly descended, it being early September, and they departed for the slaughterhouse in their two vehicles, Felham carrying no weapon whatsoever. The road to hell was quiet. Muppet expressed some surprise at how peaceful the town appeared. Not a single cop or trooper anywhere to be seen.

Felham sensed the danger from the moment they passed the guard station. There were cars all over the parking lot, but no people. Not a soul. Muppet had given the guard the name of a shipping deputy director who was expecting them, or would have reason to expect them, according to Lucy. It was not risky because there was in fact no way to call him, since he worked on the *floor,* where the noise made telephoning useless. You'd have to know that, and so the guard let them through with a routine flourish of his hand.

Once they were in, the guard ducked down.

Lord God Almighty, who didst well that thy only-begotten Son, Our Redeemer, should be born in a stable, and lie in a manger between the animals; bless, we pray thee, this stable ... that for cattle and other living creatures, it may be made a wholesome place, and safe from all aggression, and in his spirit we undertake to revenge your heart and your only Son, oh Lord ...

It was Muppet who prayed silently as the two old buddies parked their rental cars out of sight of the peripheral video – they knew how to do that quite proficiently – taking out those weapons they thought they'd need, and quickly moving in under cover of darkness.

"Yes, that's right," Jerrasi mused quietly and matter-of-factly to Madrid. "That's got to be them." Both men's eyes were captured by the first true glance of the suspects. It was a brief one at that, but a revelation all the same. For Madrid's part, he almost wavered just inches away from some kind of admiration. As for Jerrasi, he had not given the weapons scenario one percent chance. He knew his *Animal.* The two FBI special agents were waiting a mile away, in a State trooper van with video connect.

Jerrasi stared at the frozen image, locked in as the two men disappeared inside. *After all these years!*

With dozens of Texas Rangers and local police surrounding the slaughterhouse, staring it down with long-range night scopes, in addition to thirty Federal Bureau investigators, there was no road, no dune buggy path, no jeep trail in a radius of three miles, that had been left unattended.

Was it that morning, that Jerrasi had stumbled through the rubble in Maryland, having been up all night, following his mother's funeral? The compression had him slightly dazed and jittery, a bit of jetlag, as well. Thinking about the energy of those two men. A little frightening. It was dangerous, after all. He wanted to go in now after them, but the plan – as Madrid pointed out, and as they had carefully worked through on the trip to Texas that afternoon – was to give them fifteen minutes inside. The Bureau needed evidence.

Suddenly, the video trail went blank.

"Got it," Felham whispered. He'd just cut the main overhead wires going into the factory, and now shimmied back down the pole.

"What the fuck? Call, call the guard station!" Jerrasi ordered a State trooper standing by. The man did not take kindly to the FBI's tone of voice, but did what he was asked.

"They've cut all communication. Guard shack's down," the trooper acknowledged. Both he and Madrid knew that that would complicate things, since video cameras had been placed in every quadrant of the enormous plant.

"They know we're here," Felham stated, as they made their assault from the railroad depot side, trundling M-60s and long hanks of taped-together magazines – thousands of rounds. They were dressed to take out your average SMSR, Standard Metropolitan Statistical Region. But they did not expect to be alone, alone with tens-of-thousands of restless, wondering cattle. And it didn't take the acute senses of a Zen master to appreciate the setup.

"Lucy?" Felham asked.

"No. I don't think so," Muppet frowned. "Did you call anybody ...? Well, did you?"

"Jessie," he admitted.

"Hmmm," Muppet thought. He considered saying something like, *I told you,* it was the reason they'd sworn off contacts long ago, but there was no point, not now. A verbal bickering would accomplish nothing.

"She said something about being pregnant."

"You??"

Felham nodded resignedly, beaming inside.

Muppet quickly repealed his condemnatory tone. "Congratulations," he gleamed, happy for the both of them ... saddened by his adult virginity, which winced at more than one realization sweeping over the floor before them.

"My picture was on TV, Mup. And there was a composite sketch that looked a little like you."

"Ahh. Well then." He contemplated the reality out loud. "Did they have my ponytail?"

"What colour were my eyes?"

"Charcoal."

"Pricks."

"It had to happen," Felham said, with a slight sigh that might have been perceived as relief, but not really.

"I know. It doesn't change a thing," Muppet said. "Let's move. By the way, what's it going to be?"

"What do you mean?"

"Boy or a girl?"

"I don't know. What would you want?"

"A girl."

"Then a girl it is."

Jerrasi hovered over his watch. Fifteen minutes. That had been the plan. He wanted to call Kinesey and tell him. To alert the reserves, and State troopers over at the weapons factory who'd been diverted by the National Security directive of the CIA. But he knew they were under strict orders to keep to their positions, until *The Animal* was under custody.

There was another reason, sweeter and just edging on the vindictive, that Jerrasi restrained himself from calling anybody: he'd seen through to Felham, understood him. It was his boy. Nobody else was going to take credit. They had them, alright. They had them surrounded with something like one hundred and fifty men, in all.

Felham and Muppet had planned to string up the killers, onto the conveyors belts, and do them in – all of them – in the manner to which the cattle were accustomed. And they'd devised a special treat, for whatever chief executives they might find, one of whom worked late into every evening, according to Lucy. They'd intended to turn him into sausage, highest grade. To get him all the way through the system, into a nicely printed box, into a refrigerated crate, onto the train, and off to America. Same genre, though more ... meaty! as that headache pill scare some years back. But it wasn't in the cards, not tonight, anyway.

I stare into the mirror and feel the urgency. Kant's *Critique of Pure Reason* swelling like a glandular abscess, in that part of the grey matter given over to ethical deliberation. My contacts with the world, friends, family, relations, ideas, aspirations, have become dark, unclear, wobbly. A gun will get me into more trouble than I'm perhaps ready to endure. He's taught me that. But there's got to be a way to vent this, this feeling. Paying a ransom, buying them – as if they were Jews – won't resurrect the broken promise.

What's insane, in this world? What is sentimental? There will always be those who call it rational, and those for whom it is irrational. We know this to be true because of the courtesies that are applied during a war. Humane treatment of prisoners, privileges to officers. Niceties and protocols, and formal bows during negotiations. What could be more insane? A war is a war, the result of mounting dementia. There can be no half-steps. I have nothing to fear from my parents, who are dead. No fear of the shame. My wife will either accept it or not. My son is still a baby. He'll remember nothing. The reprisal – it must come – but what of it?

How will it come? Like this, men at the door, vacillating, changing plans, a setup?

They stood alone, on cold concrete, amid some thirty thousand Santa Gertrudis and American Brahmans, that seemed dumbfounded by the unprecedented surcease in operations. That multiple look, alone, may have made it all worth it. That connection with eyes and brains larger than our own, which forgave, whilst acknowledging a bittersweet twist in the savage soul of fate, however temporary. They were like extraterrestrials, those cows; original inhabitants of Eden, and they were staring gratefully at Felham and at Muppet. Animals that had been left in the very midst of their destruction, ankles and shoulders chained, fellow cows partially hoisted up, others still dangling, many dead from the weight that stopped their blood flow upside down. Thousands milled around in the square inches allotted them, with bars holding them back, and electric locks and metallurgic compounds on every side of the known universe.

Both men had soft wax Parisian earplugs in their noses to keep out the overwhelming onrush of blood stench. Such odours were enough to disarm a warrior, Muppet had remembered.

They knew without surveying the many acres of the plant that it had been evacuated, that it was only a matter of minutes, probably, before the cavalry came in. They knew what to do. It had been their plan all along, the one logical buffer between them and capture.

"What is it?" Felham shouted, his hands at the electronic security pad controlling the closing and opening of bars.

"A-C-AA," Muppet began.

Felham punched in the letters.

Eureka! Lucy had done good.

"Number 2?"

"A-C-AAB," Muppet cried out.

Again, it was there. And all the others. Three minutes down.

"The shackles!"

Shackles, shackles ... It was key, of course. Muppet read off a single page. It was one time when he had to carry it, evidence or no evidence. He just hadn't the presence of mind to memorize. Not with so much hinging on it.

Whatever sense of fatalism had entered their veins, vanished at that moment. There was a little girl to live for. *Uncle Muppet.* He liked the ring of that in his ears. Nor were they going to die ankle-deep in cow blood, on cold concrete, in Texas. That had never been part of the plan.

"Six-six-six."

"Six?"

"Three sixes, goddammit!"

"But that's my lucky number."

"Just DO IT!"

Felham adjusted his heavy machine gun on his shoulder – the strap was slipping – and pushed three heaven hopeful sixes on the electronic key pad.

Like magic, all across the darkly illuminated bovine interior, mooos of bewilderment, moaning upwards like spiral neuralgias in the night, ancient genes perplexing in the reincarnation of mournful chains, the shackles snapped open; it had been an 'ALL RELEASE' code, never used, and only implemented for emergencies, like fires, that sprung every manacle throughout the entire industry of death, where my older brother and his best friend stood, as we'd all stood since childhood, since my little black poodle, Buckingham – I'd named him – was first hit by an automobile at rush hour. And I just managed to avoid getting hit as well, but he died, died quivering, his back broken, bleeding in my arms and looking me in the eye with the pure and infinite pleading of millennia. And there was absolutely nothing I could do to save him. I've never gotten over the unfairness of that, but the cattle at least, the cattle, you sonofabitch, you unreachable deaf-mute, you human nature, were now free – if they'd only take the hint – to stampede!

And Felham and Muppet stood to the side and looked at one another for the last time. Maybe.

"LET'S GO!" Jerrasi ordered, withdrawing his semiautomatic.

"We're moving in," Madrid relayed over an open radio channel to all the forces.

Guns were raised. Huge HMI spotlights were now thrown onto the one guard station, where the entrance road snaked through the high barbed walls, covered in broken glass shards, as a barrage of State trooper vehicles converged on that same point, and an ace SWAT team, covered in total body protection garb, headed towards the main building with the determination and experience of Force Recon, or NAVY SEALS.

"I want them taken alive." Jerrasi and Madrid waited outside in the congested semicircle, kneeling behind the van, where at least fifty bolt-action sniper rifles, with .308 calibre match rounds and infrared scopes, were aimed at the four-story high, corrugated, aluminium barn-style doors, that opened to the interior. Long-riflemen, the best of the veteran Rangers, spotters, German shepherds rearing violently on their chains in anticipation, a bevy of helicopter action out beyond the junction, and layer upon layer of backup, were all in place. Once the situation was stabilized inside, Jerrasi and Madrid would head in, to make the formal arrests. Then the press would be allowed to descend.

This was the scenario that Madrid had fantasized. The orgasm scenario of FBI school. He and Shelley and the rest of the gang had – how many times – hoped for just this? Hoped on behalf of their boss, Robert Jerrasi, whose life meant nothing if not this moment. Justice, the American way, all that bullshit which only amounted to something when the real shit came down, when the bad guy had to stand in the light and be made naked before his crimes. And it was only the cops, the FBI, the arresting officers, the quiet team, which had spent years conducting a background investigation, that could possibly have made it all happen.

Except, that that too was a bunch a crap. And Jerrasi knew it. The evidence had avalanched at the last moment, by luck. Tyre marks in Marin County. That was Baggot's department. An off-duty date, who gave away the brother. That was Madrid's horny good luck. Two eyewitnesses in Maryland, whose information wouldn't have mattered, if the Bureau hadn't already gotten to the brother. And a wiretap on Jessie Moran. None of it required much intelligence, and little or no skill. Just plain luck and the dogheaded obvious, and eight previous years of his life, and the life of his son, down the tubes.

At least this night would quench Jerrasi's wrath. No more weak chin. It was over.

It was over. Iyura was at work. The cops had turned around and sped away from the house hours before. No explanation. Left heavily to my thoughts. As usual. But now, all the difference, made.

No more could these matters profitably languish inside my head. Those days of doubt, that anger towards Felham, had vanished, like the dwindling flame of a candle. The process by which this has happened is designated by some academic mental disorder, I suppose. Whereby a world I once trusted and believed in, has collapsed. Is it true paranoia, or is the fear well-founded? Is the world really like that? I don't know, for sure. But like a cancer of self-abuse, the abuse I've stomached for so long has come full circle. The *abuse* is real, both inside and outside, I know that much. Whether it was always my particular weakness to dwell on it, to look out on a sunny morning and yet continue to think of the moon, rather than something else, something cheerful, Christmas, or my wife and kid, all my good fortune, I leave to the psychiatrists. The dialogue must be my own, and it is likely that no one will ever know how I arrived at this point in time, or why I did what I must do. I certainly could not have predicted the outcome.

He was such an ordinary yuppie they'll say. *From Santa Cruz, no less. He used to play Puccini on the CD in his office. 'Tosca' was his favourite. 'The whole world's like Scorpio,' he once told me. I had no idea what he was talking about ...*

And Iyura; I can see her describing my condition to the police: *It was no accident, no imitation of the absurd. He'd played the game all of his adult life. As long as his brother was alive – in his mind – he was the freest of men. I never had any idea how sick he was. He imitated his brother. But who did his brother imitate? A suckling infant, a wild beast. Which? I don't know. The delirium of demons pursuing him. I guess he brought them to fruition.* She'd invite the officers in for coffee ... *Jason has been under a lot of pressure at work ... He doesn't have a brother!*

I might have given all my inheritance to various animal charities. But I didn't. I guess I needed a more personal link to the pain. To my own pain.

I knew any gunsmith off the street could convert an AR-15 into a full automatic M-16, the standard Vietnam weapon. I just didn't know whether I could really use it.

I can't save the world. But maybe I can protect and harvest my own soul. The soul is being pursued. The soul must fight back. It took forty years of knowing Felham, to reach that conclusion. The conversion of St. Paul? Every child kills, and then buries an animal at least once in his life.

Every child becomes that animal. Every adult chases it down. I had returned to childhood.

It happened that afternoon, that night, the next morning. A revelation in Texas. That's all.

First, I went out onto the street, south of Market, and obtained a fake driver's license from Arkansas. Any colour printer in the hand of a wiseacre can accomplish it for ten dollars in five minutes.

Then I went out and bought a barcode software program for fifty bucks.

I printed out countless numbers, standard American issue – hundreds of them. I had counted twenty-seven large grocery stores in the Bay Area, that kept tanks filled with live lobsters. *Homarus americanus.* Some nearly thirty-five pounds. Eggs can take a year to hatch. And the lobsters are about as smart. I'm told they walk along the ocean floor as far as two hundred miles to mate. That's love, though scientists have preferred to focus on their alleged bellicosity. Just like scientists to do that. Gives them more of an excuse for poking around, slicing off nerves, and then eating them. *That's* bellicosity!

My impulse had been to steal them. To repay cruelty with anger. But I had twenty-seven stores to deal with, and I wasn't eager to get caught, though I'd made up my mind that I was prepared to get caught, to cross that line between apathy, safety, law-abiding normality – the simple, quiet life most people live, as neutral and uninvolved and bland, as the U.S. Post Office – versus the condition of my brother.

I had definitely made up my mind. And the barcodes were the trick. Because no grocery store is geared up to do an on-line transaction check. The meat departments simply wrap it in paper and stick a barcode on top of it. The checkers pass it over the computer. They don't know anything. The computer's always right. I simply change barcodes, and the lobster goes from costing ten, or twenty, or thirty dollars a piece, to thirty cents. I don't even pay for that, but use my fake ID and write bad cheques.

I did it twenty seven times in one day, having outfitted the largest U-Haul truck available with a shallow, water-filled steel container. And by evening, I'd written a few hundred dollars worth of bad checks and saved hundreds of live lobsters.

I then drove out to China Beach in the dark. It was kind of hairy, even wearing thick gloves, getting the tape safely off their claws, releasing them into the waves. God, how I love those lobsters, whose intelligent dexterity and animated, all inquisitive eyes should convince anyone of their sensitivity. And how they raced towards freedom, devouring the waves and slipping into the cold comforting abyss. I became the lobsters, marvelling at their good luck, compared with mine, a man who had no choice but to live as a man among men.

Sure, I could have purchased the animals, but what was I to do, continue to purchase them? Buy off the lobster trawlers, buy off the whole industry – tens of millions of dollars every year? From Maine to Alaska?

The grocery chains were not even on to me. They didn't have a clue, I figured.

I was into it. The next evening, I visited an animal shelter with an M-16 concealed inside a plastic doggie kennel which I walked in with. I wore a black stocking over my face, just like Felham used to do in the good old days. And without much trouble, or risk, or even fear, I set some eighty dogs free, into the woods near Skyline Ridge. There were some problems, of course, which I won't go into, but with a tough guy brio and bank robber's getup, I was emboldened beyond my wildest dreams. Clinically speaking, Felham's war had pushed me over the edge, in the space of a single week, after half a lifetime of trepidation. Crazily, some of the dogs wanted to hang around. But I'd come prepared with about a hundred chocolate hostess twinkies, which I tossed up the hill, away from the place where they were destined to be put to sleep with injections, if nobody took them after nine days in residence.

I made love with Iyura both of those nights. Ecstatic love. She even mentioned it. I haven't felt so good since, since before Mom and Dad died.

And the next morning, at eight o'clock, I went out down the street and waited for the cunt, bolstered by my two spectacular successes, thus far.

And sure enough, it wasn't too long before she showed up with her dachshund. The same dreary routing. My weapon was well concealed.

Hurry up, Schmo, she called the dog Schmo. But she didn't kick him this time and I found myself standing there feeling somewhat helpless, or ridiculous, because I had an M-16 in a golf bag amid my woods and irons. But she didn't kick the dog. The goddamned lady was a schizoid. For days, weeks, I'd seen her kicking Schmo. Now, suddenly, Schmo had learned. He's doing his business. And the wave rushed over me and passed back out to sea. It's like a fucking comedy.

And as I walked back up the street, through my gate, and kneeled to pick up the morning paper, feeling – WONDERFUL! – three police cars came skidding to a halt there, not twenty feet away, and I looked up at the front window and saw Iyura slowly suckling Bart in so very Japanese a style, a demure elegance that transcended the ages, and I was struck from behind, by the furious dreadful pride-lending words, FREEZE! YOU SONOFABITCH!

THE RAPTURE

"Start that sucker. We're on our way," Muppet said, speaking into their one remaining mobile phone.

Micky received the message.

"Shall we?" Felham said, strengthening himself. They stood behind the agitated huddles of all those cows and bulls, perhaps twenty-five million pounds of scared weight.

Muppet pulled Felham to him, grabbing hold of the hair on either side of his head and kissed him full and passionately on the cheek. Felham reciprocated by brushing gentle fingers over Muppet's eyes.

Both men then raised their weapons, and with a tandem terrified battle cry, sent hundreds of rounds up into the aluminium rafters ... and thousands of cows forward launching with a ferocity that gathered hormonal group speed and frenzy.

Just as the troopers were advancing in formation towards the doors on the outside, undergoing maneuvers as choreographed as any ballet.

Now, hearing the enormous fray from within, the troops ducked down, just as the massive aluminium doors came crashing forward with an explosive force none of them had counted on.

"Jesus, they've stampeded the cattle!" a top executive with the company, standing near Jerrasi, exclaimed. His throat was choked with its realization.

Jerrasi cried out, he should have known better, guns blazing forward in a panic to check the impossible. The cattle bore down, one acre after another of avalanching anger bursting from inside the killing ground, wrathful hooves and desperate snorts and matted fur. The front guard of Texas Rangers and SWAT men simply disappeared, shells firing upwards towards the stars from abandoned bodies, exo-skeletons muted in the crushing free-for-all. Ten seconds later, the semicircle of patrol cars were inundated, the forty-mile-an-hour breakaway mass careening unavoidably onward. A patrol car exploded, others were jettisoned, as men were gored and tossed about like Styrofoam mannequins, sucked downwards into the meat grinding dust, while choppers overhead thrust their lights upon the massacre and radio transmissions back and forth ejaculated like so many firecrackers.

The cattle kept pouring out, like blood from a jugular, fleeing forward into the night air, towards Panhandle liberation. A hurricane of atavistic impulses. And somewhere in their midst, or just at the tail-end, were Muppet and Felham, racing to keep up, or riding buckin' bronco style, or hanging on to tails, for no one will ever know with certainty, and in dust sped out away from the factory, though little noticed.

And it was my older brother at the wheel. And there was nothing that was going to stop him. He had a date with a redhead, after all.

"DROP IT!" the rear officer shouted.

Iyura ducked behind the curtains.

I stood with my arms spread upwards, the golf bag falling to the grass.

"MOVE AWAY FROM THE BAG AND LIE DOWN ON THE GRASS. KEEP THOSE ARMS SPREAD. NOW!"

I knew what was happening, half-a-dozen officers standing all over me, black leather boots crunching down on top of my hands, my ankles. It hurt. And then my arms were flipped roughly behind me, a joint distended, and I was handcuffed and I heard the familiar Miranda rights being read, about my securing a lawyer et cetera, certainly more courtesies than were extended to Lee Oswald, I suspect, and they flipped me back around and searched me real good, poking into the golf bag and recovering the weapon, along with a number three iron.

"JASON, WHAT'S HAPPENING?" Iyura screamed, running outside with Bart still clinging to her.

"STAY WHERE YOU ARE!" an officer shouted. "PUT THE BABY DOWN AND GET YOUR HANDS UP!"

And I could see neighbours accumulating on one side staring from their gentrified abodes of grass and eucalyptus and palm trees. There were Morton and Delila, a semiretired couple. She had been a school teacher for twenty years, and he had invented a very clever, rimmed metal container, which guaranteed them two cents on every can of tuna fish ever manufactured. Morton had had second thoughts about his invention, being from the Bay Area, and a long-standing member of the Friends of the Earth, but now it was too late for moral scruples. Like everything else.

Iyura remained steadfast, not about to put Bart down.

Guns were aimed in an orgy of force over defencelessness.

"That's my wife and she knows nothing about it," I shouted angrily, very annoyed by the handcuffs.

"About what??" she appealed with a high-pitched plaintive cry, an innocence that yanked at my tear ducts.

They then placed me in the back seat of one of the patrol cars and the Sergeant explained to Iyura what I had done, and the five witnesses who'd identified me at the pound, and others who'd seen me putting the lobsters into the water, and butchers in the seafood departments of a dozen grocery stores, who were eager to see my kind locked away behind bars. And then there was the weapon, which appeared to be the same one used the night before.

It was all appearances and hearsay, for now, at least in legal terms. But one final look from her was the real heartache, because I hadn't explained anything, all this time, and she was in the dark – she thought I'd said they were after some drifter – seeing me driven off that way. And in my head the images kept recurring, the howls and squashed brains, hearts lifted out of live dogs, electric shock after shock, delivered with prongs, to the cows and the cats, the hamsters, the monkeys looking and the rats pleading; wave after wave after relentless generation, of rodent and mammal and primate and fish, and every heart-stopping love-seeking species our one supposed Lord vivisected and cruelly, unspeakably dispatched to human Hell. It gave me strength that what I'd done was right, as the cops drove me away, and I had to admire the speed with which they'd found me out. I would never have believed it, and it gave me that much more admiration for my brother, and for Muppet, and all the planning and care they must have taken to have gone so far, so successfully, in their day.

If only they'd had their day.

I was not scared any more. It was over and I had done it. Nobody had been hurt, because I'm basically a coward, a dreamer, lost in poetic disbelief. It was more than Iyura or anyone who knows me, would have believed possible – that I should have forged bar codes, gone to the grocery stores and stolen *Homaridae,* liberated dogs, carried a weapon. That I should have seen the light in so clear and heroic a manner, after the suffering I've gone through. Why, it's a miracle, I tell you. Redemption.

And the dogs were roaming free to prove it, running wild in the redwood forests of Skyline Ridge, and the lobsters were partying under the Golden Gate Bridge, and Jason Felham could sleep easily for the first time, really, in years. In all the excitement, the realization that cows were cows and dogs were dogs – that one of these days they'd be hauled back to the pound, and recaptured on the northern plains of Texas – had not yet sunk in. For a few hours, even atop hard pillowless wood with dubious bedfellows, I felt euphoric, re-created, delivered ... the words escape such feelings, for having done something. SOMETHING.

The booking, the manhandling, nothing mattered to me. Iyura's brother used a bondsman friend of his. I spent the whole day, and that night, in jail but was out by nine the morning after, for ten percent of the bond, or ten thousand dollars. My having never done anything wrong – not even a traffic violation – certainly helped. Still, the charges were serious enough and included assault with a deadly weapon, reckless endangerment, illegal possession of a machine gun, conspiracy to steal lobsters, and a felony charge on all those bad cheques, as well as a counterfeiting charge, because of the barcodes business. They couldn't get me for anything having to do with Schmo – one consolation – since I never removed the weapon and it wasn't loaded. I guess I'd just meant to scare her with it. There was an added legal ambiguity, in that they could not prove the gun was loaded the night I freed the dogs, either. To be honest with you – it wasn't. There was no way I would ever risk that enormous gun going off.

And there was yet another consolation: Robert Jerrasi never had the pleasure of knowing that *The Animal* was ever even dimly concerned with his worthless existence. For Felham, the FBI had never even entered the equation. What neither he nor I anticipated, however, was one tenacious cowboy named Madrid.

I had a month to ponder my defence tactics. Akira, Iyura's brother, believed that I could beat some but not all of the charges, and that I was probably looking at twelve months in jail and three years on probation, at best. At worst, depending on the judge I was assigned, twenty-five years. If that were the case, Bart would be a grown man when I got out. Six presidential elections would come and go. Iyura would become old. We'd never have another baby, which we'd planned. There were not that many books that I wanted to read.

"Why did you do it?" a psychiatrist asked me, just like that, in private consultation. Akira thought my seeking help, voluntarily, would strengthen our case.

I wanted simply to scream. Not to cop to an insanity plea – never – but really and truly to scream. Because the questions and my answers were utterly predictable. In reality, there was nothing I could ever say. Scream, yes. Say, no. As if I were being crucified from within, by my own irreversible storehouse of mental notes and feelings, and along comes this unfazed, untouchable, scholastic, nine-to-five rational side, wondering whether there's something troubling me. Where did it begin? Where might it end?

"Was there some event that triggered it?" the psychiatrist went on, attaining new reaches of the banal, pushing, I'm sure he figured, into dark and dangerous territory. "Or some person who coaxed you into it?"

About a week before I was to stand trial, something very strange happened. I still can't explain it, any more than a man can know how the world views him, or what he really looks like, or really is. It came to me in the form of a simple message – revelatory, absent-minded, a light piercing the window, a phone call, or a telegram, maybe it was a letter, or just the thought of one. A vision at night, a *deja vu* one morning – of a complete stranger, a voice new to my insides, who sported the possibility that everyone was going to be fine. That there was a way out, after all. Not for the billions of animals already dead – they'd be dead in me forever – but for the others, the ones still living, a world still filled with little Barts, and ducklings, and a horde of mentally unstable brother's keepers. People wrestling with every agony, everyday. Good people, sad people even happy people, or at least those who could still manage a happy face ... Some of them were living out their days in disguise, the voice explained, at a Rat Temple in Rajasthan. That's right.

"Who are you?" I pressed, the only child in me suspecting everyone. "What are you telling me?"

Had I actually heard the words? Read the message? Or simply encouraged myself with more invention? After that one enlightening night in jail, I would have to assume the latter. But it does not matter, now.

I will admit that India had been on my mind for some reason; its cows, its vegetarianism; a place, I imagined, that would absorb any eccentricity or faith, even an outlaw like myself. And perhaps this India of mine was like Iyura. When I first fell in love with her and thought of nothing but her and would have done anything to be with her. Crossed continents, suffered fools, vanquished enemies.

Akira, after settling down some, was unclear about existing extradition laws between India and the U.S., especially if religion was involved. But he strongly discouraged me.

I mentioned it to Iyura. Well, more than mentioned. I prepared her for the conversation.

"What's there?" she asked intently. I assumed she'd never leave San Francisco, but I was not prepared to abandon the marriage without at least offering her this one option. Jail was out of the question. I just couldn't handle living in a cage, any more than a chicken could.

"It's a white marble Hindu temple in the desert," I explained. "Quite beautiful, I expect. Peaceful. And filled with thousands of rats which the local Hindus have worshipped for centuries as gods. And they feed them. And they're of course totally tame, even playful. Nobody's ever been bitten. Only a few toes nibbled now and then." The nibbling of toes had stuck with me.

"What's it all for?" my wife asked, not sure whether to laugh or to cry.

"Well, evidently they believe that someday the rats will be reincarnated into people, and that the Hindus will become rats. A little like Doctor Dolittle. And the cycle will continue forever and ever."

To my surprise, Iyura laughed. It must have been the Doctor Dolittle part, which, she said, she'd read as a little girl in Japanese. All of my misgivings about her possible reaction dissipated there and then. She turned out to be something of an animal rights Samurai when given this chance – and to think we'd never really discussed any of my problems. I hadn't had the courage to raise the spectres inside me out into the open. Not with her, not with anyone. I had lived in shame, in panic, in horror and outrage, up to the minute of my deliverance, when I went out and purchased a weapon. But she turned out to be devoted to what I had done, or imagined, or hoped for. I fell in love with her all over again. Which isn't to imply a necessarily happy ending. My older brother might have been a mirage, but not the animals. Not their colossal world shattering pain.

Iyura didn't quite know what to make of my own inner struggle, once I tried to explain it. Though I didn't actually detail *all* the aspects of my intimidation, the host of visitations that plagued me in the guise of FBI men, the hearing of voices, snippets of dialogue, birds in Thailand, turncoats and moral enigmas, the so-called Association for Biological Animal Research Units in Maryland, of cows in Texas, and the two of them, Missouri-bred Muppet, and my own Jason-bred Felham, and certainly not Jessie – but she seemed to understand that whatever had tormented me all these weeks, and months, indeed, these many years, that this was part of my humanity, of working out something not easily achieved, or understood; a philosophical argument, however envisioned, as big as Hiroshima, as small as one man's heart, that might normally have just gone on arguing and creating and fearing and raging, sinking deeper and deeper into the malaise of what being human is all about, without ever reaching a resolution.

Whereas I'd been lucky, transforming mere solipsism into active therapy, if one is prepared to call the commission of a crime, therapy. It's doubtful the California State Criminal Psychiatric Board would view it in so generous and uncommon a light. Nevertheless, I'd somehow made it through the waist-deep waters; I'd reached solid land, sunlight. A starting point. And I hadn't even killed anybody. Or not yet.

On the other hand, I also knew that my rival phantasms had never actually confronted one another, nor did I see much hope of putting my brother, and a Robert Jerrasi, in the same room together. Even in my mind.

India nevertheless loomed with viable, not imagined, coordinates. A real place. Iyura, graciously, and with a youthful sense of starting over, was willing to accept that. And she did.

In the coming days, we obtained forged passports somewhere south of

Market Street, I knew the right crowd by that time, and made our roundabout way out of America. The moment we passed through customs, I knew that this was forever. Once in Pakistan, we trekked east across the border, stopping in the ancient city of Jaisalmer for a few nights before heading into the heart of the desert, past silken mirages, long-haired nomads and minarets of eroded sand.

Bart rode between the camel's humps and seemed to enjoy the ride, while I whistled my favourite arias, by Zucchini.

I took to camels immediately, but was greatly disturbed to see some of the local herders overloading them with enormous bundles and beating them unmercifully. Thirty miles into the desert, two days away from the legendary Rat Temple, I heard rumours of slaughterhouses throughout the land of Gandhi and I already knew that it wouldn't be long before my brother, damn you, Felham! started making more trouble.

About the author:

Michael Tobias is the author of 25 books, and the writer, director and producer of over 100 films. This diverse body of work has been read and/or viewed in over 80 countries. Tobias lives somewhere in Asia.